THE
COURT
OF THE
UNDEAD

F.M. ADEN

NORTHERN LIGHT PRESS

TORONTO

ISBN: 978-1-7389631-1-9 (e-book edition)
ISBN: 978-1-7389631-0-2 (print edition)

Northern Light Press
Toronto, Ontario

To Mom & Dad—for always believing in me.

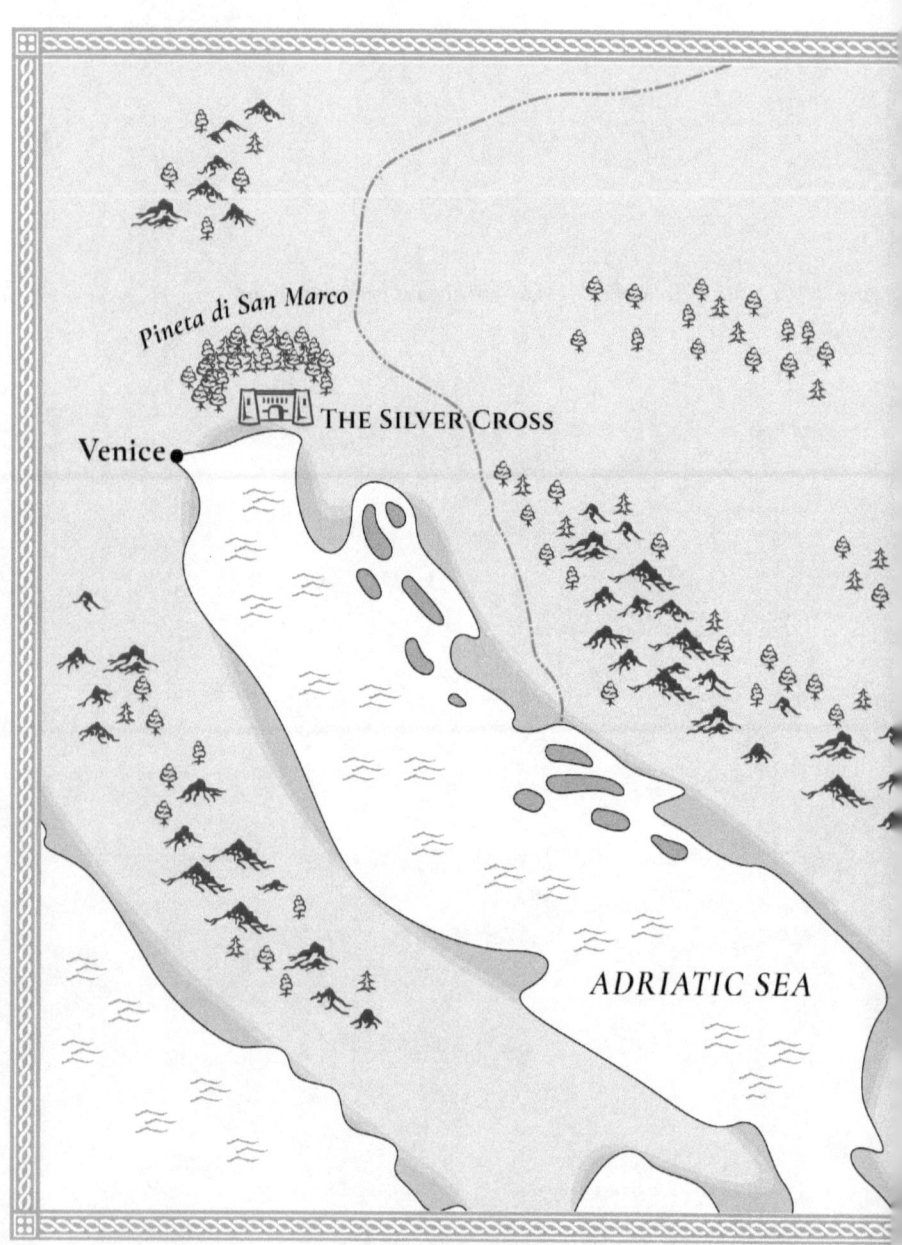

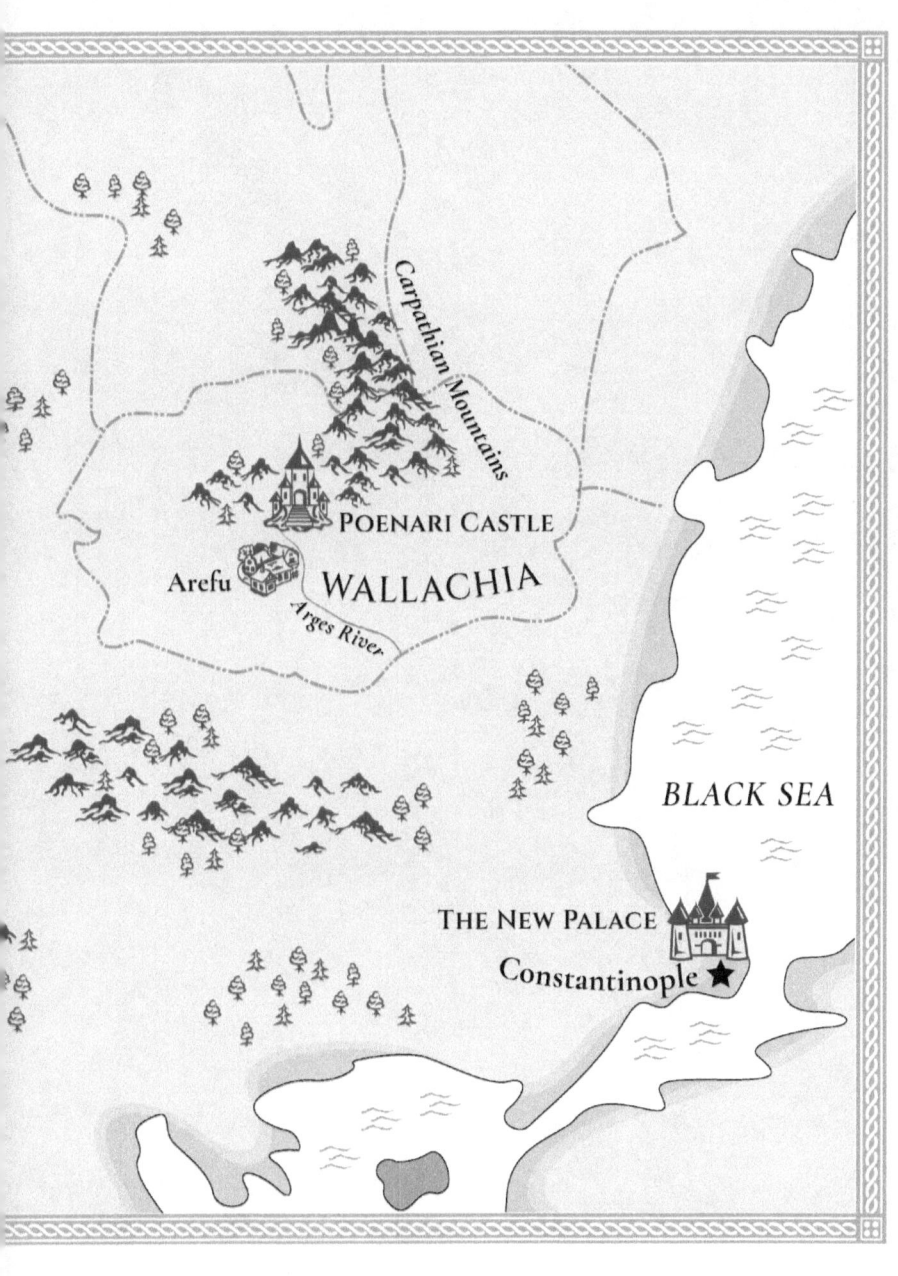

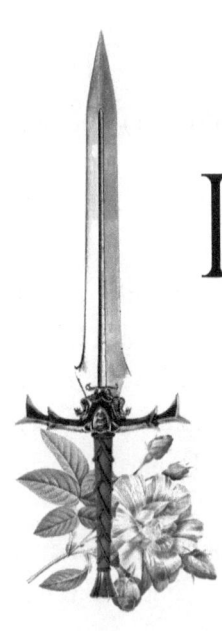

I

THE NEW PALACE, CONSTANTINOPLE

IT HAD BEEN a brittle night in the first week of October when Sevda Ghulam, a nursemaid to two willful girls, sat before them on her spindly knees and shared one of her famed tales. A stark Turkish winter rattled the windowpanes of the New Palace like the bones of the dead, and a thin, white sheet blanketed the ground. Snow rushed down like fresh tears, soaking the ground in its misery and fog.

The girls had just eaten, and their stomachs were full from their plates of rice pilaf and their cups of sharbat. From the way Aylin bounced on her bed, Sevda could tell the young girl had drunk more than one cup of the sugary drink. Their linen *gömleks* billowed around them like ghostly apparitions, and Sevda smiled fondly at them both.

She had watched these girls blossom, unfurling like tulips in the courts of the sultan. While she had not been young when they arrived, she had never felt so old as she did now. Her bones creaked when she walked, and her figure hunched as if she would fold in upon herself at any moment. At times it felt as though the only thing preventing her from returning to her Lord was her willful charges. She recalled the day they had arrived at the Ottoman courts from some distant place in central Africa. Their father had amassed great power in the Turkish court as the chief Black eunuch, and his daughters were soon raised in esteem and bundled in great promise.

"Settle down, girls," Sevda said with a wave of her wrinkled hand. Yara was the first to sit at her feet, chin perched on her palm. It took Aylin longer to stop jumping and settle down beside her sister, collapsing in a heap of limbs. Her dark hair curled around her brown face like that of a charming woodland creature. Unlike Yara, she could not sit still long enough to have it plaited.

"Will you tell us a frightening tale, Aunt Sevda?" Aylin asked. "I tire of those fairy tales that are not really fairy tales, but lessons disguised as fairy tales. It is never any fun when we know that the thief will always be punished, the prince will always marry the beautiful girl and the witch will always be burned."

"It is so wretched outside," Yara whispered, curling beneath Aylin's arm like a kitten seeking warmth. A fire burned in the hearth, but still the cold was harsh enough to freeze a babe in the womb. The trees in Constantinople had grown frail and crooked that year, blackening like sour grapes. Even the Erguvan tree the sultan favored had been struck by the ill fortunes of winter. "I want a happy tale, please."

"It is my turn to pick," Aylin said. "And I want something vicious. A story with teeth."

"Just nothing about the djinn," Yara rushed. "I don't like those stories."

Aylin snickered under her breath. Last time she had asked for a story of the djinn, Sevda had told her of a djinn who loved a woman so ardently he had possessed her. Aylin had loved the idea of someone loving you so much they chose to live in your skin. Yara had hated it, even though the tale had a happy ending. The woman had ended up going to an imam to have potent *ayahs* read on her to exorcise the djinn. It hadn't made a lick of difference to Yara, who had slept in Aylin's bed for two weeks and jumped at every shadow that curled along the walls.

Aylin had wished that the story didn't have a happy ending. The world she knew was not a happy place. Even at the tender age of twelve, she knew that there was evil lurking among them. But it was not the djinn who frightened her, but mortal men.

"No djinn," Sevda said, stroking her chin. She was filled with so many stories that Aylin imagined that if one were to cut her skin, she would bleed words. "Ah, there is one my *nene* told me of creatures who live among us. They go by many names in many cultures, but us Turks call them *ubir*. But they are also called *strigoi* and *vampir* in other tongues."

"I've never heard of them," Yara whispered.

Aylin elbowed her between the ribs. "Don't interrupt."

Sevda waited patiently until they had stopped their chatter. She despised disruptions, and it was several minutes later when she began to speak while they sat as silent as mice.

"These creatures belong to the night. Birthed of death and sorrow, they have risen from their graves to feed on the essence of us. To feed on the blood that fills our veins."

Yara shivered, biting her lip hard. Her hand shot up to ask a question, or rather a plea to change the story, but Sevda gave her a stern look before she continued with her tale.

"They prowl in little villages and exist in the shadows. While some claim that they are as ugly as a newborn donkey, others claim that their beauty can lure in the most pious slaves of God," she said. "If you listen carefully, you will hear the trickle of news of a child found with bloody stamps on their neck and wrist. Wretched tales carried from the winds in Moskva to Constantinople. Women whose scarves were peeled back to find that their skin had been mauled." Sevda turned to the window, her wise brown eyes looking into the rustle of snow that swirled in the distance like a darwīsh in flares of white robes. "During the winter you must never travel alone. Should the *ubir* catch a whiff of the blood that stains your veins, they will devour you. Or if you are truly unlucky, they will offer you eternal life, and you will walk among them, cursed and despised by God."

"How does one kill an *ubir*?" Aylin asked. Sevda rarely shared the important answers that Aylin wished to know. Even now she merely pointed a stern finger at them both.

"Into bed, both of you," she said. "If your father discovers you out of bed at this hour, he will have my head."

Aylin crawled beneath the heavy fur, sinking into the mattress. Sevda blew out the candles and placed a warm kiss on both their foreheads. The door had barely sealed shut before Yara leaped from her bed and curled beneath Aylin's covers. Aylin felt her cold feet tangled between hers.

"She never tells us how to kill the monsters," Aylin said with a huff.

"With prayer," Yara said. "Ask God for help and he shall help you."

"I would much rather ask my blade," Aylin said. "Is it not God who provides us with weapons to kill the wretched and protect the innocent?"

"I don't like when you speak so violently," Yara whispered. "It is unbecoming."

"You don't like a great many things, Yara," she answered with a sigh. "Attempting to please you is like pleasing the sultan. Tedious, and you never know if you will get the chance to kiss his ring or meet the point of his soldier's blade."

Aylin toyed with the end of her sister's braid. Yara was truly a foreign creature to her. She never understood why she was so gentle. Sometimes she feared if she held her too tightly, she would crack and splinter into a thousand pieces like a clay vase. Yet despite it all, she loved her sister, most fiercely.

Aylin stared off at the window, listening to the soft, faint sounds of her sister's breathing. She never fell asleep until Yara did.

In the distance, Aylin imagined an *ubir* standing in the midst of the storm. Pale faced and sharp toothed. He would crawl in through the gap of their window and walk on both hands and feet till he stood above them both. He would pat their heads, place a *kazandibi* on their tongues and wait until the rice pudding melted in their mouths. And then without warning he would bend down and drink the blood from their veins until they died.

Aylin wished Aunt Sevda had shared that tale; it was certainly more chilling than her tale of morals and caution.

Everyone knew there was nothing sadder than dead children.

II

THAT MORNING YARA read a book of Arabic poetry while Aylin painted a portrait beside her under the Mediterranean cypress. Her Arabic wasn't as strong as her Turkish, Latin, and Greek, but she was determined to master the language. Yara adored challenges. It was why she was so passionate about solving puzzles. She was rarely seen without a board of pieces in hand. Aylin, on the other hand, hated sitting still for long and rarely helped her finish the puzzle sets their father would bring back from his trips. Streaks of paint coated her sister's skin like the lines of a map, and she smelled of pigment and linseed oil.

"What are you painting?" Yara asked curiously.

"Ilyas," she said. "He is the newest member of the Janissary. They brought him in from Transylvania with a few other boys. I found him crying yesterday. He was so upset that I caught him crying that he choked me."

Yara gasped. "He choked you? Will you tell Baba?"

Their father was a powerful figure. Yara would sit up straight anytime he entered a room, and many knew of the power of Beşir Ağa. He was the closest advisor to the sultan and oversaw his entire administration. Yara had always had a fascination with politics. It reminded her of one of her puzzles. Sometimes she would bribe the guards with sweet cake and *baklava* to let her into the fourth courtyard, where the sultan's meetings were held. She'd hide behind the nearest pillar and listen to him plot against the Venetians and discuss the increase of taxes from the vassal states.

"So, he can be punished?" Aylin asked with a click of her tongue. "Not a chance. Besides, I'm making this for him as a welcome present."

"But he hurt you," Yara said, bewildered.

"He's confused," she said. "He's just arrived in a foreign country and speaks not a single Turkish word. He will be forced to serve in a pitiless war against his own people. Is it not a miserable position?"

Yara hadn't thought of it that way. Aylin was a year older than her. Fourteen to her thirteen, but sometimes it felt like she was far older than Yara. She was firm minded and never fretted about anything. Baba always said she had a strong head on her shoulders, whereas Yara's only defining characteristic was her beauty. It was no secret that she was beautiful. Yara had heard it for as long as she could remember. She heard it in the market when she was looking for ripe fruit and from the pashas who came to court. Her cheeks were rounded with twin dimples, and her body was soft and pliant as clay like most of the noblewomen. It was preferred that a woman appear well-fed to befit her station and wealth rather than thin and sickly.

"Why is his head so big?" Yara blurted. The painting of this Janissary boy was appalling, to say the least. His head was big and lumpy, and dark hair grew like roots from his head. His mouth descended in a frown, and his nose appeared almost hound-like.

"I think I will have nightmares," Yara whispered.

"Ilyas would love to hear that," she said. "He finds himself so fearsome. Even when he's crying."

Aylin stared back at her grotesque painting with a pleased smile on her face. She blew on it and trotted off in the direction of the barracks. Yara couldn't help but follow her. Sevda called her Aylin's shadow. She was always one step behind her.

"Have you seen Ilyas?" Aylin asked one of the passing soldiers.

He pointed faintly at the back of the barracks, before swiftly turning his attention back to Yara.

"Salam, Yara," the young boy said with a bright blush. "How are you this morning?"

"I'm well, thank you," she said. Yara tried to peek over his broad shoulder to look at Aylin marching around the barracks like she was the lieutenant. Her back straightened when she came upon her target—a pale boy with a shaved head. His face was still as he marched around the field being commanded by Ahmet Efendi in his serge cloth and red collar. Oftentimes the collar stitched to a soldier's greatcoat signified their rank. The boy marched alongside other pale-faced boys whose skin resembled the color of milk. Their eyes were blank, and Yara's chest tightened when she thought of what Aylin had said. That they were displaced and sad. Sometimes she would look upon her father's face and see a melancholy that made her ache. His black brows would be coiled like a serpent and his fingers would absently stroke his beard.

"What hurts you, Baba?" she'd ask, startled that he could feel an ounce of pain. He had always been the second-strongest person she had ever met. The first being Aylin.

"I miss home, little one," he'd say. "But you must never tell anyone that. The sultan is most gracious, and he despises ingratitude."

"Will you tell me about home?" she asked. He never shared stories of his boyhood with her. He never told her about his love for Bornu, where they had been born.

He shook his head. When her father had been brought to serve the sultan, he had left Aylin and Yara behind with their mother in Africa. It wasn't until he had amassed power that he had sent for them. By then their mother had succumbed to an infection that doctors said was caused by the mosquitoes. Aylin had buried her in the back plot while Yara wept in a corner. Their father had arrived twelve weeks later, after their mother's corpse had grown putrid in the soil. During those lonely months, Aylin would hunt squirrels for dinner and Yara would sometimes sing for spare coins. Though there wasn't much coin to be gathered from those who struggled as terribly as they did. Aylin would hold her every night while she wept, as if the strength of her arms would keep Yara from falling apart.

Their first few days in the New Palace had been strange. Everyone spoke a language they didn't understand and worshipped a God they had never heard of. Their faces had been scrubbed and they had been bestowed with Muslim names and converted in a mosque with beautiful pillars and lush crimson carpets. Yara would spend her days getting lost down the twisting palace hallways, staring wide-eyed at the ornate trimming and the lapis lazuli and turquoise tiles. The high arches and the floral motifs that covered the rugs like a silk veil would unravel before her like a procession. She'd spend her mornings admiring the pavilion and wandering the four main courtyards. Her favorite was always the third courtyard, where she'd often disappear beneath the Gate of Felicity and wander the looping garden path and smell the windflowers and tulips.

"You know you girls cannot simply interrupt training," Ahmet said, beard flicking in the wind like a waving flag. "Your father shall hear of this, Aylin!"

Aylin ignored him, as she did all authority. Ilyas's face twisted in distaste when Aylin poked his shoulder.

"Give me one moment," Yara said to the poor boy who sought her attention. She wanted to see Ilyas's full reaction to Aylin's portrait and approached them as discreetly as possible, stifling a giggle behind her palm.

"What is that ugly creature?" he demanded in a cracked voice that lurked between the paths of boyhood and manhood.

Aylin's brows furrowed as she stared at her portrait. "It is you, of course."

"Me?" he asked.

"It is a gift to welcome you to the Ottoman court," Aylin said looking a bit hesitant. "Do you not like it?"

Yara could see that he disliked it a great deal, but for some odd reason his hand wrapped around the canvas, and he tucked it beneath his pit.

"I have to resume training," Ilyas said. "Don't disrupt us again."

Aylin shrugged. "I don't take orders from you or any man."

Yara wondered almost wistfully what it would be like to speak her mind so freely. Nobody flinched when Aylin shared her provoking thoughts. Or tramped into the barracks without supervision. Her *salwar* was stained and her *gömlek* creased. Shockingly she did not even wear an *entari* to protect her modesty.

Yara prayed that she was always this brave and nobody ever doused the flames of her soul until she was nothing but ashes.

III

SWEAT COATED AYLIN'S back, and her limbs shook as she awakened from another nightmare. She couldn't recall what the nightmare had been about. Only that it had left her bones chilled. She stared into the warm brown eyes of her nursemaid and chaperone, Sevda Ghulam, whose scent of lilies instantly soothed her, as did the trace of her wrinkled hands over her brows. While she appreciated her soothing presence, Sevda didn't dote on them like children anymore, and it made her frown at the gesture. Aylin had turned nineteen this past spring and Yara had turned eighteen at the year's start. By all accounts, they had been long past marriage age. If it were not for their father's insistence that they find a match who was not only suitable but whom they loved, as he had once loved their dead mother, they would have both been wed at fifteen.

An echo hung in the air. The bell. The bell had been struck.

"Are there invaders?" she demanded. Her fingers swept beneath the linen enclosing her pillow and wrapped around the handle of her dagger. Sevda's old face twisted in shock at the sight of a young maiden so bluntly wielding a dangerous weapon. Her hand clutched her chest dramatically.

"Where did you find such a ghastly thing?" she demanded.

The dagger was ghastly—nothing like the ornate pieces the nobles wore as they perused the court gardens. It was given to her by Ilyas, one of the sultan's treasured Janissary. He was training a small company in the barracks and had been appointed as Çorbaci a few months back. Ilyas had taught her basic self-defense and had given her this blade on her nineteenth name day with a warning to not poke out anyone's eyes.

It was a wonder she could still shock the older woman. Sevda knew that Aylin had never been the gentle doe her sister was. And while Sevda had tried her best to raise them properly so they'd find suitable matches, Yara was the only one who dutifully attended her lessons on etiquette and primed herself on the duties of a wife and mother, Aylin would disappear into the garden maze or play a spitting game with the guards or, some days simply deal cards. Much to Sevda's dismay her skin had darkened from languishing in the sun without the proper head covering to shield her delicate skin, and her brown eyes held a shrewdness that her nursemaid had often described as being distinctly *male*.

"Is it the invaders?" Aylin demanded. "In the name of God, I swear to cut their throats and eat their entrails."

"*Audubillah!*" Sevda gasped. "Where did you learn such a thing?"

"Where's Yara?" she asked, staring at the empty bed to her left and the scattered pillows. Dread pooled in her stomach.

Aylin was devoted to Yara. Her younger sister was the jewel of the palace. The sultana was fond of her singing and often let her perform in the audience hall and behind the harem walls. Even the imperial prince held a fondness for her. It was whispered by all that good things were coming her way. Yara the Beautiful. It was what the courtiers called her.

"My darling girl, your father is assembling men to search the city," Sevda said gently. "Yara seems to have disappeared. We were at the *pazar* earlier that day. Perhaps someone or *something* caught sight of her."

"Yara is gone," Aylin whispered.

"I heard rumors of young men and women disappearing into the night. Their bodies appearing in canals and the deserts of Arabia, drained of blood, strange bite marks adorning their bodies," Sevda said.

Sevda clasped the end of her chain, which held a dangling painted indigo charm that was made to ward off the evil eye. She was a superstitious woman. And would often share her family's tales of the djinn and their ability to possess the innocent during the evenings while they sipped their linden flower tea. But Aylin's favorite tales had always been of the blood drinkers. In her smoky, bruised voice, Sevda would tell them of how God had cursed the pagans to drink blood forevermore. She would tell them how insatiable these creatures were, and how one rarely survived an encounter with them. And while they were just tales, her sister had always believed that there was an ounce of truth in them.

"I fear she was captured by a dark soul," Sevda said, a shiver racing down her spine. "I fear she is in hands far worse than the Byzantines."

<hr />

Aylin tossed on her *salwar* and a pair of cowskin boots. She found an old, hooked belt of Ilyas's and tied her *kilij* to her hip. Her fingers quickly braided the length of her hair, and she cursed her shaking fingers for slowing her down. Yara. Her sweet sister, with her dimpled smile and raven curls, was gone. The Byzantine slaves called her Aphrodite in reference to their old goddess. The one who represented beauty. And Aylin knew that it was a curse to be a beautiful woman in this world. One that she was pleased had skipped her. But Yara had not been so fortunate. Any number of harms could come to her.

Aylin recalled those lonely weeks after their mother's death. The stifling walls of their home and the endless rain that patted the ceiling with rough strokes. She remembered Yara, small and nimble, eating around a piece of mold-covered bread. Aylin remembered how her heart had caught in her throat and how she had made a promise that she would do anything to protect her. To build her a better life. If their father hadn't come for them, Aylin had every intention of keeping them far from the hands of poverty and illness.

Aylin had promised herself that night that she would always protect Yara. And she would not become an oath breaker.

"Aylin, my darling girl. Please sit down. It will worry your father if anything should happen to you as well," Sevda said in a rush.

"You said she was captured by a dark soul," Aylin said. "Was there someone watching her? And please don't speak in riddles."

"Not just her. He was watching all of us," Sevda said. "Like he was looking for someone."

Aylin hesitated. "You said she was with people worse than the Byzantines? Who did you mean?"

Sevda stared into her eyes and shook her head. "I am an old woman, Aylin. Filled with superstition and myth. Perhaps it is merely in my head."

"I want to hear it," Aylin said tightly. "I want to hear *all* of it."

"There have been rumors of dead people found with their blood drained. It's gone as far as Transylvania and the neighboring vassal states," Sevda said. "There are creatures, older and more powerful than us. I fear that Yara caught the eye of one of them."

Aylin shivered and recited a small *dua* to protect them from evil. Yara had always believed in monsters and magic, while Aylin firmly believed that there wasn't any need to believe in monsters when humans were already monstrous. She had heard tales of the fall of cities and villages pillaged and burned. How Mehmet II had broken the Theodosian Walls that had once protected the Christians from the Rus and the Bulgars, strangling their flow of imports and exports on the Bosphorus. She knew that holy men raped innocent women, and children became slaves to empires. Even now in the Ottoman courts, there were plenty slaves of wars. Greeks and Romans and Africans whose miserable faces haunted the halls and whose lips curled in scorn at their captors. Sometimes she wondered if she would be down there, stifled and broken among them, if her father hadn't raised his station.

Aylin didn't believe in folktales because history was far more terrifying than any old maid's story.

Aylin left her bedchamber and marched down the hall. She would go to the *pazar* and search the city. She wouldn't rest till Yara was brought home safe and sound.

A large, meaty hand gripped her neck, and Aylin felt someone raise her from the floor. Her head spun to glare at Ilyas. Only a few years older than her, he was a mountain of a man who used his great height to carry her around like a stray cat anytime she made him mad. With his raspy voice and dark stubble, sometimes she forgot he was the thin boy with the long limbs who chased her in the garden maze during high summer when she'd sneak away to the barracks filled with the newest batch of Janissaries.

Aylin hadn't known when she first met Ilyas that he was a Balkan slave. His brown hair and pale blue eyes had been striking, and she remembered Yara claiming to be madly in love with him. But Ilyas had been as rabid as a stray dog. He had bitten her once when she offered him a loaf of bread. She still had the mark on her hand to prove it. But he wasn't that Christian boy anymore. He had raised his station, gained the favor of the sultan and been elevated to the role of *Çorbaci* with his own cavalry, and he was now a devout Muslim.

"Go to bed, Aylin," he said in that dry tone of his.

"Put me down!" she growled. "I swear, Ilyas, I will cut your—"

He shook her hard enough to make her teeth rattle.

"Go. To. Bed," he said slowly. "The palace is on lockdown."

Aylin twisted and turned, but the brute was too big to injure. She tried to claw his hands, but from the small tilt of his lips, he enjoyed it far more than she'd like.

"Please, Ilyas," she said, and when her voice cracked it wasn't a ploy to soften him. She was truly rattled by Yara's disappearance. "I need to find her."

Ilyas released her, and his face softened when he looked at her. "Your father is going to search the city, and we'll turn over the palace. This could be a personal attack on your family. It is important that you stay in your bedroom or go to the sultana's room. She was fond of Yara' perhaps you'll be of comfort to each other and seek solace in prayer."

Her lips curled at his suggestion. "Sit around and weep when I could be turning over the city. *Never.*"

Before Ilyas could catch her, Aylin raced down the hall. She could hear him cursing behind her and the heavy thud of his footsteps. While he outweighed her in height and muscle, Aylin could run circles around him any day of the week.

The gates were parted for the men who would aid in the search. At the center was her father, his white beard stark against his dark skin. He was in the middle of his speech, and they were all too distracted to notice the slip of a girl who disappeared past them toward the assembled horses.

Ilyas yelled for them to stop her just as she unwound the harness. Aylin jumped on the horse and spun in a quick circle, hearing the movement behind her. Her heart thumped and the only sound it said was *Yara. Yara. Yara.* Nothing mattered but finding her sister. She would deal with the punishment for her actions later.

She turned around to lock eyes with her distraught father and a furious Ilyas, whose big fists were clenched at his sides. Aylin didn't think he could hear, but she spoke the words, nonetheless.

"I'll find her, Baba," she whispered. "I'll find her."

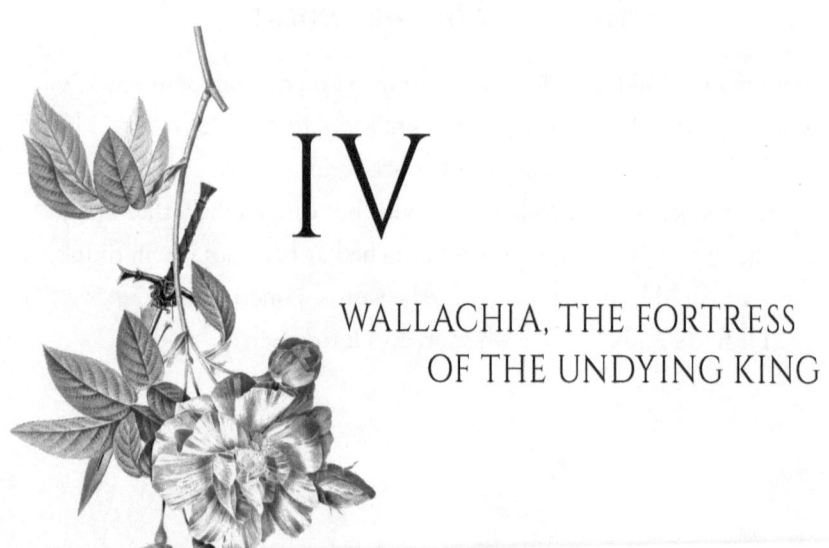

IV

WALLACHIA, THE FORTRESS OF THE UNDYING KING

YARA'S LIMBS TWITCHED with fear. Her eyes were sealed with a handkerchief and the darkness was never-ending. She opened her mouth to speak, but a rag had been twisted around her mouth. The cloth was sour and filthy. Bile coated her throat, and she swallowed it back, desperate not to choke to death. The platform beneath her feet swayed, and she couldn't tell if she was on a boat or cart. Either option frightened her. Either one meant she was far from home.

Was Aylin with her? It was wretched of her to think it, but she wanted Aylin to be there. With Aylin by her side, she had a chance of survival. Her sister was the bravest person she had ever met. She liked to joke that if the sultan ever began to recruit women in his army, then they would flee at the sight of Aylin and her spine-tingling roar.

Footsteps creaked before her, and the blindfold was ripped from her face. Yara stared at an unfamiliar face. He was a hard-faced fellow with a pointed nose, flat lips, and a beard. Yara twisted her arms, but she was tied to a post and the rope only rubbed her skin harshly with each pitiful attempt.

"Careful," he said in a thick accent. "You are hurting my precious cargo."

"Where am I?" she demanded, even though the answer was rather clear now that she could see. She was on a cargo ship, surrounded by boxed goods marked and stamped in Turkish lettering. But that was not the worst of it. There were others. Some were tied to the opposite post and others were chained to the beams. What concerned her most was the youth that marked their faces. The youngest was fifteen and the oldest must have been twenty. Yara was somewhere in the middle at eighteen.

"Wh...what are you going to do with us?" Yara asked.

His eyes were unbearably cold, and all she could think was that wherever he was taking them, it would rival hell. Prayers floated in her mind, tangling around her in temporary comfort. As much as the words coiled around her mind, they didn't suckle the cold from her bones.

"Get some sleep," her captor grunted. "You are going to need it."

<hr />

The air was harsh, slapping their cheeks with its invisible hands, stuffing their noses with its icy fingers. The captives were marched forward as if they were being led to their execution, with their hands shackled and burlap sacks covering their heads. The captors had made them climb a set of stairs—a never-ending ascent that knocked the breath from her lungs. It had taken two hours to climb to their destination. With nothing but their sweaty palms gripping the rail and the whistle of the wind that promised a swift death if they missed a step. They were pushed with hard iron prods anytime they stopped. Yara had never felt her muscles twitch so painfully, and the knot in her side had grown from an uncomfortable pinch to a stabbing sensation that made her want to curl into a ball.

At last, Yara heard the creak of an iron gate to welcome their arrival. It was warmer the farther they walked. A hint that they were inside. Yara tried to remember her steps and the turns they made. It would help when she plotted her escape, and she would escape.

"Is this the new batch?" a gruff voice asked.

"Yes," their captor said. "I'll make introductions to the nobles, let them have their pick."

It was a moment before the other man responded. "I'm sure Lord Dracul will be pleased. He expects your finest."

"As my lord commands," the bearded man purred.

The clink of their chains was deafening in the silence. Beneath her bare feet, Yara could feel polished marble and smell the faint trace of soap.

They entered a humid room, and her nostrils burned with the smell of salts and scented lavender oil. The blindfold was ripped from her eyes, and she stared at the pool of shallow water that made the baths. Servants flooded the room, one for each prisoner. Yara stiffened at the sight of the young girl before her with a thin dagger clasped firmly between her fingers. Slowly and efficiently, the servants began to tear off their clothes.

"Stop," Yara hissed. The girl didn't shift, and she wondered if she had even heard her. Cool air grazed her naked skin, and her shackled arms twitched to cover herself. The others protested, but their words fell on deaf ears. In the corner, she saw the bearded man, their captor, eyeing them all with glee. When his gaze struck her, she flinched.

The servant girl washed her, slowly and methodically. It was the most demeaning thing she had ever experienced. For a small moment, she wondered if she were being sold as a slave to a Byzantine, but the more she stared at her fellow captives the less that theory seemed to hold. Several of them were fair-haired Byzantines, several of them were Turks, a few looked Balkan, and she was the sole African Turk.

Once they were washed, they were clothed in a manner that could only be deemed offensive. The men were given white loincloths with gold harnesses and the woman were given lacy pale nightgowns that stopped at their thighs. They were translucent, so you didn't have to imagine what they truly looked like. This was worse than the bath. Yara wished the floor would open and welcome her into its maw. It would be preferable to this shame that sunk beneath her skin and burrowed its way into her flesh.

They were marched like cattle down a dark hallway. The windows were boarded up with planks and bars much like a fortress. It was dark and gloomy with high-arched hallways, crimson carpets, and vaulted ceilings. They came upon a pair of iron double doors. Two sentries stood on either side, and when Yara looked into their eyes she gained the distinct sense that there was something terribly wrong with them. Their gaze was devoid of humanity and their skin looked hardened, like a yolk covered it. Both were deathly pale and frightening.

They entered a grand hall that was slightly decrepit. Beyond the veneer of twinkling candlelight that shone from iron caskets and re-flected in golden goblets. A thin film of spiderwebs spanned the pointed ceiling, hanging from the wooden beams like a stretched crucifix. There was a dais and a man sitting upon a grim throne—a bleak structure made to resemble a crow with fanning black wings. Before him was a banquet table with food. A woman lay naked on the middle of the table, sprawled like some unholy sacrifice to a false deity, legs spread between baskets of apple and peach. Her eyes were frozen staring up at the ceiling, and several puncture wounds covered her torso and breasts. Yara stared at the guests to see if they were horrified by this sight, but they mingled and chatted like there was not a dead girl lying on the table full of piercing holes. The girl beside Yara shrieked in horror, and silence descended in the room. It seemed that the silence was worse than the noise. When these strangers looked at her, Yara felt as though she were looking into the eyes of death. They all looked alike. Tall and lithe beings with kaftans of the finest brocade and jewels that gleamed. Their skin was as varied as the captives'. She noticed Yemenis, Algerians, Venetians, and Indians, all with regal features and skin that looked like it had been deprived of sunlight. Their pallor was so weak, Yara wondered if they suffered from some deficiency. The few that smiled had unnatural canines that descended like wolf's teeth, and a few were stained with blood, but Yara told herself it was wine. It had to be wine. The ones who were sitting held slumped humans dressed exactly like the captives in their slips of clothing.

They prowl in little villages and exist in the shadows.

Aunt Sevda's warning twisted in her mind. The tale of the *ubir* and their ability to devour one's lifeblood. This was neither a small village nor the shadows. They were in the forefront of this place, unconcealed by darkness. Not merely existing but thriving.

Yara shivered, eyes desperately searching the room only to come across several inhuman gazes. They licked their lips when she looked to them for help. Their noses twitched like they smelled something divine.

"Fresh blood," a dark voice bellowed with joy.

Yara stared up at the man on the dais, the one who sat upon the vicious throne. He appeared both old and youthful. With a thick black beard and short-cropped hair, he looked neat and orderly. But there was a flicker in his eyes, one that warned of madness, of years festering in debauchery and living in heresy.

"Welcome to the Court of the Undead," he announced, spreading his arms dramatically.

Yara shivered at the power of his voice. It was wild and booming, as if it possessed a life of its own. The creatures who sat so still in their chairs grew even more rigid.

"I'll be making the rounds to see which noble picks from the stock," her captor said. He dragged the seven miserable souls forward. Yara stumbled when he yanked the chain. The girl beside her whimpered and moaned. The fair-haired boy to her left stared bravely forward with his jaw clenched. Yara found herself caught between fear and determination. She knew if she panicked it would scramble her wits and destroy any chance she had to escape. But to pretend as if she were not affected by this new reality, was falsehood.

Someone whistled, and Yara's head snapped up to stare into their red eyes. Two figures sat alone in a corner. A wide berth away from the guests, as if people knew better than to come close to them. They were identical in every manner but their hair, which was both long and straight as a pin. One had hair as white as snow and the other had hair as dark as the night sky. Their faces were beautiful and youthful, like they were carved from marble. Plump lips and pointed cheekbones descended into firm jaws.

"The Demirci Boys," her captor whispered. "The dark-haired one is Eldar and the fair-haired one is Volkan. Shall I make introductions?"

Yara shook her head, but it was too late. He had unhooked her from the others, who were being led around the room by one of the sentries her captor had whistled for. While the hard-faced man on the throne frightened her with his gleaming gold rings, something about these young men made her knees knock together like she was a newborn colt. It was their eyes. Empty and lacking any human sentiment.

"They are a hard sell," the captor explained. "Prefer the hunt rather than my procurements. But occasionally I strike true, and from the way they are looking at you, I may leave here twice as rich." He laughed, cruel and bitter.

"You are not one of them," Yara said. "Their eyes are red."

"Keen-eyed girl," he said with a hearty thump to her back. "A starved creature's eyes are red, while a fed one's are black. Beware of the red-eyed ones."

Her captor had pale blue eyes. A burst of color in a sea of predators. It was how she could make out the humans. That and their
flimsy cloth that she realized had more to do with ease of access than
anything else. She could see the faded bruises and teeth marks on
their bodies. There was a strange haze in their eyes, almost as if they
were drunk.

"Why are you doing this?" Yara asked. "Do you not fear God?"

"Because it pays well, and the devil fears no God." He shrugged.
"The vampir can't walk in the light, so I bring them the finest blood
slaves in the prettiest shells."

Yara tucked that bit of information away. Did he mean they could
not walk in sunlight? And he called them vampir—it sounded Hun-
garian, which explained his Latin accent.

Now that she was up close, Yara felt herself tremble. Her eyes
flickered between the dark-haired one and the fair-haired one. They
had Turkic names, and she hoped that would fill them with some
form of sympathy for a fellow countrywoman. There was something
distinctly feminine about their faces. Beauty that pure was rarely
reserved for men. Kohl painted their red eyes, elegant and pointed at
the ends.

"I brought this one from Constantinople just for you both. I know
how picky your tastes run, and your inclination to share," her captor
said. "She is well-known in the sultan's court. Sings like a nightingale,
they say, with the voice of an angel. She's young. Has a few good years
of life left, and plump enough to keep you warm at night should you
wish to bed her."

Yara flushed. She had always known she wasn't as slim as Aylin.
Her stomach dropped and her breasts could barely be held by the
flimsy strands of this nightgown. While immodest on the other girls,
it looked vulgar on her. But nobody had ever spoken so shamelessly

about her, stripping her agency and power with a few scathing words. Poking at her like she was livestock and not a person.

The white-haired one appraised her thoughtfully while the dark-haired one simply stared ahead, bored and picking at his nail.

"Hi, pretty bird," the fair-haired one cooed. There was something wrong with his eyes. Like they were drowning in madness. His gaze lifted to her captor. "You may leave while we determine her suitability for our lifestyle."

Her captor frowned. "I don't want you to damage the goods."

The man dug into his pocket, revealing several gold coins. "Half now and half if we keep her. Either way, you got half your price."

"No, don't go," Yara whispered. "Please..."

Her captor disappeared into the crowd, greedily counting his coin. Yara stared at them both. A chill ran down her spine. Now that her chains were left on the ground, she was free to move, and she didn't hesitate to spin around and rush to the door. She had scarcely made it one foot when her chains were yanked back roughly. She stumbled backward, falling on the lap of one of the twins. She twisted and turned, stabbing her elbow into his stomach. He laughed wildly, like they were playing a game. But then his arms shackled around her, and he squeezed tight until she cried in pain.

"Let us save the games for later, shall we?" he whispered. His teeth grazed the shell of her ear. The wet point made her shiver. It had to be as long and abominable as the others, like the rest of his kind. *Monsters.* She had found herself in the midst of monsters, and Yara had no idea how she was going to survive.

"What do you think?" he asked. It took her a moment to realize he wasn't speaking to her. He was speaking Greek, and because she was so visibly an African Turk, he had assumed she didn't know the language. Her father had made sure that Yara and Aylin had all the makings of noble girls. She was well-versed in languages, music, etiquette, and the art of running a household.

"Her scent is too distracting. We need our wits about us," his brother replied.

"Speak for yourself, brother," he said, inhaling at her throat. Yara tilted her neck to get as far away from him as she could, but when he chuckled, she realized she was giving him far better access than he'd had initially. "I don't share your lack of control."

"We had a rule, Volkan," he said through gritted teeth.

"I'm tired of rules," the one named Volkan said. The one with hair as white as frost. "I want her, Eldar."

His brother didn't seem pleased by this, and neither was Yara. To distract them, she kicked Eldar in the shins. Hard. She expected a reaction—anger, fury, something—but he only blinked at her like she was an insect crawling over his polished boots. Nothing more than a nuisance.

Volkan laughed, a warm, tinkling sound, before he flagged down her captor. Within a matter of minutes, Yara was sold as a blood slave.

<hr />

Volkan did not waste any time tying her to the bed while his brother disappeared to his bedroom. It was a relief that she was only dealing with one of them instead of two. She fought and kicked, but Volkan possessed both strength and speed that could only be described as demonic. At times he was merely a blur of color. His black kaftan and pale hair danced in the dim light as he made his way around the bed like the Angel of Death. Yara would much rather be taken by the true Angel of Death and find her path to God than be shackled with these feline men who pounced upon her like she was a fresh slab of meat.

The bedroom was dark with no windows, and a circular bed with dozens of pillows lay at the heart of the room. Volkan tied her arms and legs to the carvings that held the canopy of the bed, knotting the silk cords tight with his long fingers.

"What shall I call you, my pet?" he asked once he had finished. His long finger drifted down her chin.

Yara curled her lips and spat at him. If Aylin were here, she would be proud. Proud that she was fighting and not crying in a corner like she ached to do. Everything she did from this moment forth would be for her sister. Aylin would never forgive her if she stopped fighting. She missed her so much it hurt. And for one terrible moment, she ached to give in to the pain and weep.

Volkan wiped his face and when he looked at her, he was scarcely human. His pupils were dilated, and his lips curled back to reveal his monstrous teeth. Before she could scream, he had leaned over her and sunk his teeth into her throat, tearing at the delicate skin. At the first draw of blood, Yara found her fear ebbing away and morphing into a spike of pleasure. Her body relaxed and she released a deep sigh. She sank deeper into the bed, feeling the weight of his palm on her hip.

"You just couldn't help yourself, could you?" Eldar asked. He leaned against the wall, watching them intensely as if he were reeling himself back from joining in. Yara saw his face transform with hunger. His teeth lengthened, descending far past his lips.

But when she looked at him, she didn't feel fear, she felt safe.

"Just wanted a little taste," Volkan said, drawing back and wiping his bloody chin. "Look at her. How she stares at me so sweetly."

Yara felt his hand stroke her cheek and she leaned into his touch, much to his delight.

"Go to sleep," he said. "Now."

Yara felt her eyelids grow heavy and before she knew it, she had fallen into a deep slumber.

Eldar watched his brother feed on their new toy. The girl had spat in his face. Little did she know, Volkan was as unpredictable and unhinged as they came. He hadn't been the same since he had been freed from Titus and Pomona's imprisonment. It had been their Lord Dracul who had sentenced him to fifty years in their care for slaughtering that noble girl Volkan had been obsessed with. Eldar had worked tirelessly to have it reduced to three years. But those three years in imprisonment had changed him.

Eldar knew his brother like the back of his hand. Volkan hadn't hurt the girl. He wasn't a fool. The nine trueborn were vampir royalty. Even Volkan, who had a blood thirst like no other, would never dare touch a strand of their hair. Someone had set up his brother. It was why Eldar was back at court. To find the culprit and to punish all those who had condemned his brother all those years ago. He wouldn't settle until the Draculesti line had fallen and all their supporters had burned with them.

The door to the girl's bedroom clicked shut and Volkan stepped out, tying the long strands of his bone-white hair into a knot. He stuck that strange finger bone between the strands to hold it in place. From the elongated structure of the finger and the thinned claw, it looked to be from a dead vampir. Volkan was terribly sentimental about his kills. It was disturbing. He always grabbed a keepsake. He had a trove of mismatched rotting teeth, bones, and lumpy blackened hearts in a chest in his bedroom.

"László says the girl is a well-known courtier. Sings for the sultana. Even has the imperial prince wrapped around her little finger. Quite an accomplished little thing," Volkan said. "It feels good to be given someone so prestigious. I tire of the village girls."

"I don't care about the history of my food," Eldar said. "Don't tell me you plan to obsess over this one. We have bigger problems."

Volkan waved his ringed fingers dismissively. "Yes, yes, dethrone

Vlad, claim the seat as Lord of the vampir and the title of the Undying King."

"A bit of discretion and tact goes a long way," he hissed. There were people listening everywhere, and they possessed superior senses to humans. It bothered him how Volkan wasn't taking this as seriously as he was. He never took anything seriously. Yet it continued to surprise Eldar how he had survived this long with that careless attitude.

Volkan leaned forward with that infuriating smile on his face. He cupped his hand behind Eldar's neck and dragged him till their foreheads were pressed against each other.

"I will do as you ask, brother," Volkan said. "I've accepted long ago that while I was blessed with all the good looks, you were gifted with that devious brain of yours."

"We are twinned, you fool."

"But only one of us was given hair as fair as a young maiden's and frosty lashes to match."

Volkan thought he was a gift to the world. That he was the most beautiful bastard to exist. Eldar didn't even have the luxury of insulting his appearance without insulting himself.

"I'm not going to sit here and compete over who is prettiest," Eldar growled, smacking his hand away.

"Because you'd lose," Volkan said, pressing his lips to Eldar's cheek in an affectionate kiss. Eldar swatted him away and leaned forward, staring at his board filled with pieces. The game was called chaturanga and involved strategy and wit. It was a little game he'd picked up during his travels to India. But his set was more personal—it was an intricate board Eldar crafted to resemble Dracul's court. On the right-hand side were Dracul's allies and on the left-hand side were those with no direct allegiance but whose fear of Dracul kept them in line. In the middle were the lesser vampir, those who didn't come from the trueborn families and were no longer tied to their deceased master or mistress by their sire bond. Between Volkan and Eldar, there were three hundred and fifty members under the House of Demirci. Some of them sired by the brothers and others who had once served their father and his father before him.

Eldar knew which four great houses would be easiest to win to their side. It wouldn't be easy to convince them. Fear was an excellent motivator, and Dracul cradled their fear in his palm. The vampir didn't fear Eldar, not yet at least. And Eldar had a plan—one that would require both cunning and brutality.

V

IT HAD BEEN two days since Yara had disappeared. Aylin had wandered the *pazar* until her feet had formed grooves in the grass. It saddened her to think that her father would be worrying about them both now. That she had put him in a terrible position that no father would ever wish to be put in. But she knew if she returned to the palace, she would be truly helpless, locked in her bedroom like those princesses in the fairy tales. Staring forlornly out from her tower while her sister was drawn farther out of her reach with each passing day.

"I knew I'd find you here, you wicked girl."

Aylin's head snapped up to find Sevda glaring at her. Aylin had been sleeping beneath an abandoned cart the past few nights. She hadn't brought any silver *akche* with her to purchase any food or board. It was the start of September and the nights had already begun to grow colder. The chill had nearly kept her awake at night.

Her stomach ached in hunger, and the sight of the *börek* in Sevda's wicker basket made her half-feral. She reached for it and tore her teeth into the baked flesh, chewing the lamb meat and dried apricots. A moan slipped past her mouth as she tore off another piece.

"I should alert the guards," Sevda said, staring at her crossly. Her foot tapped restlessly, and her arms were folded tightly across her chest.

"But you won't?" she asked.

Sevda sighed. "You will only escape again. Besides, I think I know someone who might be of help."

Aylin sat up straighter. "You do?"

"I believe the *ubir* took your sister. The tales I've told you are truth," she whispered. "It is why the pagans of old would cremate their dead, so they wouldn't rise against them. It is close to winter and the nights will grow longer. It is easy for them to snatch us up. Children go missing daily, and no common thief would dare commit crimes under the sultan for fear of losing their hands. It is them who have taken our precious Yara."

Sevda clutched her hand with bruising strength, her eyes filled with fear.

"There are whispers of an order in the Republic of Venice that hunt these creatures. They call themselves the Silver Cross. You must implore them to provide you aid. Ilyas shall travel with you," Sevda said. "They will not be receptive to your faith or ethnicity. But the crusaders have taken up a different torch, one that burns for the wicked. It is a war between men and monsters, and not the gods they worship."

It would be suicide to attempt to cross the shores of Venice. Ever since the Ottoman-Venetian war, when Sultan Mehmet had fought for the ports on the coast of the Aegean, tensions between their nations had mounted. There were no vessels that would carry Aylin and Ilyas to port, and their fate if caught upon their shores could cost them their heads.

"Ilyas will never take me there," she said. "I don't know if I even believe this. Or if I'm willing to lose my head over it."

"I'll take you," Ilyas said in his gruff voice. The shadow of his large form darkened her little hiding spot. "But you will listen to every order I give you."

Aylin nervously looked behind him to see if he had assembled the palace guard. This could be an elaborate ploy to drag her back to the palace. Perhaps Sevda and Ilyas were conspiring to bring her home.

"I don't trust you," she said with narrowed eyes.

"Of course, you don't," he said. He looked at her like she was an irritating insect that he was desperate to squash beneath his boots. "You rarely know what is good for you."

"Take that back, Ilyas," she snapped. "Or I swear to God, I will stab you."

"That is enough," Sevda said. She raised her head to the sky like she was begging God for the patience to deal with them. "Ilyas shall take you to Venice. And from there you must find your own way."

"It is ten days' travel if the weather holds steady. We'll have to cut through the Sea of Marmara to the Adriatic Sea," Ilyas said. "I've packed us some clothes and dry bread and dates."

"*You* believe it was these monsters who took Yara?" she asked, staring at Ilyas incredulously. He was so faithful; she didn't think he believed in superstition.

"My great-grandfather told me of villages ransacked by beasts who left behind corpses drained of blood. They are wiser now and don't draw attention as they once did, but they still exist in the shadows. They still torment the living," Ilyas said. "We found a boy in our farm once, drained of blood. It was said to be wolves, but wolves do not leave behind flesh."

Aylin shivered. She could picture vividly the gruesome sight of a young boy with tangled limbs and glassy eyes.

"We need to leave," Ilyas said curtly. "Your father is going to search the ports today, and we need to be on the ship before we are caught." He offered her his hand and Aylin let him help her up.

Once she was settled on her feet, she wrapped her arms tightly around Sevda's thick waist, inhaling her scent of oranges and sweat. Her dry lips kissed her forehead. "May God keep you and Yara safe."

"Tell Baba I will return with her," she said. "Tell him I won't rest till she is found."

Ilyas gripped her hand, tugging her impatiently away from the tear-stained Sevda. He led her to the bustling port and showed their forged paperwork to the official who sported the fashionable moustache all Turkish men had. Aylin caught a glimpse of the paperwork and was surprised to find that he had given her his surname: Aylin Çorbaci.

"You made me your wife," she snarled when the official had waved them to board. Ilyas's hand, which had been tight on hers, shifted to her waist.

"Do you think I am proud to be walking with a wife who is covered in mud and sweat? Her clothes torn to bits and pieces?" he asked, wrinkling his nose as if he could not bear the smell of her. "It is more humiliating for me than it is for you."

Aylin felt a strange sense of glee when the boat rocked. He could barely keep his footing, and his fingers immediately gripped the railing. His cheeks were flushed, like he was about to be sick. And when the ropes were unknotted and the sails dropped, Ilyas hung over the rail, heaving violently.

Aylin cackled at his misery.

It was going to be a fun trip to Venice.

For the next few days, Ilyas either dozed off or vomited violently or prayed fervently that God protect them from the turning tide. He was a terrible companion. Aylin dabbed his forehead with a wet cloth, and his knitted brows relaxed under her touch. They had a small room with two beds nailed to the floorboards and a corner that held the heap of their belongings. For a moment she had worried that they would give them a single bed to share as husband and wife.

"You are not such an unpleasant wife," he murmured.

"You are a weak husband," she said. "A privateer from a rival nation could assault our vessel, and you would be here flat on this bed."

"I do not get a reprieve from your insults even when I'm ill?" he asked with a raised brow.

"Only death could protect you from my harsh tongue," she said.

"We must discuss what awaits us in Venice," he said, attempting to sit upright. It took him a few minutes to sit without heaving up his guts. "We will be foreigners in a country that is not our own, and the dangers we face are unfathomable. I will reclaim my Christian name and if they ask, we will tell them the truth: that I was paid as a debt to the sultan from the vassal state of Transylvania and was initiated into the Janissary. I have escaped and wish to build a life in Venice with the blessings of the papacy and the doge. I will join the ranks of this Silver Cross and, when the time comes, I will root the monsters out. And if, God willing, Yara is alive, I will bring her back to you."

"Why don't we just pay them to help us retrieve Yara?" she asked.

"Because I didn't bring enough money to pay a ransom. Unless you had the foresight to bring any coin?" he asked. He paused awaiting her response.

"No," she mumbled. "But we can ask them for help."

"They are soldiers and as soldiers we do not compromise our mission for unpaid and unrewarded side quests. Besides if I am being honest no Venetian man will care to save a Turk girl. If anything, we can learn much from them and leave to find Yara. But we need intel first."

"What about me?" she asked. "Nobody will believe I am your wife. The Janissaries are celibate. Their duty is to God and the sultan alone."

They had all taken a vow to neither wed a woman nor father any children.

"I will convince them that their vows were not of worth to me. It was all a pretense, and I secretly took a wife," he said.

"I won't sit in some house awaiting your return. I intend to join this legion. To learn about these *ubir*," she said. "You are not the only one who knows how to wield a blade."

"These hunters are trained Christian *men*," he said. "You are a Muslim woman, Aylin. Do you know what they do to women like you?"

"No, what do they do?" she asked innocently.

He swallowed, the lump beneath his throat shifting beneath his skin.

"A man cannot speak of such things," he murmured.

"I won't let you go off on this crusade without me," she said. "If it is men they want, then I shall make them believe I am one."

"How will they believe that, Aylin?" he asked. "A man would have to be blind to assume otherwise."

Aylin was rather thin and short. Unlike Yara, who had a bosom that was the envy of any woman, Aylin was as flat as a board. Besides her long, wavy black hair that fell to her knees, there were not many womanly traits about her. Even Ilyas had the long, fingered lashes of one of the beautiful women in the sultan's harem, and the dark kohl he wore to protect himself from the sun only enhanced his pretty blue eyes.

"I'll cut my hair," she said. The thought made her shudder, and she wrapped her hands around her knees to force her resolve. Her hair was the prettiest thing about her. Ilyas liked to touch it when he thought she wasn't looking, and Yara always said she would trade her soul for it. Aylin had always felt a strange pride when she came upon a looking mirror. Her face was far too sharp and hard, and her lips and eyes had always appeared too big for her slim face. But her hair... her hair almost made her appear beautiful.

Ilyas's eyes widened like she had threatened to cut her limbs instead of her hair.

"There is no need for any drastic decisions," he said in that calm voice of his, but he sounded rattled. Aylin touched the heel of her palm where Ilyas' small teeth were forever punctured into her skin from that fateful day he had attempted to punish her for all the sins of the Ottomans, cursing at her in his foreign tongue. She wondered if he remembered his early days at court. Back when he had a different name and worshipped a different God.

"Will you be punished for leaving your station?" she asked.

Ilyas was silent for a long while. "Perhaps. Perhaps not."

"Ilyas, I'm serious," she said. "You could be executed as a deserter."

"Or I could be hailed as a hero for returning your sister to court," he said.

Aylin knew that the sultan was fickle. He could grant him estates and wealth for the safe return of Yara. Or he could have him strung up on the city gates as a warning to any Janissary who thought to flee his God and duty.

"When Yara is found, I think we should stay in Venice, once she safely sits on a vessel bound for Constantinople," she said. "We should carve out some type of life for ourselves away from the tyranny and stifling rules of court."

Ilyas stared at her as if she had suggested they chuck off their clothes and dip into the Sea of Marmara for a midnight swim.

"I will never turn my back on my empire, my sultan, or my faith," Ilyas said sharply. "If he decides that my death is deserved, then I will tilt my neck for his blade and pray for God's mercy in the hereafter."

"Don't be a martyr," Aylin said, wrinkling her nose in disgust. "It doesn't suit you. Tales of martyrs keep no one fed but the poor and the pious."

His lips tilted slightly. "Are you frightened I'll be executed for *you*?"

Aylin scoffed. "My life will be far more peaceful without you. No woman needs a husband as lazy as you."

"No man will touch the gates of heaven with a wife like you," he said. "You could try the patience of an *imam*."

The boat lurched, and his face turned deathly pale. He turned to the side of his bed, desperately grasping for the bucket to heave his guts in. Aylin was gracious enough to push the pail toward him with her foot, but not so courteous as to hold back the chuckle that escaped her.

⁕

On the eighth day at sea, Ilyas bribed the captain and secured them a boat with a narrow helm and two oars that stuck out like wide ears. They twisted down the northbound canal of the Adriatic Sea, while the small vessel occasionally rocked from side to side. Ilyas took the oars and pushed with all his might. His dark brown hair swayed beneath the breeze, falling into his light eyes.

Aylin toyed with the ends of her braid and gripped her blade in her other hand, contemplating shucking the whole thing off. She wouldn't sit idle while Yara suffered at the hands of these monsters. She wouldn't let Ilyas take the brunt of the risk. If she wanted to join and train alongside these men, she would have to discard the only piece of herself that ever mattered to her. It was vain to be so obsessed with her hair. It wasn't a limb. It would grow and recover when severed, blooming like a wildflower. A lump scratched her throat, and she held the blade to her scalp.

"Aylin. Don't," Ilyas said. She felt the shudder of the oars being slammed into their slots just as she cut through the braid. She held it in her palm, and her fingers grazed the prickly torn ends. It felt like the stump of a sliced tree, flat and uneven.

"What did you do?" he whispered.

"What I had to do," she said in a firm voice. Aylin couldn't stop touching her shorn hair. Ilyas stepped forward, the boat swaying precariously beneath them. His palm stroked her head, long fingers running through the frayed ends.

"You're a fool," he snapped. "A fool with a terrible cut."

"We will tell them I am fifteen. That we are brothers."

"We look nothing alike," he said.

Ilyas was a fair-skinned Transylvanian whose skin had turned a golden bronze like fresh-baked bread during his tours with his cavalry through the scorching deserts of the sultan's region. His eyes were a pale blue, like a sheet of ice that covered the ground during the wintertime. For those who didn't know him, he could come across as cold, with a firm line for a mouth that rarely rose into a smile. His fingers toyed with his silver necklace, the one with the crescent moon and the star.

"Half brothers," Aylin corrected. "You will have to pretend to like me."

"How are we supposed to do that? You cannot speak to me without insulting me," he said.

"You make it quite easy," Aylin said. "Besides, you *always* glare at me. I've never seen you smile at me except when you beat me in combat."

"There we go," Ilyas said, returning to his seat. "We are a miserable pair, and nobody will believe that we're related."

"I will do anything to bring Yara back home," Aylin said. "I will smuggle my way into Venice and join this band of Christian men to bring my sister home. And nothing you say will stop me."

Aylin frowned. "If I have to pretend to like you, so be it."

"Don't sound too excited about it," he said dryly. "You may exert yourself."

Aylin's lip twitched, but she bit down on it. She would never give him the satisfaction of thinking he was funny. Ilyas surprised her when he took the severed rope of her hair and tucked it into his pocket like it was a keepsake. Her mouth parted to speak before she decided she didn't exactly know what to say to him.

"What shall we pick for my name?" she asked. "I want something pretty and strong."

"What a dilemma," Ilyas said with a dramatic huff.

They drifted in a sea of ghosts, sprays of the water stroking her face with icy fingers. The edges of her kaftan were stained with dirt from her travels. It was a finely made cloth intertwined with black wool with metallic silver threading. Fur lined the collar, and the sleeves billowed with each stroke of the wind. The *hassa nakkaşları* were the finest designers in the Ottoman court. While Aylin was not important enough to have her clothes commissioned by such talented hands, Yara was given access to the highest reaches of the court. Her friendship with the sultana and companionship with the prince raised her in esteem among the *bey* who travelled from their *beyliks* for court functions. It felt right to be cloaked in her sister's robe while she hunted her captors. It smelled like her, like jasmine and the warmth of the sun. It felt like rosy cheeks and wide-toothed smiles. It felt like Yara.

Aylin felt the stinging graze of a tear roll down her cheek. It slipped into her collar, disappearing into her flesh like a carp swallowing a row of eggs. The boat picked up speed as if Ilyas could sense her distress. She was grateful that he was so ill-equipped in handling weeping girls. He didn't speak of her torment.

And Aylin did not wish to discuss her pain.

———

The story Ilyas weaved was spun with all the grace and decorum of a seasoned storyteller. He had given her strict instructions to let him do all the speaking, which was fine by her. Her Greek was rather poor and her Latin even more tragic. All those lessons under the tutelage of the stern Ibrahim Hoca, who prided himself on being the hand that shaped the imperial prince, had left her with a bone-cracking yawn and a growing desperation to stab him in the eye with her quill.

Upon arrival at the Port of Venice, Aylin was overwhelmed by the loud bustle of the city. Buildings made of wooden stilts and the razor-thin tip of the cathedral's arm winked in the distance. There were military vessels and cargo ships docked on the harbor and gondolas owned by wealthy patricians in the canals. Aylin had read in a book once that Venice possessed as many canals as it did roads. Men with wooden crossbows perched like crows atop the ledge, and she could see their gilded blades holstered to the hips of their commanders. Aylin stared warily into the distance as if the Venetians could smell their traitorous blood.

The city twisted and writhed like a phantom before them. The Republic of Venice. The constant enemy of the Ottomans, who refused to bend to the sultan. They were in enemy waters, and her skin shone as brown as the sand that layered their shores. Her foreignness could not be ignored. She worried for a moment that this had all been a foolish endeavor. That they were sailing off to their deaths. It

calmed her that they'd had the sense to pray earlier. They had dutifully rinsed in the strait, coating their skin with the cold water before Ilyas led her through prayers. His soft, scratchy voice a soothing
balm.

"If they grow suspicious of us, they will hang us as Ottoman
spies," Ilyas said. His dark brows crumpled like parchment. "We will
not live to see the next morning prayer."

"God help us," she whispered.

"Amen," he breathed.

Ilyas stared at her strangely. They were only twenty minutes away
from docking.

A surprised yelp escaped her when his hand gripped her by the
nape and drew her into a forced embrace. Her palm lay flat on his
thigh, and she felt the muscle shift under her touch. It was a rough
hold. A gesture more comfortable between soldiers than man and
woman. His hand held her with the dominant force of a man who was
used to bending others to his will. Aylin had seen him once from
behind an orange tree, commanding his cavalry. His face had been so
severe she had hardly recognized him. She knew then that there were
two Ilyases—one was hers and one belonged to the sultan.

"Do not get yourself killed?" he whispered harshly. "If it ever
comes down to your life and mine, you choose yourself. Always. I am
a trained soldier. I was destined for death the day I left that idle farm-
house in Transylvania and my fingers unclenched from the apron of
my mother to grip the sultan's blade."

"You should have joined a traveling troupe, not the military," she
said. "Your flair for theatrics would make you a crowd favorite."

"I know you joke when you're scared," he said. His breath stirred
her hair, and the intimacy of the embrace made her stiffen. Ilyas was
not one for touching. He was rather religious and kept a wide berth
from women, lest he be tempted by them. His gaze was always low-

ered, as was *sunnah*. So, for him to embrace her so candidly felt rather grave and ominous. It was unspoken, but she knew that they could die before they ever reached her sister. This could be their last moment together.

"The situation must be dire indeed for you to be so tolerable."

Ilyas released her, sighing as if she were a nuisance. But she caught the mild twitch of his lips. He gripped the oars like they were his sword and he pushed forth, cutting through the water like Prophet Musa did the Red Sea.

The moment they docked, the Venetians swarmed them, sensing something amiss. It wasn't every day that a small boat with a dark-skinned girl and a giant man slid into the Venetian port. Their language flitted by her ears like the churning flaps of a bird's wings. They spoke far too fast for her to understand. She struggled to capture a trickle of Latin that escaped their pale mouths.

Ilyas spoke slowly enough for her to grasp enough words to form a sentence.

"We seek asylum with the Republic of Venice, with the permission of the doge and the pope," he said. "My name is Elijah Cazacu. I hail from the Ottoman vassal state of Transylvania and was sold into military service and forced conversion while my mother was sold into household service with one of their *bey* lords. I escaped with my brother. He is of both Transylvanian and Turkish blood."

A cross-eyed man of about fifty stared at them with disbelief. He looked at them from head to toe. A slow perusal down their persons, as if he would find their guilt written on their clothing.

"How did you escape?" he asked suspiciously.

"I stole from the aǧa. He was fond of me and permitted me to visit his home to dine from a shared platter with his wife and child. I used the coin to forge paperwork for my brother and I to flee that cursed state and seek refuge with my brethren."

The man looked at his compatriots. Their eyes spoke words she could not understand, and she struggled to keep her fidgeting at bay. Ilyas's presence soothed her. It comforted her that he was taller than the men who enclosed them in a circle.

"You will be questioned individually," he said. "Should your answers be satisfactory, you will be taken to the nearest chapel to seek refuge with the pastor. If there is a slip of untruth to your words, the punishment will be harsh indeed. You will be sent to the execution block, and that is only after you are tortured in the doge's dungeon for months on end. Your limbs hacked off one at a time and your faces carved till there is nothing but bone."

Aylin swallowed as one of the soldiers grabbed her elbow.

Before they were drawn apart, she curled her smallest finger around Ilyas's thumb, holding on to it for what felt like an eternity. His eyes locked with hers with a steady warning that said, "Be brave."

Aylin was yanked toward a small office. It was damp inside and smelt like salt and sweat. The soldier who had led her in sat in a wooden chair that creaked beneath his weight and folded his pockmarked hand atop his drooping stomach. He stared at her with relaxed eyes, as if he didn't hold the weight of her future in his palm.

"Do you speak Latin?" he asked.

"My Greek is better," she said.

"How does the bastard child of a Turk noble and a Christian woman speak our civilized tongue?" he asked.

"I was taught by my brother," she said. "He ran into his mother during a trip to the market and she told him of my existence. We would find ways to visit each other. To understand our different lives. He taught me his true faith, the one he carried inside him all this time, and I nurtured it inside me."

"Sing me a psalm," he said. "A beautiful one about the Virgin Mary."

Aylin glared at him. "We were not sitting around singing psalms. We were plotting our escape and understanding the differences in our life. It isn't easy to discover you've had a brother this entire time. One whose heart yearned for freedom the way a babe yearns for milk."

"Your brother is prettier than you and built like an ox, while you look like an unfed orphan," he said. "Are you sure you're related?"

"I'll let him know he's caught your eye," Aylin said with a smirk.

His face turned a mottled shade of red. The heavy thud of his boots was the only warning she received before his hands wrapped around her throat, squeezing tight until tears sprung to her eyes. Aylin scratched his hands, skin caking beneath her fingernail, but he refused to release her as she desperately gasped for air.

"I could kill you and not lose a wink of sleep, Ottoman scum." He spat. "You call yourself a man. Disgusting."

The door banged open and the officer who took Ilyas stepped in. His beard drifted like a hoisted flag as he looked between them both.

"The boy's a trueborn Christian; we cannot turn him out," he said. "Release the cretin. He is fond of the boy, even though his blood is polluted with the sins of our enemy."

Aylin fell to her knees when the soldier released her, choking madly on the air that her windpipe hungrily sought. Her throat felt raw, like it had been scraped clean.

He kicked her. A hard jab of his boots to her ribs that made her groan.

"Get up," he said.

He gripped her by the collar and pulled her out the door. Ilyas stood there, his lips pulled into a thin line.

"Is this the Christian goodwill you give to those seeking refuge?" Ilyas demanded. His finger trembled when he touched her reddened throat. Aylin swatted his hand, glaring at him. He was treating her like a delicate woman when she was supposed to be a *boy*.

"You're lucky I didn't cut his tongue for his disrespect," he growled.

This time it was Ilyas who glared at her, and Aylin quickly looked away from his frigid blue eyes. They could make a grown man flinch.

"I'll discipline him," Ilyas said. "It is clear to see our mother softened him. Tolerated his disobedience for far too long."

The officer grunted. "You're a wise boy."

He led them to a gondola and paid a small sum to have them taken to a chapel. She and Ilyas were packed onto the small bench. The officer who questioned Ilyas sat before them. It was a tight fit, and Ilyas's big thighs swallowed up majority of the space. Aylin had half her torso swinging precariously close to the murky water.

The streets were barely contained by the influx of vendors, civilians and patricians who went about their day.

Ilyas's posture was rigid, assessing their surroundings as if a threat would assault them at any moment. His shrewd eyes looked at every passing civilian and studied them before dismissing them as irrelevant and moving to the next.

"You have the trained eye of a soldier," the officer said. "You should consider service to his lord, the doge's army."

"Once I am settled and honest work is found for my brother, I shall consider going back into service. It feels unnatural to walk without a blade in my hand," he said. As if his blade wasn't hidden in the confines of his boot.

"I wish you the best, my boy," the officer replied, clasping him firmly on the shoulder. "This is not your country, but we welcome you all the same."

It shouldn't have surprised her that they respected Ilyas for his fair skin and the fluidity of his tongue. It was strange to rely on him.

To look to him for guidance in this foreign country where, unlike in Constantinople, it was now she who stood out while he fit in perfectly. She knew Ilyas secretly enjoyed leading the charge, being the one to concoct his ingenious plans.

They were brought to an old chapel with cobwebs covering the ceiling while a pair of orphan boys diligently scrubbed the floor panels with soap.

Aylin stared at their temporary home until they found this cabal of hunters. Aylin wondered if perhaps Sevda had misled them. If they had traveled all this distance and risked their necks for nothing. Staring around at the small, dilapidated chapel stuck in the middle of the bustling streets of Venice, Aylin couldn't help but feel hopeless. It was musty inside, like the windows hadn't been drawn open in some time. The pointed roof was water-stained and cracked. A man in weathered robes lit candles on the silver candelabra. At the sound of their footsteps, he turned around, peering at them curiously.

"And who do I welcome to the house of our Lord?" he asked.

Ilyas stepped forward with a thrust of his hand. "Elijah. I've returned to join the flock of our Lord with my brother, Aydin."

They had decided on a Turkish name for her because it fit the folds of their story of being the son of a noble and a slave woman. And besides, she had wanted something similar to her own name. Something she wouldn't forget.

"Welcome, my children," the pastor said. He had a warm smile and a comforting disposition. Aylin felt instantly soothed by his presence. The officer bid them farewell, and the pastor led them to the only available room: the bell room. He didn't ask them any questions, and she figured they weren't the first refugees he had taken under his wing.

A single cot sat in the corner with woollen blankets that looked chewed thin by rats. And hanging in the center was a rusty bell shaped like a fallen tulip.

"I am terribly sorry to say we have but one bedroom available," the pastor said. "I can hunt for some fresh blankets, but this is all I have."

"This will do, Father," Ilyas said politely.

The door clicked shut behind them, and Aylin had scarcely made a move before Ilyas had her pinned to the wall.

"What did you say to provoke him?" he demanded. "You had to have said *something.*"

"It was a joke," Aylin said. "From his reaction, you would think there was some truth to it. That he truly did desire you!"

"I don't care if his mother desires me," Ilyas said. His mouth tightened into a grimace as if he were disturbed by his own words. "And neither should you."

"You forget I am not a trained soldier. I cannot compose myself as well as you. I will do better to keep my words to myself."

If she didn't make an effort to apologize, then they would argue till the end of time. Ilyas could hold a grudge for decades.

"He could have cut out your tongue," Ilyas said. "And he would have been within his right to do so."

"I'm sure it would please you to not hear another word from me," she said.

Ilyas pushed away from her like he couldn't tolerate her presence for another second.

"Bolt the door," he said. "It's almost prayer time."

Aylin locked the door and frowned when she had done it. She was finding it far too easy to accept his commands, and she regretted doing it so quickly, but it would be far too immature to unlock it now. He placed the blanket on the ground, and Aylin drew the second blanket atop her head in an act of modesty. Ilyas read the verses of the Qu'rān in a faint whisper. She felt calmer in the end, as if her fears were floating away into the abyss.

"I will go around and question them about the Silver Cross," he said. "They will be more receptive to me."

"And what shall I do?" she asked.

Ilyas shrugged. "Whatever it is you do that doesn't involve getting us killed."

"I don't want to sit around. Yara is *my* sister," she said. "I want to do as much as possible."

"You think I don't care about Yara?" he asked tightly.

Aylin stared at him strangely. She wondered then if he had risked everything for her sister because he liked her. Yara certainly thought he was handsome. She batted her long lashes at him anytime he would go on his patrols. If she was feeling terribly bold, she'd whistle and dart behind the rose bushes, leaving Aylin to fall under the scrutiny of his hard gaze.

"Do you like her?" Aylin asked. She was surprised by the sharpness of her tone. It wasn't that she cared if he liked her sister. Every warm-blooded man was obsessed with Yara. She simply didn't like secrets and half-truths.

"Do you forget that I've sworn under the sultan to take no wife and father no child?" he asked with a single raised brow.

"That doesn't mean you don't feel attraction," she said. "Do you like Yara?"

"No, Aylin. I don't like your sister. I dare say my vow of celibacy is safe with her," he said in a dry tone.

"Have you ever been tempted by a woman?" she asked curiously. She sat atop the thin cot, hearing it creak miserably under her weight. A small smile graced her lips when she saw him tilt his head to the sky as if he were praying for the patience to deal with her. His throat rippled with his swallowed words.

"There is one right now who is *tempting* me to kill myself," he said.

"Very funny," Aylin said. "And entirely *haram*."

She lay down in the bed and stared at the ceiling, at the spider-webs that drifted like clasped palms. Her eyes felt heavy, and she found herself drifting into a deep slumber.

VI

YARA WOKE UP disoriented. It was dark in the room, and her shoulders ached, as if she had performed an excruciating task the night before. At the sight of the silk cords on her wrists, it all came tumbling back: the kidnapping, the sale, the feeding. Her eyes frantically searched for her new captors, but the bedroom was empty. All except for a young girl who dusted the mahogany armoire and whistled an unfamiliar tune. Candles had been lit and the curtains were still drawn, so she could not say how many hours had passed.

"Good morning," the girl trilled, in an oddly chipper voice. She released the cloth she used to wipe the wardrobe and retrieved a letter made of fine paper and sealed with red wax.

"Shall I read you the note left behind?" she asked. "Can you read?"

Yara could read perfectly well, but she shook her head. It was best if they thought she was uneducated. While her captor had revealed a bit of her status in court, he had not relayed how powerful her father was or his close ties to the sultan. They had spoken Greek comfortably before her, so they were yet unaware of her vast education, and she wanted them to underestimate her.

The servant girl read:

Good morning, pet,

You looked rather pleasant sleeping in my bed. It wasn't difficult to imagine how you'd look dead. Still and haunting and utterly beautiful. Fear not though, my wicked love, for dead maidens don't keep us nourished. Feel free to explore the lodgings of our host until dinner. You are expected to arrive at eight and dress accordingly. I've laid out a dress for you to wear.

Yours,
Volkan.

Yara shivered at the macabre words. He was doing it to frighten her. Volkan was the cruel brother. That much she was certain of.

"Shall we prepare you for dinner?" the girl asked.

"What time is it?" Yara asked.

"Oh, a little after sunset."

Yara blinked in alarm. She had slept through the entire day. That was unlike her.

"It is the way of them. To sleep during the day and rise at night," she said. "We all follow their schedule."

"I...I didn't want to sleep. He told me to sleep and I just..." Yara had blacked out. She would have never slept if he hadn't commanded her to do so. Her mind had been too disturbed to rest peacefully. Her fear far too heightened to soak herself in the comforts of sleep.

"When they feed, you become susceptible to their suggestion. They can make you do just about anything," she said. "You will learn soon enough that we are weaklings before them. In this world, they are our dark gods, and we are their broken supplicants."

There was a dull acceptance to the girl's words. Yara noticed faded teeth marks on her pale wrist. Her hair was knotted in an intricate braid that wrapped around her head. She couldn't have been older than sixteen. Yara felt her heart clench for the young girl.

"What's your name?" she asked.

"Elisabeta," she said. "And yours?"

"Yara."

"You have a beautiful name," she said with a gentle smile.

"Are you a blood slave?" Yara asked.

"No, my brother was sired by Volkan," she said. "When my brother transformed, he couldn't bear to leave me behind. So, he brought me with him to the Demircis' family manor in the Ottoman empire, and now to the estate of Lord Dracul in Wallachia."

So, they were in Wallachia then. It was a small relief that they remained in one of the sultan's vassal principalities. The vaivode of the province would be oath-bound to return her to Constantinople if word was brought to his attention or even to one of the boyars, and she could perhaps find safe passage back home.

"Why would your brother bring you to this ungodly place?" Yara asked.

"It is safer to live with monsters than to live away from them and constantly fear when they might strike," she said. "Besides, the brothers aren't wretched to their sired. Anyone under the House of Demirci is offered their protection."

Elisabeta began to unknot the silk knots, and Yara rubbed her wrists once she was free. Her eyes darted to the door, and Elisabeta gave her a sympathetic look.

"It is sealed shut. All the front doors, that is," she said. "Impenetrable during the day. And heavily guarded at night."

"There must be a way," Yara murmured.

Elisabeta crouched down till they were eye to eye. "The only way to survive is to keep your head down. Be dutiful and never disobey a vampir."

Yara shuddered at the word. To invoke their name was to accept that they existed.

"If they ask to feed from you, it is better to be gracious." Elisabeta continued. "Reluctant prey only whets their appetite."

Elisabeta dressed her in an Egyptian *kalasiris*. It concealed little and was made to be worn in severe heat and not inside the cold walls of a Wallachian fortress. It was a shade of saffron that was agreeable with her pallor and made her brown skin shine.

Elisabeta led her down the gloom-stained hallway. Shadows lurked in the crevices and the faint flicker of candlelight illuminated the space. Grand stone doors crystallized with ornaments led into different rooms painted in dull coloring. Most rooms had a hearth that crackled with fire to keep one warm while the decor hinted at traces of various cities. Ceramics from İznik perched on low tables, silks from India decorated tablecloths, polished books from Baghdad were tucked between the shelves of the library, while weapons from Venice hung from the wall.

Seating corners were filled with brocaded pillows with dangling tassels. Velvet curtains hailed from ceiling to floor like frozen sentries. Gilded portraits and paintings of pale-faced men and naked women covered the walls. Iconographies of saints from Rus lay on the mantel beneath a wide-framed portrait of the Virgin Mary cradling a sheep in her arms.

"It is called Poenari Castle," Elisabeta said, as they swept into one room after the other. "Dracul found it and reconstructed it as an eternal home to the vampir. It was constructed long ago as a fortress to protect against the Mongols. It has never been breached, and you must climb over a thousand steps to reach the top."

"I know," Yara said dryly. "I climbed it. And I nearly punctured a lung for it."

Yara was not like Aylin. She wasn't slim and coated in muscle. Her thighs rubbed together when she walked, and her stomach drooped like a wilting flower. Any form of activity tired her greatly, and she would have nightmares of that journey. She could still feel the faint echo of a twinge in her side when she walked.

"How has the sultan or the vaivode not heard of it?" Yara asked. "Even a passing boyar?"

"The villagers of Arefu have an understanding with Dracul. They pay tithes, and in return they receive his protection. It is why blood slaves are brought from neighbouring cities. It is because of the pact."

"To turn a blind eye to this monstrosity is unholy," Yara said with a click of her tongue.

"In time you will learn to relinquish your beliefs," she said. "You will find that it is easier to accept them than to risk their wrath."

"I will never forsake my stance," Yara said. "They are unnatural, and I pray that Volkan burns for his sins someday."

Elisabeta nervously looked around, as if someone would punish them for her words. It was silent as they perused the empty hallway.

"Will you tell me of them?" Yara asked. "Of the Demirci boys? That is their name, correct?"

Elisabeth stiffened. "I do not wish to gossip."

"I am only curious," Yara said. "And I have no power to harm them. Only to understand them."

The lie was heavy on her tongue, but Yara looked at Elisabeta in a manner that she hoped was soothing rather than calculating.

"Volkan is unpredictable. He enjoys wild parties filled with debauchery, and his wicked tongue will make the most innocent of maidens' blush," she said. "Eldar is rather austere and keen eyed. One can never quite tell what he is thinking."

"They are nobles in this court, yes?" Yara asked. Though she had a feeling she knew the answer to that. They carried themselves with power and dignity.

"Yes," Elisabeta said. "There are nine trueborn families. These are people who are born human and naturally transition and become vampir, whereas a sired vampir is made."

"How does one kill a trueborn?" Yara asked.

Elisabeta shook her head in silent warning.

"It is late. We must dress you before Volkan arrives," she said. And without another word she turned back around toward the prison that was Yara's bedroom.

⚜

Elisabeta dressed her as though she were the bride of Death, in a black lace dress with a plunging neckline.

Her dark hair had been raised in an intricate style and pinned with a jeweled comb with onyx shells. Thick dark kohl covered her brown eyes, and Yara couldn't help but think that she looked enticing enough to eat. It dawned on her that she was no better than livestock. A blood slave. A role that was emphasized by the collar Elisabeta abruptly snapped on her neck. She barely glimpsed the sigil of two black scorpions whose shell arms were intertwined in comradery. The sigil of her captors. It had been sealed onto the wax of *his* letter.

"I'm sorry," Elisabeta said. "Their blood slaves always wear this. The chain will be held by your masters." She attached two long iron chains to the rings on her collar. Yara felt suffocated, and while she knew the collar didn't suppress her breathing, the weight on her chest made her gasp. It was demeaning. Far worse than this scrape of a dress. She could sacrifice her modesty, but she could not do the same for her humanity.

"I don't want this," Yara said, her fingers scratching at the iron as if she could pry it off with sheer will.

"It is better this way," Elisabeta said gently. "Remember what I said. It is easier if you do not resist."

A knock sounded on the door, and Yara swallowed down her panic. The door opened to reveal both Eldar and Volkan standing side by side in ink-black kaftans. Their long hair fell in wisps down to their waists, almost maidenly in their design. Their faces looked ethereal, as if God had painstakingly taken his time to craft them both. Their pale skin was lustrous beneath the light. One mouth was tightened in a scowl and the other raised in a wolfish grin.

"Spectacular," Volkan said. "You look good representing our house. Does she not, Eldar?"

Eldar grunted and looked down the hallway. "I'll meet you in the Grand Hall."

He disappeared without sparing her a second glance. It unnerved her to see that Volkan's eyes were red. She recalled what the seller had mentioned: that red eyes indicated hunger. If that were the case, then he was *starved*.

Yara took a step back, much to his delight.

"Has our pet shared her name with you, Elisabeta?" he asked.

"Yes, my lord," she whispered. "She goes by Yara."

It didn't hurt Yara that she so easily betrayed her confidence. Elisabeta would not have shared her advice to not resist them if she did not follow it herself.

"Yara," he said tasting her name on his tongue. "*Yara.*"

"My father will pay you if you release me," she said. "I will not speak a word of what I witnessed. Of the...of the unnaturalness I've seen."

Elisabeta disappeared down the hall when Volkan waved his fingers at her in dismissal. They were alone. Somehow, she wished Eldar were here. He seemed to be his brother's moral compass.

Volkan stepped into the bedroom. His steps were slow and leisurely, as if he possessed all the time in the world. He continued to prowl toward her until her back was pressed to the armoire.

"Yara, do I look like a peasant hungry for a spare coin?" he whispered.

"I cannot speak my mind freely," she said. "I haven't forgotten your nasty temper."

"Speak freely," he said. "I wish to know your true thoughts."

"Then yes," Yara hissed. "You look like a street rat."

Volkan stared at her for one silent moment before he laughed. That ringing melodic sound made him seem less villainous and far more human than she'd like. It was jarring, for someone who appeared so predatory to possess human characteristics.

"Nobody has ever insulted me so viciously before," Volkan said. "Even Eldar knows better than to pick at me. I was a rabid dog when I was young, who would tear the arm off anyone who looked at me wrong. Even before I transitioned."

"When did you transition?" she asked. She didn't expect him to answer, so she was surprised when he did. She was curious to know what it was to "transition." And the more she learned, the more it improved her chances of escape.

"All vampir from the noble bloodlines—that is the trueborn—transition at twenty-five to thirty. Eldar and I transitioned prematurely. Mine occurred at eighteen and Eldar's at nineteen. He thinks he's older than me since he transitioned later. But I came out the womb first, which makes me oldest, do you not agree?"

"He is certainly more mature," she said under her breath.

"Do you know we also have a keen sense of hearing?" Volkan asked. He bent down to trail his nose along her cheekbone, inhaling her scent deeply. "If you seek to insult me without me knowing, you'll have to keep it in the recesses of your mind."

He tangled his hands in the separate chains, clutching them like they were the reins to a horse. "Come along, my love. We do not wish to be late."

He led her down the hallway. Yara stared at the portrait of a man on a throne, who sat alongside other related faces. They all shared the same dark hair and empty black eyes, like they could see into one's soul. Beneath the portraits were plaques that said their names and titles. Vladislav Dracul the II, the Undying King, the Leader of the Draculesti line. Mircea. Radu. Mihnea. All were titled the Undying Princes. They shared the same cold eyes and tight lips, like someone had suckled the life out of them. Yara wondered if these creatures were immortal. While their faces appeared youthful, their eyes struck her as old. They were eyes that had feasted on wars and survived devastating plagues. Even Volkan, for all his humor and biting snark, had ghosts dancing behind his eyes. Not as old as these creatures, but something haunted him. Yara would have to discover what it was.

"I expect you to behave yourself tonight," Volkan said. "As much as I enjoy our conversations, you will practice obedience. Speak when addressed and refer to me as your lord. If you do anything untoward, I will have to discipline you, and that won't be pleasurable for either of us."

Yara scoffed. "I'm sure it won't be pleasurable for you at all."

He caught her chin, yanking her head toward him. He licked his lips, revealing the sharp points of his canines. "Perhaps I should drink your blood and force you into submission."

Yara shuddered, thinking of the way he had put her to sleep last night. That loss of control frightened her. It was one thing to be paraded around in vulgar clothes and be led by a brutal vampir. It was another to be robbed of her senses and agency.

"I will behave, my lord." The words tasted like acid in her mouth.

"Will you?" he pressed. The nail of his claw dug into her flesh enough to slice the skin. Yara hadn't realized it before, but he had small, black-tipped claws perfect for puncturing skin should his teeth fail. Blood trickled from the wound, and he pressed his mouth to her chin and sucked hard. Her eyes fluttered shut. An intense spike of pleasure churned in her gut when he opened his mouth wider, and his lips traced the outline of her bottom lip.

"Answer me," he said against her skin. Her mind was hazy, but his words were not a command. Relief almost made her knees buckle. She could curse him if she wanted to, and she was tempted to try.

"Yes, my lord," she said.

The doors to the Grand Hall were drawn open. The room resembled a cathedral, with high wooden beams and a great archway with ribbed vaulting. There were sectioned alcoves covered with stained glass where couples disappeared for privacy. Yara wondered with a deep shudder exactly what occurred behind those confessionals. She had seen a similar pattern in the Hagia Sophia.

Hundreds of candles were strung on the ledges, illuminating the dark room, and long wooden tables sat laden with feasts. Volkan led her to a table, and her stomach grumbled at the sight of the food. Yara noticed a flag descending from the wall to hover above their table. A black flag with two white scorpions. All the tables at the front had flags of various sigils, while the tables in the back had no markers.

There were dozens of people at this table, and at the center was Eldar. His shrewd, cold eyes searched the room like he was hunting for some unseen prey. It soothed her to know that nobody was staring at her or mocking her. All around her, blood slaves were treated wretchedly. Some were sprawled on tables and devoured by multiple vampir, while others smiled dazedly as they were led to those alcoves. Those were the ones who frightened her. The ones who enjoyed the torment and were influenced by their bite. It had subdued her last night, and she had fallen susceptible to his whispers.

She was trapped in a room full of devils.

A young man drew back Volkan's chair and for one horrible moment she thought he intended for her to sit on his lap, but the words he uttered were far worse.

"Kneel," he said. Like she was a dog. Like she was not the daughter of Beşir Ağa. The noblest servant of the sultan. The backbone of Constantinople.

Her skin burned as chuckles drifted from the table. Volkan sat back, expecting her to crawl into the gap between his legs. He was testing her, seeing if she would go back on her word.

Yara swallowed her pride and turned to sit between *Eldar's* legs. A tactic to get under Volkan's skin.

Eldar's feathery brows twisted in irritation to see her half-leaning against his calf. Volkan's lips had tightened to a thin slit, and she resisted the urge to smile. She had humiliated him, and it felt wonderful.

"Don't do that," Eldar said in that pretty, lilting voice of his. Somehow his face was harsher than Volkan's. Or perhaps it was his permanent scowl that made him so unapproachable. His cheekbones were thin enough to cut through his flesh, and his nose was strong and pointed like an arrow.

"Do what?"

"Come between my brother and I," he said.

"I wouldn't dare," she said.

Despite the humiliation of sitting on the ground, Yara liked that she was partly hidden beneath the table and enshrouded by his long legs. Yara stared at him as his gaze shifted around the room. She knew that look from the sultan's court. It was the look of someone who sought to advance their position and was searching for cracks in the armor of their opponents.

Yara stared at him for what felt like hours, studying the small shifts on his face. The way his brows furrowed when he pieced something together. The way his lips tightened when he was displeased. The way his fist closed when he was angry. He was a fascinating creature who revealed nothing unless you studied him. Much like a predator studied their prey before they attacked.

Yara felt her stomach growl in hunger. His head snapped down, as if he'd just realized she was still sitting at his feet. A frown darkened his face, blooming like a stain on his beautiful features.

"Volkan, feed *it*," he said. He punctuated this lovely comment with a hard nudge of his knee for her to go to his wicked brother. Yara glared at him, but his attention had returned to survey the room once more. Yara despised the yank on her collar and crawled to Volkan, resisting the urge to bite his leg.

"Come, sit on my lap," Volkan said with a snap of his fingers. Yara opened her mouth to refuse, but the more she thought about it, the more it seemed preferable to sit up top than curled by his feet like a kitten, eating the scraps from his palm.

"How could you do this?" Yara snarled under her breath the moment she perched awkwardly on his thighs. "How could you treat your own countrywoman so poorly?"

Volkan drew her back till she rested on his chest. Her posture was stiff, and she could feel her spine straighten at the graze of his kaftan. His fingers were cold and spindly, the joints stretched in a manner that provoked discomfort. His nails were pointed and retracted into his skin at will. But he didn't hide it now: his monstrosity, his otherworldliness was there for all to see. Even his teeth were stretched, sheathed in ivory porcelain.

"We do not care for race or faith in these halls," Volkan said. "Look around you. Look at the vampir and the humans."

Yara looked at the Turks and the Egyptians and the Spaniards and the Chinese and the Greek and the Venetian and the African. They mingled, dressed in the exquisite fabric of their nations. In beautifully dyed silks from Aleppo and Damascus, in bright cotton stained with pigment of cochineal and lac. Shoulders masked in fur-lined kaftans, chests draped in brocade coats decorated in gold appliqué and colorful beads. Some women's heads were laden with a kaşbastı, the diadems gleaming under the candlelight. Others wore the vibrant swatches of east African turbans.

The blood slaves were just as diverse, with no indication that they had been picked based on anything other than the blood that ran in their veins.

"We are still cut from the same cloth," Yara whispered. "Even if you deny it."

"I'm only half-Turk," Volkan said. "And you? You don't look Turkish."

"I'm from Bornu," she said.

"How did you find yourself in Constantinople?" Volkan asked. "It is quite the journey."

Yara kept her lips sealed. She knew what he was doing, prying into her life to figure out anything he could about her.

"How did you find yourself as a vile creature who feeds on the innocent?" Yara asked.

"I'll answer your question if you answer mine." His eyes sparkled as if he found her amusing. Yara watched as he cut a piece of lamb-stuffed quince and held it up to her lips.

"I can feed myself," she said.

"Let me," he insisted. Yara opened her mouth to protest but he was quick, and the sweet and savory flavor burst on her tongue. Her stomach clenched, starved for the delicious food. Volkan was quick to retrieve a second bite, and she accepted it only because his hands moved far more quickly than her own. She didn't have to wait long to fill her stomach. He rotated between spoonfuls of almond *pilaf* wrapped in flatbread and eggplant paste drenched with stewed mutton on top.

"You didn't answer my question," Volkan said.

Playing the role of the illiterate girl hadn't worked for her, so it was time to change tactics. She would wield her upbringing like a sword. It wouldn't make him mistreat her any more than he already had. Perhaps he would think twice about shackling and chaining her like an unruly beast and treat her more like a genteel woman. Or so Yara hoped.

"My father is the *kızlar ağası* to the sultan," she said. "I'm certain he's rounded up a thousand men, if not more, to retrieve me."

"I could kill your father's men with my eyes closed," Volkan said with a faint smile. "Chief Black Eunuch a powerful role, but one steeped in blood and prejudice and hate. Tell me, my pet. Do you despise them for the pain and suffering they brought your father? For tearing him from his country and forcibly castrating him and erasing his language and faith and destiny until he was nothing but a docile servant?"

Yara clenched her teeth. She was not a child. She knew the Ottoman Empire was imperfect. Ever since Aylin had told her that Ilyas was torn from his family to serve and die in the sultan's never-ending war, she had devoured books of history. She had read upon the fall of Constantinople, which had once belonged to the Byzantines, and the torment of the Christians, who had died and been enslaved. She knew of the fate that was bestowed on the eunuchs who oversaw the harem. She knew the pain her father endured as he was torn from their home and taken to Egypt to be castrated and then put before the sultan for service.

"I know the world is unkind to the weak," she said tightly. "I know that men are selfish and cursed and ungodly. If you think your words will hurt me, it is no new information to me. Better to be a slave with power than one without."

"What a unique perspective," Volkan said with a stroke of his chin. His inhuman hands snagged her attention, and she shuddered. If you spoke to one of them long enough, you could *almost* forget their nature. "You are a brave one, my pet. Braver than most."

"Now that you know the unfortunate circumstances of my birth, will you tell me of your origins?" she asked.

"I am a man of my word," he said, relaxing in his high-backed chair. Yara's eyes drifted to the dais, where a blood slave lay with her limbs sprawled while the vampir sucked on her wrists and ankles. Her glassy eyes looked up at the beams that criss-crossed the ceiling, barely clinging to life. She wouldn't last another hour, and that greatly saddened Yara. She made a promise to herself that she would do everything in her power to prevent herself from meeting such a fate.

"The Demirci are an old family with vampiric roots for as long as one can recall. In the early days we were blacksmiths before we shot to power in the courts of Osman the I. Before vampir transition, we are weak creatures not any better than the mortals we feed from. Anywhere from the age of twenty-five to thirty is when we die and return as immortals driven by blood lust. We tend to retreat from the humans and return to our ancestral home once transitioned and rotate between there and Dracul's Court of the Undead."

"How old are you?" she asked, her eyes wide in horror. "Did you walk the earth with the early prophets?"

Volkan scoffed. "No, Eldar and I are mere children at court. We are not any older than our true age. I propose we are now twenty-one, but I will have to confirm with Eldar. I don't quiet keep track of my years I suppose it doesn't matter once you've stopped aging. I dare say you and I are not too far apart in age. So, you may stop looking at me as if I were a decrepit old man preying on your youthful soul."

"If that is truth then why are you so cruel and hardened?" she asked.

His eyes drifted away from her in a manner that almost appeared thoughtful. Behind his red eyes she could see a glimmer of childish innocence, as if he had grown up more quickly than most. She wondered what type of life one must have lived to become so ruthless.

"I haven't had an easy life," he said. "Eldar was always better at controlling himself than I was."

He straightened his shoulders, a mask covering his face to hide the truth she had barely caught hold of. "I tire of these questions. Go dance for Eldar."

"I don't dance," Yara said. "I can sing."

"I didn't ask you to sing," Volkan said easily. "I asked you to dance. If you succeed in entertaining my brother, neither of us will drink from you tonight. If you fail, we will take a wrist each. Is that understood?"

Her heart thudded. "It doesn't need to be this way."

"We are not equals, my pet," he said, stroking her cheek absently. "No amount of your invasive questions will bridge the gap of our nature. You were made to sustain us, and we were made to break you."

Yara stood up, wiping her sweat-stained palms on her dress.

Volkan pushed her toward his brother. Eldar had dragged his chair back to continue his inquisitive staring, picking apart their surroundings like they were a board game. There was enough room before him for Yara to thoroughly humiliate herself.

"Volkan has asked me to dance for you," she said.

"I heard," he said.

Yara frowned. Of course, they could hear perfectly well in a crowded room. They were predators.

"Will you pretend to be entertained?" she asked. "*Please.*"

Eldar blinked in offense, as if she requested, he join her for her dance.

"If you make it quick and don't speak to me for the rest of the night, I will," he said. His eyes were already beginning to grow glazed with boredom. He waved a hand for her to proceed. Yara took a deep breath and swayed her hips like she had seen the court performers do. It wasn't beautiful and sensual like the women who danced for the sultan. Her limbs were rigid, and her footing was slippery. But she kept it brief.

"Marvelous," Eldar said. His voice thick with sarcasm. "That was certainly not a waste of my time."

"You are immortal," she said. "You can sacrifice five minutes."

"Not for you," he corrected.

It stung but she was getting used to his harsh tongue. While he didn't toy with her the way Volkan did, he still despised her.

"Speak frankly, brother," Volkan said. "Are you entertained?"

Eldar looked at her. Yara bit her lip, pleading with her eyes.

"It was adequate," Eldar said.

"Yes or no, Eldar," Volkan said. "I don't like riddles."

"Yes."

A sigh escaped her lips.

Volkan's brows furrowed. "So, you do not mind if she dances for us every night. For the next sixty odd years or however long her mortal life prevails."

"I would rather poke my eyes out with hot needles," Eldar said.

"Then it is a no?" Volkan continued. "She was a dreadful bore, admit it."

"Stop it," Yara snapped. "It was a yes or no question, and he answered."

Volkan's lips twisted in a smile. "I never said I was fair."

Eldar rose, fixing the loosened lapels of his kaftan. "I have better things to do than play a role in these childish games."

"You've scored a point," Volkan said mildly impressed.

Yara had barely released release a sigh of relief before he spoke his next words.

"But I intend to score the next."

VII

AYLIN STRETCHED HER stiff limbs. For a moment, panic spread beneath her skin, unfurling like the peel of an orange. Then she spotted Ilyas curled on the floor near the door, and everything came flooding back in a rush. Her heart twinged at the absence of her sister. It grew even more knotted at the sight of Ilyas coiled into a ball as if he were a stray dog. Aylin crossed the narrow room to offer him the bed; she didn't think she could return to sleep if she tried. The floor creaked when she lowered herself to her knees and his eyes instantly swung open, his fist latching desperately on to her throat. Aylin whimpered in pain. Her skin was still sensitive after the officer had choked her. Her throat had darkened to a vivid shade of blue black, like the sky before sunrise.

Ilyas released her, sitting upright in concern.

"I'm sorry, Aylin," he whispered. "Did I hurt you?"

"No," she said. "Why are you half-awake?"

"A soldier always sleeps with one eye open," he said. "Especially when he has a charge to protect."

Ilyas pointed to the corner. There was a tray with dry bread and onion soup alongside a tin of water.

"I've brought you food. And there's a bucket with water and soap for you, if you wish to bathe," he said.

"Thank you," she said. "Any word about these creatures who took Yara?"

"There's an old man who lives behind the chapel. His name is Father Lorenzo. They say he's a recluse. They say he's seen things that would frighten any mortal man. He hasn't left the confines of his home for almost a decade and doesn't take any visitors."

"Did you speak to him?" she asked.

He shook his head. "I thought that we would go together."

Aylin's lips peeled in a wide grin, and he blinked as if he was startled. She reached for him and squeezed his hand.

"Thank you, Ilyas," she said. "I know that we bicker like a pair of old wives, and we don't always get along, but I'm glad that you are here. That you are risking everything for me and Yara. I don't know what I'd do without you."

His face softened. "Always."

That small word slithered beneath her ribs, sinking into the flesh of her heart. It warmed her like a cup of mint tea on a winter's night.

Once Aylin had eaten and bathed, Ilyas began to tug on his boots, lacing the knots rapidly.

"Let us go to him now," he said. "If he has any information, we can steal a horse and leave at first light."

Aylin followed him down the narrow staircase into the chapel. They slipped out the back doors into the thicket of woods and darkness. There was a house sitting in the center of the woods, shrouded in moss. It hung like a thick drape on the side of the little house like a flaky beard. It reminded her of the hut of a *cadı* in a fairy tale. A beacon for djinn and evil and vile bargains. Yara would hate it. Aylin happened to love it.

Ilyas rapped his big fist against the door. Loud enough to wake the dead.

"Leave," a withered voice said.

"I wish to speak with you, Father. It is regarding a most delicate matter," Ilyas said.

"Leave," he repeated. "I don't take visitors."

"This is important," Aylin said. "Someone that we care for is in danger. She's been taken by these creatures. In the Turkish tongue they are called *ubir*, but perhaps you have another name for them. They are creatures who feed on the lifeblood of honest men and women."

The door cracked open just a sliver and was drawn forth rather ominously. Almost as if the shadows were luring them into its hungry maw. It smelled stale in the house, and a faint trace of iron burned her nostrils. The man before them sat cross-legged in the darkness. His hair had grown unbearably long. It scraped the floor like a carpet. His skin had a strange pallor, and his eyes were as black as the shadows he had taken as his comfort. He looked like a forest cryptid, a being that had forgone civilization to disappear into the wilderness.

"Foreigners," he breathed with a sharp inhale as if he could smell their otherness.

There was no sitting area, and when Ilyas sat down cross-legged before him, Aylin followed suit.

"We are brothers from Constantinople," Aylin said. "We've heard you are well traveled and possess many stories to share. We hope that you will tell us more of these creatures."

"I will share my secrets, but I will expect a favor in return," he said in that hoarse, broken voice. She wondered when the last time had been that he had spoken to someone. His words were cracked and slipped from his mouth in an ill-fitting manner, like a coat that fit too snugly.

"We won't make a deal without knowing the terms," Ilyas said.

"Smart boy," Lorenzo replied.

It felt like forever until he spoke again, and when he did, Aylin straightened till her back was as tight as an arrow.

"I ask that you kill me," he said. "A blade to the heart. That is my request."

She and Ilyas exchanged a look, wondering if this was a test. Did he suspect they were Ottoman spies? Did he want to see if they would attack a countryman?

"We are here as refugees. If we are found killing people, what do you think they'll do to us?" Aylin asked.

"No one shall mourn me. My death will be a great service to my countrymen," he said in a bitter tone. "Should I share my tale with you, you will know why I need to be released from this abominable life."

Aylin and Ilyas shared another look. They communicated with their eyes.

He's going to get us killed, Ilyas's eyes said.

He might give us the answers we seek, said Aylin's.

As usual, Ilyas ignored the words her eyes had so eloquently spoken.

"Return to our room," Ilyas said aloud. "If this is some test, then I will pay for it with my life alone."

He could only enact his will through shared glances for so long. His forced tongue, as usual, demanded her obedience. "If not, I will return with the answers we seek."

Aylin gritted her teeth. "I'm not going anywhere. We are here to find Yara. *Together.*"

Ilyas didn't seem pleased by her words, but before he could argue some more, Aylin turned to their host.

"You have a deal," she said, staring at the strange priest. His eyes darted between them like he was faintly amused.

"I first came across them during my travels," he said. "I had been a young man, fresh eyed and oblivious to the evil that roamed this earth. A mere cleric with grand ambitions until I came upon *her*. She had appeared as a distressed woman on the side of the road. Her cart had been broken by bandits, she claimed. My gallantry allowed me to fall for this elaborate ruse. Unbeknownst to me, I was her prey. Her face was bloodless. Her hair pale as silver. Her eyes crimson. It was like looking into the eyes of a monster. A beautiful monster."

Aylin shuddered, goosebumps tracing her skin.

"She feasted on my blood," he said. "There are venoms that coat their teeth that trick your mind to believe you are safe. It can almost be pleasurable."

"What happened next?" Aylin whispered.

Ilyas elbowed her. "Don't interrupt."

"I'm not interrupting. I simply don't like dramatic pauses," she said.

"May I continue?" Lorenzo asked dryly.

"Please," Ilyas said.

"After this encounter I grew frightful and prayed for days on end, locking myself in a room. Until I heard the whispers of those who hunted these blasted creatures," he said. "I came to Venice and joined the brotherhood."

"Do you know where they are?" Aylin asked. "The Silver Cross."

Aylin smelled ink and heard the scratch of a quill on parchment before he rolled it up and tucked it into his pocket.

"Complete your end of the bargain and take the address from my corpse," he said.

"I'm afraid we must refuse," Ilyas said. "The risks are simply too great."

"That's a shame," Lorenzo said in his raspy voice. It sounded oddly sinister in the dark.

Aylin barely blinked before she felt a hand coiled around her neck, raising her till she dangled off her feet. Somehow, she was in Lorenzo's arms when she had been halfway across the room. He possessed a brutal strength, and speed. Despite her nails digging into his flesh, it refused to tear beneath her touch, almost as if he were made of stone.

"Il...Ilyas," she gasped. She couldn't breathe.

"I didn't finish my story," Lorenzo said calmly. "There were hazards to the job of being a hunter, and sometimes your prey gets the best of you. I was killed and awakened to resemble the very ones I hunted. A cruel punishment, indeed. I've prayed for God to give me mercy and to strengthen my hand enough to take my wretched life. If you won't grant me that, then I will make him my partner. A companion in this miserable immortality."

He held her at an odd angle, but Aylin did everything in her power to look upon him. From the ashen look on Ilyas's face and the unnatural way Lorenzo's flesh did not splinter or tear beneath her nails, she suspected the man behind her was scarcely mortal.

In the pale moonlight, she looked upon a monstrosity she could not name that iced her veins with its frigid touch. His teeth were sharp, thinned points intended to slice through flesh, and his eyes were a crimson so startling it made her flinch. A shiver coasted down her back, wracking her entire frame in fear. As much as she had trusted Sevda's judgment, she knew that a part of her resisted the absurdity of monsters among them. Even though she believed wholeheartedly in Islam and the existence of djinns, she did not believe in this corruption. It had to be *sihir*. It had to be a trick of the eye. But it felt real. His punishing grip blistered her skin, and she could feel the incisions his claws made, breaking flesh.

"All I've ever wanted was to be given the mercy of a quick kill,"

Lorenzo said. She could hear the misery that coated his words. She wondered how long he had lived in this sad little house with the stained walls and moss-covered floor. How many years had trickled away in prayer and torment, begging for a release that would never arrive.

"Release him," Ilyas growled.

"Kill me," Lorenzo said. "Or I swear by Christ I will drain him and make him one of us."

"Your wish is granted," Ilyas said with a brutal smile. He raised his *kilij* and struck between the gaping of her arm, piercing his heart. It made a squelching sound before Aylin crumbled to her knees. Lorenzo was gone. Nothing but his lifeless eyes facing the downtrodden ceiling revealed the absence of his cursed soul. His face looked weathered, devoid of its youth to reveal the true signs of its age. By the fine-lined wrinkles that creased his flesh, he had lived a long, torturous life. She pitied him, pitied the life he had been forced into. It spoke volumes that he would prefer the company of death to this miserable existence. To this monstrousness.

In the tangled remains of his priestly robe, she hunted for the promised address and clutched it in her fist.

Ilyas whispered a verse of the Qu'rān. His voice strangled in disbelief and fervency.

"Let me see." He crouched down, reaching for her neck. Blood trickled slowly from the wound.

"Don't fret," she said, raising her hand to stop him. He could be fussy when he wished to be, and he easily swatted away her hand.

"I'll clean it when we return to our bedroom," he said. "We'll pack and steal a horse. Is the address legible?"

Aylin nodded, staring at the slanted handwriting. There was a faint description of a forest and its name.

"To think of Yara trapped with these creatures, and at their mercy." Aylin shook her head. "It makes my blood run cold."

"It is worse that they seem to be able to infect us," he said. "I wonder for how long he lived with this disease. I pray that he is granted some measure of relief in the afterlife."

"His face was wretched," she whispered. "I will have nightmares of it."

"Come, we don't have time to waste," he said. "We need to disappear before daybreak."

"What do you think he fed on?" she asked.

"I saw some animal carcasses and fresh-plotted earth during our walk," Ilyas said. "I reckon he drank animal blood and buried them to prevent suspicion."

Aylin shivered. They walked in the dark back to the chapel. She felt hollow from the ordeal and the thought of her sister in danger. She prayed that they weren't too late. That the *ubir* hadn't feasted on her innocence and turned her into one of them.

The sun burned her skin, and the mare trotted beneath them, unused to carrying such weight. Most of their travel to their destination had been done through gondolas and waterways. They had sold their stolen horse and purchased another one, once they were closer to the island of Lido. It was said to be home to a variety of monasteries and convents. So, she was hopeful they would come across the brotherhood.

Ilyas was big enough to require a stallion, but the little grey mare was the best they could find. The poor thing swayed beneath their weight, wobbling on its weak hind legs. Aylin's back was stiff from the brutal pace they kept, and Ilyas refused to stop until they reached their destination. Aylin found herself supporting her weight on his chest. He inhaled sharply, and Aylin knew she shouldn't be so improper, but God, her back was prepared to snap in half.

They were in the depths of Pineta di San Marco, a small pine forest with towering trees and gnarled branches. A gentle breeze swayed the cropped strands of her hair, tickling her scalp. They came upon a bone-white chapel with a red thatched roof. Beside it was a worn-down estate with big windows that looked like eerie eyes. It was a big building that spanned acres, almost appearing quaint though its structure had been rusted by time.

"Seems rather serene," she whispered. "I don't see a crop of trained soldiers."

The door to the chapel opened and a man stepped out. He couldn't have been older than twenty-five and had a beautiful, slim face and pale blond hair that fell to his shoulder. He walked with a grace that spoke of a noble birth. He wore a black robe with a white priestly collar and his hands were folded pleasantly before him.

"Good evening," he called. "Are you lost, my brother?"

Aylin opened her mouth, but Ilyas squeezed her hip, silencing her efficiently. Her heart stumbled beneath his touch, and she struggled to ignore the groves of his fingers clinging to her bone.

"We have come with a purpose," Ilyas said. "My name is Elijah, and this is my half-brother."

"Salvatore Di Mazi," the man said.

"I will be frank with you, Salvatore," Ilyas said. "We were led here by a priest named Lorenzo, who had been taken by a most ungodly illness. My brother and I believe that our sister has fallen into the hands of creatures that are beyond our prayers and must be destroyed lest they ruin us."

Salvatore looked at them both with shrewd brown eyes. Aylin shivered when his gaze fell on her. The warmth that coated his words didn't seem to reach his eyes. In fact, he looked rather wary of their arrival.

"We only accept Venetian Catholic men to take up arms against the *vampir*," he said. "Your presence will sow descent among the men. They don't take well to foreigners."

"Our sister is in trouble," Aylin said. She hopped off the mare, her bones creaking in gratitude that she was finally standing upright. Her temper had reached its pinnacle. She had crossed seas to come here, cut her hair, and was tolerating Ilyas's brutish presence. She had sacrificed everything to find her sister. And she would not be denied by a haughty priest.

"You claim to be a man of God, but you would turn us away for nothing more than the color of our skin and the land of our birth," Aylin snapped. She stood before Salvatore, craning her neck to look upon his eyes. "Answer me!"

"You are young and willful," he said. "And while I commend your bravery, we are not letting children fight this war. Perhaps an exception can be made for Elijah, but not you."

Salvatore looked bored by her insistent nature and turned on his heels to leave.

"Elijah, come with me," he said. "The boy will tend the stables or clean the chapel to earn his keep."

Aylin lunged for him, before he could take a single step forward, he spun around and caught her by the throat.

"Your temper is a nuisance," he growled. "I'm surprised your parents didn't beat it out of you."

"I won't clean up the muck and polish your boots," she spat. "I'd much rather slit your throat in your sleep."

"Aydin," Ilyas said sharply. "Behave."

"Listen to your brother," Salvatore said with a faint smile. He released her, letting her stumble backward. "If you complete your tasks in a satisfactory manner, perhaps you will have time to train with us, boy."

He disappeared into the chapel.

"Can you believe that bastard?" she hissed. "If you complete your tasks in a satisfactory manner." Aylin mocked his voice.

"Are you done?" Ilyas asked.

Aylin nodded.

"There was no need to provoke him," he said. "He has a point. As a woman, you can pass for being nineteen, but with your haircut and your short stature you look like a boy of fourteen, at best. No child should fight a war they do not understand."

His eyes were dark, haunted. And Aylin felt a pinprick of unease. He had been fifteen when he had come to the Ottoman court and was swiftly trained as a Janissary. It seemed silly to complain of Salvatore's injustice when Ilyas had suffered more than she could ever understand.

"I'm sorry," she whispered. "I'll try to control my temper."

"Will you?" he asked skeptically.

Aylin nodded and almost smiled when she saw the crinkle between his brows disappear. He was so easy to please.

If she had to brush the mane of a few horses to train with the men, then she would do it, but she would find her way onto that training field. She would do anything it took to become stronger.

It wasn't the first time she had been underestimated by someone. She had grown up as a woman in a world that saw them as delicate creatures. A world where her roughness and sharp tongue were considered unnatural. Aylin would prove that high-handed Salvatore wrong. She would prove to Ilyas that she could be patient.

And when the opportunity presented itself, her aim would strike true.

VIII

VOLKAN WAS RUNNING late that night, and Yara found herself in the company of his stiff brother. Eldar held the chain of her shackle far from his body, as if the taint of her inferiority would pass on to him if he stepped too close. Yara was pleased that it was him instead of Volkan. She hoped whatever task occupied him would take him at least a few more hours. She felt as though she could break through to Eldar. He seemed far saner and more rational. Perhaps she could provoke some manner of sympathy from him. He sat down in his seat, and she dutifully sat by his feet. She would try to lure him in with sweetness. If that didn't work, then she would insult him until he had risen to a temper. Anything to draw away the indifference that cloaked him.

"You look handsome," Yara said pleasantly. And then as an afterthought, she added, "My lord."

Eldar stared down at her, surprised, like he had forgotten there was a girl curled between his legs.

"And you sound pathetic," he said, returning his gaze to the court.

He had that same look in his eyes. The one that meant he was being calculative and deceitful. That he was picking apart the weaknesses of the courtiers to use to his own benefit.

Yara opened her mouth to respond, but he cut her silent with a scathing comment.

"Silence. Before I muzzle you," Eldar continued. "Food is made to be seen, not heard."

"I can help you," Yara said, ignoring his half-hearted threat. He didn't even care enough about her to fully threaten her.

"And what can a powerless, little girl like you do for me?" he asked. He clicked a finger along the wooden armrest. His iron ring with the familial sigil of the Scorpios clicked in an infuriating manner.

"I grew up in the Ottoman court in Constantinople," she said. "I know how to play games."

Her words weren't merely bluff. While Aylin had been chasing soldiers, Yara had been making herself known in the high circles. Flirting with men of status and giggling with women of noble birth while sipping on *kahve*. Yara knew how to lie through her teeth and how to sow deception.

"This is not the silly game of mortal men who fight over whose god is best," Eldar said. "This is a spider web, and if you're not careful you can get your leg stuck and eaten by your own blood and flesh."

"I know I'm not the strongest person in the room. But I am clever and...and I am beautiful."

The words tasted wretched in her mouth. Her entire life she had despised her beauty. Aunt Sevda once told her the world was kinder to ugly girls. She recalled men her father's age wiping their dry lips on her cheek, lingering until she felt bile climb up her throat. She remembered the imperial prince staring at her chest when she sang for him, and she had felt both sickened and pleased that he found her exceptional. She knew she would never be powerful enough to be his equal. She would only ever be another jewel to adorn his harem. To be beautiful was a curse disguised as a blessing.

"Our kind have lived for centuries. We've seen a variety of beautiful women. Another one is of no special interest. If that is all you have to say for yourself, then this conversation is over," Eldar said. His gaze wavered, and Yara desperately clutched his cold hand. It stiffened beneath her.

"Give me one hour," she said desperately. "One hour to sweep the room, and I will impress you with what I learn."

"You just want to run," he said with a dry chuckle. He shook her hand off his and without any tact rubbed her touch off with a handkerchief, wiping neatly between each finger as if she were tainted with the plague.

"I won't run," Yara said. And she wouldn't. Not until she had gained his trust.

Eldar stared at her. "No, you won't."

He reached for her wrist, and she knew what he was going to do before his lips even closed around her skin. He sucked a few drops of her blood. And when her mind was hazy, he whispered to her that she was to not run away from him tonight.

The shackle around her neck was removed, and Yara felt the temporary relief of freedom as she gulped in deep breaths. Even though the shackle didn't affect her breathing, Yara felt her lungs hum in victory. She stared at the room, hunting for the key players. Shivers ran down her back. To think that she, a mere lamb, expected to trick these wolves was beyond her. But she was ready for the challenge. It filled her with a sense of purpose, and while she knew Eldar's command soaked into her bones and the door offered her no freedom, she could not help but glance upon it.

Yara appraised the one they called the Undying King. The First Vampir. He was a big man with a stern face. By his feet sat a pale-haired girl and boy. Every so often he would bend down and help himself to the offering of their necks.

Her strategy began to unspool in her mind, and Yara spotted them: the princes from the portraits. They sat closest to the dais, a signifier of their importance. They must have been direct relatives of Lord Dracul.

She crossed the room to their table. Their boisterous voices made her flinch, but Yara steeled her shoulders and came to the one who seemed to be leading the charge. Above them was a banner of a dragon in the same black-and-white coloring as the Demirci scorpions. Its reptilian tail disappeared into its mouth. The one with dark hair that fell to his shoulders and a patch covering his eye smiled at her. This one was Mircea. The Undying Prince she'd seen in the portrait.

"A gift from the brothers?" He licked his sharp teeth.

"I'm afraid not," Yara said. "I was hoping for an audience with the king. I wish to recite a song that should please him."

He raised a brow as snickers drifted around him. A wheat-haired woman beside him ran her forked tongue above her ruby lips. Yara could see the stitching of thread that prevented her tongue from healing. It sickened her to think of the pain she had suffered for such a mutilation.

"You wish to entertain the Undying King?" he asked.

"I've sung before the sultan," Yara said. "I have experience entertaining kings."

His companion spat on the table. "Filthy humans don't count."

Yara didn't flinch; she held her ground. Mircea arose and held out the crook of his arm.

"Let us see then if my brother finds you amusing or if you will die for your impudence," he said. Judging by the thrill in his voice, he was hoping for the latter. The others stared at her as if she were a jester come to entertain them all with her death. It felt strange climbing up the stairs, hearing the flutter of her skirts. She was glad she had been put in this frothy black gown. It was far more appropriate than what she had been brought in with last night. Much more fit for an audience with the Undying King.

Mircea pushed her before the Undying King, and she fell to her knees, feeling the painful sting of her skin peeling. The floor was made of black marble with glimmers of white, as if milk had been poured under it.

"What is this?" Lord Dracul demanded. His voice was deep and booming, like a gong that had been struck. It commanded attention and spoke of great power. Her father had always said you could tell the power of a man by the strength of his voice and the grip of his palm when he shook your hand.

"The girl seeks to amuse you with a song. She says she is well-known in the Ottoman court," Mircea said.

"Is that so, child?" Dracul asked.

Yara slowly raised her head to meet his gaze. It was black as midnight. His hair fell to his shoulder, and a widow's peak parted the front. He could have been handsome if he did not look so harsh, as if God had been angry when he shaped him. He could not have been older than thirty-five. But the youth of his face was lost in his eyes. His eyes had seen a thousand lifetimes and contained every inch of cruelty to be found in the world. They had burned and torched and maimed and killed. All the vampir's faces were carved from stone, beautiful and immortal. It was their eyes that gave away their inhumanness. It was their eyes that revealed their monstrosity.

Yara nodded. "Yes, my lord. I have the perfect song if you wish to hear it."

"And what do you wish for in return?" he asked. "You humans are eager for escape, are you not? Do you wish to be released once your song has concluded?"

His claw scraped ominously along the handle of his chair. It took everything in her to control her flinch.

"No, my lord," she said. "I only wish to be in your favor and show myself to be greater than my brethren. There is more use to me than the blood that travels in my veins."

The Undying King seemed amused by her response, or so she thought, from the unnatural curve of his lips that could scarcely be called a smile. He fluttered his fingers for her to proceed with the performance. His blackened claws drifted lazily in the air before settling down.

Yara didn't turn to the audience. She folded her hands before her and sang a sweet tune of a forlorn maiden whose lover was to go out to war as commanded by the sultan. It struck her then that the room was silent, everyone enraptured by the girl in the dark dress with the sad song. Her voice echoed around the high ceilings beautifully, and Yara found herself overcome by the music, by her rapt audience, by her desperate hunger for freedom. Singing had always unburdened her soul. It was a secret she had learned could move even the most despairing souls and a powerful tool in her arsenal. It was a wonder to think this court of creatures could sit as still as marble and listen to her with honesty and an attentiveness that was almost humane.

When the song ended, Yara had forgotten she was performing before a court of bloodthirsty villains. So captured was she in the performance it had almost felt as if she were at home, sitting in the lily-scented chambers of the sultana or standing before the golden pillars of the main court. Applause sounded, carrying through the room like a goblet drum, and her heart clenched as she looked at the Undying King, wondering if her gamble had paid off. His face was difficult to read. He could be experiencing any number of emotions. Perhaps he would kill her for wasting his precious time or grant her his favor for being a delight. Sweat beaded down her skin, slipping into the nape of her dress. She shifted from foot to foot, wrangling her stiff fingers.

"My lord?" she asked in a strangled voice. Had she been too presumptuous? Had she foolishly gifted him her death?

"Excellent," he said with a wry smile.

"Thank you, my lord."

"Come here," he said. "Kneel."

Yara kneeled before him, and his thumb pressed to her forehead. His claw pierced her skin, and she flinched as it twisted in a circle. Blood dripped into her eyes, and for one terrible moment, she wondered if she had miscalculated, and he would disfigure her before he killed her.

"You are under the protection of the House of Dracul and the Undying King," he said loudly. "Any vampir who harms you will be punished by the method of defanging and then impaled on the court gates for a hundred nights.

"You will serve my court until I see fit," he said. "You have earned my favor, child."

Yara stared at him, stunned. "I will not be harmed?"

"As long as it pleases me."

"And the twins?" she whispered. "Will I return to them?" She shuddered to think of being alone with Volkan. There was something unsettling about the way he looked at her. Like she was his possession, and he was her thankless master.

"No, you are under the House of Dracul," he said in an irritated tone. "See to it, Mircea, that she is provided a tutor. Her naivety is unbecoming."

"Come," Mircea said, clasping her elbow. "You have much to learn, pup."

Mircea dragged her to sit by him. She exhaled a breath of gratitude to be seated in a chair like a person rather than an animal. A plate of food was brought to her, and she dug in, scooping a handful of rice, and tearing into her meat with abandon. She guzzled a sweet berry drink from a chalice after assurance from Mircea that it was not wine.

It shocked and overwhelmed her to think she had succeeded in her mission. She had caught the attention of the king *and* secured protection until he grew bored with her. Her gaze wandered the room till she landed on the twins. Volkan glared at her with a hatred that made her flinch. She didn't know when he'd arrived, but it was clear to see that he had been privy to her rise in station. It was almost as if *she* had betrayed him. Eldar looked at her like he was seeing her for the first time. There was an interest in his eyes that frightened her more than it should have.

"Here." Mircea offered her a handkerchief. "Clean your blood. It does no good to tempt us when we cannot act on our impulses."

⟡

Her new bedroom was spacious and airy, with a gossamer canopy and thick grey wolf fur to drape herself in when she was cold. There was a stunning fresco painting that overtook the ceiling. It depicted ancient Egyptian deities with the sky painted behind them, burning under the glow of the sun. Yara blew out all the candles but the one by her bedside. It didn't feel safe to trust the night. Not after all she had experienced. It seemed almost too good to be true to be provided with her own chamber.

She crawled beneath her blankets and fell into a restless sleep.

Yara awoke to a dull thud. A sound that seemed to be coming from the ceiling. And when she looked up, she was horrified to find a person hanging from the edge of the ceiling like a spider. Before she could scream her throat dry, the intruder fell gracefully to their feet, revealing Eldar's tall frame. He patted his hair down to fix the way-ward strands as if hanging from a woman's ceiling was a common occurrence. Yara stood up abruptly.

"We must speak," he said.

"Why were you climbing my ceiling?"

"Because I can," he said. "Sit down."

Yara was about to sit when she realized that his command was harsh, without a "please" in sight. She folded her arms across her chest, and he sighed like she was a misbehaving child.

"Very well. Stand then," he said. "But you will listen to me care-fully, and you will do as I say if you wish to gain your freedom."

"My freedom," she whispered.

Eldar was a shadow in the dark. He moved with a grace and speed that was unnoticeable to her human ears. She was surprised to find him so close to her. Yara tilted her neck as far as she could to accom-modate his unnatural height. She came to the middle of his chest, and she felt oddly childlike before him.

"You're in a unique position with access to the heirs," he said. "You may not know much, but Dracul's brothers and his son are next in line to the throne. The brothers, Mircea and Radu, are scheming for power, and young Mihnea, his son, has barely transitioned, so he is of no interest to me."

"You want me to spy on them?" she asked.

Eldar only blinked, neither confirming nor denying her statement.

Yara bit her lip. Eldar roughly yanked her chin down till her lip popped free from her teeth.

"If you're going to be my eyes and ears. You need to control your expressions," he said harshly. "You will also need to practice being calm. We can hear when your heart races and smell your sweat."

"I haven't agreed to anything," she said. "I could lose my life for doing as you ask. I was lucky to catch the Undying King's favor. I am *safe* for now."

"For now," he clarified. "I assume the goal is to return home."

"Always," she said.

"I can make that happen, so long as you do as I say," he said.

Yara didn't have a plan to return home. Her first step had been bettering her station, and that had been accomplished. It was as she had told Volkan. Better to be a slave with power than a slave without. Her second step was to return home, and if she had to get into bed with the devil for it to happen, then she would. She would do anything in her power to return home, to return to her family.

"I accept," she said.

"There is another house of importance: the House of Maleinos. The heads of the family are Titus and Pomona," he continued like he'd known she wouldn't turn down his offer. His jaw ticked when he spoke of them, and the first hint of deep emotion crossed his face. It wasn't superficial like all his other emotions. Whatever thought crossed his mind just then seemed to slice him. "They will be arriving tomorrow. Ensure that you are in their immediate circle."

"How will we communicate?" she asked.

"Volkan or I will come to you," he said. "Don't seek us out."

Yara shook her head. "No. Not him. I hate him."

"He is my brother. You will give him respect," Eldar said tightly.

Yara glared at him, but he was adamant about involving his brother in his schemes.

"If he touches me, I'll kick him between the legs," she said. Aylin said it was the best way to break a grown man.

Eldar appeared thoughtful before he said, "He'd love that,"

"Of course, he would," she muttered. Yara yawned, and Eldar nodded to her bed. "I will let you return to your rest."

It shouldn't have surprised her when he leaped up and crawled along the ceiling, slipping out the doorway. Even if he looked and talked like a man, Yara had to remember he was anything but. He was a vampir. A hunter and natural-born predator. Though they could retract their teeth and claws to appear innocent, Yara promised herself that she would never forget that she was amidst monsters.

IX

ELDAR WAS NOT surprised to find Volkan surrounded by naked limbs and drinking from a bejeweled chalice while his admirers cooed and kissed his bare chest. He hadn't been pleased that the Undying King had taken his plaything from him, and he hadn't left his bed all day. Even now his silk sheets were tangled around his torso while he drank from the wrist of a young human boy.

"Go feed my brother," he said, patting the boy's head affectionately. Eldar hadn't fed all day, and he accepted the boy's offering and cut into his wrist, hanging it above his mouth. Warm blood trickled down his throat, and he felt the pounding in his head slowly fade away. It was an intimate act, drinking one's lifeblood. Eldar had never enjoyed the way his body responded to his prey, almost as if he were controlled by them. He exercised control so thoroughly that he despised being led by his appetite. Rarely did he let his teeth sink into their flesh.

"Thank you," he said, wiping his mouth.

"It's my pleasure, my lord."

Eldar searched for Thaddeus, who sat in a corner writing his soppy poems. His pale blond hair occasionally drifted into his mismatched eyes while a slave girl brushed it back every so often. Eldar had warned Volkan numerous times about the importance of siring soldiers and not bratty noble boys who penned erotic rhymes during their spare time. Thaddeus was descended of a long-dead emperor of the Byzantine Empire. Not that he ever let anyone forget. He was lazy and a waste of immortality, in Eldar's opinion. But he was Volkan's best friend, and he could be of use once in a while.

"May we speak in private?" Eldar asked.

He stared up at him and sighed so loudly you would think he had been asked to prepare the feast for the night.

"I have a few more lines to write before the Muses take their leave," he said. "Can it wait?"

"I've listened to your readings when you subject us to them. The Muses never took pity on your work, and I don't see why they would start today," Eldar said. "Come along, I don't have all day."

"Cursed to eternal darkness, but fear not, ye weary souls, Lord Eldar is as warm as the sun itself," he said with a lazy grin. "And as handsome as the devil."

"I promise to cut off your tongue if you flirt with me again," Eldar said with a dark glare. Thaddeus arose and followed him out of the bedroom, likely sensing his rising impatience. But Eldar wasn't lucky enough to be subjected to silence.

"Do you know when I first met you, I thought you were a eunuch?" he said with a boisterous laugh. "Isn't that funny?"

"Not particularly."

"How do you relieve your urges?" he inquired. "Volkan says you are as innocent as a virgin maid. As untouched as the day you were bo—"

Eldar pushed him till his back collided with the wall and pinned him with his elbows. Cracks danced along the wall from the weight of his body. Yet his attack didn't have the desired effect. Thaddeus only grinned in return, revealing his sharp teeth. Like Volkan, Thaddeus enjoyed infuriating him, but he wasn't in the mood today. Weeks of plotting and scheming had exhausted him. Especially since he had come to an undesirable decision about what was required for his rise to power. It involved securing an alliance by means of betrothal. The thought of taking a wife sickened him, but Volkan had refused to take on the duty before he had finished pitching the idea. And as the older of the pair, Eldar had accepted the unflattering task himself.

"Are you going to bite me to prove your dominance? That's what you lords do when your sired steps out of place, is it not?" he asked. He tilted his neck. "Have at it then. I've always found it rather erotic."

Eldar scoffed. "You would like that far more than you will this."

Eldar dug his hand into Thaddeus's chest, breaking through bone to feel the stillness of his dead heart. There were three ways to kill one of their kind: rip out their heart and burn it, stand in the sunlight, or drive a blade through their heart.

"Do you know what I do to my sired?" Eldar whispered in his ear. "I rip out their heart the moment they awaken and keep it locked in a cage with their name. If they ever displease me, I simply set it on fire. It doesn't matter how far they run to escape me; so long as I possess their heart, I can kill them at any moment. Sounds rather godly, does it not?"

"Abusing your sired has been outlawed," Thaddeus said. "You are not allowed to hold their hearts."

"Who will tell on me?" Eldar whispered. "Certainly not the 'abused' sired, as you so sweetly put it."

Thaddeus's frame tightened beneath him. "Volkan will not allow this."

"He can be appeased with a new toy," Eldar said.

"I won't poke fun at you anymore," Thaddeus said at last. "Promise."

"No, you won't," Eldar replied. He ripped out Thaddeus's heart and watched as his bones shifted back in place and his skin slid shut. Volkan liked to draw lines in the mud between their sired vampir. But Eldar didn't care as long as they were made by a Demirci they were fair game.

"Give it back," he growled.

"Do as I bid, and if you are well-behaved, it will be in your possession once more," Eldar said. "If not..." He licked the wet pulp that was the boy's heart, enjoying the flicker of fear that crossed his blue eye and his black eye. Sired vampir always kept their eye color from birth, whereas the trueborn vampir's eyes were black when satiated and red when starved.

Thaddeus's chest was rising and falling in rage, but he bit back whatever insult danced on his lips. If Volkan had disciplined him earlier, it would not have come to this. He would have listened to Eldar's command, and they would have bypassed this tedious exchange.

"Titus and Pomona are arriving this afternoon," Eldar said, finally getting to the purpose of his visit.

"Those bastards! If they so much as look at him, I'll tear out their eyes," Thaddeus promised. His teeth elongated at the thought of violence.

"I need you to keep an eye on Volkan and ensure that he is nowhere near either of them," Eldar said. "I don't want a scandal."

"Volkan cannot be controlled."

"He can and he will. The House of Maleinos will fall, but we must practice patience, and that means making sure that Volkan doesn't lose control."

"I'll do my best," he said.

"If he cannot be stopped, bring him the human girl. The dark-haired one with the short stature. He is obsessed with her."

"She's under His Lord's protection. What if he breaks her?"

"Make sure he doesn't."

———◦∘◦○◦∘◦———

Yara stared at herself in the gilded mirror. At the length of her hair that swept down her back, her brown skin that shone with lavender oil and shimmering gold paint. Her lips were painted with rouge and kohl lined her eyes. For the first time in a long time, Yara felt like herself. The way she felt in the Ottoman court, finely dressed and pretty. While Aylin preferred a dagger, Yara had always preferred face paint as her protection. It hardened her face, sweeping away the softness and lifting her eyes in a manner that suggested a cruel nature. A black diadem of onyx jewels covered her head and the elaborate red silk *entari* with a jeweled belt paired with a shimmery gold salwar was far more modest and appealing than the clothes she'd worn in servitude. Her skin burned to think of Volkan dressing her like a doll and parading her like a tamed house pet.

"You are favored by the Undying King," Elisabeta said. "And you shall be the gem of his court."

When Mircea brought her a ring of human servants who looked at her with curled lips and hissed at her that she was no better than them, Yara had requested Elisabeta. To her surprise, considering she was a servant under his household, Mircea notified her that Eldar had relinquished her to Yara's service.

"Does that upset you?" Yara asked in case she was mistaken, and Elisabeta hated her too.

She was prepared for them tonight, for the vampir. With her armor of cloth and jewels and her wits sharpened, she would do what Eldar asked of her. She would win her freedom the only way she knew how: by playing court games.

"No," Elisabeta said. "You were wise to ignore my advice. I suppose keeping your head down and being dutiful only applies to the weak, and you are no coward, Yara."

"Nor are you," Yara said.

Elisabeta was silent as she worked to fix her clothes. As if she were lost in thought.

"Everyone is excited for the arrival of a family...what are they called?" Yara pretended to hunt for their name.

"The Maleinos. They're an old family. Almost as old as the Dracul clan, who are the first of their kind," she said.

"I wish to make myself more knowledgeable about the court and these familial clans," she said. "It is different here. Where I am from, the God you worship decides your political allegiance. There are no such barriers here. I see the Byzantines and the Turks, and the Africans and the Chinese embrace each other with no scorn. But those who despise each other are not so obvious."

"There are feuds. The oldest is between the houses of Demirci and Maleinos. It has lasted for centuries," she said. "The Maleinos also have a feud with the Osakwe and the Kuznetsov family. But the Maleinos are also closely aligned with the House of Dracul by the betrothal of young Mihnea to the daughter of Lord Titus and Lady Pomona, young Vita."

"That is a lot," Yara murmured.

"I haven't even walked you through the sire bond, the structural hierarchy of the High Houses and who has taken whom to bed recently," she said with a conspiratorial wink.

"I will hold you to that lesson," Yara said with a smile. "The Undying King did say I was to be educated, and Mircea isn't breaking my door down with a ring of tutors."

"I'd love to be your tutor," Elisabeta said. "All eyes shall be on you, and the Maleinos, of course."

Yara didn't think that many eyes were to be on her. She was a mere entertainer among nobles.

"Oh, you head on without me," Elisabeta said when Yara looked at her for guidance. "Servants do not attend court dinners."

"Then I bid you good night," Yara said with a warm smile.

Yara drifted down the hallway. There were no guards at every corner like in the sultan's court. Nor were there polished, gold-trimmed pillars and extravagant finery. It was harsh and brutal in Dracul's court. A never-ending winter devoid of any warmth.

Yara bumped into a figure. One that was rather pretty for a man. With curled blond hair and a mischievous smile that could tempt a virgin to sin.

"My apologies," she said.

"No worries, my dearest," he said.

His smile was wide and unrelenting, and Yara instinctively took a step back, only to feel the press of a second body, and the ghost of a cold breath. She spun around and her stomach churned at the sight of Volkan. His white hair fluttered like a cape behind him.

"You can't hurt me," she said firmly. Dracul's cut on her forehead had turned to a dark scab and eventually, it would fade into a scar before it disappeared. Until then she was safe. So, long as his mark graced her skin, she was untouchable.

Volkan's lips tilted in a cruel smile. One that filled her with instant dread.

"Where is your brother?" she asked. While Eldar, with his permanent glower and cold disposition, wasn't much better at the very least he didn't seek to hurt her.

"Fond of my brother, are you?" he asked. "The hero and the villain. Are those the roles you've cast us in, in your performance? I've always been fond of destruction. Isn't that right, Thaddeus?"

"Yes, my lord."

"And I am rather possessive of my belongings, am I not? My sired, my lovers, my blood slaves."

"Most viciously, my lord."

"I am not yours," Yara snapped. "And if you touch a hair on my head, I will see to it that the Undying King makes an example of you!"

It was silent for one long moment before they both began to laugh. The musical sound made her teeth grind, and she lifted her hand to push Volkan, but he effortlessly secured her wrist in his hand like she was a child. Her breath caught in her throat, and she hated the spike of fear that warmed her belly. She hated that she was powerless and weak.

"I will release you," he said, "if you beg me. Beg me as your lord and you, my devoted servant."

Yara struggled against his grip, but it was like pushing against iron.

"It seems she needs some encouragement," Thaddeus said. "Perhaps a bite to make her more pliant."

Volkan smiled, revealing his pointed teeth. They descended past his lip, and she could see the hunger in his eyes. It even felt like his claws were lengthening, grazing her skin in a monstrous caress. He appeared more beautiful like this, with his fine-boned features and red lips. His ghostly skin shined with a porcelain nature, like he had been carved to precision by a sculptor. Yara couldn't open her mouth. Her fear was so overwhelming and potent that she noticed his nostrils twitch like he had inhaled the sweetest perfume.

"Volkan." His name was called in a voice identical to his own. Relief flooded her when she saw Eldar coming over, and she twisted harder to get to him. His presence renewed her vigor, and she scratched at Volkan's hand. But before she could slip free, Volkan dug his teeth into her neck. The pinprick of pain was drowned under the luminous fingers of pleasure. Yara had never felt this tingle in her limbs before, like she would combust at any moment. She became far too aware of his touch. His hand draped around her waist and the other cupped behind her neck, gripping her tightly. It lasted seconds before she was ripped away and pushed behind someone.

"Beg me, Yara," Volkan whispered. His words drifted into her mind like a lullaby, and she found herself falling to her knees. She wanted to please him as he had pleased her when he drank from her. There was a voice inside her mind screaming beyond the veil, but she could not hear it.

"Say it, Yara. My Yara."

"Enough," a voice growled, loud enough for a trickle of clarity to draw in. When Yara found herself on her knees, horror assaulted her along with a heavy dose of shame. It was made even worse when Eldar gripped her beneath the arms like a child and stared at her in disgust as he raised her to her feet.

"You crossed a line, brother," he said. They often spoke Greek, but Eldar was so furious he spoke rapid Turkish, the words intersecting like knots. "She is under the protection of the Dracul clan. Do you wish to be imprisoned again? Do you wish to be sent to the Maleinos again? And you." He spun on Thaddeus and gripped him by the neck. He lifted him till his feet dangled. "You incompetent bastard."

"Put him down," Volkan said. A crack sounded, and Thaddeus fell in a slump, his neck twisted at a terrible angle. Yara screamed so loud she could feel her ears ring. It wasn't until Eldar barked "shut up" that she clasped her mouth shut.

"So, she obeys you but not me?" Volkan said, staring at her like she was a puzzle. His eyes were filled with bitterness. "And you don't even have to bite her for it."

"Is he dead?" she asked, staring at the boy. His eyes stared blankly at the ceiling.

"Unfortunately, no," Eldar said. "Once his neck heals, he will be back to torment us with his idiocy."

"I'm going to tell Mircea," she said. She didn't care if she had a deal with Eldar. Volkan would suffer for hurting her, for humiliating her.

"You won't tell him anything," Eldar said. "Because you wish to escape this place rather than stick around and be the lowest member of our hierarchy. This is not the sultan's court, and you are not special."

His words stabbed at her chest, and despite her best efforts she couldn't hold back the flinch that crossed her face.

"You are no better than your brother. You simply hide your cruelty better," Yara said.

Eldar smiled—not the sharp grin Volkan had, but a cold one, devoid of any feeling.

"Stay away from me," she whispered. "Both of you."

"So long as you uphold your end of the bargain," Eldar said, "we need not cross paths. Come with me, Volkan."

Volkan sighed and followed Eldar, but when he turned back, he gave her a look. One that said he was not done tormenting her.

<hr />

Eldar stopped walking and gripped Volkan by the neck, his claws twitching in anger.

"This needs to stop," he said through gritted teeth. "This destructive behavior. It is going to ruin everything for us."

When he had asked Thaddeus to use Yara as bait, he had expected some harmless flirting, considering she was under Dracul's protection, and she was *not* to be harmed. He hadn't expected to find her on her knees with hazy eyes and a leaking neck. Anyone could have come across them and reported the incident.

"You mean it will ruin everything for *you*," Volkan spat. "You've always hungered for more. Mother said you'd fight me for breast milk when you'd had your fill. Nothing is ever enough for you. You are blinded by power."

Eldar felt his eye twitch. His grip on his brother's neck tightened, and Volkan glared at him.

"I want revenge," Volkan said. "But you want a throne."

"And you are satisfied riding my coattail," Eldar snapped. "You possess no ounce of self-preservation. At times I feel as though I have been burdened with a child. One who I constantly have to look after for the rest of eternity."

Eldar regretted the words when he caught the flicker of pain across his brother's eyes. He sighed deeply, rubbing his mouth.

"I'm sorry, brother," he said. He softened his grip and let his claws soothe his skin in a rare show of affection. Volkan brushed his hand aside.

"You don't need to look after me, Eldar," he said with his lips curled. "I can take care of myself."

Eldar cursed under his breath when he brushed past him, making sure to dig his shoulders into his chest on his way to the Grand Hall.

Not long after his dramatic departure, Yara arrived, fixing her hair and drawing her collar up to hide the puncture wounds on her neck.

Eldar's lips curled at the sight of her. The human girl was more trouble than she was worth. Volkan was obsessed with her because she challenged him with those haughty eyes and that disrespectful tongue. If she were more respectful, Volkan wouldn't hunt her at every turn. He would grow bored and forget her, but she was determined to poke him. To prove that she was as strong as them. Even as a blood slave, the fire had never left her eyes.

"Behave," he warned.

"You're not my father," she said with a wrinkle of her small nose.

"If I were your father, I would have taught you manners a long time ago," Eldar said. "And I'd have taken you over my knee should you ever forget."

Yara stared at him like he was an insect beneath her shoe.

"I should thank God you are not," she said.

Eldar was distracted by shouts of alarm. He left her, disappearing in a blur of speed and walking straight into chaos. The Grand Hall was filled with blood; it leaked through the marble cracks like water. The scent was stale and bitter, hinting that the person attacked was nonhuman. He recognized the big frame on the ground as Titus Maleinos, his face squeezed in a grimace. His torso was littered with arrows, but strangely, none pierced his heart, as if the attacker did not wish to kill him. Pomona lay by him, just as riddled with arrows as he was. She screamed at her legion of guards to find the attacker while blood poured out of her mouth. Their guards, along with the court guards, leaped into the ceiling beams, searching for the assailant.

For one terrible moment, Eldar feared that Volkan had been driven to madness and fallen into bloodlust. His eyes desperately searched the hall, and relief crossed him when he saw Volkan in the corner, arms draped around a girl and whispering in her ear. Eldar knew his brother well enough to suspect that, while he played at being distracted, he was thrilled by the events unfolding and had likely had a hand in them. Eldar couldn't confront him. Not here, where eyes would be on them, first and foremost. Ears picking at their every word.

He had to proceed with his night as usual. His eyes scoured the room for the Ramose family. He was to meet their daughter today and outline the terms of the betrothal. They were an old and traditional Egyptian family said to have been walking the earth since the first pharaoh's time. Eldar felt dread at the thought of entangling himself in a permanent union. While both parties would likely take lovers years down the road when they grew tired of each other and perhaps even take separate homes, Eldar would have to have children, since he and Volkan were the last of the Demirci line, and Volkan was certainly not doing anything to extend it. It was the thought of children that worried him. He wasn't prepared to be a father.

He came across Bahiti, the family matriarch as she was making her way to the exit.

"Eldar," she said. "We were just about to head to the safety of our chambers. There seems to be an attacker not yet captured by Dracul's soldiers."

"May I walk you to your rooms?" he asked.

"That is most generous," she said with a dim smile. Around them, other families were following her lead and being led back to their chambers by their family guards. Eldar's own legion hovered at the corner of his eyes, awaiting his signal. "You may walk with Akila."

Eldar stared at his future bride—if negotiations went in the direction he hoped. She was a shy, sullen creature who was always caught with a book in hand. Eldar much preferred it this way. He was not a man of many words and he aspired for the same in his bride. Silence was his favorite companion.

"Hello," she whispered.

Eldar gave her a smile, and when she stared at him in alarm, he realized he was grimacing.

It was going to be a long night.

⸻

Yara trailed after Mircea. It was clear to see from the bloody vampir's pierced with arrows that singing was not on her schedule tonight. It had been jarring to see the man and woman lying there, their faces twisted in pain. They had been taken out of the hall by their guards, who shielded them as they exited, protecting them from the unknown assailant.

"Stop following me, pup," Mircea growled.

"I'm bored and I don't know anyone but you," she said.

"You don't know me," he said, offended that she would suggest such a thing. Behind them was his brother Radu, who stuck close to his heel.

"Those people attacked, they are the Maleinos family, are they not?" she asked.

He didn't respond, so she took that to be confirmation. They climbed up the dais and Yara followed, sticking close to the hulking figure of Mircea. He was tall and broad, like a tree that had been uprooted and made into a man. Radu was the opposite slim and gangly with a sharp, pointed face and a long chin that he often stroked when in thought. He could be handsome if he didn't look so spindly, like he was recovering from an unknown illness.

"The attacker?" Vlad barked. He didn't seem pleased by the state of the Grand Hall. All around them, people were either dining like nothing was out of sorts or fleeing like they were in the middle of a war zone. It was utter chaos.

"Gone," Mircea said. "He shot from the beams. We had a shipment of servants this afternoon, and we suspect he arrived under the guise of being a servant."

"The Maleinos will demand blood," Radu said. "They are saying Pomona was with child. That the child is lost."

Yara shivered at the thought of a dead child. To attack a pregnant woman was unthinkable. This depraved place grew more dangerous with each passing day.

"Who would dare defy me this way?" Dracul growled. His lips peeled to reveal long canines. The dark fur that covered the shoulder blades of his kaftan bristled when he exhaled a sharp gust of wind.

"We don't know," Mircea said. "The Maleinos have many enemies. The brothers, the Osakwe, the Danesti, and lord knows who else."

"The fair-haired one is temperamental and unpredictable," Yara said. "Volkan, that is. I wouldn't put this past him."

"He does have the most reason to orchestrate this attack. And where is his brother?" Radu asked. "Did anyone account for him?"

"I saw him outside before I arrived," Yara said.

"He's busy courting that timid daughter of Bahiti," Mircea said. "Saw them walk off together."

"We'll discuss this more thoroughly in the war room," Dracul said. "Mircea, check on the Maleinos, assure them that we are hunting the attacker."

"Yes, my lord."

Mircea gripped her elbow, and for a moment she thought he was going to chide her for pushing her nose into political affairs that did not concern her. But he lifted her above the ground and before she could blink, he ran. The walls blurred around them, and her stomach churned dangerously as he tore down the hallways. He released her, and Yara fell to her knees. Her vision shifted, and she imagined this was what it felt like to be filled with wine. Broken fragments pieced together to showcase Mircea laughing at her heartily.

"I don't feel too well." She groaned.

"No, I don't reckon you do," he said. "You're desperate to be in the middle of our court politics. Don't tell me a little dizziness has scared you off?"

Yara stood up on shaky legs, desperately trying to keep her stomach contents inside their chamber. It helped that she hadn't eaten dinner yet.

Mircea didn't wait for her to catch up. He knocked on the double doors until a grim faced man opened the door.

"My lord." He bowed.

"Are Titus and Pomona healed enough to talk?" Mircea asked.

"Yes, my lady is most distressed," he said. "As you know, she was with child, and I'm afraid the child is lost."

Mircea walked inside. The room was spacious. There was a seating section filled with embroidered pillows with gold tassels and thick Persian blankets covering the distressed woman at the heart of it all. Her flaxen hair was streaked with blood and her eyes were rimmed in pink, like she had been crying. She was beautiful, with alabaster skin and a face that looked distinctly feline. Beside her was a man with auburn hair and a thick beard.

"It was Volkan Demirci." Pomona growled. "I want his head! If you had seen the way, he smiled with satisfaction as he kissed that harlot. It was no different than if he were to spit in my face."

"We have no proof," Mircea said. "Until the attacker is found, we won't know who sent him."

"It is the Demirci boy," Titus growled. "Have him brought here for questioning."

"You forget yourselves," Mircea said tightly. "He is not your prisoner anymore, and he is still trueborn."

"He murdered an infant," Pomona said. Her face tightened until her teeth descended. "What is the sentence for that?"

"Death," Yara whispered.

They stared at her as if realizing for the first time that she stood in the room.

"The sentence should be death," she said.

"Who are you?" Pomona asked with a curious tilt of her head.

"Yara, Daughter of Beşir Ağa," she said.

"My brother's latest trinket," Mircea said with a heavy sigh. "And my newest responsibility."

"A pretty trinket," Pomona said. "Can she be trusted?"

"She's arrived recently. She hardly knows what we speak of. Let alone has the sense to betray us," he said, speaking as if she were not in the room. It infuriated her that he was so dismissive of her. Perhaps this was why Eldar had approached her to act as his spy. Nobody noticed her if she didn't speak. Nobody was frightened of a mortal girl.

"Our existence must be a shock to her system," Pomona said thoughtfully. "Very well, she may stay."

She turned her sharp gaze back to Mircea. "I will get you the proof you need. That idiot is no doubt hungry to boast of his scheme. We'll invite him to dinner, fill him with wine, and gain a confession."

"I'll send you one of Dracul's trusted men. He'll hide in a place of your choice and ensure that this confession is valid on behalf of the throne," Mircea said. "Your family feud has existed for centuries, and you understand we simply cannot go by your word. Evidence is key."

Pomona's lips curled in distaste, but Titus nodded.

"As you wish, my Undying Prince," Titus said.

"My condolences," Mircea said before he turned on his heel. Yara rushed after him.

"Do you think he did it?" Yara asked in a whisper the moment they stepped outside.

"It doesn't matter what I think. Only that the punishment for murdering an unborn child of one of the trueborn may entail his life," Mircea said. "We haven't executed a noble in centuries; it should be a fun affair."

"Volkan may die?" she whispered. While she took no great pleasure in suffering, she could admit that the world would be a far better place without Volkan Demirci. There was no shortage of cruel men, and if she could help rid the world of one of them then she would consider her life a fulfilling one.

If Eldar inquired about this information, she would lie to him. She wouldn't tell him of the plot against his brother.

In the end, if he caught wind of her betrayal, she would claim that the Greek they spoke was beyond her fluency.

Volkan Demirci was set to die, and Yara would not interfere with fate.

Yara awoke that night to the distinct sense of being watched. She sat upright, holding the furs to her chest. The room was silent and dark. There were no windows in the fortress since these creatures could not tolerate the light. All the windows that had once existed had been covered with brick. The candle she had left to burn had been doused. It was strange to sleep without Aylin's warmth. It made the dark feel hostile and the night unbearable.

Yara crawled out of her bed, feeling vulnerable in the open space. Her sleeping tunic fell to her ankles. The pale color of the fabric made her appear ghostly. She hoped it frightened the intruder.

Fingers wrapped around her wrist, and she stared down at a man of shadow.

"We need to talk," Eldar said.

In the dark, she couldn't make him out. Just the blur of a shape. He was sitting on the indigo chair in the corner. As if he lorded over *her* space. She wondered how long he had sat there and if this were a means to rattle her.

"Do they know who the attacker was?" he demanded.

"No," she said. "They believe he escaped."

"Do they have suspicions?" he asked. "Any nobles they think were behind this?"

"I don't know," she lied. "I don't understand them when they speak. I am an African Turk, as you know. And you all speak Greek."

The hand on her wrist yanked hard until she fell on his lap. His hand clamped down on her mouth to muffle the surprised yelp that escaped her.

"Do you think I am an idiot, Yara?" he hissed. She could feel the sharp point of his teeth grazing the shell of her ear. She shivered, holding as still as possible, like he was a wild animal prone to attack at the smallest inconvenience. "Volkan upset you, and you've decided to get some revenge, have you?"

He lowered his hand for her to speak.

"That's not true," she said.

"I can hear your heart racing," Eldar snapped. "Tell me what you know."

"Let go of me," she said, squirming on his lap. He had an arm secured around her waist and the other wrapped around her neck like a shackle.

"Answer me."

"Not like this," she said. "I am not your blood slave anymore. You will respect me, or I'll find someone else to free me."

He tilted her neck, and Yara could faintly make out the shadow of his monstrous face, the slope of his sharp nose, the tilt of his jaw, and those dagger-like canines. She could feel the wrath of his anger. It pulsed between them like a living, breathing entity, coiling around them in a suffocating grip. For a moment, they were suspended in silence. Their hatred was the only thing that they shared, a cord that wrapped around both their chests.

"Do not test me, Yara," he whispered. "I am worse than my brother when I am provoked."

Yara stared at him blankly, refusing to fall to his whim. Their relationship was mutually beneficial, and she would not let him treat her as any lesser.

"Are you going to bite me?" she asked. "Force me to reveal my truth?"

"No," he said. "Torture is more Volkan's style. I have my own method of gaining results."

"How?" she asked.

"There is a man raising havoc in Constantinople. Hunting for his missing daughter. The Chief Black Eunuch, Beşir Ağa," he said, slowly. In that soft, hypnotic voice of his. She wouldn't know that it was threats he was weaving with his pretty voice if it weren't for his harsh grip. "If you don't tell me what Titus and Pomona are plotting, I will have his finger brought to you. One for each night that you keep your mouth sealed."

Yara folded her arms across her chest. The mention of her father brought a tight knot to her stomach. She missed him and Aylin so much that it ached. Despite herself, she felt a stray tear slip from her eye. It rolled down her cheek, and she felt the warm slide of his tongue capturing her pain like it belonged to him. The cold graze of his breath soaked her skin.

"They are going to invite Volkan to dinner," she whispered. "They expect him to boast about his hand in the attempt on their lives. There is going to be a representative of the Undying King's hidden away to confirm his guilt. Mircea says he will be executed for the death of the unborn child."

Eldar cursed beneath his breath.

"Let me go," she said.

"You deserve to have your neck snapped for even attempting to withhold such information," Eldar growled. "Lie to me again, and I will carve your father to pieces. I will also find anyone you've ever loved and ensure they suffer a similar fate."

He released her, and before Yara could speak he had disappeared.

A gust of wind slammed her door shut, and in the dark Yara released the sob that had steadily built in her chest from the moment he threatened her father. She allowed herself that one night to mourn the young girl who had arrived cloaked in innocence and purity. She cried for the girl who would shame God with her hunger for vengeance. She cried for the girl who existed before the Demirci brothers found her.

Tomorrow, her tears would be a painful memory.

Tomorrow, she would be stronger.

X

AYLIN AND ILYAS had been given a small room in the house. There were three floors, and all of them were filled with broad-shouldered Venetian men. These were not nobles, but rather uncouth men raised in farmland and sailing ports with a rabid glint in their eyes. They hungered for death the way a newborn babe ached for milk. Aylin felt unbearably different because of her skin color and her short stature and thin frame. She didn't know what they fed these men, but all of them were big, with swarthy skin and dark hair and their swinging silver crosses. The only exception to this was Salvatore Di Mazi, who was thin and tall and fair-haired like a gazelle.

She and Ilyas descended the spiralling stairs for dinner after taking a quick bath and donning fresh clothes. He had disappeared while she bathed to speak to Salvatore. It made her skin itch that she had not been privy to that conversation. She could hear the loud masculine laughter and the coarse sound of their chatter as they approached the double doors.

"It will shock you, the way men speak in the privacy of their own company," Ilyas said. "But you must bite your tongue and laugh at their jokes."

"I will try my best," she said. "Self-control isn't my best trait."

"For me," he whispered. "You will do so for me."

It was such a strange sentiment that the words shifted like tangled insects beneath her chest. She couldn't bring herself to nod or confirm it. Because a small part of her, beneath the barbed shields that covered her heart, *wanted* to please him.

The room went silent upon their entrance. A hundred eyes blinked at them, and her breath stilled. She hadn't expected this many men. Hope blossomed in her chest, unfurling like a wildflower. Perhaps they stood a fighting chance against these wicked creatures.

On the dais sat Salvatore, and beside him was an old man with weathered lips and tufts of snow-white hair. To his right was another man with a grim face who looked to be about thirty.

"Ah," Salvatore said, raising his chalice. "May I introduce the newest initiate to our circle, Elijah. He is Transylvanian and has come to honorably aid our fight against the vampire. Many of us have lost our loved ones, or worse, watched as they returned to us with an unnatural hunger in their eye. We welcome Elijah to our ranks. To our war upon the vampire and an end to their unholy race."

Cups were raised to him, and a chorus of welcomes rang around them. Salvatore didn't bother to introduce Aylin. Not that she was surprised or offended.

Space was cleared for Ilyas at the nearest table. Across from them sat a burly man with a thick beard and a boy with spiky blond hair that looked like it was made of thorns and a cruel glint to his eyes. The boy had massive fists that could no doubt bludgeon one to death, and those fists were curled around his cup as if he imagined it was Aylin's neck.

"The name is Borza," the man with the beard said. "This ill-tempered one is Domenico. Fair warning, he bites."

Domenico didn't look away to greet Ilyas; his gaze was latched on Aylin when he spoke. "What's this Ottoman scum?"

"Careful," Ilyas said, darkness threading his words. "You speak ill of my brother."

"Brother?" he asked. "I take it your mother was a whore then."

"Yes, she was, and your father was her first patron," Aylin said. "Who knows? Maybe you're one of our bastard brothers."

Ilyas clutched her shoulder, squeezing in warning. Rough laughter danced around them at her comment, and Domenico's face reddened to an unhealthy shade.

"The servants eat in the kitchen," Domenico said. "I take it from your bony frame and pretty face you are not here to serve our war."

"I intend to serve," she said with a serious nod. "My spit in your food, that is."

Domenico stood up, and Aylin relished the chance to run circles around him. Her fingers reached for her *kilij*. Her hand wrapped firmly around the enameled handle, safe and sturdy in her palm. How delighted she was that she and Ilyas had the good sense to smuggle their Turkish weapons into Venice.

Ilyas yanked her behind him.

"We've had a long travel in search of your Order," Ilyas said. "My brother is more companionable after a night's rest."

Domenico brushed past them, but not before he whispered a word of warning in her ear.

"Don't let me catch you without your brother," he said. "I'll show you a true Venetian welcome."

Aylin snarled at him, enjoying the wrath that flared in his pupils. If he laid a finger on her, she would cut him from his stomach to his groin.

Ilyas lowered her into a chair, still gripping her like she was an ill-behaved child. She shrugged off his grip. Domenico had started it with his hateful words, and all she had done was defend herself.

"I apologize for his rudeness, my boy," Borza said with a frown. "Domenico is a wild animal. Even Father Salvatore has little hope of molding him into a soldier."

"Then why bother?" Aylin asked. "Maybe he should be tossed onto his behind and we should pray that, God willing, his bones get picked by wolves."

Borza laughed, revealing his stained teeth. There was something comforting about the big fellow.

"Well, his father is the right hand of Salvatore, the *Reverendo Don*." He pointed his hand at the man with the dark hair. "Father Cristifano appointed Salvatore as the head of the Silver Cross, the holy brotherhood tasked to eradicate these creatures, just last spring. Before that, it was Cristifano who led the order, which is why Domenico Zancherelli acts like a spoiled brat."

"I won't tolerate him targeting my brother," Ilyas said. "Anyone that strikes him will be treated as if they struck my own flesh."

"And the same goes for anyone who comes for him," Aylin said, pointing at Ilyas. Though she couldn't think of a single reason why anyone would torment Ilyas. He was big and menacing. One would have to ache for death to willingly attack him.

Borza whistled. "I wouldn't dare cross you."

Aylin smiled. She liked him.

⸻

Aylin couldn't sleep that night. She stared at Ilyas's sleeping face. They slept on twin beds that faced each other, and the light trickle of his snoring soothed her. She felt a wash of gratitude cleanse her bones. She was glad she had him to lean on. His skills and training and even his pale skin had gotten them a lot further than she would have on her own. She wished she could repay him by some means.

"Aylin," he said in a harsh breath.

For a moment she thought he had awoken, but his eyes were sealed shut. A ghost of a fleeting smile crossed her lips. She hoped it was a good dream and she wasn't tormenting him in his sleep. If that were the case, it was no wonder he was so distant with her in the mornings. She ruined his sleep every night with her presence. She ruined his nights *and* his morning.

Aylin reached for him, slowly, gently. She would rouse him lightly so he could stop this nightmare, where she was probably breaking every rule, he set and fighting strangers for looking at her wrong. Her fingers lightly grazed the stubble on his cheek. She felt the weight of his face tilt into her palm, resting on her, and her name once more passed his lips in a soft exhale. Her heart thudded and she tried to withdraw her hand, but he clasped her wrist, holding her hostage.

Aylin couldn't draw it back, not without rousing him. So, she closed her eyes and slipped into a dark, empty slumber.

⸺◆◆◆⸺

Aylin awoke to a sore wrist. There was a chair tucked beneath the doorknob as Ilyas prayed *fajr*. Aylin sat upright and watched him finish up. His vivid blue eyes met hers as his thumb stroked the *misbaha*. The rhythmic click of his prayer beads filled the room. There was a firmness to his mouth, and when his gaze dropped, she knew there was something amiss. Several long minutes passed before he spoke.

"I've left some water if you want to perform ablution," he said. He still wouldn't meet her eye, even when he spoke.

"Are you well?" she asked. "I'll admit the food they cooked last night was rather bland. I understand if your stomach and taste hasn't settled with it."

"You are the pampered one," he said. "Not me."

Aylin hopped off the bed and sat before him, crossing her legs. Her eyes flickered to the left, and she realized that he had moved his bed. It was on the other side of the room, beside the door. Her skin warmed and a flash of shame rippled through her stomach. She shouldn't have touched him so intimately, and she should have ripped her hand away instead of leaving it there as if it belonged on his skin.

"For propriety," he said, following her gaze. "You are still a woman, Aylin."

"Of course," she said. She smiled, hoping to brush off the lingering awkwardness. "I hope this doesn't mean you will hold the door for me and fill my plate before yours."

He laughed, a warm sound that trickled down her nerves like fire. "I wouldn't dare do that. Not even in the palace. You'd bite my head off for it."

<hr/>

It brought a sour taste to her mouth when Ilyas was pulled for training while she was led to the stables. Her skin twitched like a trapped rabbit, and it took everything for her to follow the young girl down the green path. There were only two women on the estate. One was the cook, Gratiosa, a hot-headed woman with a limp that made her hobble around the heated kitchen, and her daughter Leandra, a girl of seventeen with a thin frame and slightly buck teeth.

"And your name is, *Don*?" Leandra asked.

"Aydin," she said.

"I'm Leandra," she said. "Your Latin is most unique."

Aylin knew she meant it was rather broken. Ilyas had said her accent was "charming" in a tone of great sarcasm.

"Thank you," she said.

"You must be proud of your brother," Leandra said. "I was peeking behind the door when Father Salvatore introduced him. He is fighting for an honorable cause."

"I want to be training alongside him, but that cursed Salvatore clearly despises foreigners," Aylin said. "He thinks I should be cleaning up after his filthy horses instead of wielding a blade."

"You mustn't speak ill of him. He's a good *Reverendo Don*," she said uneasily. "Kind and gracious."

There were stalls for about fifty horses in the stables. Leandra advised her that she would clean the manure first and then soap the floors. She led her to a small cabinet that held all the supplies: soap and water and brushes to comb their hides and a stick with clawed fingers to scrape the floor and accumulate the dirt-stained leaves.

"Call me if you need anything. I will be in the kitchen, kneading dough," she said. She bent her head in farewell and trotted off back to the kitchen.

A deep withered sigh escaped Aylin. An hour. She would go at this for an hour before she found Ilyas and forced him to train her. Salvatore be damned.

⁂

Sweat coated her brow as she made her way to the field behind the house. There were men training all around her.

She could see Ilyas learning the glide of his blade. It wasn't the sharp, curved blade preferred by the Turks, but one that was rather long and slim. His brow furrowed as he adjusted his grip. He swung rapidly at a straw figure, tearing off its head. The men cheered, a chorus of "Elijah" filling the air. On the opposite end, she saw Domenico training with Salvatore, whose pale hair was knotted above his head. His tunic had long been abandoned and sweat gleaned on his abdomen. Aylin looked away in disgust.

"Aydin," Ilyas called, curling his finger.

Salvatore frowned at the sight of her, and she smiled at Domenico, whose nostrils flared.

"If you tell me to return to my bedroom, I will cut you," she said to Ilyas.

"Grab a blade," he said, pointing to a hooked board from which hung a range of weapons. "Find something light with a small handle that fits your grip."

Aylin perused the selection. Most of them were heavy and wrapped in guarded *ricasso* and hilt rings.

"A sabre would best suit you," Salvatore said, wrists neatly folded behind his back. "Inspired by the Ottoman Turks."

"How apt of you to make such a startling observation," she said. "I am indeed a Turk."

"Or perhaps a schiavone," he continued as if she hadn't spoken, "a favorite of the Slavonian, Dalmatian, and Croatian mercenaries who guarded the Doge of Venice." His hand intimately stroked the thin blade. "Both are lighter and can reach farther than your short arms."

Aylin stared at him warily. There was no way he had come to help her. This was all some ploy to get rid of her.

"If you truly want to join us," Salvatore said, "you will pick three men. Whoever draws blood first wins."

"I pick them?" she asked.

Salvatore nodded. "That is only fair."

Aylin grabbed the sabre, the closest thing to the *kilij* she had trained with back in Constantinople. Aylin looked at the men and assessed them for weaknesses. The one in the corner with the missing tooth preferred his left to his right and he didn't protect his weak side. Another one was young, probably sixteen; he moved with speed to hide his lack of finesse. Brash and reckless, he would be a good second pick. Her eyes fell on Domenico. He hated her passionately. Emotions were a weakness, and he would be sloppy. Even now he stared at her with his fists closed, as if he were resisting the urge to beat her to death.

Aylin pointed at her three marks.

Ilyas frowned. "Domenico isn't a wise choice. I've watched him fight, and he possesses a savagery that makes him rather unpredictable."

"I'll survive, brother," she said.

Salvatore nodded. His handsome face did not show an inkling of surprise at her choices. He called the three men forward, and they lined up to the side. The rest of the men slowly came forward until they formed a circle around her, their grime and sweat-stained faces grinning from ear to ear as they rubbed their palms at the thought of bloodshed.

"On my whistle, you will begin," Salvatore said. "First to draw blood wins."

Aylin cracked her neck and fell into her battle stance. All those years of Ilyas training her to protect herself ran through her mind. She intended to make him proud and ease the strain on his face. The bump on the column of his throat shifted, and she knew he prayed for her. And God seemed to favor Ilyas as his prayers were rarely left unanswered. She hoped that favor touched her today during this trial.

The man with the missing tooth grinned at her.

"I've never fought a boy so pretty," he said. "You look like my childhood sweetheart."

It was a curse that Aylin made a decent girl but a pretty boy. Her face had always been harsh, or so it was described by the courtesans. Hamid Bey had once told her she looked distinctly "African." And when she had curtly asked for an explanation, he simply meant she looked "stern and unapproachable." It was strange that the ethnicity they loathed in her was the same one they adored in Yara. The sultana herself had once said Yara was a true Turk and commissioned her artist to paint a portrait of her so she could find the finest suitor.

While Yara had a soft, round face with wide eyes and sweet dimples, Aylin had cheekbones carved with a blade and a flat nose.

Aylin's hand tightened around her blade. She was glad she was not pretty. Being pretty hadn't saved her sister, but perhaps her mediocrity would save them both.

Aylin waited for her opponent to lunge. She always let her opponent make the first move and played defense until they grew tired. Their blades clashed in a loud, ringing sound. As expected, he favored his left side and tended to attack on her right side. The first thing Ilyas had taught her was to train with both arms.

"Soldiers are trained that way, in case their dominant hand is ever injured or severed," he had explained.

The man was quick, and he nearly caught her cheek before she ducked. Aylin switched the blade to her left hand and caught him unexpectedly on the side. Blood welled from the small tear, and he looked down, surprised.

"Christ," he hissed. "He caught me."

"Out," Salvatore said a bite to his words. "Pietro. In."

Aylin rolled back her shoulders and crouched. He was young. A few years younger than her, which meant he had much to prove to this lot. The whistle to commence had barely left Salvatore's lips before he dashed forward with speed. Their blades collided with such force that a painful ring slammed down her wrist. Her teeth clenched, and she waited for his next attack. Aylin could see the sweat dotting his forehead from the excursion. His first attacks came in quick succession without a break or pause, but they were getting slower and sloppier. Aylin lunged, aiming for his knee, and just when he lowered his blade to protect his lower half, she switched directions and sliced his stomach.

"Pietro. Out," Salvatore barked. "Domenico. In!"

Aylin took in a deep breath, flexing her aching fingers. He would be the most challenging. She hadn't seen him fight in order to gauge his strengths and weaknesses; she was going in blind. He peeled off his shirt, leaving nothing behind but the silver crucifix around his neck with blood-red rubies encrusted within. He stared at her and licked his lips. There was a crazed gleam in his eyes that made shivers race down her spine.

Salvatore whistled, and she expected Domenico to lunge, but he didn't move. He stood as still as a statue. He didn't move or raise his blade. He simply stood there, and Aylin realized that he didn't have a blade. It seemed too good to be true. She stared at him cautiously, wondering what game he was playing.

"You're defenseless," she said. "It seems almost cruel to best you."

Domenico didn't respond. He curled two fingers as a signal to attack. Aylin lunged for him with her blade raised. He bent down, evading her attack unscathed, and it shocked her when he barreled into her. The brunt of his shoulder dug into her torso, knocking the breath from her chest. Aylin fell on her back, feeling the painful collision of his body and the weight that suffocated her. Her hand grappled for her fallen sabre, but he pinned her wrist to the ground with his own. Aylin grabbed a fistful of dirt with her spare hand and tossed it in his face. He released her to rub away the dirt, and she crawled away, fingers hooked in the curved hilt.

"You want to play dirty?" Domenico growled. "Let's play dirty."

His thick hand wrapped around her ankle, and he dragged her back. He slapped her, so hard it brought tears to her eyes. A small moan slipped past her lips, and she was rewarded with another slap.

"Did you think you would best me, boy?" he said, leaning down to whisper in her ear. "Do you think I cannot end you?"

Blood welled up from her bitten tongue, but she swallowed it back, refusing to give him the satisfaction of winning.

"You slap like a little girl," she said provoking him. He raised his hand to retaliate, leaving her hand briefly untended. Aylin raised her hand to his neck and scratched hard, tearing past skin and sinking into his flesh. Blood trickled down to his collarbone, and she grinned in victory. He roared a hollow sound that made her insides shake, and before Salvatore could call the end of the match, Domenico bent down and bit her ear. A scream bubbled up her throat, and for a moment she thought he would tear it off.

"Release him," Ilyas said in a cold voice, "or I will slit your throat."

Domenico stilled, and she felt the slow release of her ear from between his sharp teeth. He grinned. A wolfish smile stained with her blood and pain. Aylin cupped her ear, struggling to staunch the bleeding. Ilyas had his blade pressed to his throat. His body trembled with fury. She had never seen him so enraged, like he would tear out of his skin if he didn't end Domenico.

Salvatore came toward them.

"Stand down," he said, pressing a firm hand to Ilyas's shoulder. "That was not good camaraderie, Domenico."

He looked at Aylin, lips pressed into a firm line. "We begin training at daybreak."

Aylin felt something wet strike her cheeks, trickling down her skin. Domenico turned around after spitting on her. Aylin was prepared to throttle him for the indecency when Ilyas gripped her shoulder.

"Let us get you cleaned," he said.

"Leandra in the kitchen should be of help," Salvatore said. "He's lucky Domenico didn't mutilate him."

"Thank you," she whispered to Ilyas, as they walked down the empty hallway. His frame was wracked with small tremors, as if he would come undone at the barest provocation. When Aylin pressed her hand to his elbow he stilled, and his body relaxed beneath her grip.

"Aylin," he whispered. "You will be the death of me."

"I would follow you in death," she said. The words were supposed to carry an air of levity as all jokes did, but they sounded oddly heavy. As if she relied on him so thoroughly even God couldn't take her from him.

"That almost sounded like a gift. A better one would be *not* following me, so I am not miserable in this life and the next," he said.

Aylin laughed, almost forgetting the piercing wound on her ear. It stung anytime the wind licked it. And she could feel the blood pooling on her shoulder. It was a deep cut, that much she was certain of.

Leandra was not surprised by her battle wounds. She brought a ton of water mixed with salt and poured it on the wound, making Aylin flinch before she carefully wrapped it in a clean cloth. Aylin realized she was moving a bit stiltedly, as if she were terribly self-conscious. She realized the source of this affliction when Ilyas began to ask a string of questions about everything from the possibility of an infection to the healing process to whether she would be scarred. Leandra looked at him beneath her lashes, pushing a strand of her fair hair behind her ear. Her skin turned a blotchy pink that spread to her neck as she stumbled over her words.

Aylin felt a strange stab in her chest and folded her hand in her trousers, so she didn't reach for him. So, she didn't dig her nails into his flesh to remind herself that he belonged to her. He had always belonged to her.

"I'll change the wrapping tomorrow," Leandra said. "It should be sealed up in a few days. You're lucky to have an ear!"

"If I catch that bastard on his own, I'll carve him up," Aylin growled.

"Language," Ilyas snapped. "Just because you are surrounded by filthy soldiers, I won't have you speaking like one."

"My apologies, Father," she said.

Leandra left them and Ilyas placed his big hands on her hips, drawing her down from the stool. Warmth spread from where his fingers were splayed on her hipbone. His smallest finger rested on the band of her trousers.

"I can walk perfectly well," she said. "You don't need to act like a doting mother."

"First I am a stern father and now a doting mother?" He raised a brow. "I suppose I can't ask if you're in pain for fear of being compared to another familial figure."

"It's a dull ache," she lied. "Barely feel it anymore."

"I feel as if I'm not doing enough to protect you," he confessed. She could feel the warmth of his breath when he spoke, and the trailing whisper of his brown hair stroking her forehead. "I feel as if I am failing you."

It was his nature to protect. Even when they had been young, his eyes would always trail both her and Yara, a deep scowl on his face anytime he caught her being mischievous.

"You are doing perfectly," she said. "Thank you for letting me fight for her. Thank you for not trying to stop me like all of them. I'm beginning to realize the sad truth is that it doesn't matter if I look like a man or a woman, I will always be despised for my skin. I will always be the most hated person in every room, I will always be considered inferior, and I will always be unwanted."

"You will always be important to me," he said with no hesitation. His words were smooth and assured, as if he were stating mere fact. "You will always be superior to all, and you will always be wanted."

She felt a hard knot in her throat and a stinging sensation in her eyes. She didn't know the last time she had been spoken to like that. And while her father and Yara were duty bound to love her, this felt like the first time anyone outside her family had expressed such blind devotion. Her heart swelled, and she could scarcely breathe from the emotion that wracked her small frame.

The door creaked open, and his hands dropped abruptly as the cook stepped in.

"Leave," she snapped. "I've told you filthy boys to leave my kitchen alone! If I find you've stolen a single pastry, I will skin your hide!"

Aylin stifled a giggle. She and Ilyas disappeared down the hallway like a pair of misbehaving children. The phantom touch of his words drifted in her mind, warming her from the inside out.

You will always be wanted.

XI

ELDAR HAD BARELY had the self-control to tear himself away from the girl. The urge to punish her, to squeeze her delicate neck until she was gasping, was overwhelming. If it wasn't for the knowledge that Volkan had tormented her enough for them both, he would have made sure that she regretted lying to him. The mention of her father was a good touch. He made it his mission to know all there was to know about his network of spies. Anyone who was not sired by him was liable to betray him. And that included the devious Yara. She was a good liar he'd give her that. Her heart hadn't skipped a beat until he touched her—then it had shot like a trapped hummingbird eager to break free of its cage.

True to her word, the next evening a page was sent to deliver a letter requesting the presence of his brother for a dinner hosted by Pomona Maleinos.

"It is a trap," Eldar said.

He could feel Thaddeus glaring at him from the corner. Still upset that Eldar had immobilized him last night and now possessed his heart. His fingers bristled as he swirled the raven feather in ink and lamented his woes.

"Of course, it is a trap," Volkan said. "They want me to confess. Idiots."

"They have a member of the Dracul clan in hiding, prepared to capture this admission of guilt," Eldar said.

"Did your little spies tell you this?" Volkan said. "How many do you have in every family?"

He had six spies among the noble families, and Yara was his seventh. It was his first time implementing a spy in the House of Dracul. Only two houses remained unfiltered. One of them happened to be his betrothed's family, so that left just one untouched.

"We must stay united," Eldar said. "Represent our family. They will goad you with your suffering, but we must stay strong."

Volkan's eyes grew clouded, and Eldar knew he was back there, trapped in the cellar beneath the Maleinos stronghold. When he had been released, Eldar had barely recognized his brother. The haunted look in his eyes. The way he flinched from his touch. Eldar had wished many times that he could carry Volkan's pain as his burden. Volkan had fallen deeply into his vices, using wine and warm bodies to cope with his misery, but distractions only numbed his pain. They didn't erase it.

Even now, when his mind was far from him, Eldar did not know what to say or do. He didn't have any words of comfort to share or a brotherly hug to offer. He felt relief flood him when Thaddeus wrapped his arms around Volkan and kissed his forehead.

The Maleinos family would fall.

Eldar had sworn it to his brother the day he was returned to him a shell of the boy he had been when he left.

Tonight, they would toy with Volkan, but not once would they gain the satisfaction they expected. This was the first strike of many to come.

"Did your attacker escape?" Eldar asked.

Volkan hesitated.

"I know it's you. Just answer the question." Eldar sighed.

Volkan grinned. "He did."

"Good," Eldar said. "If you intend to strike again, I'll help you. Just don't go off on your own again."

"You swear it?" Volkan asked. "You won't dissuade me?"

"On our mother," he swore. It was better to plan with him than to be blindsided again. If he hadn't had Yara in place to act as his eyes and ears, he could have lost his brother.

Volkan smiled. "Well, brother, then let us prepare for dinner with our enemies."

The doors were parted for them upon arrival, and Eldar caught sight of her before he could assess the room for exits and entrances or scrutinize the staff for any suspicious behavior. Yara stood by Pomona and held a chalice of wine, but she did not sip from it. For a moment he wondered if Pomona had dressed her, as she favored the Greek designs. Yara wore the Grecian robes like she had been born into it, as if she had come out of her mother's womb swaddled in the fabric. A thin veil of crimson fabric knotted around her neck with a gold pin, and a short slit revealed one brown-skinned leg anytime she walked. When she turned, he saw the slender curve of her bare back.

"Magnificent," Volkan breathed.

Eldar tore his gaze from her and hunted the room. It was empty but for Pomona, Yara, and Titus, who sat at the head of the table. He wondered faintly how Yara had secured herself an invitation. A small part of him was impressed.

"Our guests have arrived," Titus said in his deep, booming voice.

Pomona spun around to face them. Her blond hair was knotted in a tight coil, revealing the stern lines of her face. Her pale eyes latched on to Volkan, and beneath the mask of anger that clouded her eyes, Eldar could see the poisonous depths of her desire. She had always been obsessed with Volkan. Before he had been placed under her thumb, her eyes had always been locked on his at court. They had been young during their first foray into court barely fifteen and not yet transitioned.

"We were surprised to receive your invitation," Volkan said. He walked around the space like he owned it. Fingers lifted the baubles that decorated the little entrance table. He began to play with a small wooden elephant, twisting it in the air as if it were galloping. "I would have thought you'd be recovering after the attack."

Pomona crossed the room in a blur of speed, and Volkan caught her by the neck.

"I know what you did," she hissed. "You took my child away from me."

"You are not worthy to call yourself a mother," Volkan said, his lips curled in disgust. Her fingers dug into his hand, tearing the skin, but he didn't so much as flinch. "Any child of yours would be an abomination."

His hand was clasped so tightly around her neck, her next words were a gasp.

"What was that?" Volkan taunted, drawing her closer.

"Our child," she said.

Volkan released her, and she crumbled to the ground. To Eldar's surprise, Titus didn't interfere with the rough treatment. Perhaps it was their plan for Pomona to rile him up into a confession.

"Liar," he said in disgust.

Pomona smiled for the first time since they arrived, and Eldar itched to carve it off her face.

"It's the truth," she said. "It was yours, and you killed it. Who is the monster now?"

"That is enough," Eldar said. "We didn't arrive to be accused and disrespected. If that is all you wish to convey, we'll take our leave."

"Perhaps it wasn't him who orchestrated the attack, but you," Pomona said, rising to her feet. "The clever-eyed Eldar Demirci, who always has a card up his sleeve."

Eldar didn't justify her ribbing with a response; he looked at Volkan and nodded to the door. They turned on their heels when she called out.

"When you're caught for your lies and the Undying King asks for your death, I will ask him to give you to us for the rest of your immortal life. Titus and I shall be your keepers once more," she promised. "Your torment in the past will be pleasurable compared to what we do to you. You won't be kept in a cage this time. You will be dragged on our chains in court naked and blood hungry."

Volkan shot forward, but Eldar caught him, and he dragged him out of the room. It took great effort to pull him down the hall and pin him to the wall. His eyes were feral with a bloodlust that would make any mortal man cower.

"Enough," Eldar growled.

"It's not mine," he growled.

"No, of course not," Eldar replied. "Who knows who Pomona has opened her legs to? I reckon it's Titus's spawn."

"They never touched," Volkan whispered.

Eldar frowned. "No? They share a child."

"I believe they only ever coupled once to conceive that child."

"That doesn't mean there wasn't someone else," Eldar replied.

"All they ever touched was me," Volkan said in a small voice. "They never looked at each other the way they look at me."

Eldar stiffened, Volkan rarely spoke of his time in imprisonment.

And while he had always encouraged his brother to speak to him, at this moment all he wanted to tell him was to stop.

"It was never-ending. The pain and pleasure. The blood starvation was worse. I would think Titus was you, and when he'd touch me, I'd think you were embracing me, and I'd feel relief. But it was never you. I thought you were a ghost when I returned. I couldn't believe you were real."

Their mother would say that they were two sides of the same coin.

Volkan was his only weakness. The only person that could ever be used to break him. Eldar never felt pain or anguish, but when they had taken Volkan from him he had felt himself splinter. While it might have been Volkan in that dark cellar, Eldar had been punished alongside him. He had hated himself for failing to protect him, for not thinking quickly enough to save him, for letting them carve a piece of him away. His bright-eyed brother had not been the same since his release.

"I failed you, Volkan," Eldar said in a tight voice. "I didn't have the time to color my hair before they took you. I would have taken your place. I need you to know that. If you are ever in any trouble, I will *always* take your place."

Volkan shook his head. "It is better this way. You can barely stand anyone's touch now. Imprisonment would have broken you."

"I don't care if I am broken," he said. "So long as you are whole."

Volkan pulled him in a tight embrace. He stroked Eldar's hair like he was the one in need of comfort. Like he was the broken one.

<hr />

Yara stared at the wretched face of Pomona. Her fury could not be masked as she broke the delicate dinner plates. The loud crash of a jeweled chalice being thrown at a wall echoed along the ceiling. Her pale hair came undone from its careful coil, wrapping around her like serpents.

Titus caught her arms, and she sobbed, breaking down onto the floor. Yara felt like she was witnessing a private moment, and she slowly crept toward the door.

"*You*," Pomona said harshly.

Yara turned to face her, surprised by the hatred that flooded her eyes. She had been welcoming when Yara arrived to impart a message on the prince's behalf. She had pulled her arm and told her to stay and hailed her servant to dress her in these robes, as if they were the dearest of friends.

Pomona stood before her in the blink of an eye.

"Why was he looking at you like that?" she asked, a bit wild-eyed.

Yara thought of Eldar and the way he had pinned her with his stare the moment he entered. She hadn't looked away from Pomona, but she'd felt the dark trail of his eyes lingering down her form. No doubt still angry that she had sought to trick him. To lure his precious brother into a trap.

Did Pomona suspect that they were working together?

"Eldar is a complicated creature," Yara said. "He looks at everyone so intensely."

"Not Eldar," Pomona spat. "Volkan."

Yara frowned. "He was looking at me?"

Yara stared at the jealousy swirling in her eyes. It was deeper than jealousy; it was a consuming desperation. Yara hadn't fully understood the hate spewing between them both. All she knew was that Volkan had been imprisoned, and she and Titus had been his unfortunate wardens. She was shaken by their altercation, by the venom in Volkan's eyes. It made her shiver to think what cruelty Pomona had subjected him to.

"I should return to Mircea," she said. "He expects me."

She had a performance tonight at the Grand Hall, and she wouldn't upset Dracul by arriving late. Pomona stepped away from her with a snarl.

Yara breathed a sigh of relief when she escaped the room. She traced her path back to the hall, surprised by Pomona's anger at her. She had pretended to be so kind and innocent, as if she truly wished for them to be friends, but the moment she had fallen under Volkan's stare that truce had splintered. Yara pitied her for the loss of her child. But none of these creatures were soft or sensible.

They were monsters. Every last one of them.

Yara touched the blunt tip of the dagger strapped to her concealed thigh. The one Mircea had given her. He had crouched down from his immeasurable height and stared at her sternly. At times he reminded her of her father. It was the beard, she supposed, and the way he patted her shoulder awkwardly, as if he did not know how to behave toward a young girl.

"The sharp point is for stabbing," Mircea said. "Aim for the crotch. You are far too short to reach their eyes."

Yara playfully aimed for his eyes. "I could have blinded you."

"I am bent down to see your eyes. Your opponent won't do the same," he said.

While she was no expert swordswoman, Yara felt safe with the weapon. She understood then why Aylin always had one securely tucked beneath her skirts.

When she came to the Grand Hall, she was surprised to find it empty.

"The celebrations are being held in the Bone Garden," a guard said. He led her to the barred doors at the back of the hall. Her heart raced at the thought of going outside and inhaling the crisp air. It cracked open, and she stared at a garden that was both beautiful and grotesque. The plants and flowers were crisp and hemmed in by well-tended hedges. There were pillars with chains decorating the outer rims like a fence, and on these chains were desecrated creatures. Blackened and charred to a crisp, they were scarcely recognizable—all but the sharp points of their teeth, which remained untouched even in death. Bile crawled up her throat, and she couldn't turn her eyes away from the horror.

She jolted at the touch of a cold palm resting on her bare back.

"The Undying King hangs his enemies at nightfall. When the sun rises, they burn, their skin melting off like wax, their hair singeing and flesh boiling like cooked meat. If you take a deep breath, you can smell the char mixing so sweetly with the hyacinths," Volkan whispered. "A perfect execution."

Yara shivered at the strange stroking touch of his claws.

"He should string you up next," she said boldly. "The world would be a far kinder place without you in it."

He laughed in that strange, whimsical manner.

"You shouldn't spend time with the Maleinos," he said. "They are abominable creatures."

"And what are you?" she asked.

"Turn around," he said. "Face me."

Yara turned to look at his angelic face. It was the hair, she supposed, that made him appear divine. The palest white, it mimicked the bones of the dead.

"I'm not afraid of you anymore," she said. "You don't frighten me."

"No, I dare say your heart doesn't race like it once did," he said. "The king's mark has made you mistakenly believe you are invincible."

Yara stared into his red eyes, and when he licked his lips, she felt that familiar trickle of fear mixed with something else...the strange desire to feel the pressure of his teeth sinking into her. To feel her limbs loosen and her mind relax, and her emotions melt away like smoke. It was an addicting feeling, to be free from the demons that shackled her mind.

"Does it sicken you to know that I am out of your reach?" Yara asked. "That I won't kneel for you and feed you and exist for you."

"No," he said with the barest hint of a smile. "Would you like to dance?"

"Never."

His hand wrapped around her waist, and he led her to the crowd of dancing people. Volkan spun her like she was a doll. They moved in a manner of such intense speed they were merely a blur to her human eyes, ribbons of color and skin. Her feet swept off the floor, and her dress twisted indecently.

"Volkan. Stop," she breathed, clutching on to him for fear that she would break her neck if he performed any abrupt stops. He was moving so fast her stomach churned. She clutched the fox fur that decorated the collar of his kaftan, wrapping herself in his arms, and she wondered if this were his ploy to torment her into embracing him.

"I can't stop," he whispered, teeth grazing her ear. His mouth drifted lower until he was buried in her neck.

Yara felt a strange burst of pleasure, and she realized that he had bitten her. The sharp pinprick of pain was washed by pleasure so intense it made her knees shake. It was like her body craved the poison of his bite. It was more intense than the last few times, like he was inside her skin. His hand tangled in her hair, releasing the pins that held it up. Yara moaned when he licked the cut sealed, and his lips pressed a gentle kiss to her neck.

"Shall I tell you a secret?" he said against her skin. "I could make you do any number of wretched acts with a simple whisper, but I will ask you for one."

Yara was still dazed.

"Pretend that you like me," he said.

Yara felt her lips turn up in a smile, and she stared at him without any hatred, but a feeling that closely resembled tenderness.

"You are very pretty," she said. Her finger drifted across his jaw.

"Prettier than Eldar?" he asked with a sharp grin.

"Not quite," she teased. It was strange to feel this lightheartedness inside her. She hadn't felt it since she had arrived at the Court of the Undead. "I loved dancing in the sultan's courts. It was filled with such vibrant colors and the most delicious feasts. I remember spinning with Aylin as she scowled during the entire scene. She was much like your brother, drawn to the shadows rather than the light."

"What else did you love?" he asked.

"I loved the court games," she said with a wistful sigh. "It was fun and distracting. A game of cat and mouse. I couldn't get enough of it."

"You are still playing games, are you not?" he asked. He lifted her and spun her, the flare of her dress twisting around her knees. "You've secured yourself the blessing of Vlad Dracul. Mircea looks upon you like you are his daughter. Even Eldar respects you."

"He respects me?" she asked.

"He will never confess it, but I think so."

"And you? Do you hate me?" she asked.

"I hate all mortals. For their weakness, for their softness, for their mortality," Volkan said. "But you are not like them, are you, Yara? You are like us. You hunger for more."

Yara could feel the lightness in her fade like it was melting from her skin. Her senses crept back in, and when she realized what he had done, anger coursed through her veins.

He sighed. "I see you've broken my charm."

"If you bite me again, I swear I'll tell the Undying King," she said. "I won't listen to your brother again."

"I should have commanded you to forget that you were bitten," he said.

"Why me?" she asked.

There were hundreds of blood slaves. She had seen them at his dinner table. He had the prettiest men and women offering him their wrists and necks. He had his choice of the human feast that surrounded him.

Volkan's lips lifted in that wicked grin like he knew a secret she did not. He released her and fell into a deep, mocking bow.

"Until I see you again," he said.

Yara turned away from him. Standing alongside the banquet table filled with food, she saw Pomona's eyes on them. Her gaze was filled with hatred for them both. She did not look at Yara as she had before, with curiosity, but with a wrath that begged to unravel and consume her.

After her brief performance, Yara stepped down from the podium that housed the Undying King's throne. Her eyes critically scanned the garden. For the first time in days, the possibility of escape was within reach. The doors were always sealed and there were no windows to attempt to scale, but here, outside, there was hope. From her vantage she saw how truly domineering the fortress was. Big grey walls with pointed arches and slim towers.

There were stone chimeras guarding the back door of the courtyard. Beyond the crowd of dancing and drinking courtiers was a dark maze. The gaping mouth taunted her with the promise of escape, and Yara couldn't resist the urge to disappear into the unknown with the hope that there would be light on the other side.

She traveled into the maze, and her breath caught in her chest. It was dark and barely illuminated by the torches hung up every few feet. Her breath grew foggy in the air, and she wondered how the season had changed so rapidly. It must have been at least a month since her capture. It had been September when she had been kidnapped. And she presumed it to be October now.

She felt the tingling sense of being watched, but anytime she looked behind her there was nobody in sight. She picked up her pace, her white slippers soiled by the mud and squelching miserably with each step. It was impossible to be discreet with the noise she was making. The sense of being followed heightened with each turn in the labyrinth until Yara began to run. Sweat began to trickle down her forehead until she bumped into someone. Her hand pressed to his chest to control her balance.

"God, not you!" she exclaimed. "You and your brother will be the death of me."

"I was wondering when you'd figure out that there is no exit. It's a never-ending maze," Eldar said, his lips tilted in delight. "But you humans are no better than the beasts you whip. You lack any form of higher thinking."

"What?" she whispered.

"Vlad thought it humorous to build a maze with only one exit: the entrance," Eldar said, leaning against the hedge. His dark hair swayed under the breeze.

"How do I get out?" she asked.

"Prayers and sheer luck," he said. "It took me months to map it out in my mind."

He turned on his heel, and Yara saw him bend slightly forward to no doubt race into the distance. She entangled her arms around his torso, feeling his entire body stiffen at her touch.

"What are you doing?" he asked gruffly.

"My feet ache and I'm exhausted. I don't want to find the way back by myself," she said. Yara knew she was whining, but she was far too tired and frustrated to care. This venture had been a great waste of time. How could she have been so foolish as to think escape would be that easy? This was no estate; it was a fortress.

"Could you not take me with you?" Yara asked, smiling at him sweetly.

"I am not your savior."

"Just this once. Volkan bit me again, you know. If you lead me out of this hell, I won't tell Mircea," she said.

Eldar's gaze darkened, and he pursued his lips. "Have you forgotten that your father's life rests in my palm? Say my brother's name one more time and you'll regret it."

He sealed the space between them, and Yara stumbled back. She could feel thorns digging into the flesh of her bare back.

Her chest rose and fell heavily, pressing against him with each deep breath. He was so close she could feel the weight of his leg slip between her own and tangle in the fabric of her dress.

"Say it," he whispered. His fingers lifted to catch a stray curl. It wrapped languidly around his pale finger, and he tugged hard. "Go ahead, little mouse. Say *it*."

Yara hated him. It burned in her chest, a strange, unfamiliar feeling. It was nothing like how she hated the others of his kind. Far more than she hated Volkan. This was primal. It felt as though she had *always* hated him.

He released her hair and drifted a claw down her throat. Softly stroking her skin. But danger lurked beneath his touch.

Eldar laughed, a dry sound. "You mortals are pathetic."

"And you monsters are cruel abominations," she hissed.

"I'd rather be the wolf than the mouse," he said. "One of them is destined to *always* be devoured."

Yara blinked, and he was gone. Nothing remained of him. Not even his footprints. Only the unrelenting silence.

At first, Yara continued to travel the labyrinth, determined to prove him wrong. She didn't need him. She never had. But as the night progressed and her weary feet gave out from under her, coated in fluid-filled blisters, and her skin sealed in sweat, Yara began to weep for the second time since she came to Wallachia. It felt good to feel her skin shudder with torment and her eyes burn. Like she was cleansing her soul.

She missed her family so much that it hurt. And now with the grim knowledge that she could die here in this maze, her pain felt heightened. They would never know what became of her. Aylin would never know how hard she had tried to be strong for her. For her beautiful, brave sister.

Yara felt her eyes slide shut, and she fell into a restless slumber.

Something shifted beneath her, and Yara felt her eyes open to stare into a beautiful, familiar face. Relief flooded her at the thought that he had come back for her. He lifted her into his arms, and she wrapped her hands around his shoulders. She was shaking, and she worried that he could feel the tremors of her body. She didn't want him to know how frightened she had been. How every rustle of the hedges had grown ominous in the dark. How every graze of the breeze broke her skin out in goosebumps. How the cold had made a home of her bones.

"I hate you," she whispered, as she clung to him tightly. The green walls passed them in a burst of speed, fading into nothingness.

"I hate you too," he confessed.

Before she knew it, they were in her bedroom, and he was laying her down gently. A strange contrast to his unbidden cruelty only hours earlier. He stared at her with those black eyes. And it felt like looking into the void.

Yara knew then that she would do everything in her power to become strong enough to destroy him. She swore to herself that she would see him on his knees someday.

"Don't look at me like that," he whispered. His thumb drifted along her bottom lip, claw scratching her soft skin. "It arouses me."

Yara bit his thumb hard, surprised when he didn't flinch. He only smiled. That wicked, demented smile of his. She turned her head away from him. He was just as mad as his brother, and she wouldn't humor him with her anger.

The door clicked shut, and she released a sigh. Even as her eyes slid shut, Yara felt as though she were being watched. As if he still stood over her like the Angel of Death, haunting her till her soul departed her body.

In the dark, she whispered a prayer of protection and hoped that it would save her from the dark and the monsters it birthed.

XII

AYLIN HAD FELT lighter the past two weeks. Every morning after praying *fajr* she would go to the courtyard an hour before the men trickled in with stretched yawns and their customary glares. She could feel a shift in their distaste toward her each day that she showed up with her sabre and her fists bound in cloth. Her bruises marked her determination, and slowly the mistrust in their eyes faded until they began to greet her with a curt nod during their morning training.

All except for Domenico and Salvatore. They remained united in their stance. Domenico that she was unworthy and Salvatore that she was too young.

So, she was naturally surprised when Leandra claimed that Father Salvatore wished to speak with her.

They travelled down the empty hallways. The estate was suppressed in color and art. It was a grim place built as an extended barracks rather than a home. With thinned carpets and walls decorated by weapons it wasn't particularly welcoming. Leandra led her to an old study. Salvatore wasn't there yet, and she knew it was a power tactic. To keep her waiting as if she were his lesser. The door clicked shut behind her, and she perused the room with her hands neatly folded behind her back. There was a bookshelf that held Latin titles and a mahogany table rested atop a frayed grey rug. There were a few letters atop the table. She scoffed when she made out a letter he was writing to the pope. Of course, he was in cahoots with the papacy. It seemed the entire Catholic Church was aware of these creatures. She wondered if the sultan was aware of this blight or if word had not yet crossed to his borders.

"Are you spying on me?" Salvatore asked. His collar was so stiff she wondered if it merely mimicked its master.

"You mean your boring letters convincing the pope that you are handling the task discreetly and appreciate the funds being funneled into your greedy hands?" she asked. "I didn't know the Church was so involved."

"You didn't think a sect run by a *Reverendo Don* and called the Silver Cross was run by the Church?"

"I thought you were a bunch of religious fanatics," Aylin said, sitting in his chair. His lips thinned into a slim line, and she thought he would demand she rise from his chair, but he sat opposite her in the guest chair. She smiled at his glare and continued, "Who simply liked to play dress-up. You are far too young and cruel to be a priest."

"Cruel?" he asked. "In what manner?"

"I've seen the way you look at me. I dare say you've never seen anyone who is not Venetian," she said. "But you don't look at Elijah that way, and he's Transylvanian. I suppose you are only shocked by people darker than you, not fairer."

"That is untruth," he said. "I told you that I didn't want children fighting my war."

"I'm no child. I'm nineteen!"

Salvatore stared at her warily. "And I am thirty-five."

"I do not jest," she said.

"Even if that is true, you do not have a soldier's physique. These creatures possess inhuman strength and power," he said. "You would be snapped in half if they ever got their hands around you."

"Even if I were as strong as you so fondly claim I am not, you would still find some fault within me."

"I do not hate you, Aydin," he said almost gently. "Truth be told, you remind me a lot of myself when I was young. You have fire within your guts and a sharp tongue. I do not envy your brother's duty to keep you out of trouble."

Aylin could almost believe him. His pale blue eyes stared at her with such conviction, and his handsome face appraised her like she was a fascinating creature. She didn't see the hate she had once seen. It didn't burn like Domenico's.

"I require your assistance in a discreet matter," he said.

Aylin sat upright. Of course, he had been softening her for his request, filling her with compliments until she was half-bloated with pride.

"Don't look at me like that," he said. "Every word I said was the truth. Besides, I believe this will be of interest to you and your brother."

"How so?"

"You said your sister was taken by these creatures," he said.

Her breath stilled in her lungs, and she hung on to his every word with desperation. Aylin couldn't stop herself from reaching for his hand. Her touch made him startle, but he didn't pull his hand away.

"Tell me," she said. "Please."

"How sweet you can be when you want something," he said with a faint smile. "We've captured one of them. They were prowling the plains for weeks. The villagers called upon Father Alexander, as they believed a demon was haunting them. But it wasn't a demon leaving their cattle empty, bloodless husks, but rather a vampir."

"You've captured it?"

Salvatore nodded. "She is confined to a room under heavy guard. We have been studying her flesh. Their ability to heal is fascinating. There is much to be learned."

"What do you want with me?" she asked. "To use me as bait?"

"Nothing so distasteful," he said. "It seems she doesn't speak any language but Turkish."

Aylin sank back into his chair with a languid smile. It felt good to be needed. To see his lips thin into a firm line the longer she remained silent. It wasn't until his left eye twitched, and his hand fell ceremoniously down on the table, that he spoke.

"Will you translate for us?" he asked. "We wish to know where the rest of her kind is hiding."

"I don't know," she mused. "I've felt rather underappreciated since I've arrived. It's almost as if I'm not a person."

"I gave you the opportunity to prove yourself," Salvatore said. "I've allowed you to train freely with no restriction."

Aylin had every intention of helping him, but it was fun to pull his leg for a bit.

"Why didn't you ask Elijah?" she asked curiously.

"Because he needs to remain focused on his training," he replied.

"Right," she said bitterly. "And I don't."

Of course, she would speak to the vampir. If it meant she was one step closer to Yara then she would do anything he asked of her. It had been a little longer than a month since she last saw her sister, and with each passing week, she couldn't help but feel as though all hope was lost.

But she didn't like how he implied that her training was not as important as Ilyas'.

"That was not an insult," he said gently. "I think highly of you and while you may not possess his strength you are a brave and zealous boy."

"I'll speak to her," Aylin said. "Where is she?"

"She is recovering from a few inquisitive tests we've performed," he said. "I will summon for you when she is capable of speech."

"By inquisitive tests you mean torture?"

"Good day, Aydin," he said. A hint that their conversation was over.

Aylin left his study and had just turned the corner when she bumped into a broad chest. She stared up into the gruesome face of Domenico. Unsurprisingly, his tunic was missing, and her palms had fallen upon his bare skin. Aylin had barely blinked when he shoved her into the nearest wall. Hard enough to make her teeth rattle. His thick fingers coiled around her neck, pinning her like she was a rabbit caught in his snare.

"Where's your brother that you always hide behind?" he asked. She felt the wet slide of his tongue running down the tip of her injured ear to the lobe. She had removed the wraps as Leandra advised since it had sealed neatly with a scab over the past few nights, but she regretted removing the cloth when she felt the flat of his tongue. Shivers wound beneath her skin as she remembered the pain of his bite. It felt dangerous to be so close to that feral mouth of his.

"He will kill you if you hurt me," she said. She hated how small he made her feel. How frightened she was in his presence. Judging by the vicious curl of his lips, he could sense her fear like the predator he was. He could hear the thud of her racing heart, and it only seemed to whet his appetite.

"I'd like to see him try," he said. "Maybe I should get rid of him first. Slit his throat in his sleep and then come for you."

Rage burned through her like wildfire. It was one thing to torment her. It was another to bring Ilyas into it. Before Aylin could talk herself out of it, she raised her knee and slammed it between his legs. It was the first thing Ilyas had taught her in their training. If immobilized, don't be afraid to do anything to survive—including using a man's weakness against him. His face crumpled in pain, and he crouched down, breathing like a wild beast. Aylin tore off into the distance. She could hear the thud of his footsteps behind her.

There were a group of men coming down the hallway, and she exhaled in relief at the sight of Borza. Besides Ilyas, he was the only person she trusted in this place, along with Leandra, who reminded her painfully of her sister.

Domenico grabbed a fistful of her short hair, and she screamed as he dragged her back to him.

"God above," Borza snapped. "Release him, Domenico."

"I'm going to punish this brat until nobody recognizes him," he snarled. "I will tear him to pieces."

Borza crossed the space and pried Domenico's fingers from her hair. Her scalp ached the moment he released her, and Aylin spun around, gathering a wad of spit. Satisfaction curled in her belly when it struck his face. She didn't think his face could get any redder, but it did. He looked like he was going to come undone. If he wasn't planning on murdering her before, he certainly was now. It took three men to subdue him. He writhed like a man possessed, struggling to reach her.

"I'll kill you," Domenico roared.

"Not if I kill you first," she snapped, writhing in Borza's arms. She would never give him the satisfaction of knowing she feared him. So, she pretended to struggle as if Borza's arms were the only thing keeping her from destroying him. "I will paint the walls with your blood!"

Aylin felt a pair of arms wrap around her, pulling her from Borza. She knew that scent of woodsmoke and mint leaves. Ilyas clasped his hand around her mouth. If it were anyone else, she would bite them until their blood filled her mouth for even attempting to silence her. But she let him pull her away, half dragging her, half carrying her.

"You missed all the fun," she said when his palm slid from her mouth. He held her chin between two fingers. Ilyas was not a man of many words, but his silence made her uneasy.

"He started it," she said, knowing how childish that sounded. It was the same excuse she'd tell Baba when Yara attacked her for ruining her puzzles and Aylin rightfully defended herself. It wasn't her fault she enjoyed ruining a puzzle as much as Yara enjoyed solving it.

"He threatened you," she said. "I was protecting your honor."

"Why does this mouth of yours always get us into trouble?" he asked. His thumb tapped her lips twice, and she stilled.

"I...it doesn't," she said. Her skin felt warm and feverish. Ilyas wasn't one for touching, and she was glad for it. Her mind couldn't string together a coherent sentence to save her life. He had turned her into a blubbering fool.

"Then why is it that Domenico looked prepared to tear you apart at the seams?" he asked. "If it isn't your mouth, then what is it?"

"He doesn't need an excuse to hurt me. He's been out for my blood from the moment we arrived, and you know it!"

"I doubt your sweet temper and pliant words have soothed the matter," he said.

Aylin smiled at him from beneath her lashes. "I can be sweet-tempered and pliant."

Relief coursed through her veins when he laughed. Ilyas had once said she was the only person who could make him laugh, and she took her duty *very* seriously.

"What will I do with you, Aylin?" He shook his head.

Aylin wrapped her arms around his torso, seeking a comfort only he could provide. She felt his big palm settle on her head. It seemed every day that passed, her heart grew fuller, like it was expanding beneath her bones, and she didn't know how to stop it or even if she *wanted* it to stop. She had never felt anything like it before in her life. From the moment she had met Ilyas, she knew he was special. She could see it in the way he held himself. He had been fifteen and frightened, but not once had he let it bring him down. He had taken the wretched cards dealt to him and built a life from it.

"I wish I could be like you. I wish I could be strong," she said. "Sometimes it's easier to let my tongue run wild than to admit that I'm afraid."

"I'll speak to Domenico," he said. "If he comes near you again, I won't be held responsible for what I do."

"And if he threatens you again, *I* won't be held responsible for what I do."

Two days passed before Salvatore summoned her. It was a rare day of rest and she had been slowly losing her mind in their bedroom. Ilyas slowly sharpened his blades, occasionally pausing to run his fingers affectionately down his blade.

"I feel like I am intruding on a private moment," Aylin said. Her hand curled beneath her head as she watched him work. Ilyas did not believe in rest. Idleness was the devil's playmate, he liked to say.

"Why is that?" he asked.

"Because you are making love to that blade," she said. "Or as the Venetian men say you are *fucking* that blade."

"Aylin," he said sharply. "Behave."

She giggled, thrilled that she had gotten a reaction from him. She wondered how far she could push him before he unraveled.

"What do you think it is like?" she asked. "*Fucking.*"

Ilyas exhaled a sharp breath. "Who have you been speaking to?"

"Pietro," she said. "He has taught me a lot. You will not believe the positions he spoke of—"

His blade cluttered to the ground, and she felt his thick palm land on her mouth. He was so close to her; she could feel the heavy weight of his body as he leaned over her. Aylin realized then just how close they were. Her heart thudded as she studied his handsome face covered with dark stubble. He was beginning to look like these rugged Venetian men. His brown hair that had slowly begun to grow to his shoulder. Aylin playfully bit his palm, until he lowered his hand.

"They are corrupting you," he said darkly.

"I like being corrupted," she said. "And not being treated like precious glass,"

He opened his mouth, perhaps to lecture her on the company she kept, so she swiftly changed the subject.

"Should I cut your hair?" Aylin asked. Her finger slipped into the silken strands as if she were taking measurement.

"You don't like it?" he asked.

"I do," she said. "But I thought you wouldn't like it. You always kept it short when you were serving in the army. Is this not a form of service?"

"I will leave it be," he said with a faint smile. "Since you like it so much."

Aylin released his hair, curling her fingers tight to her chest to stop herself from reaching for him. She hated this feeling blooming in her chest, unraveling like a sick flower with its petals covered in mold. She despised how her heart galloped and leaped like a wild mare void of leather strappings. She wanted to dig her fingers in her chest and rip away this growing affection. She knew better than to develop feelings for a Janissary. Even if he was far from court, he would always be a Janissary. He would never betray his oath to the sultan. He would never wed or even touch a woman in a manner that carried any affection.

He was far too close to her, and she was far too tempted to seal the space between them. A small taste of the future they would never share.

"I should go speak to Salvatore. He expects me," she said, sitting upright. Aylin didn't look at him when she tugged on her boots, afraid of what he'd see in her eyes. He opened his mouth to perhaps ask what Salvatore required of her, but she had blindly fled out the door and up to Salvatore's study before he could utter the words.

She cracked the door open with little interest in announcing herself to Salvatore. The thought of catching him unguarded was particularly appealing. He was penning a letter, candlelight stroking his face like an absent lover.

"You are sitting in my chair," Aylin said.

He released a sigh. One so deep and harrowing that Aylin almost pitied him. She needn't be so insufferable, but it was delightful being a thorn in his side. Especially since he provided her with the reaction she wanted.

"Follow me," he said curtly.

Salvatore stood up and spun around, the tail of his robe sweeping the stone floor. He slipped a key into the wall. The keyhole was placed beneath a decorative shield that he discreetly raised. And when the key twisted, he pushed the wall forward revealing a hidden passage. It was small and damp inside, and she followed him into the dark. A part of her wondered if it was wise to come without Ilyas and not even share this information with him so he knew her whereabouts. But Salvatore didn't have to lure her into a secret passage to kill her.

They came upon a bolted door where a man with a stern face stood guard.

"Evening, Cesari," Salvatore said.

"Evening, Father," he said. "The blighted wench was screaming all morning. Nearly made me deaf."

"We will see what she is hiding," Salvatore said determinedly. The door cracked open, and Aylin was not surprised to see that the creature was chained to a slab of stone as if she were being laid to rest. Thick silver chains covered the entirety of her torso, and a gag had been inserted in her mouth. Aylin could see the sharpness of her unnatural teeth. Her dark hair was thick and covered half her face in a mask. Her eyes roamed wildly around the ceiling before settling on the two of them.

"Remove her gag," Salvatore said.

The guard worked carefully to unbind her mouth.

"I didn't think their prestigious order accepted outsiders," she said in Turkish. "Why is one of our kind helping these vile heathens?"

Aylin narrowed her eyes, warily staring at Salvatore, who stood in the corner. His shrewd blue eyes focused on them both. If the creature expected her to hold some faint trace of camaraderie because of their shared background, she was mistaken.

"Tell us where my sister is," Aylin said. "She was captured by your kind."

"I haven't fed for days. Not since I was captured by these fanatics. If you give me an ounce of blood, I will answer your questions."

"What does she say?" Salvatore asked.

"If we give her blood, she will answer our questions."

"Never," he said. "She will answer our questions, or we will cut her from her chest to her legs."

"He says he will torture you if you don't answer his questions," she relayed.

"Ask her where her kind hide," Salvatore directed.

"Where do your people live?" she asked.

"Everywhere," the creature said.

"One of them took my sister. Her name is Yara, Daughter of Besir Ağa. Have you heard of her?"

She stared at the ceiling thoughtfully.

"Yara, you say," she said. "Would this be a Yara with an angel's voice?"

Aylin's heart thudded. Her palms grew slick with sweat. It had been weeks since Yara disappeared, and this news was sweeter than honey. Aylin leaned forward, peering down into her dangerous face. Salvatore clasped a warning hand on her forearm.

"Not too close to her. Not while her mouth is unbound."

"Yes," she said. "Where is she?"

The woman smiled. A wicked, feral smile that brought a shiver down her chest.

"Give me a half cup of your blood and I will tell you all about your little nightingale," she cooed.

"What does she speak of?" Salvatore demanded. He left his perch on the wall to hover over her shoulder.

"She says she knows where my sister is," Aylin whispered.

"You can't let her twist your mind," Salvatore said. "Ask her where her kind resides. Warn her under punishment of death."

"Where are your people?" Aylin asked. "And tell me where my sister is."

"I will not speak a word until the fire that burns my throat is soothed," she said.

"She refuses," Aylin said.

Salvatore's face tightened. "Very well, a few more weeks of torture should loosen her tongue."

Aylin frowned at the resolve she saw in the woman's eyes. She wouldn't tell them a word until she had her blood. If Aylin hoped for any answers, she would have to make a deal with the devil. Somehow, she would have to visit her without Salvatore and give her what she wanted.

The door clicked shut behind them as they returned to his study. Salvatore returned to his desk, a pensive look in his brown eyes.

"We will pick this up in a few weeks' time," he said.

"What if she doesn't crack?" she asked.

"We haven't brought in Domenico yet," he said. "Once he has an hour with her, she will sing like a canary."

The thought of spending an hour with Domenico *without* torture chilled her. She couldn't imagine what it would be like *with* torture.

"On the topic of Domenico, you have both been assigned to go hunting for tomorrow's meat. We have a rotational system for hunting our meat," he said. "It will give you both a chance to put this rivalry to bed."

"You want me to go into the forest with Domenico carrying hunting weapons?" she asked. "Only one of us will return alive."

"I don't care," he said. "I tire of hearing reports of your disagreements. Men who do not trust each other cannot fight alongside each other."

Aylin stared at him warily. This was a terrible idea. She couldn't think of anything worse than being stuck in a forest with Domenico.

Aylin figured if she survived a day with Domenico without killing him *or* herself then she would be brave enough to face her sister's captor.

XIII

ELDAR STARED AT the scroll of paper, and then he stared at his betrothed, Akila. Her slim, nervous face was partly hidden by the gossamer veil she wore. Bloodred rubies covered her throat like a shackle and henna stained her fingers as they tapped restlessly on her knee. Volkan stood by his shoulder as his family witness and made little effort to hide how bored he was by the affair. This was the third time he'd yawned in the past five minutes. He discreetly kicked Eldar under the table in a gesture to speed along the proceedings.

Eldar's feather felt heavy as he scrawled his name. Under his name, Volkan wrote his own in his scratchy handwriting. A year from now, they would host a grand celebration in Cairo and consummate the marriage and the betrothal would be complete. He felt sickened by the thought of both bedding her and tying himself to the inconvenience of a wife.

"May we speak?" he asked Bahiti. As she was the matriarch of her family, their relationship would be far more critical than the one with his betrothed. Akila was merely a pawn in his machinations. The true prize was Bahiti.

"I'm surprised you were willing to settle down," Bahiti said in the privacy of her bedroom. Her long fingers twisted the chalice, and her kohl-lined eyes scrutinized him. Bahiti was a fearsome tale in North Africa. Rumor of a beautiful woman who hunted the desert had risen in the late thirteenth century. At times a sired vampire's master or mistress would die, and they would seek to create their own clan. While they couldn't make their own vampire, they would often recruit strays. Bahiti would strike down those who sought to live like the trueborn, killing dozens as she traveled. Any lesser vampire was punished for desiring more by the vengeful Bahiti.

"The men of your line lack any manner of domesticity. It's why your line is left to you and your brother alone."

Volkan and Eldar had sworn long ago that their line would end with them. They had been children when they had made that pact. Tired and abused by their father Cetin Demirci. Cetin had despised Volkan because he would spend more time combing his hair than wielding a blade. So, he would beat him unconscious anytime he disappointed him. And when Eldar defended his brother, he would hurt Volkan twice as hard. Cetin had learned early on that Eldar did not cry. He *never* cried. No amount of pain could break him. So, he hurt Volkan to pull any type of reaction from him even if it was anger. Even if it was rage.

"I require allies, and your family is a loyal breed," he said.

In other words, he would accept domesticity so long as it benefited him.

"Will you tell me more or is this cryptic answer all I will get?" she asked. "I am not foolish enough to believe you love my Akila."

"Only a fool shares his plans," Eldar said with a dry smile. "Should the time come, your family will protect mine as if we were your own."

"Should I be concerned?" she asked. "We don't wish to be dragged into a personal feud. And the Demircis have a web of enemies."

Eldar blinked at her. If only she knew that the feud, she spoke of was far greater than that. A war was coming. There had never been a shift of power. Since the dawn of time, it had been the Dracul family exchanging the throne between their kin. It was they who banded their kind together. But they weren't the oldest family, nor were they the first. Nobody quite knew who was the first. They had all simply decided that Vlad was the first and it had stuck.

It had been his father's dying wish to seat himself on the throne, and when Eldar had torn out his heart and ate it, he had felt that ambition become his own, just as his power had flooded his vein. The Dracul family had outlawed cannibalism on the basis that to consume the heart of a vampir would inflict untold damage upon the psyche of the vampir, especially if it belonged to one of noble blood. It could lead to madness and the possible exposure of their existence to the humans. But Eldar didn't feel crazed, he felt powerful. His speed had increased, and he could go longer without feeding. His strength far surpassed his brother's. They had been wrestling one day, and he had shattered Volkan's wrist unintentionally, the bone grinding to dust beneath his grip. They had always been so evenly matched it had shocked his brother.

"We are family, Bahiti," he said. "You must learn to trust me."

"I've never trusted you, Eldar," she said. "I'd sooner trust your brother than you."

"That makes you an intelligent woman," he said. "A good trait to have in an ally."

"And you are unpredictable," Bahiti said with a tight frown. "A terrible trait to have in an ally."

Eldar pressed his palm to her cheek. "Akila will have a bright future if she is by my side in the end. And you will do exactly as I say because you only want the best for her."

Several long moments passed before she nodded. Her eyes were flooded with curiosity. She couldn't help but be tempted by power. It was like dangling a carrot before a starved horse. She couldn't help but bite.

Eldar returned to his bedroom and stared at his board of pieces. He moved the piece of Bahiti to his side of the board. Satisfaction ran beneath his skin to see their side growing and expanding. It would be a long while before his army could rival the Dracul family and their allies. But this was far more than his father accomplished during his quest for power.

He had taken his broken legacy and crafted it into reality.

Sweat dripped down her back as she lunged forward. Yara glared at Mircea, who sidestepped her attack with grace. He moved with the poise of a refined dancer even though he was rather broad and muscular. He was rather fleet-footed.

"You're too fast," she said.

"And you're too slow, pup," he said. "You complain about being mistreated by our kind, yet you flinch anytime you strike true. Do you wish to be as wretched as us? Or do you wish to be a child hiding behind the mark of someone more powerful than you?"

Her blood boiled at his goading words, and she was pleased to find her dagger sinking into his hip, blood spouting like a fountain from the wound. A smile tore up her cheeks, and she jumped in delight. Mircea stared at her almost fondly and patted her head.

"Not too bad," he said.

"I think Pomona hates me," she said, bending down to catch her breath.

"It is Volkan Demirci's flirting that she hates," he replied. "She is obsessed with him."

"I suppose it doesn't help that he got away with the attack," she said, crouching down to rest. He handed her a tin of water, and she gulped it down gratefully.

"No, it does not," he said darkly, as if he too wished to see Volkan punished.

"I think they are keeping secrets," she said. "I think they're interested in the throne."

"Why do you say that?" Mircea asked curiously.

"I see it in his eyes. Eldar's, that is," she said. "He hungers for more."

"Are you certain of this?" he asked. "I already have Radu to contend with for the throne when Vlad steps down. And young Mihnea when he grows older. I don't need to be blindsided by power-hungry nobles as well."

"His brother, Volkan, is interested in me. I'm sure I could get answers from him if I tried," she said.

Yara was playing a dangerous game. But she couldn't find it in herself to feel an ounce of guilt. Eldar had threatened her. He had purposely been cruel to her simply because he could. It was tiresome being a little mouse, as he so mockingly called her. It was time for her to become more.

"Will you?" Mircea said. "And what is it you want in return?"

"I want to be released from here once I've given you sufficient information to prove Eldar's betrayal. And I would like to be compensated for my capture. I'd like land and property under my name and enough payment to keep my family and I satisfied for the rest of our mortal lives. But mostly I want to be freed."

"Is that so, pup?" he asked teasingly. "You're becoming as ruthless as us. Why would I wish to let you go?"

Yara felt something within her. A strange need to make him proud. Mircea had never mistreated her, and it was easy to develop a sense of loyalty toward him. She respected him, and he deserved to sit on the throne for that alone.

"Do you know how long it has been since I arrived?" she asked. Without the sight of the sun, she did not feel the passing days. But it felt like forever. It felt like a lifetime.

"We reach the end of October," he said. "Only a week and a half left."

Yara sucked in a sharp breath. Almost two months. She had been trapped in Dracul's lair for almost two months.

"Oh," she whispered.

Mircea nudged her with his elbows. "Do not see your time here as waste. You are wiser. You are stronger. You are harder."

"Why are you so nice to me?" she asked.

"If you think I am nice then you've certainly been treated most wretchedly," he said.

"I suppose I have," she said.

"There is a way for you to never feel that fear again," Mircea said. He paused as if he were allowing the temptation within her to grow. "I could make you one of us."

Yara stiffened. Of course, she knew that one could be made into them; she'd heard about the "sired." The ones who had been made and were not trueborn.

"Nobody would mistreat you. You would not have to rely on the protection of another. You would be a force of nature. A beautiful predator," Mircea said.

"I don't want to be a monster," Yara said. The thought of her with sharp teeth and those small claws made her shiver. But the thought of power enticed her. To be feared was a divine thought. "I would never see my family again."

"You would have a new family," he said. "You would be my sired. My daughter."

Yara hated that his words touched her, softened her, as he clearly wanted them to. While she liked Mircea, she could not forget that he was as manipulative and wicked as the rest of his kind.

"I wouldn't see my sister again," she said. The thought of never seeing Aylin again was harrowing. Her sister was as vital to her as the heart that beat in her chest. It was for Aylin that she refused to become one of them. While she adored Baba, it was Aylin who would always carry a big piece of her heart.

Still, the thought of seeing the surprise on Eldar's face when he looked upon her transformation almost brought a heady smile to her face.

"I don't wish to be a slave of the night."

"There is a pleasure to be found in darkness," Mircea said in that silky voice of his.

"Not for me," she said. "Will you honor my terms?"

"I will," he said. "You will work with my Mistress of Spies. There is much to learn from her, and she will teach you her ways."

⸺⸺◆⸺⸺

Yara was nervous to meet his Mistress of Spies. Mircea bragged that she could collect the secrets of the dead, and Yara hoped she had not discovered that she had once agreed to spy for Eldar for her freedom but had betrayed him for her Lord Mircea.

The woman before her was tall and beautiful, with deep ebony skin and braids that fell to her waist. She wore a white *entari* with silver details that made her look angelic.

"My name is Zuri," she said. "I'm the Mistress of Spies for Lord Mircea Dracul. I've personally trained his network of spies, and you will be trained in those arts much like the others." She snapped her finger, and a boy stepped inside. He was human; Yara could tell by his pretty green eyes. "I've mostly trained our kind, but Lysander is one of our human spies. He is an exemplary spy and is what you should aim for during our lessons."

Zuri stepped into Yara's room in a whirlwind of directions. Lysander sat upon her bed like he owned the place, stretching his limbs intimately atop her coverlet.

"Humans have two tools at their disposal. One, they are insignificant, and nobody cares if they are in the room, which makes it easier for them to listen in on important conversations," Zuri said, striking up a finger. "The second is that we naturally desire humans both for sustenance and to use for our pleasure. So, we are drawn to them and cannot exist without them."

"I don't think being insignificant requires any lessons," Yara said. "I am rarely looked at twice in any room I arrive in."

Lysander laughed, staring at her with a bright smile like she was a delight.

"I am quite certain, my dear, that men both human and vampir look at you when you enter a room," he said.

"This is a game of life and death," Zuri said with a grim look. "Spies are killed upon the barest suspicion. If a noble family suspects you are an implant sent from another rival family, they *will* kill you. And while I will train you as best as I can, I've lost some good spies and don't wish to lose any more."

Yara nodded in understanding. While her circumstances protected her, namely the carving on her forehead, Yara knew that survival was an important skill to learn, especially in this depraved palace. Zuri stared at her sharply. "Tell me a lie."

"Eldar is the kindest person I've ever met," Yara said.

Lysander snickered in the corner. He bit his lip when Zuri glared at him, stifling his laughter.

"Your heartbeat was a bit irregular," she said. "If you don't believe your lie, your body will react. Try to believe your lies as best as you can."

Zuri made her lie through her teeth for an hour until she could do it efficiently without her heartbeat racing. She ran her through a brief history of the vampir, the court system, and the monarchy. It was so different yet similar to the Ottoman Empire. But here it was not faith that guided them, but rather power. And a family was only as powerful as its allies. There were nine trueborn. Usually, the families closest to the Dracul family were of higher status than the others. There were some families who stayed far from court and only attended for large functions whereas there were many who stayed at court for seasons at a time before returning to their ancestral home.

"The namesake of our kind fluctuates with each language and culture. We are not aware of our origins only that the trueborn came into this world born to transition into a creature of the night," she said. "And the sired were made."

"Is a sired vampir sworn by duty to serve?" Yara asked. "Like the Jannisary. They must serve under threat of death."

"A sired vampir cannot hurt their master. It goes against their nature," she said. "They are born to serve the nine."

"There are tunnels beneath the manor," Zuri continued. "An intricate network that Lysander will show you. It is where we speak in private. Vampir have sensitive ears, and while this floor is only accessible to the Dracul family, it is best to practice caution at all times."

Yara nodded. Interested to learn of the tunnels and pathways.

"A good start for today," Zuri said. "We will practice some more tomorrow. Lysander will escort you to dinner tonight."

Yara frowned. "Why do I need an escort?"

"He will be training you on the second portion," she said. "Seducing is more than merely spreading your legs. It is the act of carrying yourself with intrigue and sensuality. At times standing in the corner is insufficient, and catching the eye of a person works to your advantage."

Yara stared at Lysander. He looked like a doll with pretty, fair hair.

He reminded her of Volkan's friend, the one with the mismatched eyes. They both had a gentle beauty like deer grazing in a meadow.

"Lysander will have a new wardrobe fitted for you," Zuri said. "We'll have garments brought from all over. You will be known for your beauty, cherished by the court, and when you steal their most treacherous secrets, they will be none the wiser."

As promised, that night a trove of chests arrived, carried by seven supple servants. The first held dresses, the second jewels, and the third all manner of adornments from gold headpieces to decorative bangles.

The servants didn't disappear once they put down her new possessions. They drifted around her, combing and untangling her hair, lathering jasmine oil over her body, and draping her in a peach-colored *entari* that shone brightly against her dark skin. Her dressers had foregone the matching *salwar*. It didn't surprise her that their strange customs appreciated immodesty. She was grateful that the *entari* fell to her ankles.

They placed a gold headpiece that tinkled anytime she moved upon her head, and a gold necklace that both fashionably and strategically protected her neck. She wouldn't let Volkan bite her again. If she couldn't tell the Undying King about him because of his unhinged and fiercely protective brother, she would do her best to protect herself. The strap of her dagger weighed heavy on her leg, and the cold graze of the metal against her thigh reassured her.

Lysander arrived promptly at eight and offered her the crook of his elbow.

"You look beautiful," Lysander said. "I see why Prince Mircea picked you."

"Is that a part of the job, being beautiful?" she asked. "Because you have that in spades."

"It's difficult being a human. You are always the weakest person in any given room. From the moment I was brought here in chains, I sought to distinguish myself," he said. "If seducing and lying will raise my station, then I will do what I must."

"Have you ever thought of escape?" she asked.

"At first, yes, but then I grew a love for this strange, dark place," he said. "This court of hedonism and indulgence, where you may be as wicked and depraved as your heart desires. I've found a comfort in the absence of God's light."

Yara could see the appeal. Women were treated as equals. They were predators like the men. Their teeth just as sharp. They danced and drank as raucously as their male counterparts.

"I see," she whispered.

"Do you long to return home?" he asked, staring at her with his pale blue eyes.

"Most desperately," she said. "I miss my family."

"There is far more pleasure to be found here," he said. "Do you not think you can grow to love this place?"

They arrived at the Grand Hall, thousands of candles illuminating the dim room. Many faces were cast in shadow, and her gaze fell on Eldar, who took languid sips from his chalice. His dark hair was drawn back in an elegant tail. Yara studied the harsh angles of his face, and when his eyes met hers, his lips lifted in a menacing smile that brought shivers to her flesh. He was cloaked in his garb of black. She rarely saw him with any flash of color on his person. Even the sole ring he wore, with the interlocked scorpions that represented his family sigil, was a bland, old iron ring. In a court filled with vibrancy and elaborate jewels, he was painfully simple.

"No," she whispered. "I hold no fondness for this place."

"Eldar Demirci is a beautiful man, but his eyes are frightening, almost divine with the knowledge they hold," Lysander whispered. "I've always felt rather unsettled in his presence."

"He is crueler than his brother," she said. She still remembered the horror of the maze. Of the cold sheathing her in its frigid arms. The shivers that wracked her body and the terror that made her weep. The hatred she felt for him seemed to grow the closer they got to his vicinity. Lysander was leading her around the room, telling her little bits of information about every person. It was hard to focus on the gossip. She could feel Eldar's eyes on her, burning her skin, following her every move.

"Give me a moment," she said. "One second!"

Yara crossed the room to Eldar, and she tapped him on the shoulder. He turned slowly, staring at her from beneath his long lashes. It was a dismissive gesture. One that made her fists curl.

"You should apologize," she said tightly. "For the other night."

Eldar stepped away from the crowd, and she took several steps back until she was pressed into one of those secret alcoves. The ones they disappeared into to feed and caress their blood slaves. This one was covered by a black filigreed sheet with gold animals painted across it, depicting a glorious menagerie of birds and wolves and serpents.

"Is that all you came to say?" he asked. "Why don't you force me? Or are you too weak for that?"

Yara drew out her dagger from between the buttons of her dress, which gave her easy access to reach her weapon. He was too fast for her to attempt to press it to his neck, so she pressed it between his legs.

"I hope you have no intention of having children," she said.

Eldar stared at her with a small tilt of his head before the unthinkable occurred. He lowered his tall frame till he was on his knees.

Strangely and almost suppliantly he looked up at her, revealing the pale column of his throat. Yara felt dazed, like she was in the middle of the forest staring into the eyes of a wolf, uncertain as to when it would pounce and knowing full well that she could not outrun it.

But it was too good to be true. Eldar hadn't bent down to beg for her forgiveness. She knew it the moment his teeth elongated, and his crimson eyes focused on her like she was not a person, but mere sustenance wrapped in a dress.

"Don't you dare," she whispered. Her dagger pointed to his eye. Eldar grabbed her wrist and squeezed until it clattered to the ground.

"Just a taste," he said. "Don't be selfish."

Before Yara could come up with a retort to that, she felt his teeth sink into the flesh of her thigh, disappearing between the gaps between her buttons. Her head fell back as she felt the pleasure flood her stomach. Her senses felt heightened, and a small growl escaped Eldar, like he was feeling the same wondrous torture she was. Her body felt limp and her head light-headed. It struck her that he was feeding longer than usual, but she was far too dazed to care.

Eldar drew back at last, his canines sliding out of her skin with a squelching sound. Blood trickled, and he didn't lick it and heal the skin like Volkan did. He let it drip down her leg and placed her dress back in place with oddly tender fingers.

"It feels good, doesn't it?" he asked. His palm grazed her cheek, the gesture almost fond. "It feels even better for me. I see why Volkan tempts the wrath of Dracul for a sip from you. Your blood carries all the joy and pleasure you seem to lack."

"You didn't heal me," she said.

"That pain is a small reminder of what awaits you if you ever betray me." He leaned down to whisper in her ear. "Never hold a blade to me."

"Or what?" she asked.

Eldar was gone, not deigning to respond to her insolence. It frustrated her how he so easily overpowered her. She looked down at her barren fingers, and anger flooded her veins. He had stolen her dagger. Her gift from Mircea and the only thing that made her feel safe these days. The urge to scream made her dizzy. It took her several minutes to collect herself and return to the room of monsters.

Eldar wiped the blood from his mouth with a handkerchief, tucking her dagger into his pocket. His head felt fuzzy, the way it always did when he drank too much, and his senses were sharp and keen. He didn't know what possessed him to drink from her so intimately, like she was his lover. Volkan always teased him for holding bloody wrists above his chalice, but Eldar had never enjoyed the intimacy of drinking directly from the source. But he *had* enjoyed feeling the soft grip of her skin beneath his fingers and the tremors anytime his claw scratched her. The way she had responded to the fluid that coated his teeth and softened for him had felt oddly satisfying.

"Does Volkan know?"

His head snapped up to see Thaddeus, whose lips were curled in a smile.

"Know what?"

"That you are just as obsessed with his woman."

"Do you not have anything better to do than speak hearsay?" Eldar asked. "Should I give you a task to keep you busy?"

"I saw you on your knees. Your face stuffed between those delicious thighs," he said. "I was tempted to join you both."

Eldar paused to glare at him. Ever since he had taken his heart, Thaddeus had been a rather unfortunate gnat on his shoulder. He followed him everywhere he went. Earlier that morning he had arrived in the bathing pools, watching him rather avidly as he lingered in the warm water. And late that night he had found him on his terrace, staring off into the Bone Garden. Thaddeus had had the gall to disturb him with a recitation of a rather unfortunate poem.

"Am I being replaced?" Volkan asked, draping an arm over them both. "I thought I was the one who sired you, Thaddeus."

"You are, my savior," Thaddeus said kissing Volkan's hairline. "No one shines as bright as you or rivals your gentle beauty."

Eldar's face scrunched up in distaste. He didn't know how Volkan could stomach the words that spewed from his mouth. It was one thing to hear his terrible poems and another for him to speak in that familiar manner. If he were Eldar's sired, he would have been strung up in the Bone Garden merely for existing or had his tongue ripped out from the filthy orifice that was his mouth.

"I am throwing a celebration a few nights from now. For you and Akila," Volkan said. "To celebrate your betrothal."

"Please don't pretend as if you are doing it for me," Eldar said. Volkan would use any excuse to throw a celebration.

"We should invite your Yara," Thaddeus said.

"Of course," Volkan said. "I've had her invitation sent to her quarters."

"Do you truly want that insufferable girl?" Eldar asked. "She's ill disciplined, haughty and foolish."

"I find her intriguing. So much anger in her eyes, it makes me wish she had true power to see just what she'd do with it," Volkan said.

"You know who else finds her intriguing?" Eldar said. "Pomona."

"I know a third person who wants her as well," Thaddeus said coyly.

Eldar glared at him before returning his gaze to Pomona. She had been watching Yara rather devotedly since that night. It must have been Volkan's interest that put her under her sights. It was clear to see she was planning something for Yara, and that jealousy had infected her.

"If that hag lays a finger on her, I'll break every bone in her body,"

Volkan growled. "The death of her unborn child will be a mercy compared to what I'll do to her."

"If she attacks her, it's a good thing for us. She'll anger Dracul. He marked the girl," Eldar said thoughtfully. Perhaps he should find a way for Pomona to strike the girl. It would suit him well if Pomona fell out of favor with the Undying King.

"Don't you dare use her as a pawn," Volkan warned. "The girl is mine."

Eldar didn't take his words to heart. Volkan had a new obsession every week. The tides of his affection were ever changing. Eldar left them both to their bickering and idle chatter. He caught the eye of Mircea, who raised his cup to him in salute. They hadn't spoken in months. The tension between them had always run high, even before Eldar had begun to hunger for power. Whatever cordial relationship they had had been fractured since Volkan's imprisonment.

Eldar crossed the space to the pillar he leaned upon. Mircea cut a frightening figure with his thick brows and heavy beard. Eldar felt oddly boyish beside him. At times he wished he had transitioned later in life, when he was more man than boy. More fierce than beautiful. He hadn't had the chance to develop muscles and while he wasn't starved, he wasn't big either, but rather tall and slim. So he was stuck in this frame for the rest of eternity.

"My favorite Demirci brother," Mircea said. "How do you fare?"

"Better than you, I suppose. Your pallor is faint. Have you not been sleeping well?"

Mircea laughed a dry, rough laugh. "Have you not heard that you're supposed to lie to a royal?"

"Well, I've never been a desperate courtier before. Would it ease you if I were?"

"I wouldn't believe it for a moment," he said.

"Do you think it will be you he picks?" Eldar asked, staring at Vlad

Dracul, the Undying King. He was a long-haired man with a sharp face, a flat nose and a mouth always sealed in grimness, with a chin that belonged to an aristocrat. He was old and more powerful than them all. Eldar wouldn't win in hand-to-hand combat with him. He needed to be stronger, more vicious, and more brutal to unseat him from his throne.

"You think it will be Radu?" Mircea asked, staring at his brother. Mircea was the wiser option. He was rational and not easily given to his temper. He could be stern should it be required. He would be who Eldar would pick if the choice was his.

"I know it will be Radu," Eldar said. Vlad had never liked Mircea. Perhaps it was because they were far too alike. Perhaps it was some private history between them both that brought forth his disdain. When you were immortal, small grudges could be held for decades, even between brothers.

"You know, we could work far better together than against each other," Mircea said, staring at him with interest. "You're clever and sly. I've always liked you, Eldar."

"What makes you think I'm working against you?" he asked.

"I'm not a fool. And I don't want to see you executed," he said. "Our families can be allies."

"I will not ally myself with anyone who supports the Maleinos," Eldar said.

"Your brother killed the daughter of a trueborn. He was lucky he wasn't executed," he said. "He's also lucky he got away with that attack against the Maleinos. Pomona is still calling for his head."

"Volkan is innocent, then and now. The feud between the Maleinos and our family has always been taut. I wouldn't be surprised if she framed him for that murder. She always wanted him, and you know it."

"Think about my offer, Eldar," Mircea said. "An alliance with my family, once I'm seated on the throne, could be beneficial to your family."

Eldar sipped his drink but didn't bother to offer him a response.

"Because, if I find out about any treachery that you're plotting against the throne, I'll make sure you and your brother are imprisoned by the Maleinos. And once that sentence is complete, I'll string you both up in the Bone Garden until you're nothing, but a husk and the Demirci name is lost to the hands of time. Is that understood?"

"Don't threaten my brother," Eldar said sharply. "It is the best way to make an enemy of me."

"Not a threat, a warning. You'd be wise to heed it."

Their conversation was cut short by the swelling sound of Yara's singing. The court was in rapture, swayed into dance by her delicate voice. Eldar stared at her beside the Undying King in her beautiful clothes. She cut a striking figure, standing on the dais, and commanding the attention of the room. He felt his fist curl in anger. He wanted to rip her away from their greedy eyes and lock her somewhere only he could access.

Eldar was surprised by his reaction, and he wondered if it was her blood making him this possessive. If it was, then he couldn't feed on her again. He couldn't afford distractions, not when he was so close to his goal.

Not when he could taste victory.

XIV

IT WAS DAWN when Aylin went to the forest, strapped to the teeth with all manner of knives. She had folded a scabbard around her chest with six different blades sheathed in the slots. When Domenico had told her gruffly to be saddled and prepared to depart at first light, she had woken up even earlier to find the best horse in the stable and ensure she was armed to the teeth. She hadn't told Ilyas she was departing to hunt for meat with Domenico. She didn't want to be the girl who hid behind him instead of fighting her own battles. If Domenico so much as looked at her incorrectly, she would slit his throat.

"I'm surprised you're not weighing down the poor beast with all that silver," Domenico said. "Do I frighten you, little boy?"

"Not as much as my existence threatens your sanity," she said. "I've infected your mind without even trying. So, you tell me, who holds the true power?"

He clenched his fists around the reins until his knuckles turned white. And without a word, he disappeared into the thicket. Aylin followed him at a safe pace. They moved in silence. The only sound was the crunch of leaves and roots beneath the hooves of their horses. It wasn't until they had come upon a clearing that Domenico hopped off the horse and began to tie the reins around a birch tree, wrapping them tight around the ivory trunk.

"We will go on foot from here on out," he said.

Aylin didn't like the thought of descending from her horse to walk alongside him, but she was better equipped for a fight while he only seemed to be prepared for hunting. He had a steel crossbow slung across his broad shoulders, which wouldn't be of much use if they engaged in close combat. He kneeled before a bush, and Aylin mimicked his gesture. She didn't know the first thing about hunting. While she didn't mind sticking a knife in any man who attacked her, the thought of bringing down an innocent creature made her stomach churn.

The deer were cloistered in a small herd. Their graceful necks bent down to the grass, they chewed leisurely, unaware of the hunters in their midst. They looked so peaceful and delicate, it seemed unnatural to disturb them.

"Here, you take the shot," Domenico whispered.

"You take it," she said. "I've never fired one of those things."

"Take the shot," he said. "Before I change my mind and start hunting *you.*"

Aylin unwillingly clasped the crossbow. It was heavy, and her arms quaked from the effort of holding it upright.

"I can't hold it," she said. "What is this made of? Salvatore's pride?"

She was not surprised he didn't laugh at that one. He grabbed her roughly, supporting her upper arm and slapping a hand on her jittery thigh, before sliding it up to rest on her ribs and fix her posture.

"Focus," he growled. "You have one shot, or we lose them all."

Aylin took a deep breath, ignoring how close he was to her and the fact that he was touching her where no man had touched before.

She released the trigger and watched the cocked string detach. It sank into the thin neck of the closest deer. A bloom of red spilled down the column of its neck and soaked the grass. The other deer scattered wildly, disappearing into the forest without a single glance backward. Domenico released her, and she was surprised when he lifted the beast onto his shoulder, as if it weighed no more than a feather. He tied the deer to the back of his horse, leaving her to drag the heavy crossbow behind her.

He mounted her horse and coiled his hand around the reins of his horse with the deer mounted atop.

"Get off my horse," she said between clenched teeth. If he thought he could steal her horse and leave her behind in unfamiliar terrain, he was sadly mistaken. She would heave this monstrosity over her shoulder and pierce him with as many arrows as it took for him to fall.

"Either we can share, or you can walk back," he said evenly. "The choice is yours."

Aylin stomped over to him, lugging the heavy crossbow. He hadn't left her with much of a choice. They would have to share a beast, which would be just as uncomfortable as when he had steadied her hand.

"Take it," she snapped.

He easily clasped the crossbow and used the straps to hang it from his back. Aylin sat in the small space before him. With the crossbow behind him, sitting in the back hadn't been an option. She felt suffocated by him, enclosed by his massive frame. While he was as big as Ilyas, he didn't bring calmness to her but rather an unease that crawled beneath her skin. Her back was as stiff as a rod. It had been a twenty-minute ride to the clearing, and the idea of being near him for that long was unthinkable.

She felt a sting on her back and realized that he had hooked a finger beneath her scabbard only to release it.

"Stop that," she said sharply. "You won't like it if I'm mad."

"Won't I?" he asked. And he did it again. Harder this time.

"Do you wish to provoke me?" Aylin asked. "Did you not learn your lesson yesterday?"

A ghost of a smile crossed her face at the thought of spitting on him again. He had deserved it.

"That reminds me," he said. "I still owe you for that."

They stopped by a small stream, and Domenico dismounted.

"Why are we stopping?" she asked.

"Because you are not the one covered in deer blood," he said. "My shirt is soiled."

He began to tie the horses to the tree and removed his shirt to rinse himself in the rushing water. Aylin began to pace, keeping an eye on him. She unraveled her scabbard from her chest letting it dangle from her fingertips. It was beginning to tire her, and she wouldn't dare sit down when Domenico was around or let her muscles slacken for a moment. He wasn't being as violent as usual, but she didn't trust him one bit. Her gaze was wary when he walked toward her. His green eyes were as unreadable as always.

"Give me your tunic," he said, running a wet hand through his short, cropped hair. He had cut it recently, and all that covered his scalp now was blond fuzz. It suited him. Though she would *never* dare tell him so.

"Never," she said. Her hackles rose.

"Give it. Before I tear it off your back," Domenico demanded.

Aylin laughed, but it sounded weak and hollow even to her ears. He couldn't take her shirt. It was one of the two garments that concealed her womanhood. He lunged for her, and Aylin scarcely had time to fight him off before his hands had clasped the fabric and roughly pulled it from her head. She always wore two tunics stacked atop each other to conceal herself, but in their struggle, he happened to peel them both.

"Stop!" she cried. But the brute didn't listen, not until he held the twisted fabric in his palm. Aylin spun around, covering her nakedness. She covered her chest with her palms and felt her limbs shake so hard she thought she would collapse. He was going to tell Salvatore. He had seen her. She knew from his widened eyes and gaping mouth that he had seen.

Everything was ruined. Ilyas wouldn't forgive her for this recklessness. For being so foolish as to go anywhere with Domenico without telling him.

Domenico came around. He stared into her eyes curiously.

"I always knew you were hiding something," he said. He pulled her tunic back over her head and roughly grabbed her hands to fill the sleeves.

"Will you tell Salvatore?" she asked, wrapping her arms around herself.

"Are you an Ottoman spy?" he asked.

Aylin gave a stark laugh. "The day the Ottoman Empire recruits woman for spies will be the day they dominate all nations."

"I cannot fathom the meaning of your words."

"No, Domenico, the Ottomans haven't utilized or yet discovered the effectiveness of woman spies."

"He is not your brother, is he?" he asked with a curl of his lips, almost as if he hated Ilyas more than her. "No brother stares so ardently at their flesh and blood."

Her cheeks warmed. "He is helping me find my sister. She has been taken by the vampir, as you call them. I've sacrificed much to be here, Domenico. As much as you hate me, everything I've done was to protect my family. Every lie I've spoken. Every sin I've gathered has been for my family. I've traveled farther than most and lost twice as much to be here."

It felt like hours passed while he merely appraised her with those unreadable green eyes.

"This isn't ideal," he said with a frown. "I was going to kick you between the legs for doing the same to me yesterday, but it won't hurt."

Aylin didn't know if she should laugh or cry at his nonchalance. The surprise had melted from his face, and he looked far more like the ruthless Domenico she had met her first day here. He grabbed her chin and yanked her close. He hooked his thick fingers in her mouth, and she felt the wet slide of his spit falling into her gaping mouth.

"That's for spitting on me yesterday. From now onwards, we will use our words to convey our anger. Despite what you may think, I do not beat woman," he said. He had his palm clasped firmly on her mouth to prevent her from spitting out *his* spit. Aylin stepped on his foot, enjoying the furrow in his brow. "Swallow or I'll ring every bell in the chapel and have you sent before the doge for crimes against the Venetian Empire. Once I release you, you will apologize for stepping on me."

With a glare that could burn, she swallowed at his behest and when he released her, she let out a meagre apology, not looking him in the eye when she spoke.

"Good girl," he said. "Or shall I say, good boy? Which do you prefer?"

Aylin didn't bother answering him. She stomped to the horse and sat upright, waiting while he undid the straps. He moved slowly, taking his precious time, no doubt to irritate her. He finally climbed up behind her, and she stiffened. It had been unbearable sitting beside him as a boy, but as a girl it felt twice as bad. She could feel the broad expanse of his chest, and she could have sworn he sat closer than before.

"You never told me if you'll tell Salvatore," she said.

"Perhaps, once I tire of you and you no longer surprise me," he said. "I suppose that means you'll have to work hard to keep my attention."

"Is there not a single ounce of human decency in your bones?" she asked.

"No."

He clicked his tongue, and the horse dug into the thicket, carrying them back home.

Ilyas was waiting at the edge of the forest, brows creased in worry. Aylin felt a breath of relief escape her at his handsome face. She swung a leg off and hopped off the moving horse, an antic that could just as swiftly break her neck as it could deliver her to his arms. Her arms reached forward to wrap around him, but he placed a palm to her stomach, holding her back.

"We have an audience," he whispered.

Aylin turned to find Domenico staring at them with a dark look in his eyes. His pale skin had reddened from the sun. It brought an angry flush to his cheeks, as if he had been stricken twice.

"Did he touch you?" he asked.

"I'm offended that you speak of me so poorly," Domenico said with a pointed grin. His white teeth looked predatory from this distance. "He has all his toes and fingers intact."

He said the word *he* in a mocking manner, and she was glad Ilyas did not pick up on it. That he was too busy eyeing her body like he would find any evidence that proved otherwise.

"He also has a bit of my fluid inside him," Domenico continued. "Isn't that right, my boy?"

His words sounded vulgar, and Ilyas trembled until she quietly clarified that he had paid her back for spitting on him.

"If you touch a hair on his head again, I will kill you," Ilyas promised.

Domenico did not rise to that bait and merely led the horses to the stables. Aylin didn't hold herself back from wrapping her arms around Ilyas's torso the moment he disappeared. He folded himself in half to wrap her in the entirety of his body. She felt hollow knowing that Domenico knew her deepest secret. She didn't know how she would sleep tonight now that he had discovered her identity.

"I lost my mind when I didn't find you in bed," he said. "I almost attacked Salvatore when he told me where you'd gone."

"I'm fine," she said. "It wasn't a pleasant experience, and I never wish to go hunting again, but I survived."

And she would continue to survive, so long as she got rid of Domenico. It was not an appealing thought, but Aylin knew what she had to do.

She would have to ensure that Domenico didn't live long enough to share her secret. To rob him of the breath in his chest before he used it to bring her down.

She would have to kill Domenico Zancherelli.

XV

THERE WAS AN invitation on her pillow in the stark handwriting of Volkan, welcoming her to the betrothal celebration between Eldar Demirci and Akila Ramose. Her heart thudded and her finger grew slippery with sweat. She didn't know why this news shocked her. Eldar's eyes were so cold, she could not imagine him looking upon his wife with any sort of affection. It felt unnatural for him to take a bride.

Yara was curious to see him interact with his betrothed, so curious she knew she would accept this invitation.

Yara began to slip off her headdress when she felt a hand grip her throat. It wasn't light and deadly like Eldar's grip. It was a painful, crushing hold that choked the breath out of her lungs. It squeezed until the air was robbed from her chest and her vision darkened. Till there was nothing but a dull, black void.

Yara awoke to a terrible pounding in her head. A weight hung from her wrists, and she realized she was shackled to the wall. Fear twisted

in her gut and memories flooded her mind of when she had first arrived, when she had been tied to Volkan's bed. Except it wasn't Volkan
who stared upon her with his gleeful eyes this time, but the dreadful
figures of Pomona and Titus.

"What do you want?" she asked hoarsely. "I am under the protection of the House of Dracul, have you forgotten?"

"No, my dear," Pomona said, crouching down before her. "It's hard
to forget when you remind us so often."

Her nail scraped down her cheek, drifting lazily down her skin.

"Your death will solve two of my problems," she said.

Yara stiffened. "You can't kill me. The Undying King will make a
cruel example of you and that fool." She jutted her chin at Titus, who
sneered at her.

"Nobody will know it is us. Volkan has not made his obsession
with you a secret," she said. "He will fall for this. Titus, do you, have
it?"

Titus had a kaftan, which he suspiciously draped over Yara.

"Volkan's scent will cover your dead body. It isn't the first time a
girl who snagged his attention died horribly," she whispered. "It
seems to be a habit of his."

"Why do you hate him so much?" Yara whispered. It seemed Pomona's entire life revolved around the pale-haired man. "Did you kill
her? The first girl? The one that led to his imprisonment?"

Elisabeta had told her one lazy afternoon of the unfortunate
events that led to Volkan's imprisonment. He had barely transitioned
when it was said that he had killed a trueborn girl. It seemed highly
unlikely that Eldar wouldn't have covered up the murder, if Volkan
had killed someone. It stood to reason that he had been wrongfully
imprisoned for three long years. And she suspected the culprits of
that crime now stood before her.

It had begun with Volkan, and now it seemed destined to end

with him. First, he had bought her, and now his enemies would punish her to get to him.

Pomona came close enough that Yara could smell her lily-scented oil. And when she whispered in her ear, the words were a fervent caress. "I don't hate him, you silly girl. I love him. Everything I have done has been for him."

It almost sounded like she believed herself.

"He's arrived," Titus said.

"I want him to watch you die. To know that mortal affection is doomed to fade," she said. "Only an immortal can give him the love he craves."

Volkan sped into the room. Before he could reach her, his arms were snagged on either side by two hidden guards who slipped out of the shadows, converging on him. They quickly restrained him while he twisted and snarled, his teeth snapping wildly. When he looked at her, Yara felt a trickle of terror slip down her spine at the animalistic look in his eyes.

Pomona clicked her tongue. "So predictable, my precious. Running into danger without a care in the world. You know Eldar would have thought it through. So thorough that one. Never leaves a stone unturned."

"I'll tear you apart," he growled. His voice dropped several octaves till his words were a mere rumble in his chest.

"No, you will not," she said.

Pomona ran her claw down his throat. It slid slowly to his chest. She talked to him with open familiarity, like she was an old lover. Volkan flinched, turning his face away, squirming against her touch.

"Do you wish to say goodbye to her?" Pomona asked.

Titus gripped her by the root of her hair, raising Yara to her feet. The shackles clacked as she was forcefully drawn forth till she stood before Volkan. Her eyes were wide with fear, but it wasn't him who terrified her for once.

They had found themselves in far worse company.

"Kiss him goodbye," Pomona commanded.

"I don't..." Yara shook her head. She had never kissed anyone before, and it felt wrong for it to be now. For it to be someone other than her husband. For it to be *him*.

Her eyes stung at the thought that she would die at the hands of these monsters, but only after they thoroughly destroyed her soul.

"Don't look so upset," Volkan said. "There are worse things than my tongue in your mouth."

"Are there?" she snapped. "I cannot think of a single one."

He had the audacity to laugh. Pomona didn't like that, and when she nodded, Titus pushed her head forward till her forehead was against Volkan's chest. She felt the cold gust of his breath graze her hair.

"Close your eyes," he said. "I feel as though I am being blinded by the sun."

"Is my glare too much for you?" she demanded. "Or do you speak of my beauty?"

A hard nudge of her head, and Yara resigned herself to her fate. To kiss her tormentor. She tilted her chin and he lowered himself to accommodate her. His lips were unbearably soft, and she felt her stomach clench tight in surprise. Their hands were restrained, but that only made the kiss more wild, more consuming. His tongue slipped past her lips, licking her mouth with abandon. Yara was ashamed by her body's reaction to him. By the way she was leaning on him, desperate to feel his hands on her.

Titus drew her back forcefully, but before he did Yara acted impulsively. Her mouth was near the man who gripped Volkan's shoulder, and she bit him hard, blood spouting into her mouth. He howled in pain, and the slip of his hand was enough for Volkan to escape. He twisted and dug his claws into the neck of one of the guards and his fist into the chest of the other. With a hard tug, he tore out one's throat and the other's heart.

"Volkan! Behind you!" Yara yelled. Titus had released her to surprise Volkan from behind, but Volkan spun around to meet him. Pomona turned her furious eyes on Yara and backhanded her hard enough to bring tears to her eyes. She unshackled her and gripped her neck, dragging her to a corner to watch the scene before them unfold.

"You stupid, foolish girl," Pomona hissed. "Once Titus has put him down, I will cut out your throat."

Volkan and Titus moved in a blur. While Titus outweighed him in muscle, Volkan was taller and faster. At times she would swear he disappeared mid-attack. Her heart tightened in fear. If Volkan lost, then all hope was gone. Titus had pinned Volkan to the ground, his meaty fist gripping his throat. Volkan scratched his face, and when his claws lengthened, gouging out Titus's eyes, Yara felt bile crawl up her throat. His voice was raw as he screamed in pain, releasing Volkan and crawling away. Blood and fluid trickled from his shattered eyes, and Volkan gripped him by the hair, revealing his throat. He dug his nails in and, with a hard yank, severed his head.

But Volkan wasn't done; he kicked the table and tore free the broken leg from the rubble, raising it above Titus' chest.

"Don't you dare!" Pomona screeched. "This will be considered an act of war."

Volkan stared at her. With his black eyes and sharpened teeth, he looked monstrous.

"Then let us go to war," Volkan said.

He brought down the stick into Titus's chest, impaling him. Yara watched in horror as Titus' body and severed head stilled.

Pomona's hand slackened, and Yara jabbed her elbow into her stomach and ran. Volkan met her halfway, drawing her behind his back just as Pomona collided with him.

"You've ruined everything, for a mortal girl," Pomona snarled. "Your life is forfeit."

"If you speak a word of this to anyone, you will have to explain why you were going to kill a girl marked by the Undying King," he said.

"Nobody will believe that," she said.

"I'll tell them," Yara said. "I will tell them how you sought to frame him. How you did it with the ease of someone who had done so before."

Volkan stiffened. "Is that true?"

Pomona stared past him at the decayed corpse of Titus with something that looked suspiciously like sadness.

"This is the second person you've taken from me," she whispered.

"I won't stop until you're dead," Volkan said. "That is a promise."

He draped his arms around Yara's waist and led her out of the room. She leaned against him, seeking the comfort he provided. It had been so long since someone had held her.

"This is all your fault," she said.

"If you forgot, I was ambushed too," he said.

"I could have died."

"I wouldn't have let that happen."

"Why?" she asked, her eyes narrowed. "You hate me."

"No, *you* hate *me*," Volkan said.

"You don't give me a reason to like you," she said. "You've been despicable since I arrived here."

"I've been charming," Volkan said.

Yara realized that they weren't going in the direction of her bedroom. In fact, they were heading in the opposite direction.

"You'll be safer with me tonight," he said as if he'd read her thoughts. "Pomona will not let our actions go unavenged."

Yara was too tired to argue. She nodded, and he seemed pleased by her acceptance. He led her past a lavish sitting room and into the dark bedroom she had been in last time, with the great ebony bed frame and the curtains of heavy damask that she knew concealed bricked-up windows. There was a balcony, but those were only opened at night and barred by lock and key during the day. The silk cords hanging from the post made her stiffen as she recalled her brief stay in his lair.

"I won't use them," he said.

"You're hurt," Yara said, pressing her fingers to the blood on his neck.

"It's healed," he said. "I need to bathe the blood off."

Yara sat on the bed. She still felt dazed by all that had occurred tonight. She should have been used to it by now. The unpredictability of these creatures who feared no God or higher being shouldn't have shocked her. Yara began to wind her hair into a braid to soothe her shaking fingers. Volkan leaned against the wall while his eyes tracked her every move.

"How did you survive it?" she asked in a quiet whisper. "Being imprisoned by her."

Yara couldn't begin to imagine what he'd suffered. Pomona and Titus were a cruel pair. And her heart ached with sympathy for Volkan.

His eyes were haunted when he spoke. "You learn to drag your mind away from your body. You start to make a corner of your mind that remains untouched. And you exist there until it ends."

"Nobody deserves that," she said.

His lips lifted in a faint smile. "Not even me?"

"Not even you."

Volkan left the wall and pulled some garments from his armoire. He brought out a long tunic and handed it to her, folded and crisp.

"Thank you," she said. He turned to leave, and she hesitated, wondering if Titus had hit her head too hard, because the words escaped her before she could take them back. "Are you hungry?"

Volkan stood before her before she could blink.

"Are you offering, my love?" he breathed. His fingers stroked her neck gently.

Yara nodded and tilted her head. Volkan leaned down and pressed a kiss to her neck.

"Thank you, but you need to conserve your energy," he said. "They've done a number on you, and I suspect this is only the beginning."

Volkan disappeared before she could respond. Her neck tilted and skin tingled from his kiss.

Yara awoke to darkness, and she tried to recall the last time she had seen the sun. It felt like ages ago when she walked through the palace gardens, smiling under the warmth of the sun. Her feet sunk into the earth like vines, fingertips drifting along the tulips. How she craved the light. It must have been November now. Which meant she had been trapped here for two full months.

"Good morning, my dark dove."

Yara stared at the creaking wooden chair in the corner. She could just about make out his frosty hair and bright red eyes.

"Have you been here long?" she asked, stretching her stiff limbs beneath the sheets.

"All day, I suppose."

"Were you watching me sleep?" she asked.

A shiver ran down her back to think of the intimacy of it.

"I had to make sure you were safe," he said. "I protect what's mine."

He was staring at her like she was a possession. It angered her, and she parted her lips to remind him she belonged to no one but herself until she recalled her promise to Mircea. She would have to get close to him in the hopes that he would reveal his brother's treachery.

Her heart raced at the thought of tricking him. And when she looked at him, she knew he heard the lurch of her heart. He stood upright, his height surpassing any man she had met before him. He sat by her, and Yara felt the slim grip of his fingers begin to slowly unwind her braid. Yara felt her eyes slide shut, comforted by his touch.

"I forget that you humans respond far better to tenderness than cruelty," he said. "It makes sense that weak creatures are driven to weakness."

"I like it best when you don't speak," Yara said.

Volkan laughed, that lovely musical sound that made her ache to hear him sing. His voice was both soft and sharp, like the strings of a lute. She imagined he would sing as splendidly as her. That they would make a beautiful duet.

"Shall I be kind to you, little Yara?" he asked. "Will that make me less monstrous?"

"I don't think you know how to be kind," she said. "It is in your nature to be wild and cruel. You can no sooner change the print of a leopard than you can teach your kind to be anything less than what they are."

"And here I thought you were an optimist," he said. He found a pearl-encrusted comb and drifted it through her hair with a care and precision she did not expect from him.

"You cannot hold onto hope for long," she whispered. "It eventually fades."

Yara wondered then if she would ever return to Constantinople. If she would ever be surrounded by her family again, crowded around a low table and eating from a platter fit for kings. A part of her wondered if they had moved on. Her father would have to call off the search soon. While the sultan was generous, he would not let his resources be depleted, and men scouring the street day and night was not worth the trouble. She wondered if Aylin sat by the window awaiting her return, and if there would come a day when she turned away from the window to resume her life.

"You're pretty when you are sad," Volkan said.

Sometimes it felt as though Volkan saw her as a doll. A glass-eyed figurine who could be handled and contorted to his pleasure. A thing for him to lock in a cabinet of curiosities, to be admired and untouched—for him alone.

When her hair was done, Volkan left to give her time to prepare for the night. Once she had bathed and dressed, Yara stepped out the door to find Eldar glaring at Volkan.

"YOU KILLED TITUS!"

"Calm down, brother," Volkan said. "It's too early to be shouting. You'll frighten our guest."

He spun to face her. His lips curled in disgust at the sight of her.

"Of course, *she's* involved," he growled. "She's been a curse upon our lives from the moment she arrived."

"Come, Yara." Volkan offered her his hand. "Let us find something more pleasant to do than to be lectured by this surly, ill-tempered beast."

"You will both sit down and tell me everything that occurred." Eldar began to pace the room. His shoes dug grooves into the thick carpet. Yara sighed and sat down on the cushioned seats and tasseled pillows. Before her was a silver kettle, and she poured herself some *kahve*. Volkan poured a film of white sugar and stirred her cup, and she whispered her thanks for him alone.

Eldar stared at them like they were foreign beasts.

"You've bonded over the grand mess you've made," he snapped. "How touching."

"They kidnapped me with the intention of killing me. Volkan saved me and killed Titus. It was a well-deserved death," she said.

"Pomona won't tell anyone because I warned her that I'd tell Mircea she plotted to kill me. She won't say a word."

"Or she could kill you and have Volkan imprisoned or executed for killing a member of her family and pin your death on him to top it off," Eldar said. "Who is going to run to Mircea with the truth then?"

"She won't kill me," Yara said. Pomona had been broken when they left her. It would take her time to gain the energy to plot against them once more. That type of grief consumed people.

"You will stay with us until the threat has passed," Eldar said. "Your death is not ideal. It will endanger Volkan."

"How sweet of you to care for my well-being," Yara said dryly.

Volkan snorted, staring at them both with amusement in his eye.

Eldar stared at her long and hard. "Anything to share? About Prince Mircea? Did he share any suspicions?"

If he thought she was still his spy, he was a fool. Eldar had pushed her away with his threats and vileness. Not once had he treated her with a modicum of grace and kindness, unlike Mircea, who had always spoken to her with nothing short of respect. He had won her loyalty in a way that Eldar never would. When she discovered whatever plot, he was hatching against the Draculs, he would pay for his sins. Until nothing remained but bone and ashes.

"Nothing," she replied.

"Are you certain?" Eldar stared at her with his shrewd eyes. "He seemed rather suspicious of me last night, as if someone had planted a seed in his mind."

"It wasn't me," she said.

"I never said it was," he whispered. He stared at her for what felt like ages. Yara didn't turn from his gaze; she absorbed it the way one would a winter's chill should they have lost their coat. She let it sink into her skin and burn her from the inside out. At last, he turned away from her and stormed out the door. Her shoulders sunk in relief, and she turned to face Volkan, who stared at her with a crease between his brows.

"Don't play with Eldar," he said. "He can be a sour loser."

This wasn't a child's game. The stakes were infinitely higher. If she was successful with her plans, she could see herself with both her freedom and the death of Eldar. Her wicked enemy. Her tyrant.

She would see him come undone.

It was only a matter of time.

XVI

"POMONA HAS REQUESTED an audience with me," Mircea said while they sparred that night. He had taken her to the roof of the castle, where they were surrounded by the charcoal banisters. Above the embellished colonnades were grotesque animals perched on hind legs with open mouths and piercing teeth, as if they sought to devour her whole.

Yara would be the first to admit that she was a terrible swordswomen. Her arms were weak and quaked with each blow, and her footing was, as Mircea described it, "as elegant as a newborn fawn." Yet he was patient with her, and gentle. Yesterday she had cried when he blotted her skinned knee with a handkerchief and rinsed it with water and salt.

"Why do you cry, child?" he asked, confused. "I will not drink your blood. My teeth lengthen, but it is a most natural response."

Yara sniffed. "You remind me of my baba."

"Is that not a good thing?" he asked.

"It can be both good and sad," she said. "You don't think me silly, do you?"

"Never," he said.

She wondered if Pomona had come to confess about Volkan killing Titus. For some reason, Yara was desperate to protect the white-haired vampire. She didn't know when her opinion of him had changed. It must have been when Pomona had touched him so intimately and a flicker of fear had run across his inhuman eyes. He had been hurt before, and she could understand the need for a broken creature to lash out. To hurt before it was hurt.

"Did Pomona say what she wants?" Yara asked cautiously.

"Only that she requires your presence," he said.

"Anyone else?"

"No," he said.

Yara was distracted for the remainder of their session, and Mircea ended it earlier than usual.

"We will dine two hours from now in my quarters," he said.

The moment Mircea ended their sparring lesson, Yara returned immediately to the brothers' quarters. Volkan would be interested in hearing of this, and they could discuss how best to prepare for this ambush. If Pomona wished to sit down, it could not be anything good.

She bumped into Eldar and fell to the floor in an unceremonious heap. Yara was not surprised that he didn't ask about her well-being, but to not even offer his hand to help her rise was positively rude of him.

"This is not a schoolyard. Running around like a child," he scoffed. "You would do well to remember that."

"Where's Volkan?" she asked.

"Anything you wish to convey to him you can tell me," Eldar said, folding his arms across his chest. His tall frame blocked her entrance to their quarters. Yara attempted to slide by him, but he caught her by the waist and held her firmly in place. "Spit it out or I'll pry it from your mouth with my tongue."

"How?" she whispered.

He raised a brow. "Do you wish to find out?"

"No," she said. But she had no interest in telling him anything. He thought he was their master. Hers and Volkan's. As if they owed him something. But he was nothing more than a lonely, monstrous man who fed himself on the misery of others. One who thought himself superior to all and no doubt considered himself the most intelligent man in the room.

"I came to tell Volkan how much I hate you," she snapped. "How I wish I could stab you a hundred times, until you resemble a mangled corpse and not even your brother recognizes you. How I cannot believe that you were both conceived in the same womb. How only the devil could have birthed a monster such as—"

Eldar clasped a palm to her mouth. She bit him hard, but his hold didn't relent. If anything, his fingers seemed to dig into her cheek in warning.

"It's sad that you think your passionate speeches anger me. It delights me to know that I live inside you like rot, festering until I am all that surrounds you," Eldar whispered. "Love wanes and fades, but hate is consistent. It requires only the barest attention for it to be stoked into a great flame. I am pleased that you hate me, Yara. It means that I will always exist inside you."

He released her with a light shove, and before she could blink, he was gone.

How she hated when he did that.

It ensured that he always had the last word.

"Are you certain?" Volkan asked as he painted kohl on her lids. He had a steady hand, and she appreciated his need to dote on her. It made her feel strangely cared for.

"Yes," she said. "Do you think she will tell him about the fate of Titus?"

"Perhaps," he said almost absently.

He looked distressed. While he was exceptional at hiding his truth behind barbed words and mockery, Yara could sense that he was not well. She placed her hand on his arm, and he stared at her with a grim smile.

"If she tells him, I will have to stand trial once more," he said. "I can't...I can't be imprisoned again. I won't survive it."

There was a panic that flickered in his eyes that made her ache to comfort him. She let her hand drift up and down his forearm until the frantic energy inside him was silenced. She could tell from his eyes that he would never let himself be taken alive. He would kill himself before he let himself be subject to Pomona's cruel punishment again.

"I won't let her win," Yara said. "I will defend you with my last breath."

Volkan looked away from her. As if he were mulling over his words.

"I regret how wretched I was to you when you first arrived. How I treated you so abominably when I've experienced the same pain of being held captive. How I delighted in your fear and grew drunk on your pain. I would take it back if I could."

"I think I understand you a bit better now," she said.

He crouched down till they were at eye level. "Will you forgive me, my love?"

"I don't know," she said honestly.

"That is good enough," he said. "You look beautiful. I think you are good to face Pomona."

"Thank you," she said. "You are far better at applying cosmetics than I am."

"There is a reason I look prettier than Eldar. He doesn't spend a single second on perfecting his image," he said. "Sometimes I wonder if anyone can still tell that we are twinned."

Yara laughed. "I'm sure if they try hard, they can tell."

Yara had never seen two people look so alike, despite Volkan's vanity. She thanked God that they had different-colored hair, or she feared she would never be able to tell them apart.

Mircea's escort arrived at half past nine. Yara followed him, her stomach filled with needles. The last dinner she'd shared with Pomona had not ended well. In fact, it had forced Pomona to plot her death.

Mircea sat at the head of the table in his midnight-blue kaftan.

"Come sit by me, dear," he said. Yara sat to his right, pleased to be offered a seat by him.

Pomona arrived shortly after, accompanied by a man with bright red hair and a short figure. He was handsome with his hair groomed back and his shrewd green eyes racking her figure as if he were appraising her. She shifted on her chair, uncomfortable with the length of time for which he studied her. It went beyond the parameters of curiosity and felt rather invasive.

"Mircea, my favorite prince," Pomona said, bending down to place two lingering kisses on his cheek. "And Yara, a delight." Yara flinched when she pressed her cold lips to her cheek. Mircea raised a brow at her reaction, but she subtly shook her head. A sign that she would tell him after—once Pomona revealed her schemes and revealed her true character.

"You remember my cousin, Augustus," she said.

"I believe we've met briefly," he said, shaking Mircea's hand.

Yara could feel her nerves heighten the longer dinner progressed in polite chatter. They spoke of the weather and the well-cooked beef that decorated their plates. Yara learned that while food and drink did not sustain them, they still made a habit of eating. Even though Mircea had confessed that all things tasted blandly the same.

"You must be wondering why I asked for an invitation to dinner," Pomona said. "And while it's been lovely catching up, I've come here on family business."

"You've piqued my curiosity," Mircea said.

"As you know, our families have been allies for a long time, and I have a proposal to further strengthen our ties," she said. "As I see it, while the Undying King has granted Yara protection, once his mark fades there is no guarantee that he will mark her again."

"Yara is a blood slave no more," Mircea said. "She is free to choose the path of her life once she is not beholden to the king. To return to her home if she wills it."

Yara felt her heart swell at his words. That he would keep his promise to see her returned home meant the world to her.

"I think the Undying King will agree with me when I say it is time she starts to think of her future," Pomona said. "My cousin Augustus wishes to settle down and is not opposed to a mortal wife."

Yara's head snapped to Mircea to see if he found the idea as ludicrous as she did. For one, she hardly knew this, Augustus. Second, she didn't trust anybody recommended by Pomona.

"Why would you have any interest in a human girl?" Mircea asked. "Why wed a girl whose life will end in the blink of an eye?"

"She's made some powerful allies during her brief time here," Pomona said. "She seems to have the Demirci boys in the palm of her hand, and you are rather fond of her, as is the Undying King. She would make a wonderful addition to our family."

"Yara and Augustus, would you mind retiring in the sitting room?" he said. "It seems we have much to discuss."

Yara didn't like being sent away from a conversation about her. While Mircea reminded her of her father, he wasn't *truly* her father, and she didn't trust him to have her best interest at heart.

Augustus sealed the double doors shut.

"I will not marry you," Yara said. "I will not marry for anything less than love."

There was the one thing her father had stood by for his daughters, which was that when the proposals came in, he would take their opinions into consideration. He used to say the greatest curse was being trapped with someone who didn't brighten your life but dimmed it.

"What a childish notion," Augustus said. He spoke slowly, as if he were crafting each word in his mind to prove most effective. "Do you think that I could ever love the woman who has hurt my cousin so deeply?"

"Pomona deserves all of it," she said sharply. "She hurt me, and she hurt my friend."

Strange, that she defended Volkan, when a few weeks ago she would have been the one spewing insults against his name.

"And now it is our time to hurt you," Augustus said. "You will be living with us in our family home once we are wed. Far from the eye of your prince and your twins."

"Do you think you frighten me?" Yara asked. "Do you not think I have seen worse horrors than a man who promises to entrap me?"

She had been tormented by Eldar Demirci since she arrived that it had iced her heart. It no longer raced at the threats she received, but rather accepted them with no care at all.

Augustus gripped her wrist. His hand was so tight she could feel the bones beneath her skin grind. A small whimper escaped her, and she tried to pry him off, but his hard skin didn't tear beneath her clipped nails.

"Little girls can be broken," he said in that even tone of his. It was disturbing how his tone did not rise in anger or his eyes twist in cruelty. He could have been caressing her for the lack of emotion that crossed his face. "You cannot imagine the ways to break one's mind and spirit and body. Pomona would let me play with Volkan some days when she was in a good mood. It isn't difficult to break someone."

"Let go of me," she whispered.

"Everyone in our family will get their turn with you. You will spend the rest of your short life in utter agony," he promised. The door opened, and his hand dropped abruptly. A smile raised his lips as he turned to Mircea. "Thank you for being an excellent host. Yara is a charming angel, and I cannot wait to get to know her better."

"Nothing is finalized," Mircea said. "Of course, as we are subjects of the Court of the Undead, only Dracul can make the final decision."

"Pomona intends to ask for his blessings," Augustus said. He looked at her when he spoke. "I'm confident he will agree to our request."

Augustus leaned forward to kiss her cheek. She tried to step away from him, but he grabbed her arm in the same spot he had painfully gripped before. She flinched as his cold lips grazed her cheek.

Pomona was smiling when he released her. The blunt tips of her teeth elongated. Vampir could retract them to appear distinctly human but, in this moment, she wanted Yara to know that she was nothing short of a monster.

A breath of relief escaped her when they left.

"I will slit my throat before I wed him," Yara promised. "I will *never* join their twisted family."

Mircea trailed a wary hand through his dark hair. "That decision is not up to you nor I, but to the Undying King. Pomona was his lover a very long time ago, and he rarely refuses her. You are merely a pawn in this game. It is clear she wishes to strike out at Volkan with this action."

"You promised that I'd be free if I did your bidding. I've done all you asked of me," she said. "Eldar is planning some vengeful scheme against your family. I can see it in his eyes, and Volkan trusts me more with each day that passes."

Mircea sighed. "We would be fools to think the choice is up to us. Pomona came here to warn me to keep the peace between us. Vlad will step down one day when he is tired of the burden of the throne. Perhaps he will walk off into the sun to return to oblivion, or he will find other amusements. Someday, it will be between Radu and I to fight for power. Pomona came to appease me because she knows better than to make an enemy of me."

"Not enough to stop her from going to Dracul. Not enough to put this foolish scheme to bed," Yara snapped. "What good is her fear if it does not stop her? What good are promises if they are bound to be broken?"

"You are upset at me, child," he said. "But I wish for nothing but your happiness. You must believe that."

"I believe that I have nobody who loves me. Only people who care if I am of use to them," she said. A hard lump struck her throat, but she refused to cry before him.

"You must not learn to look for friends in monsters, Yara," he said softly. "You will only get bitten in return."

Mircea turned away from her, the flutter of his kaftan swinging ominously behind him. He claimed to care for her, but he would never fight for her. He found her amusing, like a trinket, but once the shine had faded, he would discard her.

———

Volkan was lounging in the sitting room when Yara arrived at their quarters. She was glad he insisted she take the bedroom there. She didn't want to be alone. He had a chalice in his slim fingers, which he placed down when she arrived. His lips were stained, and she knew it was blood that filled his cup. It didn't disturb her as much as it would have a few months ago. He stood up and silently followed her to her bedroom, clicking the door shut behind him.

"Are you—"

Yara wrapped her arms around his waist. He stilled for a second before he wrapped his arms around her, lifting her up so she could properly reach his shoulders. Her hand lightly drifted along his long bone-white hair. It fell to his back like Eldar's and was as soft as silk.

"I take it that dinner was lovely," he said.

Yara choked on a laugh. "You could say that."

"Whose neck should I twist?" he asked.

"Pomona and Augustus. But more so Augustus," she said. Her forearm ached from where he'd held her.

Volkan released her to look in her eyes. His pale brows were furrowed in confusion. "Why was Augustus there?"

"Pomona has decided that it works in her favor for me to wed her cruel cousin and live in their family house, where I was promised a life of misery and torment," she said bitterly. "Mircea says the decision is in Dracul's hand, and there is nothing he can do if he accepts their proposal."

"I knew she would strike back at us," Volkan said. "She was bound to retaliate for the attack and death of Titus. I didn't expect it to be so soon."

"What will we do?" she said. But then she shook her head, remembering Mircea's words. His reminder that she was truly alone. "What will I do?"

"You are not alone, my love," he whispered, gently stroking her cheek. "You must believe it. You protected me, and I'll protect you."

"Do you promise?" she asked. If Pomona was successful in her schemes, then Yara's life as she knew it would be over. She would be among true monsters that would put Dracul's court to shame. That would put *Eldar* to shame.

"I do," he said.

He spoke so confidently it was easy to believe him, and to seek comfort in his words. To pretend that there was someone in this place who cared if she lived and breathed.

"Thank you, Volkan," she said.

Eldar heard the grating sound of his voice before he saw him. Thaddeus was the first to enter his bedroom, followed closely by Volkan. It was the sight of his brother that made his mouth clamp shut before he barked at Thaddeus to leave him in peace.

"Who is that handsome fellow that I see?" Volkan asked. His gaze rose from Eldar's head to look at the mirror above him. "Oh, it is only me."

Thaddeus laughed in delight while Eldar sighed.

"Hello, brother," he said, folding the letters he had been penning and placing them in his drawer.

Volkan kicked off his boots and sprawled himself on his bed, and Thaddeus did the same, resting his head on Volkan's thigh.

"Is there a purpose behind this visit?" Eldar asked. Volkan and Thaddeus exchanged a look. He hated when they did that. When they spoke with their eyes. If a master and his sired built a strong enough bond, they could converse with their minds and not their tongues. Eldar had never shared such a bond with any mortal he had welcomed into the night. For a long time, he didn't believe it possible, until Thaddeus had come to him when Volkan had been imprisoned and claimed to hear his voice.

"Liar," Eldar had spat the day he had told him, convinced that Thaddeus sought to trick him. Thaddeus had been inconsolable when

Volkan had been imprisoned. He would drown his sorrows in wine. So, it was easy to believe he'd hallucinated his voice in his mind. That his addled brain had conjured Volkan from smoke and desperation.

Eldar's hand had curled around his windpipe.

"He speaks to me, I swear it," Thaddeus said, flinching from the weight of his grasp. "He told me to send you a message."

Eldar had never felt that type of rage fill his veins. For a moment he wondered if Thaddeus's mind had fractured in Volkan's absence. All he did was whimper and wail and drink. But he hadn't lied. The words he conveyed from Volkan had been a language they had crafted as children. One that did not exist in anybody's mind but their own.

And Volkan had told him he missed him.

In the present day, they both continued to speak without a single word spoken aloud to no doubt, infuriate him. Thaddeus nodded at some unspoken command, and Volkan merely smiled insufferably.

"Is there a purpose behind this visit?" Eldar asked between clenched teeth. "Or will I merely watch you both stare into each other's eyes?"

Volkan's smile dropped. "Well, we've come to discuss a serious matter. You mentioned the other day that you wish to be kept appraised of all matters."

"If you've come to ask for my permission to wed, you have my blessings," Eldar said. "You both are well suited."

Thaddeus smiled. "That almost sounded like a joke."

"We did not think you capable of such a thing," Volkan said with wide eyes.

Eldar stood up to stretch his legs. Their presence was beginning to tire him. He could handle them, perhaps, one at a time—Thaddeus with threats and Volkan by merely staring at him in silence. But when they arrived together, it was almost as if he were facing off against the same person in different cloth.

"It is about Yara," Volkan said.

Eldar's foot froze mid-step before he resumed his walk. He hated how the mention of her name visibly affected him.

"What of her?" he asked.

"Pomona has made her move," Volkan replied. "She intends to seek Dracul's permission to wed her to Augustus."

"And?" Eldar asked.

"What do you mean, 'and'?" Volkan asked. "They are luring her into their 'family' to punish her, or rather punish me by punishing her. This is for what I did to Titus and to that devil child in her womb. She is going to take Yara away from me, away from us."

"First of all, Yara does not belong to *us*," Eldar said sharply. "She is neither sired by us nor is she, our blood. Any fate that befalls her is of her own doing."

Eldar felt his teeth sharpen and his claws lengthen. He was angry that she hadn't come to him. He was angry that she trusted Volkan when he had made her *his* spy. Her loyalty belonged to him, first and foremost. Her inability to do her job due to an outside threat should have graced his ears first.

"I told you he wouldn't help us," Thaddeus said. "He cares for no one but himself."

"You won't help us?" Volkan asked.

Eldar turned his back to them. "If she wants my help, she will beg for it."

"Are you that cruel?" Volkan asked. He could hear the disgust in his voice. "You would make a frightened girl beg you to protect her from *our* enemies. She was friends with Pomona before we involved her in our lives. She was safe before she met us."

Eldar laughed—a dry, mocking sound. How his tone had changed. The itch to consume her, to break her had faded from Volkan's eyes, morphing into a tenderness that disgusted him.

"I am nobody's savior," Eldar said. "Certainly not the savior of prideful girls. She will come to me with tears in her eyes and her heart in her throat before I decide to help her."

Eldar left them both behind. He wasn't surprised to find her sitting just outside his door. Ever since he had ordered her to stay with them for Volkan's protection, Eldar had been confined to his bedroom. Yara had infected every inch of their space with her scent of jasmine and the heady flavor of her blood.

He could feel the familiar ache in his teeth at the scent of her blood. He hadn't fed since yesterday, and he was tempted to sink his teeth into her.

"Why do you hate me so much?" she asked. She sat at the dinner table, neatly peeling the stem of a flower. Her fingers were tight on the knife beside her, as if she debated sinking it into him. That was another thing he despised about her, how she filled every available surface with flowers and turned everything into a holder for the loathsome plants. The fragrance, while subtle to a mortal, burned his nostrils every morning. Volkan seemed to think it was a nice touch.

From her bitter question, Eldar realized that Volkan and Thaddeus hadn't shut the door properly and she had heard every word he had said. That was good. He hated repeating himself. Her brown eyes peered closely at him, as if she would understand him better the longer, she stared at him.

"Give me your wrist," he said. He was so blood starved; he could barely think properly. "And I will tell you."

She shook her head. "No."

Volkan and Thaddeus stepped out.

"Good afternoon, my love," Volkan asked. "Did you sleep well?"

"As well as someone can sleep knowing they are set to wed a monster," she said in a scathing tone, as if it were Eldar's fault that her fortunes had turned out so poorly.

"Look at it this way: you could have been forced to marry Eldar," Thaddeus said with a sly smile.

Yara shuddered. "That would be infinitely worse."

"Don't tempt me to rip up my betrothal papers and make you eat your words," Eldar warned. "I wouldn't mind tormenting you for the next forty years of your life and watching as the light fades from your eyes. I almost envy Augustus the pleasure of ruining you."

He watched her eyes flare beautifully with anger. She was such an expressive creature; he found it fascinating watching her emotions all unravel on her face. Her chest rose and fell rapidly, and a dark flush stained her cheeks. He may not have had her loyalty or trust or even her adoration, but he had this. Her anger would always belong to him.

But then it faded as quickly as it arrived, and her voice was serene when she spoke next.

"Come feed from me," she said, tilting her neck in offering. The pulse that beat beneath her skin and the rush of blood flowing so preciously through her veins had him licking his lips. He took a step forward, but her next words had him freezing in place.

"Please, Volkan," she said sweetly. "Feed from me."

Volkan appeared amused as he brushed past Eldar. Even Thaddeus seemed to be biting back a smile. Eldar felt something he hadn't felt in a long time. He felt humiliated.

Her pretty lips rose in a satisfied smile. He watched as Volkan sunk his teeth into her neck and she lifted a hand to trail down his pale hair. Eldar didn't know why he stood around to watch it unfold. He knew she did it to get under his skin, just as he knew the pleasure in her eyes was from the poison of a vampir bite that lured their prey into a false sense of security. It was not based on any truth. Her eyes were locked on his while she stroked his brother's hair. Volkan may have had his teeth in her, but Eldar was on her mind. He had to take small comfort in that.

"You wish it was me," he mouthed.

He watched her fist tighten in Volkan's hair. She was too far gone to respond, but he did see her lips wrap around a single word. He didn't know if it was a response to his comment or if she simply wanted to provoke him some more.

She had said his name.

Eldar left the room, his fists clenched close to his body. He didn't know why he let her affect him. He wasn't a man prone to emotions. Especially not from a girl who stood for everything he despised. Mortals were made to be turned or to serve them as sustenance. She did neither and was therefore unworthy of life.

He hadn't minded her when she had been a blood slave. In fact, he had barely noticed her, but then she had surprised him with her hunger for more. First, she had ensnared Dracul and his court, then she had softened Mircea like clay between her small fingers, and lastly, she had robbed him of his brother.

She was a creature spun by the hands of the devil.

And she had come to end them all.

XVII

AYLIN CUT A thin line on her palm and let it soak the pouch in her palm until it filled a quarter of the way to the top. If the vampir demanded blood for answers, then Aylin would feed her. It was a small price to pay to find out what fate had befallen her sister. Salvatore looked up at her beneath his thin lashes, and she kept her hand in her pocket curled around the velvet-lined pouch as if he could sense her deception. She hated that she had to deface her sister's pouch that had been tucked perilously into the crease of her shawl that she had borrowed for the journey. A pair of pearl earrings had been nestled in the pouch, and Aylin had felt her throat tighten as her finger traced the smooth beads.

"I require privacy with the vampir," Aylin said. "I don't believe she will speak while you are present."

Domenico had just returned from a torture session with the vampir. He used a handkerchief to wipe the blood that stained the fine hair on his forearm. He was meticulous about getting between the creases of his finger. She recalled faintly how he had paused during their hunting trip to wash in the stream. For a man who existed in the shadows, he hated the grime of blood and filth.

Salvatore tapped a long finger on his desk, staring at them both as if surprised that they were breathing in the same room without tearing out each other's throats. His gaze darted between them suspiciously.

Domenico's gaze was latched on her, perusing the lines of her face as if he were committing it to memory.

"It won't hurt to try," Salvatore said. "With their unnatural healing, they do not feel pain for long. Domenico has hooked metal pins in her abdomen to prevent the skin from sealing. It should make her more pliant."

Bile crawled up Aylin's throat, and she swallowed it back.

"I'll see what I can find," she said.

She walked toward the door behind Salvatore that led to the prison chamber. Domenico gripped her forearm before she could pass him.

"Don't take too long," he whispered. "Or I might have to come after you."

She shivered when his mouth touched her ear. The very one he had nearly torn off weeks ago. Warm lips brushed over the scab, light as a feather. And all she could think was that at least he didn't lick her this time. Ever since the hunting trip, she couldn't read his mood, and she didn't know when he would reveal her secret. Aylin knew it was only a matter of time.

He stared at her so intensely sometimes it made her sick to her stomach.

Aylin dipped into the dark tunnel, palms sliding along the wall to guide her. The guard pulled open the door for her without so much as a nod, and she stepped inside. It smelled rancid, like something had withered and died. The woman looked nothing like she had a few weeks ago. Her skin was wrinkled and grey. There was a wound on her stomach that looked like a split mouth, and a silver nail had been plunged into the torn skin to stop it from healing. Sweat dotted her brow and her mouth was chapped, skin peeling in red blisters.

"I've brought you an offering," Aylin said. "In return for answers."

She pulled the pouch from her pocket. Her eyes followed it senselessly.

"Give...me," she said. Her fingers twitched beneath the chain.

"Half now and half when you answer."

Aylin undid the strings and poured a bit into her desperate mouth. She lapped her tongue across her lips to catch every stray drop of blood.

"More," she demanded.

The color began to return to her skin, and Aylin realized her poor state had as much to do with starvation as it did torture.

"What have you heard about Yara?" she asked. "Tell me."

"More," she said wildly, staring at the pouch. "More."

"I will spill this if you don't tell me soon," Aylin said. "Where. Is. My. Sister."

"The Court of the Undead," she whispered. "Where no mortal has ever breached unless they were brought in chains. Where the Undying King rules over the trueborn vampir. The first of our kind. Our eternal sires and dams. You have no hope of entering without invitation. Your sister belongs to the night."

"Speak freely and without riddle," Aylin said, frustrated. "Where is this Court of the Undead?"

"In the mountains of Wallachia," she said. "Do you seek to invade where no man has before?"

It was a good thing that Aylin wasn't a man.

"Wallachia spans the length of the Milcov River and the Carpathian Mountains; you must narrow it down," she said.

"I have told you as much as I can afford to share," she said.

"Does she live?" Aylin asked.

"Last I heard, your sister was using her gift of song to charm the court. Perhaps she may live to share the tale."

Aylin poured the rest of the blood into her mouth.

"You are an honorable one," the woman whispered as she licked her lips. "I hope you find your sister."

"I am sorry that they have tortured you," she said, struggling not to look at the implements curled in her stomach. "Sometimes a quick death is preferable to a long life of misery."

"They call us monsters. But I have looked upon the eyes of the fair-haired one, and there is no light to be found."

"Salvatore is an unpleasant one," Aylin said. "I am not fond of him either."

"I do not speak of the priest," she said. "I speak of the other one. The one with bruised fists and cunning eyes."

Aylin sighed. "That charming fellow is Domenico Zancherelli. If you ever escape, don't hesitate to cut his throat."

The faint sound of his steps was the only indication of his entrance.

"Plotting against me, little one?" Domenico asked. He had gone from calling her "little boy" to "little one." She didn't like it any better, but she was glad he was no longer attempting to beat her to death. It seemed there was some small trace of chivalry that prevented him from attacking a woman.

"*Plotting* implies I am keeping my hatred for you a secret," she said.

Besides, she had a better plan to get rid of Domenico. She remembered Sevda telling her a tale once, about a woman who sold poison to disgruntled wives to murder their abusive husbands. Oftentimes the poison was untraceable. Nobody could smell nor see traces of it floating in a drink. It was such a womanly thing to poison that nobody would ever suspect her—not while she was disguised as a boy. They would simply assume Domenico had died of a natural cause.

While it soured her stomach to take a life, she would be leaving the world in a far better state without Domenico Zancherelli to ruin it. Aylin disappeared down the tunnel to speak to Salvatore, but she felt the forceful weight of Domenico crashing into her like the strike of a long blade.

"Not very gentlemanly of you," she said, feeling the coil of his hand wrap around her throat.

"I haven't touched you in weeks," he said. "Did you miss me?"

"The way a soldier misses the infection that ate away at his limbs," she said. "Release me before my knee finds its way between your legs *again*."

"You are not foolish enough to repeat your past mistakes," he said. "Not when I hold your prized secret on my tongue. It would take no more than a single word from me for you to lose all you hold dear and your rotten *brother* to fall with you."

"What do you want?" she asked tightly. "These threats bore me."

"For you to answer my question: did you miss me?"

"I told yo—"

"Lie to me," he said. "Make it pretty and soft."

"I missed you," she said between clenched teeth. "A great deal."

"That was pathetic," Domenico said. "We will practice until you can express yourself more freely."

"You mean until I am a practiced liar," she spat.

His thumb stroked the pulse at her neck like she was a wild animal.

"It doesn't matter what you are," he whispered. "So long as you know that you are mine."

Leandra was weaving a basket in the grass, and Aylin sat down cross-legged before her. Leandra sat in an open field surrounded by cornflowers. In a pretty blue dress that matched the flowers around her.

"That is beautiful," Aylin said, pointing at her basket. It showed true craftsmanship. Aylin realized belatedly that a man would not take notice of such detail.

"Thank you, *Don* Aydin," Leandra said. "I was looking for you."

"Were you?" she asked.

Aylin had sought her out to inquire about the plants she required for Domenico.

Her nerves had been lit on fire since they had last spoken. How dare he call her his, as if she were a possession to be controlled by a man? Did he think because she was a woman, she wouldn't fight him as brutally as she had before? Did he think she would cower beneath his threats? Did he think he could threaten Ilyas, and she would stand for it?

Leandra tucked her hand in her bustier, drawing forth a handkerchief, the edges painted with blue poppies.

"Will you give this to your brother for me?" she asked innocently.

Aylin held out her hand. The fabric was cold to the touch, and her smile was strained when she spoke. "Of course, I'm certain he will adore it."

Leandra smiled widely, revealing the span of her crooked teeth. She was a sweet girl, and Aylin wondered if she should confess Ilyas's celibacy. In the end, she decided to leave it to Ilyas to reject the poor girl himself.

"Thank you," Leandra said. "You are an honorable man, Don Aydin."

Aylin resisted the urge to scoff. There was nothing honorable about her.

"I had a question. I wished to pluck some berries to have a pie made. It will be Elijah's name day in three days," she said. "But I wish to stay away from the inedible ones."

"Oh, that is a splendid idea! You will let me make it, of course, right?" she asked.

"Yes, I will leave that in your capable hands," Aylin said. "But I must be of some use. Will you let me help you pluck some berries?"

"Of course," she said. "Come with me. My mother taught me much about foraging. She said there are two types of poisonous plants: one that causes severe illness and one that causes death. It is easy to tell which is which based on coloring, and if you squeeze them lightly. Another way to tell is if the bush is filled with berries. If animals don't stray near it, then it means it is not fit to be eaten."

Leandra bent before a bush. "This dark one is called nightshade. Some call it belladonna. Have you heard of such a name?"

"I cannot say I have."

"It is as poisonous as they come. A long, miserable death," she said with a sad shake of her head. "Fever, convulsions, false visions. I would not recommend ingesting this."

Leandra's eyes sparkled when she spoke of the berries. She led Aylin down the path, plucking fresh berries into her basket and pointing out any to be watched out for.

"Elderberries must be cooked before eating," she said. "Raw elderberries can be fatal."

She pointed out plants that, if touched, would give one a burning rash. She was a good forager, and Aylin was impressed by it all. Impressed enough that she had plucked a handful of the nightshade berries, enfolding them carefully in the handkerchief Leandra had made for Ilyas. Aylin had every intention of washing it out with soap before she gave it to him, rather than finding blisters on her palm come tomorrow by plucking the berries bare-handed.

Leandra had mentioned that while small amounts led to symptoms, a higher dose only brought death. She would crush these berries into his wine tonight. If all went well, Domenico Zancherelli wouldn't live to see dawn.

"Ever thought of settling down, boys?" Borza asked them, biting into the white seared rabbit meat. The fare of soldiers was poor indeed, and Aylin grimaced as she chewed the stretchy meat, feeling it unspool in her mouth.

Borza liked two things: drinking copious amounts of wine and talking about his wife. He was on a mission to lure them into the fine arms of domesticity.

"I'm celibate," Ilyas said. "Perhaps my brother can be swayed."

"Celibate?" he asked. "Do you wish to go into the priesthood, my boy?"

"It was decided for me long before I could make a choice of my own," he said. "It is a duty that I had never thought of turning away from. I do not see a future that is shared with anyone but myself."

"What if you fall in love?" Aylin asked. "I have it on good authority that a certain girl is after your heart."

Ilyas cupped his chin in his palm. "Does this girl have a name?"

"Leandra," she said, placing the rinsed handkerchief on the table. It was a bit crinkled from when she scrubbed the traces of poison off it, but no worse for wear. "A gift from her to you."

"Whom?" Ilyas raised a brow.

"Ah, sweet Leandra," Borza said. "She will make a fine wife."

"Isn't she a bit young for you?" Domenico asked, sliding into the wooden chair beside him.

Borza slapped his chest, and Domenico raised his knife in warning, swinging it between his fingers like it were a child's toy.

"For Elijah," Borza clarified.

"She will be well suited for you," Domenico said. "You both are painfully boring."

"And who would ever want you?" Ilyas asked. "No sane woman would shackle herself to you for eternity."

"I've already found my woman," Domenico said. He leaned back so he hovered on the edge of his chair. Aylin wished Borza would swipe the chair's legs out from under him so he could crumble to the ground and sustain a fatal injury.

Aylin laughed at the thought of Domenico living in a small cottage with a Venetian woman who cooked him onion soup and wiped the sweat from his brow after a long, laborious day of cutting down immortal blood drinkers. She hoped whatever woman warmed his bed didn't miss him too much when she killed him.

"You didn't tell me a word of this," Borza said with a frown. "Are we not good mates?"

"I've only just met her, but I know she belongs to me," he said. "She is deceiving and vicious."

"Sounds like you intend to wed your reflection," Borza said with a hacking laugh.

"I pity that poor girl," Ilyas said.

"We'll keep her in our prayers," Aylin said.

Domenico only smiled like he knew a secret they did not know.

"The bastard is smitten," Borza said, clapping his back. "We must drink to this! I'll get us a pitcher."

Aylin grabbed her chalice. She didn't drink wine, but she had picked up a cup for her poison.

"I seem to have picked up a cup by mistake," she said. "Here, Domenico. To your woman. May she capture your attention long enough for us to stab you in the back."

Ilyas roared with laughter, and she smiled, pleased by his reaction. Beneath the table she squeezed his hand, the chalice still raised for

Domenico. Domenico snatched it from her, sloshing it on the table. He brought the cup to his lips, and her heart thudded. Nobody but her and Ilyas knew that she had given him the chalice. Borza had been the only person who shared their table, and he had disappeared to bring them more drinks.

There would be no witnesses to her crime.

Aylin watched his throat bob as he swallowed. It was about to happen. He would keel over and then his cold heart would freeze in his chest. She had squeezed twelve berries in the cup, even though Leandra had said six or eight would do the job. Aylin would not tolerate any chance of survival. Her secret would die with him. He wouldn't rob her of the chance to save her sister. She hoped God forgave her for this grave sin.

Borza returned with a pitcher. Aylin watched Domenico, and Domenico watched her. He licked his lips and she shivered, wondering when it would happen. Five minutes passed, and she was feeling a bit anxious. Something was wrong. She had to speak to Leandra.

"Excuse me," she said in a faint whisper. She left the room, moving as fast as she could without raising suspicion.

She hadn't made it past a few feet before she was shoved into a decrepit room that looked like a library. Chairs and mismatched pillows were perched in the corners. Tapestries of dancing elephants and floral motifs that looked distinctly Indian decorated the walls, while crooked shelves made of oak hosted a nest of wilted manuscripts.

"How devious you are, little one," Domenico said with a harsh exhale.

"I...I don't know what you're talking about."

Domenico spun her around, his hands flat on her waist. There was an unreadable look in his eye.

"Do you think I drank a sip from that cup?" he asked. "I know you don't drink wine, and water is always served in a small metal cup. If you picked up wine, it was for a reason. My suspicions were confirmed by the frantic look in your eyes when I didn't fall dead to my knees."

"You tricked me," she whispered.

"Is that so vile compared to your actions?"

He seemed strangely pleased that she had tried to murder him. If she had ever doubted his sanity, this erased that doubt.

"All you have ever done was hurt me and try to break me, as if shattering me to pieces will somehow fix the rot inside you," she said. "You stole my secret, and you threatened Elijah—the only person who cares about me. I won't let you hurt us anymore. I won't stop until one of us is dead."

"I'm not angry at you," Domenico said almost gently. "I told you to keep me interested, and you certainly keep me on my toes."

"I don't want to play this twisted game of yours," she said.

"You silence the demons in my mind," Domenico said, leaning his forehead on hers. He lifted a hand to stroke the short ends of her hair. A shiver ran down her back, stiffening her muscles. He looked at her with a dark obsession that frightened her. Now that she thought of it, he had always looked at her like that. Like he wanted to consume her. Even when she had been a boy. "I want to play with you forever."

From the moment she had arrived, he had targeted her. He had hated her so blindly and ruthlessly that she had wondered if she had caused some unintentional harm or slight. But it had worsened in the last few weeks, as if the knowledge that she was a woman had twisted his hatred into something deeper. Something she could not escape.

"You said you had a woman," she said. "What if I slit her throat? What if I coat myself in her blood? Will you leave me then?"

Domenico laughed, and his eyes seemed to sparkle with a mad glee. "You would kill yourself to spite me?"

The door opened, and she stumbled away from him, both startled by his words and the sight of Ilyas standing at the doorway. He stared at them, a dark frown beginning to tilt his lips downwards. His hands were clenched in tight fists by his side.

"I thought I told you to stay away from him," Ilyas said. His long legs ate away at the space in the room. He wrapped his hand around her wrist, pulling her behind him like she was in imminent danger.

"I'll see you tomorrow, little one," Domenico said. "If he touches a finger to your head, I will cut off each of his fingers and shove them down his throat."

"I'll touch him all I want," Ilyas snapped. "He is *my* brother."

Domenico brushed past him, and he couldn't resist digging his shoulder into Ilyas's side. Ilyas took a menacing step forward, but Aylin grabbed his elbow before he could attack.

"Let him go," she said. "He is not worthy of your ire."

Aylin sat on a dusty settee. How had she failed so miserably? How had she caught the attention of such an unpredictable man? She would rather have him trying to kill her than trapping her in this blackmail scheme. She would rather die than hear him imply she was *his*. How had she gone from his worst enemy to this?

"He is mad," she whispered. "There is something unholy in him. I cannot put my finger on it."

"Why was he touching you?" Ilyas asked. "You were so close, almost as if—"

"As if what?" she asked harshly. "Do you think I want to be sharing his breath, let alone whatever else you seek to imply?"

Ilyas placed his hand on her knee. "I won't let him come between us. Now, tell me what is wrong. I sensed something amiss from the day you returned from that hunting trip. He has been watching you closely, and he is never far from you."

"He knows," she whispered.

Ilyas stiffened. "How much?"

"Only that I am a woman. Though he suspects we are not related," she said. "He has been lording it over me. I tried to end it tonight. I tried to protect us, but I failed. Forgive me, Ilyas."

Aylin felt guilty. It wasn't the first time she had endangered them. She was far too impulsive and had made a grand mess of everything. Their secret lay in the hands of a man they didn't trust, and Yara was trapped in a place with a name that chilled her: the Court of the Undead.

Tired of the secrets, Aylin began to confide in him about the vampir woman locked in the prison chamber. There had been much she had kept from him, afraid that he would stop her or look at her with those disappointed eyes that he looked at her with now.

"You promised you would follow my lead," he said. Aylin opened her mouth to speak, but he pressed a hard finger to her lips, silencing her immediately. "I asked you to follow me not because I believe my-self to be superior to you, but because of my experience in the sultan's army. I've shared everything that I know, and you couldn't even tell me that you learned where Yara was being kept."

"I've been busy trying to kill Domenico," she said. "I didn't have time to sit down and tell you everything. I didn't mean to keep it a secret."

Ilyas rubbed his brows. "I don't know what I will do with you, Aylin."

"Does that mean you forgive me?" she asked hopefully.

Ilyas didn't respond, and she tugged his arm up, sliding beneath it so it fell on her shoulder.

"I'm sorry," she said. "You know I appreciate everything you've done for me. I won't keep anything from you anymore."

"Promise?" he asked.

"Promise," she said.

"I don't want us to be apart. Not for a moment," he said. "I've left you alone for a few weeks, and you've made a great mess of things. You won't leave my side from now onwards."

"And here I thought you were being sweet," she said. "That you merely enjoyed my company."

"Do you think you deserve my good temper after being so foolish?" he asked. His words were harsh, but he gripped her shoulder tight, drawing her closer to him, as if he needed the warmth of her body as much as she did his.

"Of course," she said. "You secretly enjoy cleaning up my mess, admit it."

"You want to make a liar of me?" he whispered. His breath rustled her hair.

"Leandra wants to wed you," she blurted.

"You mentioned it before," he said. His tone was teasing when he spoke next. "Does it bother you?"

Her chest stilled. Was he flirting with her? She looked up at his handsome face with its sharp features and brilliant blue eyes that looked like the Aegean Sea. It was no surprise that women were drawn to him. Beyond his looks, he had an aura, an unnameable quality that drew you to him.

"Only as much as it bothers you that Domenico wishes to do depraved things to me," she said. It didn't surprise her that her tongue ran off without her. That she provoked him so boldly. She had always hidden the kernel of her affection so deep within her. It had only begun to unravel when they had left the rigid structure of the court and he resembled less of an oath-bound soldier and more of a man.

Ilyas's eyes were wide, and Aylin stared at him pointedly. He shouldn't flirt if he didn't expect her to be twice as bad.

"I've forgotten how shameless you are," he said. "And you are a fool to think that is all I care about. He is a threat to everything we've achieved. One word from him and our plans will come undone."

"I know," she said with a deep sigh. "I was trying to be optimistic."

"Did I ever tell you what made me decide to stay in Constantinople after I had spent nights plotting my escape with the aim to slit as many throats as I could on the way out?" he asked.

"No," she said. "I've always wanted to ask if you missed your family and country, but I didn't want to bring back painful memories."

"That day you gave me that ugly portrait of a creature who had eyes like mine was the day I stopped fighting," he said. "Something inside me unraveled, and I could feel it tether to you. I knew then that you belonged to me as I belonged to you."

Aylin stroked the faint outline of his faded teeth marks on her palm.

"Why are you saying all this?" she whispered.

He tilted her chin up. "Because I want you to know what you mean to me."

"So that nothing may come of it?" she asked harshly. "I don't enjoy these games, Ilyas."

She would much prefer he tell her they were merely friends. She would much prefer he say nothing at all.

"I don't have anything to offer you, Aylin," he said averting his gaze. "Nothing but my words."

"Well, they are not enough," she said. "They will *never* be enough."

Aylin stood up and left him to return to their bedroom. It didn't help that she would see him not long after and she couldn't properly lick her wounds in private. She knew it was unfair to be upset. She had known all her life that Ilyas would never pursue or settle down with any woman, and she was no exception. It didn't stop the pain of her heart cleaving in half. It didn't stop the doubt from creeping into her mind, the fear that once she found Yara and her sister settled down with one of her many suitors and Baba grew too old to walk...

Aylin would have no one and nothing.

XVIII

YARA HAD A plan. But she needed help. Not from Eldar, who wanted her to beg him on her knees, nor from Volkan, whose only suggestion had been that he would wed her *before* Augustus did. Her entire life she had fallen in love with fairy tales of princesses being saved by the charming prince, when she should have been studying how the prince scaled such high towers and rode through cursed forests. Her baba wasn't here to protect her, and Aylin couldn't fight her battles anymore. It was time Yara got her own hands dirty.

"Yara, what a lovely surprise," Zuri said. From the state of the rumpled sheets on her bed, it seemed she had just risen from sleep. Unlike mortals, vampir didn't require any time to catch their bearings; they always woke up alert.

"I know we're not supposed to meet outside our scheduled hours, but I was hoping we could talk."

Zuri opened her door, letting Yara into her small bedroom. It was cramped with a single bed and a writing table in the corner. It wasn't like the lavish quarters of Mircea or the brothers.

"You don't seem impressed," she said, amused.

Yara's cheeks warmed. "I thought every room in this place was fit for a king."

"Not us lowly vampir. Us sired are only a step above the blood slaves in our hierarchy."

She gestured for Yara to sit on the bed while she took the chair by the table. Her hair was coiled in neat braids that reminded her wistfully of when Sevda would knot her hair like that. Yara had always had hair that swallowed combs and required patience and a handful of oil to tame it. Whereas Aylin refused to have her hair touched. Not that her sister's hair required much effort, Aylin had the most beautiful hair Yara had ever seen.

"I love how you style your hair," Yara said. "It's very pretty."

"Thank you," Zuri said. She stared at her curiously. "Mircea says you're upset with him."

Yara sighed. "I'm upset with all men. They are selfish creatures."

"I've been serving Mircea for two hundred years, and he's never cared for anyone before, but he asked me to check on you," she said. "I believe he is fond of you."

"As I was off him," she said, feeling her throat tighten. It had been easy to see him as a father figure, to pretend that there was someone who cared for her. But Mircea wouldn't defy his brother, Vlad Dracul, for her. He wouldn't jeopardize his alliance with the Maleinos family for her. At the end of the day, she was a mortal with no power and no family ties. She was alone with nobody to protect her but herself.

"There needn't be any ill will between you both," Zuri said. "I do not believe his intention was to harm."

"I cannot be focused on Mircea when I have bigger problems to rid myself of," she said. "I need your help."

"With what?"

Yara took a deep, shuddering breath before the poisonous words escaped her tongue.

"I need to kill Augustus," Yara said.

"Mircea won't approve of such action," Zuri said. Her face was calm, with no hint of shock or repulsion at her words.

"He won't know it was us," Yara continued. "I have something."

Yara unfolded her palm to show one of Eldar's rings; it was the dull iron-ring he always wore with his family sigil. He had placed it in a little jewelry box before he went to the baths that afternoon, and she hadn't hesitated to steal it. She had waited for days for the opportunity to take it. She knew it was the only thing he wore on his personhood permanently. The only thing that could assure his guilt.

"We will leave this curled in his dead fist. Eldar's ring," she said. "Mircea promised that if I proved his treachery, I would be freed. Once it is revealed that Eldar attacked a member of the Maleinos coven, he will be executed if we are lucky, and if not, imprisoned. The laws that govern your court will demand he pays for his crime, and I will be given my freedom."

Zuri tapped her chin thoughtfully. "It is a cunning plan."

"I cannot pull it off myself," she said. "I will need your help setting it all up."

"I suppose I'm not doing anything important today," Zuri said. "But if Mircea catches wind of this scheme, you will take full responsibility."

"I swear I won't say your name," she rushed. Yara felt a wave of delight. She wrapped her arms around Zuri's neck, making her chuckle. Yara was beside herself; she even kissed her cheeks to thank her for her help. She didn't know the first thing about killing a vampir, and while scheming and politics came naturally to her, murder was far beyond her grasp.

But with Zuri's help she could pull this scheme off. And the best part would be seeing Eldar's face when he was strung up for death and the crows fed on his flesh.

It was the least of what he deserved for all the torment he had heaped on her from the moment she arrived. That night he had left her in the maze had been the worst. She had never felt so afraid and small. But when she had heard how he had spoken about her to Volkan and Thaddeus, that had broken her. He didn't care if she fell for his brother's sins so long as it was not Volkan who was hurt in the process.

He would learn soon that he wasn't the only one who could be monstrous.

Zuri and Yara stood in the shadows before his bedroom in silent surveillance. The fur-lined hood of her kaftan grazed her cheeks. Hours passed before Augustus stumbled inside, drunk and tired from a night of revelry. The moment the door sealed shut, Zuri wrapped her leather-clad fingers around the doorknob and slipped inside. She said she would call for Yara when he was subdued, and that if Yara joined her, he would instantly hear her heartbeat.

Yara waited with sweat coating her nape, dripping into the dark collar of her kaftan. Her limbs shook as she thought of all the ways this plan could fall to pieces. Pomona could come to visit Augustus and catch them red-handed. Eldar could be watching her, and any moment he would pin her to the wall and demand she kiss his boots in return for his forgiveness. Mircea could discover her deceit and take back his promise of freedom. Volkan could confront her for betraying him and hurting his beloved brother.

Yara shook her head. It would work. She just had to believe it. She had prayed all night for guidance and for God to strengthen her hand to kill this vile man. Zuri had agreed to subdue him, but she had been clear when she said that Yara would have to finish him off. She was oath-bound to tell Mircea the truth if he questioned her, and Zuri refused to take the risk of having Augustus' blood on her hands.

Ten minutes later, Zuri popped her head out and whistled for her to come in. Yara cautiously stepped inside the dim room. He was pinned to the wall, his palms pierced with two knives and a third stuck into his throat. Blood bubbled from his mouth, and Yara's eyes widened in horror.

"A stab to the heart and it all ends, my precious girl," Zuri said, offering her the handle of a thin blade. The kind that Aylin would salivate over and talk about the craft and the painted hilt. It was Aylin who would face down this man who sought to trap her in a vengeful marriage and not cower at the sight of his blood. But Yara did not have a taste for violence, and her stomach churned until she thought she would be sick.

He shook his head, and the knife that pinned him screeched as it scraped the wall with his rapid movement, as if he were a butterfly whose wings had been snapped. He twitched and moaned.

Yara took a deep breath and attempted to steady her quivering hand. She couldn't look him in the eye while she robbed him of his life. So, she slid her eyes shut and dug the sharp blade into his chest, pressing past bone until it sunk into the soft pouch that made his heart. His body decayed before her eyes, as if all the years he had lived had caught up to him. In the end, he looked like a rather sad old man, and Yara's heart ached to think she had taken a life. Even if it was one that belonged to a vampir, a cursed being crafted by the hands of the devil.

Yara placed Eldar's ring in his hand and closed his fist.

"You did splendidly," Zuri said. "It is always challenging the first time, but it gets easier with practice. Someday you won't see them as people at all, but obstacles to be moved in the pursuit of greater power."

"That will make me no different than them," she said. "I'll be no better than Pomona and Eldar."

"Perhaps," Zuri said. "But at least you won't be afraid."

—————

Yara awoke to sharp voices outside her door. She wasn't surprised to find Eldar and Volkan speaking as if there wasn't someone sleeping a few feet away. Yara didn't know what the raucous was, but she intended to find out. She stepped outside her bedroom to find them in the midst of a quarrel.

"Can you both keep your voices down?" she asked, staring at them with squinted eyes.

"How could you be so reckless?" Eldar hissed. "We were lucky you got away with Titus. Do you think you can slaughter their entire line and you won't be brought forth to pay for it?"

"I didn't kill Augustus," Volkan said. "Release me before I break your arm."

"I can't do this, Volkan. I cannot continue to clean your messes," Eldar said with a rough shake of his head. "I had a plan. It required patience, but it would be worth it in the end. I would have power. I would have them bow before me. I cannot do that if I'm worried about you constantly. You ruin *everything*."

"Listen to me, Eldar," he said slowly. "I. Did. Not. Kill. Him."

"What's going on?" Yara asked.

"You can sleep well tonight. Your husband is dead," Eldar said coldly.

"He's not my husband." She wrinkled her nose. "What happened to him?"

"We have a private audience with the Undying King. They've conducted an investigation and have reason to suspect us," Eldar said.

Yara frowned. "Both of you? Even Volkan?"

"Is there a reason why they would only suspect me?" Eldar demanded.

"Lord knows I'm not the one smitten enough with you to kill your husband."

"Stop calling him that," she said tightly.

"Enough, both of you," Volkan said. "Fighting among ourselves won't fix our situation. It's obvious who the culprit behind this was."

Yara felt her heart race, and Eldar's head turned to her. She barely had time to catch her breath before he had his hand wrapped around her throat. She was tired of feeling his slim fingers constantly wrap around her neck, as if she were still his blood slave. As if he owned her.

"Your heart is racing," he said, leaning down to snarl in her face. "Why is your heart racing?"

"Because Pomona is plotting something, and her plans always seem to revolve around hurting me," she lied. "This is her first strike, but it won't be her last."

"Why would she kill her cousin?" he snapped. "One thing about Pomona is she is fiercely loyal. I cannot say the same thing about you."

"Let her go, Eldar," Volkan said. "Hurting her is not the fix either."

"She's lying about something," Eldar said. He buried his nose in her hair. "I can smell her lies." His teeth sunk into her neck, and a whimper escaped her at the sharp sting before she fell into a pool of bliss. Her body relaxed, and she felt him wrap his arm around her waist to support her. He retreated only to plunge back into her shoulder and then her arm.

"Tell me," he whispered. "Tell me everything."

"I hate you," she whispered. "I...I want to ruin you."

"And?" he demanded. "Who killed Augustus?"

"You did," she said. Her eyes slipped closed. She could feel him bite her again. On her clavicle, his teeth scraped her bones in a caress. Yara had never had a sip of wine, but she imagined being drunk felt like this. Each bite made her more intoxicated, more pliable to his questions.

"Impossible," he said. "I would know. Tell me what you know."

"I'm going home," she said. "Mircea promised. I'll see my father and Aylin. I miss them. I miss her. I miss my sister. I wish she were here with me even if that makes me weak. I wish she were here to make you feel twice as much pain as I have. I wish she were here to break you."

She felt a tear slip past her closed eyes, followed by the wet slide of his tongue carrying it away deep inside him while he fed on her pain.

"What did you promise him in return for your freedom?"

"Eldar," a voice similar to his called out. "This is not the way. You are pushing her too far. It is easy to get addicted to our bite. Do not make her a blood whore."

"I'm close to the truth," he said. She felt his teeth in the palm of her hand, and a small moan left her lips. It hurt but it felt so good. She didn't feel or think. She simply existed in this moment of pleasure.

"More," she pleaded.

His hand was gentle on her cheek.

"I'll give you everything you want," he promised. "Just tell me the truth."

"I want you dead," she said. "I'll smile when you burn in the sun and dance on your corpse."

"And what of Volkan? Have you dragged him into this scheme?" he asked. "It's obvious that you had a hand in this. Did you risk my brother's life for your worthless human life?"

"I would never hurt him," she said. "I care about him."

Yara felt him pull away from her. She slumped to the floor. Her body felt limp, and her muscles tingled. Her eyes shot open, and she watched him step away from her. She must have been truly intoxicated, because she thought she caught a glimpse of hurt in his eyes before he stormed off.

Yara felt herself slip down the wall. Volkan came to her, picking her up gently and carrying her back to her room.

"It hurts," she said. Now that he'd left, she could feel the pinprick of the wounds that littered her neck and arms. He had feasted on her like a wolf, leaving behind nothing but a broken carcass.

"I'll heal you," Volkan said, placing her on her bed. She shivered when she felt his tongue trace the wounds. He moved slowly, hovering above her. She felt her skin slowly stitching back together like the seams of a cloth. She could feel clarity begin to trickle in, and she realized then that she had all but confessed to her crimes. Eldar knew her guilt and her hand in Augustus's death.

"He's going to kill me," she said sitting upright. Her head hurt like she hadn't slept in days, and she felt weak and sluggish.

"No, he won't," Volkan said. "I dare say this little scheme will endear you to him more. I didn't know you were so bloodthirsty."

"He brings out this side of me," she whispered. "Fills me with so much anger I feel as though I'll come undone."

"I reckon you do the same to him," Volkan said. "Did you truly want him dead?"

"Yes." She rubbed her eyes. "No." Yara sighed. "I don't know."

Volkan nodded as if that were a perfectly acceptable answer. Yara tucked herself onto his chest, desperate for comfort.

"Do you hate me for trying to kill him?" she whispered.

"I would be surprised if you *didn't* try to kill him." Volkan chuckled. "Thaddeus said he wishes he had been born before us so he could lie with our mother and ensure that she conceived only me."

Yara tilted her head. "What an odd wish."

"Lord knows he'd be a far better father than ours was," Volkan said.

"Was he terrible?" she asked.

His face sealed shut and his eyes hardened. "I don't wish to speak of him," he said, tucking a strand of hair behind her ear. "Get some rest. You've had a long day."

Yara felt her mouth stretch in a yawn.

"Will you leave?" she asked.

"Do you want me to leave?"

Yara shook her head. "I don't want him to find me. Will you watch me while I sleep?"

It was a strange request, and she hated that he was the only person strong enough to protect her from his brother. The only person Eldar would never hurt to get to her. She felt safe in his arms. Safe from the consequences of her actions. She had no doubt Eldar would punish her. It was as inevitable as the sun rising from the east and setting in the west.

Volkan nodded. He wrapped his arms around her. His long fingers began to unravel the knots in her hair. It reminded her of the day she had been kidnapped and he had taken care of her. Yara found herself slowly falling into a deep sleep, exhaustion pulling her into the dark abyss.

XIX

SALVATORE STOOD BEFORE a map of the east. It was a beautifully illustrated piece drawn with a steady hand and keen eyes. There were markings, little crosses to pinpoint travel lines from Venice to Wallachia. Beside him were the other priests. Cristifano stared at them in displeasure from where he sat beside the old Antonio, who reminded Aylin all too much of a rabbit with his whiskers and bald head. Domenico sat tilted on his chair, the back of it supported by the walls. His eyes seemed to be closed, as if he were in the midst of a nap.

When she received Salvatore's request to visit him, she had brought along Ilyas as promised. The air was tense between them both, and they didn't acknowledge the words spoken between them last night, which was a relief. She didn't expect him to forsake his vows for her, and in the morning light their argument had seemed rather silly. She had the desperate urge to put it all behind her. For once, she was glad that his discomfort with conflict worked in her favor.

Aylin discreetly kicked Domenico's chair, watching it wobble precariously. He was just about to tip over when Ilyas used his big hand to steady the chair.

"This is a meeting of grave importance," Salvatore said, pointing a warning finger at her and Domenico. "I won't have your petty rivalry spoiling it."

Domenico was dressed rather formally today in a black jerkin above his doublet. Aylin assumed it had more to do with his father's presence than a desire to remain modest. He didn't look at her once, and she frowned. No insult, no threat, not even a lecherous stare. Her finger curled to flick his ear despite Salvatore's warning, but Ilyas clasped her hand in his with a single word: "Behave."

Perhaps Domenico had gotten bored with her. It was strange not to be tormented by him, but she supposed she would grow used to it in time.

Salvatore looked at her. "While it is helpful to narrow down their nest to Wallachia, we need more."

"I don't think she will tell me more," Aylin said. She had seen it in her eyes. She would protect her kind before she told the truth.

"Domenico has broken her," he said. "She will speak."

Aylin hesitated. She could only imagine what carvings Domenico had left behind. He had probably chipped at her till there was nothing left but the barest hint of a person.

"We wish for you both to join our immediate council," Salvatore continued. "We held a vote and have agreed that your brother's expertise and your tenacity will prove fruitful for our endeavours."

Aylin stared at their faces. Cristifano didn't seem pleased by their presence. He looked nothing like his son. His hair was dark, and his eyes were as black as a crow. They had the same stern jaw, but that was all they shared. His father looked aristocratic while Domenico looked rougher, meaner.

Domenico took a long gulp from his cup. She could smell the crushed grapes that made his wine. His cheeks were flushed, and she assumed he had been drinking for some time. He looked positively miserable, as if he had received a tongue lashing before they arrived.

"I'll speak to her," Aylin said, swallowing the bile that creeped up her throat. She hoped the vampir was not so mutilated that it made her nauseous. She had to do this for Yara. Her sister was worth any sacrifice required of her.

"Shall I come with you?" Ilyas asked.

She shook her head. "She is more likely to speak to me alone."

"I'll walk you there," Domenico said, rising before she could reject his offer. He peeled open the door that led to the damp tunnel, waiting for her to pass him by.

"Are you mad at me?" she asked.

"For what?" He raised a brow.

"For trying to push your chair so you'd bash your head in and die?"

She didn't include the poison. Considering it had failed splendidly, she didn't think it would do any good to remind him.

Domenico chuckled. "Your murderous intentions amuse me."

"Then why didn't you react?"

"Well, my father has an excellent gift of sucking the spirit from my soul," he said. "It's why I drown myself in drink whenever I find myself in his company."

"He does seem rather stern," she said. "I don't think he likes me or Elijah."

"He likes nobody but Salvatore," Domenico spat. "That spineless twat. He would bend over and let my father ride him if he asked it of him."

Aylin flinched. "That is an uncomfortable thought. Please refrain from painting that image ever again."

"You hate him, don't you?" she said. "It explains much."

"What does it explain?"

"Why you are the way you are," Aylin said. "Your father refused you his love, so you hurt others to numb the pain."

"If I hadn't known you were a woman before, I do now."

"People think women are weak, but men will spend their entire lives nursing a childhood slight," she said.

"Shut up," he said. "Or I'll find a creative way to do it myself."

"I'd like to see you try."

Something flashed in his eyes. A glimmer that was both dark and consuming. Aylin picked up her pace, gesturing quickly at the guard to open the door. She exhaled in relief when the door sealed shut behind her. It smelled like rot inside. Aylin saw that the woman was in a worse state than she'd imagined. Her hair had been torn from her scalp in clumps, and her fingers had been torn off and filled with iron, so they didn't heal. Her eyes were so bruised they were sealed shut.

"I pity you," Aylin said. "Nobody deserves to live a life of pain and torment."

"I was waiting for your return," she said. "You are the only good thing in this cursed place."

"If you tell me where the location of the Court of the Undead is, I will end your life. I will end your misery," she promised.

Aylin drew forth her sabre to assure her that she had the means to return her to God. Salvatore and the council would be enraged by her actions, but it soured her stomach to think that once she left the vampir behind, she would be subject to their torture. She would be Domenico's plaything for decades to come, and perhaps he would pass the tainted torch on to his offspring. Immortality was a curse disguised as a blessing.

A tear slipped from the woman's eye. "You are purer than them. These humans who believe they are morally superior to us while they kill and lie and cheat and rape."

"I will give you peace," Aylin said. "That is my promise to you."

Several moments passed before she nodded.

"It is in the village of the Arefu commune," she said. "A fortress perched on the cliffside. You cannot miss it."

"Thank you," Aylin whispered. She sealed her eyes closed. Aylin knew from Father Lorenzo that only a strike to the heart would end her life. The sabre sunk between her ribs, digging into her flesh. Her pallor grew faint, and her face wrinkled like a date, revealing her true age. Aylin withdrew her blade and wiped it on the cloth of her torn clothes, she then recited a *dua* for her. She hoped she found peace in the hereafter. The world had been far too harsh to her during her last moments.

"Well?" Domenico asked. "Any luck?"

He leaned against the wall; his burly arms wrapped around his torso. His clothes looked strange and ill fitting on him. He drew back the collar as if it were constricting his breathing.

Aylin nodded. "She talked. I know where Yara is."

"I see my ability to break a person is effective," he said, pleased.

Her face scrunched in disgust. "You are a terrible person."

They returned to the room to stare upon the expectant faces of Ilyas, Salvatore, and Cristifano. Leandra placed down cups of tea and a plate of biscuits that instantly caught Aylin's attention. It had a cherry-filled center that made her lick her lips.

"I made a deal with her," Aylin said. "In return for the address."

It was best to get it over with. They wouldn't be pleased that they'd lost their prisoner, but she had the answers they sought. It had to count for something.

"What did you do?" Salvatore demanded.

"She asked for death," Aylin said. "Now she is dead."

They cursed beneath their breaths. Under normal circumstances, Aylin would be pleased to make a bunch of priests curse, but the look on Cristifano's face reminded her far too much of Domenico's. She could see where he got his lovely temper from.

"How dare you?" Cristifano seethed. "We had much to learn about their healing. Perhaps we could have found a means to strengthen ourselves with their blood without transitioning into one of their kind."

"So, you want the benefits of being a monster without the consequences," she snapped. "How holy and pure of you. I'm sure God would approve."

"I say we execute him for refusing to follow direct orders," Cristifano continued, as if she hadn't spoken. His face began to grow blotchy and red as he spoke. Spittle clung to the corners of his lips with every harsh word that parted his poisonous mouth. "Hang him on the charges of sabotage and espionage. It is clear to see he cares for this creature, perhaps he has even fallen in love with her!"

"I killed her," Domenico said without preamble. "So, leave him be."

It grew chillingly silent. Cristifano seemed to shake beneath this admission, and Aylin flinched at the screeching sound of his chair being pulled back.

"Sorry, Father," Domenico said tightly, but it was too late. The crack of Cristifano's hand landing on his cheek echoed along the high ceilings. His ring cut a bloody path down his jaw. Domenico didn't recoil or flinch, as if he had felt it before. As if he had experience with such a gesture.

Aylin felt a burst of anger. It slithered between her bones, and she found herself withdrawing her sabre in a haze of rage. Domenico's hand gripped her wrist, drawing her back.

Cristifano barked a dry laugh. "You protect the prideful little scum." He looked at Aylin with a challenge in his eyes.

"Strike me, boy. I dare you."

"This is enough," Ilyas said.

At the same time, Salvatore said. "Everyone, please sit."

Domenico didn't return to his seat. He grabbed the jug of wine and disappeared out the door.

"Disgrace," Cristifano said.

Aylin wondered why he had covered for her actions. She intended to speak with him later tonight and hopefully gain some answers. It didn't make sense.

"Are you well?" Ilyas whispered.

Aylin nodded.

"She says they hide in a fortress atop a mountain in the Arefu commune," she said.

"Not friendly terrain for an attacker, but a good spot for a stronghold. They may see us coming. We will have to blend in with the terrain," Ilyas said. "Did you ask her for the number of guards? Trained soldiers on hand? Entrance and exit points? Weather conditions? How many steps to reach the clifftop?"

He stared at her expectantly, as if she would have thought of such questions.

"No," she whispered. Shame trickled down her spine. She should have thought to inquire more. She should not have been so weak willed, so desperate for a scrap of information that she forgot to ask the important questions.

"Excellent," Salvatore said dryly. "We are expected to go in blind."

"That boy needs discipline," Cristifano said.

Salvatore sighed. "We will need your help devising a plan, Elijah. I think Borza visited Wallachia before; we will consult with him."

"Do you need my help?" Aylin asked.

"You have done enough," Salvatore said like he was annoyed with her. "Stay behind when we finish. I want a quick word with you."

Aylin waited until all of them left. Ilyas promised he would wait for her outside, but not before throwing Salvatore a warning stare.

"I know Domenico didn't kill her," he said. "He hates the vampir more than you can imagine. He would never grant one peace. His cruelty is not much different from his father's."

"Why didn't you say anything?"

"I'd rather he be my ally than my enemy," he said. "I'm sure you are aware that being his enemy is not an enjoyable experience."

Aylin scoffed. "A miserable experience. I almost lost my ear for it."

"What changed between you both?" he asked curiously. "I know it wasn't my proposed hunting trip that miraculously fixed your rivalry."

"I confided in him during our trip," she said. "He has held on to that piece of me ever since. As if it belongs to him."

Salvatore nodded. "He needs a friend. As you saw, he and his father are often at odds."

"He has driven him to drink like a sailor," she said. "That is far more than simply being at odds."

"I suppose," he said. "Keep an eye on him. He is more impulsive and reckless than you are. Make sure he doesn't get himself killed by his father."

"I will," Aylin said.

And when she whispered the words, she realized that it wasn't a lie to soothe him. She didn't want Domenico to die because of her. In a way, she felt indebted to him after he protected her from his father, and she would pay off this debt if it killed her.

Only then could they return to their rightful roles as each other's nemeses.

XX

ELDAR COULD FEEL his anger steadily rising like a tide. He had seen nothing but red for the last few hours as he attempted to clean up Yara's mess. He had known she was devious, but this? This was pure corruption. Her time spent with the Court of the Undead had transformed her. It had broken her soft shell and revealed the rot that blossomed inside her. A rot that matched his own. If he wasn't so livid, perhaps he could appreciate her unique brand of cunning.

He stood before the Dracul family in Vladislav's private throne room. While his throne did not match the grandiose throne carved by the famed Albanian blacksmith and entirely forged of black enamel that sat in the Great Hall, it still managed to make him look larger than life. Lord Dracul's dark widow's peak was neatly brushed back, and his white claws clicked the hand rest impatiently, as if he tired of the Demircis' scandalous endeavours.

She sat beside Mircea, staring at Eldar coldly, as if her actions were justified. There was no guilt in her brown eyes except the guilt of being caught.

Eldar licked the sharp point of his teeth. A promise of what awaited her once he plotted her demise. It brought him great satisfaction when she shuddered, the barest ripple of her shoulders beneath her red *entari*.

"You stand accused of the murder of August Maleinos," Dracul said, looking bored by the entire ordeal. "Please step forward with the evidence."

A guard stepped forward, his palms cupping Eldar's ring. The family ring he had peeled from his father's dead hand with the iron-carved sigil of the twin scorpions. He didn't know whether to be impressed or outraged. Eldar's face settled into a cold mask, appraising the object as if it were beneath him.

"That ring does not easily slip off. If it was discovered anywhere, it is because it was stolen."

"Where were you last night?" Dracul asked.

"This questioning insults my intelligence," Eldar said. "If I killed him, believe me when I say I would not be caught. I would have him carved up and sunk beneath the Indian Ocean. The Maleinos have had a grudge against my family for decades. And this is another pathetic strike to besmirch my name."

He heard her release a soft breath. Did she think he would reveal her secret? Eldar had every intention of punishing her himself. He would make her regret her lies and schemes. He would reduce her to the faintest echo of the person she had once been.

He would break her.

"Lies!" Pomona roared. She looked like she hadn't fed in days. There were hollow shadows beneath her eyes, and her cheeks were sunken in. Her pale hair lacked luster, and Eldar was pleased to see her so broken. It didn't help that Volkan sat on the opposite side of Pomona. His hand flat on Yara's knee, thumb gently stroking her skin. It enraged Pomona to see him at peace with another woman and stoked her jealousy to a luminescent flame.

Perhaps that was all Pomona had in common with him. Their blind and hungry need to possess and break the object of their fascination. But while she broke her toys in order to keep them, Eldar broke his in order to keep them *away* from him.

"You have no proof beyond my ring," Eldar said.

"This is not the first time your family has disrespected our laws," Dracul said. "We have a code. One that protects those of us at the top. We do not tolerate vultures who will feed on the flesh of their equals."

"You sided with the Maleinos years ago to wrongfully imprison my brother," he said. "Once is a mistake. Twice is an attack."

"Do you threaten me?" Dracul growled. His words seemed to rumble from deep within his chest.

Eldar stared at him, unable to muster a whiff of fear to appease him.

"My apologies," he said. "I only meant to highlight the injustice. The evidence is insubstantial at best and offensive at worse."

Dracul stared at him with undisclosed hatred. Eldar blinked, awaiting his verdict. He didn't have enough to imprison him and certainly not enough to execute him. The doors were drawn open, and he saw Bahiti enter with Akila close behind her. He had extended an invitation to the trial to them. As they were his allies, any action taken against him affected their family as well. Let Dracul see that the young Demirci boys were no longer alone with nothing but their name and their legacy to gain them respect.

Dracul's eyes narrowed. If he made a move against him, then he was moving against two powerful houses. He had always hated alliances that didn't include his family.

Dracul looked at Pomona. At the withered shell of the woman, she had been before she lost that spawn and her precious Titus, her life partner who was now nothing but a faded memory. Dracul must have realized how pathetic she was. How siding with her against Eldar and the Ramose was not a wise decision.

"We will continue to monitor this in case any further evidence crops up," Dracul said tightly. "Remember not to bite the hand that feeds you, Eldar Demirci. Remember my mercy."

"He never disclosed where he was last night," Yara said in a crisp voice. She stood up, smoothing the crinkles of her pretty dress. "I have been a guest of Volkan's the last few days, and I have barely seen Eldar around. I will stand as witness should we proceed with the trial."

"Careful," Eldar growled.

She didn't look him in the eye while she spoke, and he could see Volkan tugging roughly at her dress for her to sit down, but she barely flinched.

"I won't be forced into silence," she said. "I will not stand by while an innocent man's death goes unanswered. While I hold no love for Pomona, I've come to realize that there are worse monsters than a woman scorned. To release Eldar is to bring doom upon ourselves. It is to open ourselves to a monster worse than we can imagine. I see the poison in his eyes. He craves power and he is not afraid to burn us all in his pursuit of it."

"Settle down, mortal," Dracul said with a flash of irritation. "This is a trial, not a performance. Your input is trivial and unnecessary."

Eldar smiled at the flush that creeped up her throat. She finally listened to her superiors and sat down, perched uncomfortably on her seat. When she finally gained the courage to look at him, her eyes were soaked in fear.

Eldar licked his lips and grinned.

He was going to end her.

XXI

SALVATORE DECIDED THEY would march three days from now. He had disappeared to the city for a week in preparation for their attack. When he returned, he had a handful of horses and a new shipment of weapons and armor that the men picked through with delight. It was almost December, and a slight chill swept the air, but it was nothing like the brutal Turkish winters.

Aylin felt dread as they prepared for war. As they tried on boots and sheaths of metal to protect their forearms and necks from the bites of vampir. The men cheered and celebrated the bloodshed that awaited them, but Aylin knew that not everyone who stood here would return whole. It was a somber thought, and when Borza dragged them from their quaint estate to a local *bacari* to drink and sing away their woes, Ilyas and Aylin merely went along for the company. And because Borza refused to let them stay behind.

Aylin felt Pietro's arm swing onto her shoulder as he belched loud enough to startle her.

"Cheers, to the prettiest boy in our ranks," he said loudly. "If you drink enough and close one eye and tilt your head just slightly to the right, why, one can imagine you are a girl with a terrible haircut!" Pietro followed his own slurred instruction, turning his head and closing an eye as if to prove his point. If he were not so terribly drunk, Aylin might have been alarmed.

Domenico smiled with a lazy raise of his cup. "Cheers to pretty men."

"We should not have come to this depraved place," Ilyas muttered. He sat stiffly in his chair looking ill at ease in the cloistered space. "God will judge us for this."

"God has better people to judge than the morally corrupt," Domenico said.

"Speak for yourself," Ilyas said. "Do you even know what drink you are on?"

Domenico shrugged, taking a lingering sip from his cup.

Pilgrims, travellers, and foreign merchants loitered around, drinking and eating their bland bread dipped in onion stew while raucous chatter and drunken singing—mostly Pietro in his cracked, miserable voice—filled the room. Ilyas's eyes constantly flickered to the door, assessing for invisible threats, and occasionally glaring at Domenico when he spoke to Aylin.

"Come here," Domenico said, curling two fingers.

"I'll pass," she said. She had wanted to speak with him about the incident with his father. To let him know she would pay her debt even if she hadn't asked him to take the blame for the vampir's death. But he had been avoiding her or so she presumed. He would train in private and not attend their shared dinners. And now, when his eyes were glazed with drink, was certainly not the time. He turned away from her to look upon a corseted woman in a red dress with black lace trimming. Domenico tossed a golden *zecchino* in the air, which the woman caught gracefully. She slid into his lap, curling her arms around his neck.

"Lucky bastard," Pietro said, leaning forward to whisper in her ear. "Fancy Franca. Never met a pickier whore than her. She never accepts my coin, but gladly snatches Domenico's. I reckon she likes riding—"

"Enough," Ilyas said sharply. "We'd like to keep our food in our stomachs."

Aylin looked curiously at her. She was pretty, with long raven hair and rosy cheeks. Domenico licked her neck like a rabid animal, but his eyes were locked on Aylin while he devoured her. She felt her skin tighten, and her heart burned in her chest as if it had been lit aflame. She shifted in her chair, uncomfortable at the way he looked at her while he kissed and bit Franca's neck, hanging on to her skin like a wolf. His pale hand lay flat on her stomach, the four silver rings on his hand glinting in the light, preventing her from rising, although she looked like she was pleased to be in the presence of the devil. And that was exactly what Domenico was. He was the devil.

"I tire of this place," Ilyas said, slamming down his fist hard enough to make the table rattle. He grabbed Aylin's elbow, raising her to her feet.

"Slow down," she said, but Ilyas wasn't listening. His jaw was clenched, and he walked with such speed that if she tripped over her feet, she would be swallowing a mouthful of dirt. "We didn't even tell Borza we were leaving. He might look for us."

"They are all too drunk to notice," he said tightly. "Especially Domenico, who can't help but look at you as if he were picturing your head on that woman in his lap. If he weren't so obviously drunk, I would knock his teeth out."

"Don't be ridiculous," she said. "He wouldn't dream of a fifteen-year-old boy when he had that beautiful raven-haired woman in his arms. Did you see her lovely bosom?"

"No, Aylin. I did not," he said between gritted teeth. "And you are *not* a fifteen-year-old boy; he knows that," he said, turning her to face him. His blue eyes locked on her. "And his obsession with you has grown uncontrollably ever since he found out."

"It is harmless," she said, waving her hand at his concerns. She had poisoned Domenico and attempted to knock his chair out, so he cracked his skull in the fall, and he hadn't retaliated against her. That was a good sign. "He's been tolerable ever since. Don't get me wrong, I ache to kill him most days, but he protected me before his father."

Ilyas frowned. "What do you speak of?"

"Do you think Domenico would grant his prisoner, whom he had been torturing for weeks, any respite?" she asked. "I killed her. It was a mercy kill."

"He is manipulating you, Aylin," Ilyas said slowly, as if she were a child unaware of the danger that lurked in the world. "You are too blind to see it."

"I never said I forgive him, but right now his company is a lot more preferable than yours," she said. She didn't like his tone. He spoke to her as if she were an unworldly woman who didn't know any better, as if it were his presence in her life that protected her from all the evil this world had to offer. As if she would break and crumble without him.

Aylin spun on her heels, prepared to walk back to the estate alone. He slowly walked behind her at a leisurely pace, enough for her to feel his presence without overwhelming her. He didn't speak a word, and she could feel the bristle of his anger scratching her skin. He had no right to be angry with her. None at all.

"You are going in the wrong direction," Ilyas said.

Aylin huffed in annoyance and turned right. The forest was a labyrinth that she would never understand. Salvatore had been clear that if they were going to waste their time with idle chatter and drink, they couldn't use any of the horses in the stable, who required rest before the battle commenced. So, the lot of them had walked to the *bacari*.

"Other way," Ilyas said. She hated that he had the gall to sound amused.

Before she could turn, he placed his big hands on her shoulders and maneuvered her till she faced the right direction.

"I can find my own way home, thank you," she said stiffly.

Ilyas sighed. "I don't wish to quarrel, Aylin."

Even with the quick pace of her legs, Ilyas seemed to easily swallow up the space with little effort.

"Then you shouldn't have implied that I was an idiot," she said.

"I said no such thing," he said.

"I never said you said it. I said you *implied* it."

"This is all so childish."

Aylin ignored him. If he thought her walking off was childish, then he had never experienced her cold shoulder. Ilyas caught her by the waist, his hand settling on the fabric of her tunic.

"Your hair looks pretty combed that way," he said.

Aylin narrowed her eyes. She had combed her hair tonight with a neat middle part. And she had thought she looked rather dapper for a boy.

"You can't bribe me with compliments."

He sighed. "I'm sorry. I can't think clearly when he looks at you like that. It makes me want to wring his neck."

"Jealousy does not suit you."

"I'm not jealous!"

"That's something a jealous person would say," she said with a teasing smile.

"I've forgotten you can be an insufferable brat sometimes," he said.

"And I've forgotten how jealous you are!"

Ilyas rushed for her, and she gasped when she felt the poke of his fingers between her ribs. He hadn't properly tickled her in years. Not after she had wet her pants at fourteen when he hadn't taken her pleas seriously.

"You said you wouldn't do this again," she said, struggling to escape him. Slips of giggles escaped her, caught between sharp gasps. "Ilyas, think of the incident!"

"I'll let you borrow my pants," he said with a smug smile. His fingers danced between her stomach and ribs, leaving no part of her untended. Her eyes stung with tears, and her shrieks were growing louder with each passing moment. "Admit that I am superior to *him*. Now and always."

"No," she said. But that was clearly not the right answer, because Ilyas only heightened his assault until she had tripped and fallen to the ground. He gave her no reprieve, bending down to tend to her as if she were a playful kitten in need of his touch.

"You are better than him," she said in a rush of words. "Better than all men. Please have mercy," Aylin begged.

"I like it when you beg," Ilyas said, his hand falling flat on her stomach while she lay there struggling to catch her breath. "Did you wet yourself this time?"

"You promised you wouldn't bring that up," she said with narrowed eyes.

Ilyas smiled with raised hands. "My apologies. You won't hear me say it again."

"I hate you," she said.

"You only wish you did."

Aylin stared at him. At his blue eyes that looked pale and translucent in the dark, wavering like an apparition come to haunt her. That familiar longing curled in her stomach, begging to be freed. Until the need to seal the space between them and feel his breath on her, and his warmth seeping into her skin, grew unbearable. His hand was heavy on her stomach, and she could feel the subtle flex of his fingers, slightly gripping the fabric as if he felt as uncontrolled and unstable as her.

"Ilyas." She said his name, loose and breathy on her tongue, as if her soul were wrapped in the whisper of his name.

Ilyas straightened, and he ripped his hand away from her, as if he had been burned. He stood up so fast it made her dizzy.

"Come, it's late," he said tightly. "There may be wolves in this forest."

From where Aylin sat, there was only one wolf she saw. And it was Ilyas.

⸻

They were awakened at dawn to march to Wallachia through the Balkan Mountains. They assembled outside in preparation for their journey. The exhausted men who were still not recovered from a night of drinking and revelry began to don their armor with blurry eyes and languid fingers. In the corner, Domenico lay flat on his back with a wet rag on his eyes and a grimace on his lips. Aylin skipped over to him in a good mood. The thought of being reunited with her sister in two weeks was enough to make her chest clench with joy. Aylin yanked out a blade of grass and drifted it along his lip. His mouth twitched, and she continued to trace it on his eyelids before his fair brows furrowed in annoyance, and he caught her wrist in a punishing grip. He lifted his head and the rag slipped to his lap.

"My lady has come to rouse me," he murmured.

"Shut it," she snapped, looking around to see if anyone heard him. But most of the men moved sluggishly, preparing their horses, and fitting their weapons.

"I'm pleased to see you so discomforted," she said. "You shouldn't drink so much or use the plight of poor women to bribe them to take you to bed. Everyone knows that no woman would willingly bed you."

"So nasty so early in the morning," Domenico said with a faint smile. "You almost sound like my father."

Aylin's smile dropped. She was nothing like Cristifano.

"Don't like that comparison, do you?" he asked, stretching his arms behind him. His tunic rose, revealing a sliver of skin, and she quickly averted her gaze. "Try to hold your tongue then."

Aylin stood up, but he caught her ankle until her knee buckled and she fell back down on the grass.

"Release me," she said.

"We will share a tent tonight," he said. "Pietro snores, and I intend to be well rested for the battle ahead. He also rarely bathes, and I quite like how you smell." He leaned forward, brushing his nose along her collarbone. "Like rosewood." He flicked out his tongue in a playful lick that brought goosebumps to her flesh.

"And you taste far better," he said in a heavy whisper. He had maneuvered her, so they remained hidden from the men.

"I'm not sharing a tent with anyone other than my brother," she said in a feeble voice. She hated how he had stolen her wit, turning her into this weak, blushing maid. Her back straightened, and her eyes were cold when she looked at him. "I will never share a tent with you."

"It is terrible how close you are to saving your sister, and how it can all be ruined with a single word," Domenico said. "I would hate it if your poor sister became a casualty of the vampir because her sister was too selfish to save her."

Aylin felt her hands tighten into fists. "What have I done to deserve your ire? You've hated me from the moment I arrived, and you've done everything in your power since then to make me miserable. Why must you continue to hurt me when I've done nothing to you? *Nothing.*"

Aylin hated that her voice cracked. That she minded if this idiot wished to destroy her. She hadn't cared when it had been mindless hatred, blind rage that fuelled his dislike, but she couldn't pinpoint what this was. With one breath, he protected her from his father, while he blackmailed her in the next. He confused her and he sickened her, and he made her skin prickle in unease and dread and something else that she could not name.

"It is not for you to understand me," Domenico said, brushing the grass stains from his breeches. "Only to accept me." He pressed a cold kiss to her forehead and rose to his feet. Aylin felt her hand instinctively reach for the hilt of her sabre.

He would be lucky if she resisted the urge to slit his throat in his sleep.

Sweat dripped down her back as their horses trotted through the forest on their third day of travels. Salvatore took the lead with Cristifano to his right and Ilyas to his left. They spoke in hushed whispers, and Aylin felt a spark of envy at how easily Salvatore had become friends with Ilyas. Always leaning their heads together and conspiring against the vampir. Or maybe Ilyas was ignoring her as he tended to do when they got close, as if he had to physically distance himself from her to smother the fire that brewed between them.

"Does anybody wish to hear a limerick?' Pietro asked.

"Is it filthy?" Domenico asked from where he sat upon his black steed. His shorn hair twinkled in the dark, and his words escaped him in a thick fog. A light layer of snow encased the ground, not enough to make them worry, but enough to slow down their pace.

Pietro looked thoughtful. "No."

"Then we'll pass," Domenico said.

Borza laughed in disbelief. "How was Fancy Franca? Don't tell me she's the woman who stole your heart."

"No," Domenico said. "Merely a distraction."

"Well, what is your woman like?" Pietro asked. "Big bosomed? Dark hair? Fair hair?"

"Short hair," Domenico said. "Very short. Almost boyish, but I find it rather charming."

Aylin stiffened. He couldn't be speaking of her, could he? If he was, it was clearly a tactic to get under her skin, and it was working—she was hanging on his every word.

"She's unlike any woman I've met before," Domenico said. His eyes raised to her, burning her from within, making her bones writhe miserably beneath her skin. "And nobody, not even God, will take her from me. I will kill any man who tries. I'll remove their eyes and fuck their empty sockets before I cut each finger and shove it down their throat until they choke."

Aylin sucked in a sharp breath. Borza smiled, amused by his words, while Pietro looked intrigued by this mystery woman.

Aylin picked up her pace, cutting through the line to make it through to the front. She could feel his gaze on her nape. But she didn't turn around to face him. Aylin's eyes remained fixed ahead of her for the remainder of the trek.

<hr>

"Can we speak?" Aylin asked Ilyas.

He was in the middle of pitching their tent, and she figured now was the best time to tell him he would be sharing the space with Pietro.

Ilyas didn't quite meet her eyes, and she wanted to apologize, but she didn't know what to say. How could she apologize for her feelings? They existed inside her whether she wanted them to or not. There were many times she wished she could carve them out, but God had yet to answer her prayers. It was a cruel twist of fate that she desired the one man who would never break his vows for her.

"I'll be sharing Domenico's tent," she said. "He requested my presence."

"He is not the sultan," Ilyas snapped. "You do not have to answer
to him."

"He threatened to tell Salvatore about me," she whispered harshly.
"What was I to do?"

Ilyas ran a frustrated hand through his brown hair.

"Tonight alone," he said. "You return to me tomorrow."

Aylin hesitated. "Perhaps it is best if I share with him for the remainder of the journey. I understand that you may prefer your own
space."

They hadn't exchanged more than four words that day, and Aylin
worried that her growing feelings and this blossoming tension between them would ruin her oldest friendship. She didn't want them
to return to Constantinople at odds. She was beginning to accept
that nothing would come of it. She could bury it deep inside her. She
would bury it deep inside her.

His face softened. "I am not upset at you, Aylin. If it seems that I
am distant, it is only for me to regain my bearings and learn to be
around you without this anguish inside me, and this guilt that con-
sumes me."

"I don't want you to feel guilty," she said. "I want you to be happy."

And she wanted that for herself too. It was time for them to stop
sharing space and touching each other so freely. Aylin gave him a curt
nod that was a bit more awkward than she intended and turned back
to help with the setup.

"If I am not sleeping here, why did you made me set up the entire
tent?" Pietro snapped. "By myself, may I add."

Domenico shrugged. "It's been a long day and I am exhausted."

"What of Aydin?" he asked. "He is sharing the space; he could have
helped."

"He is tired as well," Domenico said. "Good night, Pietro."

He didn't wait for another word before diving beneath the flaps. Aylin gave the red-faced Pietro an apologetic grin, which he ignored. Their bellies were warm from the fried rabbit they ate, and she was prepared to collapse in a heap of limbs. Domenico unraveled a single bedroll.

"We will have to share the bedroll," he said. "It seems we are a few short."

"How convenient," she said dryly.

"I am not pleased by the circumstance either," he said. "I am rather big and will have half my limbs hanging on the cold ground." Aylin kicked off her boots and collapsed on the bedroll. It was thin, and she winced at the impact.

"Did you think it was a feather bed?" Domenico chuckled.

"Be a gentleman and sleep on the ground," Aylin ordered.

Domenico pushed her till she lay on one half, before he spread his massive frame beside her. A possessive hand rested on her hip like a shackle.

Aylin faced the opposite side, blinking in anger. She could feel him, feel the ripple of muscle beneath his tunic and the stroke of his breath along her nape. And that hand, that insufferable hand branded her skin like scorched iron.

"If I knew my touch silenced you so beautifully, I wouldn't resist touching you so often," he said. "Especially when your mouth runs off without you."

"I'm not afraid of you," she said. "You may know my secret, but you don't know me, and you never will. We will never be anything more than enemies."

"I like when you flirt with me," Domenico said. "It makes me burn with delight."

"What is it that you want from me?" Aylin turned to face him and regretted it the moment their noses brushed. He was so close to her; their chests were pressed together. If he hadn't known she was a girl before, he certainly did now. She could feel the steady beat of his heart behind his ribs, beating in tandem with her own.

"Why did you protect me from your father? Why do you keep telling the men of this mystery woman who belongs to you? Why did you imply that it was me? What do you want?"

Her chest rose and fell in anger. Her fists curled to her sides. She didn't know what game he was playing.

"It is rather simple," Domenico said. His eyes darkened further the longer he looked at her. Staring at every inch of her face as if he were committing it to memory. "I want you."

Every word was a painful stab to her chest. A reminder that what he felt for her had grown too uncontrollable to break. That his feelings would consume her if she let them fester. She would have to put a stop to it, end it while it was still a nub and before it grew into a poisonous flower.

"To possess you, to care for you, to mold you beneath my fingers till you are as obsessed with me as I am you. I never understood it when you first arrived, but it makes sense now. You were made for me. I've always been drawn to you, to hurt you, to protect you, to desire you."

"What is it that you see in me?" she asked. Her words morbidly curious.

"I see how loyal you are to that bastard and how he pushes you away because your love frightens him. I see how much you care for your sister and how you would do anything for her. I see how you look at me with hatred but also curiosity. How you want to learn more about me, but you're scared. Ask me a question, anything, and I will answer honestly."

Aylin didn't know what to make of his words. The comment about

Ilyas hurt but it was the truth. Everything he said was true, even if it stung to hear such sharp observations. She expected as much from him. He had been watching her avidly since she arrived. More so when he learned her secret.

"Why did you protect me from your father?" Aylin whispered. Her lips brushed his stubble, and she realized how intimate their position was. How she should put some space between them. But when the men outside had slumbered and the only sound that filled the air was the chirp of the crickets, Aylin found it easy to peel away his mask, and to read him more carefully.

"I would have killed him if he raised a hand to you," he said. "It never mattered to me if he slapped me around. Since my mother died, he hasn't been himself and truthfully neither have I. She was our light, and when she left there was only darkness. I learned to accept the dark, but I would never let it touch you."

"I'm sorry that he hurt you," she said. "You didn't deserve that. You didn't deserve Cristifano."

"I thought it would please you that he put me in my place," he said with a raised brow.

"I'm not a monster, Domenico," she said. "I wouldn't wish that on anyone. Not even you. A parent is supposed to love and nurture, and to take care of you. I'm sorry that you were deprived of that."

"And you wonder why I want you," he said, raising a hand to cup her cheek.

"Nothing can come of us," she said. "I don't forgive you. I don't think I ever will."

She didn't even bother mentioning that she would be returning home to Constantinople. Or that her father would never approve of her returning with a foreigner who shared neither their faith nor culture. But most importantly, she would never forgive him for his cruelty when they had first met. For the way he had frightened her and hurt her so callously, or how he blackmailed her so shamelessly after.

"I don't need your forgiveness," he said. "I just need *you*."

"Good night, Domenico," she said, turning her back to him.

She sealed her eyes shut, ignoring his arm that draped heavily atop her waist. She was worried about the secrets he would confess that would make her pity the broken boy who had long been abused by Cristifano. The one that clung to her as if she were the answer to his prayers.

She didn't want to see him as anything less than a monster. Even if it was easy to pretend in the dark that he was nothing more than a sad boy.

XXII

ELDAR RELISHED THE fear that filled her and the way her bones stiffened anytime he entered the room. He was almost hesitant to make a move against her. There was something lovely about watching someone exist in fear. The constant turn of her neck to see if it was, he who entered the room. The eyes that couldn't quite meet his own. The way she chewed her nails rather innocently at the dinner table, as if she hadn't had a man killed and pinned it on him in the same instant.

For some odd reason, she continued to stay with them. He suspected it was to do as Mircea said and keep a close eye on them. It was easy to see that she had drawn a line in the mud. He now saw with clarity that she did not stand alongside him, which made her a liability. One who would need to be put in her place.

He found Thaddeus lounging beneath the silver fir tree. Long limbs stretched in languor while a pretty girl sat in his lap and a fair-haired boy offered his neck as a fountain.

"Rise, Thaddeus," Eldar said with a snap of his fingers. "The time for rest is over. I have a task for you. Three, to be specific. If you are efficient, I will return your pesky heart to you."

Thaddeus raised a brow. "You won't let me finish."

Eldar glared at him, and Thaddeus sighed, patting the girl's cheek affectionately while he waved away the boy.

"Do you ever get tired of being *you?*" Thaddeus asked. "Going around barking orders, plotting your secret plots, and debating whether to kill or fuck little Yara."

Eldar stepped forward till their noses brushed. "Don't make me punish you for your insolence."

"Funny of you to think I wouldn't enjoy it," he said with a wide grin.

The deviant *would* enjoy it. It was the only reason Eldar hadn't had him dragged back to their family home and locked in the cellar below.

"I require a finger. A human one, male and brown skinned. Not young but old, around fifty," Eldar said.

Thaddeus wrinkled his nose. "I'm supposed to cut off an old man's finger?"

"Precisely," he said. "Once the task is complete, you will wrap it in a box. An expensive one with black velvet trimming and a pretty bow. With a note that reads, 'One down and nine more to go.' Make sure you sign it with my initials."

"And who is it to be sent to?" he asked.

"Leave it on Yara's bed. She sleeps in Volkan's old room for now."

"Is that not a bit...well, sadistic?" he asked. "You clearly intend for her to think it is someone she loves."

"Her father," Eldar said. "It is a reminder for her not to betray me again."

"God help anyone who betrays you," Thaddeus said under his breath.

The celebration of Eldar's betrothal was a mad affair. Yara could hear the laughter and chatter outside her bedroom as she dressed. There were two boxes on her bed. One was small, and when she opened it, she was delighted to find a beautiful silver choker. Of two scorpions intertwined. Their eyes were made of polished onyx and encircled in ivory. The note from Volkan brought a smile to her face, and she didn't even quite mind his arrogance.

I want to see my jewels on your throat when you sing for me. I want everyone to know that you belong to the Demircis.

-Your Beloved

There was a second gift. A big black box with a lace bow, covered in shiny velvet. She read the note before she opened the lid, staring at the strange and cryptic remark with the initials E.D.

She cracked open the lid, and a scream bubbled up her throat at the sight of the severed finger. She closed the lid, taking several deep breaths. He had warned her that he'd hurt her father if she stepped out of line. And she had made a clear move against him a week ago. Tears stung her eyes, and a choked sob escaped her. She slumped to the ground, feeling her chest cleave in half. She wanted to crawl in bed and weep the night away, but she knew that was what *he* wanted. He wanted to frighten her. To remind her of the little girl she had been when she arrived. The one who cowered from shadows and waited for her big sister to protect her instead of learning to dance with the monsters.

It felt like hours had passed when she finally wiped her tears and picked up the gilded swan masque she was to wear with her ivory dress. Volkan had told her that they would all be in masque and costume.

Yara stepped out of the bedroom to find a crowd of bodies, spinning as they danced. Everyone was in stunning dresses and masques with bustling feathers and jeweled foreheads. Some wore frightening masques while others were extravagant. Only the blood slaves' faces were unconcealed. They walked around with diamond-encrusted leashes around their throats and silk blindfolds with the eyes cut out for them to see. One lay in the middle of the table like a pagan sacrifice, naked limbs sprawled open with an apple in his mouth. Almost as if he were a fountain dripping with blood while they held their chalices beneath his ankles and wrists. Her heart went out to the poor creatures. Silk strappings unravelled from the ceiling and lithe woman spun around the room, the curl of their toes brushing shoulders. In the corner were people perched over smoking pipes. The bitter scent of tobacco and opium stained the air. It was a night filled with hedonism and wickedness. A night to unwind and give in to one's desire.

Yara had been excited for tonight. It had been impossible to be anything but while Volkan regaled her with tales of his infamous feasts and celebrations. But as she walked around the candlelit room, she only felt a strange numbness. It struck her that she had not a single friend in this room. Nobody cared if she was hurting or dead. She was just another concealed face in the sea of people. She had nobody to confide in about the wicked act Eldar had performed. Nobody to soothe the ravaged kernel that held her heart. Her throat tightened, and it took everything inside her to not break down in the middle of the floor.

She saw Volkan standing by the wall, staring at the crowd like a sultan surveying his subjects. He wore the mask of a white wolf, and his cloak was drawn over his head. His black eyes were focused on his brother. Across the room, Eldar stood beside his betrothed wearing a similar mask—a black wolf. His betrothed was beautiful, slim, and tall with raven hair and almond eyes and smooth brown skin.

Anger pulsed in her veins at the sight of him enjoying himself while her father recovered from his mutilation. Bile crawled up her throat to think of him laughing and drinking while she stood there, miserable and broken. She wanted him to see her, to see that his terrible gift hadn't broken her spirit. It had made her only more determined to be loyal to Prince Mircea. More desperate to discover his secrets and have him brought before Dracul again for his betrayal. It hadn't broken her; it had made her stronger.

"You've thrown quite the celebration," she said to Volkan, unable to hide how impressed she was by it all.

"You think so?" he asked.

"It's not like anything I've ever seen," she said.

"No, I don't think the Ottomans would dare anger God with this display of gluttony and sin," he said.

Yara scoffed. Her finger absently traced her throat. "Thank you for the necklace. It was a far better gift than your brother's."

Volkan looked at the scorpions twisted around her neck. His eyes darkened, and she assumed he was pleased by the sight of it.

"What did he do?"

Yara thought of the finger, and of how her baba's finger had stroked her hair when she was frightened of the dark and held her hand when they went to the mosque at noon. And how Eldar had taken a piece of him as if he were an animal made to be carved. As if the sultan hadn't taken much from him already. He had lost more because of her. Yara would never forgive herself for putting him in danger. She would be careful from now onwards.

"I don't want to talk about it," she said with a shudder. "You won't mind if I don't sing tonight, will you? I know I promised but I...I don't think I can do it."

"It is fine," he said.

She turned to face him, and Yara felt a heavy dose of gratitude.

For everything. From saving her from Pomona to being an excellent host. He had brought her clothes and jewels from her bedroom and had his cook make her the finest delicacies. Even though he couldn't taste whether the food was good or bad. He had gifted her with this extravagant necklace, and he hadn't fed from her, even when she could see the hunger in his eyes. Even when she saw his muscles shake with the need to plunge his teeth into her delicate skin. He was changing, for her.

"I won't feed from you unless you let me," Volkan had told her the other day. "Does that please you, my sweet wolfling?"

"That you are practicing basic human decency? No, Volkan, it appalls me."

"You are a difficult woman to please."

"And you are a wretched beast."

It had been said in jest, but once her words had settled in her throat, she could not shake off the look in his eyes. The way he looked at her like he was thinking of feeding on more than just her blood, as if he were thinking of feeding on her soul.

Yara stared at him, and she boldly pressed her hand to his pale throat. She felt the ripple of him swallowing, and she thought of the night of the kidnapping, when Pomona had forced them to kiss. The way he had kissed her with abandon. She wanted to feel that again. To feel less alone. To feel wanted and desired. Even if she knew he was just as terrible as all of them. Even if she knew he could turn on her in the blink of an eye.

She wanted to feel something uncontrolled by Pomona. Something that belonged to her alone. She didn't want Pomona to claim any piece of her. Not even her first kiss. Yara would redo it. She would reclaim her stolen kiss.

Yara stood on her toes and pressed her mouth to his lips. For a split second, he stood as rigid as a statue. His lips were nothing but a firm, hard line beneath her mouth. But then something in him shifted, and he gripped her neck roughly, claws scraping her skin, digging deep enough to bruise. He spun her till she was the one pressed against the wall and lifted her violently, so she was pinned by the hand on her neck while the other gripped her thigh.

His mouth devoured her with a brutality that had been lacking the night they first kissed. That night he had been desperate. But tonight, his kiss was angry, almost as if he were punishing her. It was not delicate, but ruthless and consuming, as if he sought to destroy her. Yara felt her heart race and stomach tighten. It was wrong of her to desire a man who was not her husband, but she was consumed by a need so overwhelming it swallowed her guilt. She felt the sharp prick of his teeth slicing her bottom lip and then the tingling pressure of him sucking the blood clean. Yara drew back to catch her breath, and her lips parted in surprise. During their feral kiss, his cloak had slipped from his head and his dark hair had unspooled like a thread.

"Eldar," she breathed.

"I see why my brother is fond of you," he said, wiping her blood from the corner of his mouth and sucking the taste from his thumb. "If that is how you welcome him, then I can understand his obsession at last."

"How dare you!" she said, her voice shaking. "How dare you trick me."

"You are rather easy to trick," he said. "It required no great effort on my end."

Yara slapped him, the sound reverberating around them. His dark hair fell rather poetically on his face, and when he looked back at her Yara had the strange urge to flee, but she was still trapped by his body. By his hand that had returned to wrap around her throat, and the other one that squeezed her thigh in warning. His nostrils flared.

"If you do that again, I'll make you wish you were dead," he warned.

"You hurt my baba. You deserve far worse than a slap," she hissed. "You deserve to die a miserable, lonely death."

"You didn't want me dead a minute ago when your tongue was shoved down my throat and your hips were grinding on my legs," Eldar said shamelessly.

She could feel the stain of shame crawl up her throat. She would pray tonight, pray for her actions, and pray for her foolishness.

"I thought you were Volkan, and you know that."

"I think you knew it was me," he whispered in her ear. "I think you are a liar."

Yara scoffed and pushed him away from her. She slipped past him and found herself on the balcony, gasping for air. Her finger gripped the trellis as she attempted to soothe her ravaged heart. She felt like a cup filled to the brim with fear and hopelessness and this rabid desire, and one more drop would see her come undone.

I think you knew it was me.

Had she known it was him? Secretly? Subconsciously? Yara shook her head. She wouldn't let him taint her with his allegations. She didn't *want* to kiss him. And she would never kiss him again.

"Where have you been?" a soft, feminine voice inquired. Her masque was drawn over her eyes, and her intricate braids were pooled on her head like a crown. "Mircea was worried about you."

Yara stared at Zuri and confided in her the events of the past few days. After they had killed Augustus together, it felt as though they were bound by the gruesome affair. Yara trusted her more than anyone in this cursed place, and it felt good to unburden herself.

"Volkan protected me," she said. "I don't want him to be punished for Titus' death."

"Only if Pomona pushes for an investigation will we have to review it. If not, then we'll put it to bed," Zuri said.

"Eldar's out for my blood," Yara said. "He hurt my father."

"Eldar is a powerful enemy," she said. "I fear this will be the first of many attacks to follow. You will have to keep your chin up and handle his torment with grace. Do not plot against him until you are certain you are strong enough to win."

Yara nodded, staring off into the distance.

"Is there something else that weighs on you?" Zuri asked gently.

"I miss home," she whispered. "I feel as though I may crack under the weight of longing."

"It can be frightening being somewhere new around people who feed on misery," she said. "Mircea turned me when I was a few years older than you. It took me many years to adjust to this world and to the life of a vampir. Yet you are expected to do so in a matter of months. Keep your chin up. Give Mircea what he is looking for, and he will honor his word. He will free you from Eldar Demirci."

Yara nodded. The sooner she found out what Eldar was hiding, the sooner she could go home.

She had failed once, but she had learned from her mistakes.

She would not fail again.

⸻ ⋆⁂⋆ ⸻

It was time to end this blood feud. Eldar was going to kill Pomona. She would come after Volkan. If not today, then tomorrow. It was his duty as the head of the Demirci clan to protect his brother. He wouldn't let her vile plans come to fruition. He wouldn't let her punish Volkan or *her*. Yara was his to break.

He drifted a hand across his mouth and licked his lips to savor her taste. He hadn't expected her to kiss him. And while the kiss had not been intended for him, Eldar hadn't felt an ounce of guilt when he had stolen it, molding her beneath his firm hands and adjusting her to fit his pleasure.

He saw Pomona's blond hair drifting in the dark. She was taller than most women, so it wasn't difficult to pinpoint her in the growing crowd. He drew up his hood and crossed the room toward her.

"Do you miss him?" Eldar asked.

Her head spun around to face him. Fangs bared in warning.

"Titus, that is?" he asked. "Or perhaps your dead child."

Pomona lunged, and his hand ripped through her chest. It clasped her heart, wrapping around the dead flesh. Her mouth parted in shock. It was mayhem on the floor, and nobody knew his hand was wrapped around Pomona's heart. Among the swaying bodies and feasting folk, they fit in, nestled together like lovers. The murder of Pomona was not an entirely selfless act to protect his brother and the willful Yara. He needed the sustenance of feeding on her heart. The heart of a trueborn was filled with power that was cultivated by their vast lifespans. And he needed to be stronger to take down Dracul. He needed more power to unseat him.

"You will never harm a hair on my brother's head again," he whispered. "Nor look upon the human girl. You will *never* touch what's mine again."

Eldar ripped out her heart, and it felt glorious to watch her eyes seal shut and her body slump forward. He let her fall with a dull thud and disappeared into the shadows. In the privacy of his room, he looked upon his hoard. An immortal heart torn from the chest of one of the trueborn was a delicacy that surpassed even the rarest meat. It soothed a dark craving within him. His father had been his first, and this was to be his second.

Eldar didn't hesitate to eat her vile heart. With each bite he could feel his body thrumming with power. Her power seeped into his blood like poison. His veins darkened with thin black lines, intertwining like clasped hands beneath his pale skin. In the gilded frame of the mirror, he watched his pupils expand, covering his eyes in a shell of black. His teeth elongated into thin needle points, and his claws extended far longer than he had ever seen. They were now inky black at the bottom and white at the curved tips.

The door to his bedroom swung open, and Volkan entered. His masque was lifted to his hair.

"I've forgotten how much I missed when we'd switch places. It was fun flirting with your bride. What a chaste, innocent creature!" Volkan halted in his tracks. His eyes widened in horror. "What is wrong with you?"

"Pomona is dead," Eldar said. His voice sounded strange and raspy.

"That doesn't explain why you look like *that!*" he said. "What have you done?"

Eldar licked his fingers, marveling at the height of his senses. He could smell, taste, and hear *everything*. It was unlike anything he had ever felt before, heightened beyond all measure. He could hear the faint chatter in the servants' hall three floors below and smell the waft of pine and oak in the forest that shrouded the fortress.

Volkan crouched before him. His finger trailed the dark veins on his fist. When he gazed up at him, he looked unbearably sad.

"You haven't been yourself since I was imprisoned," he said softly. "I know that you hunger for power. But it is unnatural to devour the power of our dead. Beyond that, it is dangerous, Eldar. Many who've fallen down this path haven't survived. You do not merely eat their power. You eat their madness. You eat the years of their life filled with pain and suffering until you are more beast than man."

Volkan gripped his chin. "I cannot lose you, Eldar. Not to your ambition and not to this path you have fallen upon."

"Nothing will befall me," Eldar promised.

"If you fail in your pursuit of power, Vladislav will wipe out our entire line. Us and all those we've sired," Volkan said. "Is that a risk you are willing to take?"

"Yes," he said. "I swore to take down the Maleinos and Dracul.

One is gone and the other stands. I will not rest till they have both fallen."

"And what if you are gone before that happens?"

"Then you will finish my crusade," Eldar said. He could feel his gums twitch as his teeth slid into place, and he sheathed his claws. He could feel his pupils shift, but the cursed veins remained.

"Is it still on my face?" Eldar asked.

"Afraid you look ugly now?" Volkan teased.

Eldar turned to the mirror to find that his face remained untouched. But the black veins ran down his body and neck like a curse.

"You'll have to wear gloves and a high-collared tunic like an orderly priest," Volkan said. "It serves you right for tempting fate."

Eldar flicked his nose, enjoying the grimace of pain that crossed his face.

"Why did you give me hell for killing Titus? And then go ahead and kill Pomona?" Volkan asked, rubbing his nose. "And I will break your finger if you do that again."

"Pomona was a loose end. Besides, she is not the only trueborn who died tonight," he said.

"Stop with the cryptic nonsense and give me a straight answer, Eldar."

"I had Defne kill Akila's cousin Kosey," he said. "Two deaths in the same night that are vastly unrelated will draw forth suspects that don't include us both. It will be assumed that the same person killed both, and nobody will suspect that I had a hand in the death of my betrothed's family. So, I will not fall under suspicion."

"But I was just sharing a bowl of milk custard with him," Volkan said. "Just an hour past."

"Don't pout," Eldar said. "This was necessary to protect us."

And Defne, his best assassin, would bring him the heart of Kosey. It would be the last puzzle piece to ensure his power. To satiate him.

His third heart might even give him the strength to physically challenge Dracul as was customary. Every few decades it was said that a trueborn would challenge Dracul to a fight to the death in the hopes of claiming the title of Undying King. Because Dracul was arrogant he would always accept. Eldar intended to challenge him to a fight to the death. He refused to confide this to his brother who would seek to dissuade him.

"I don't know if I should be amazed or frightened," Volkan said.

"You should be pleased that you are on my side," Eldar said, fondly rubbing his neatly combed white strands.

"God help anyone who crosses you," Volkan said, raising his chalice. "To the Demircis."

"To the Demircis," Eldar repeated.

And he drank his chalice of blood to the last drop.

XXIII

SOMETHING WAS CHANGING. Yara could feel it. It wasn't merely the cold that seeped into the grey stone walls or the breeze that made the candles flicker ominously. Or the flutters of snow that encased the Bone Garden in a white blanket during the winter revels. Nor the heavy kaftan and fur caps that covered the guests. It was Eldar. He had begun to wear a set of leather gloves before winter arrived. And he was gone so often she scarcely saw him. He would spend weeks away from court. Only to return empty-handed with not a whisper of his journeys.

He hadn't spoken to her since that kiss. He didn't even look at her. And Yara had begun to feel invisible.

"An invisible spy will find it easier to get into places undetected. To listen to conversations without anyone noticing them," Zuri had told her. Yara supposed his lack of attention meant he no longer saw her as a threat. After he had gifted her with the gruesome severed finger of her father, he seemed to have put their rivalry to bed. Wrongfully assuming that she was had been put in her place.

She had been uneasy around him the past few weeks and she knew he sensed it.

Mircea was eager to know if the brothers were behind the death of Pomona. The only reason his suspicion wasn't fully cast on the twins was because another boy had died that night. And Radu and Mircea remained busy hunting the culprit behind these deaths. Each eager to win their oldest brother's favor.

Yara intended to search his bedroom that night. There were always people fluttering in and out of their quarters, blood slaves and sired vampir and servants and dressing maids. Eldar always locked his bedroom and draped the iron key around his neck. Volkan, on the other hand, didn't lock his bedroom.

"What are you thinking of, my pet?" Volkan asked as he fingered his set of cards. Thaddeus and he were playing a game. Each round, one or the other of them would slip off an article of clothing.

"I'm thinking how you both are idiots. If you wanted to see each other naked maybe you should have taken a bath together," she said. "I don't see the purpose of this game."

"It is called gambling, dear," Thaddeus said. "Except instead of coin, which we possess in spades, we trade in our modesty. Would you like to join?"

Yara wrinkled her nose. "Perhaps some other time."

"So polite," Volkan said, as he unbuttoned his greatcoat, drawing the brocade from his pale chest. Yara stood up and appraised the glossy cards in his finger. They were expensive, the kind that was illustrated. Volkan draped an arm around her waist, drawing her onto his lap. It didn't alarm her when he performed such intimate gestures. Yara told herself it was a job, and that it was necessary to accept his odd affection. She wasn't vulnerable enough anymore to attempt to kiss him. Whatever madness had soaked her bones that night had faded as easily as it had arrived.

Perhaps it had been a blessing that she had kissed Eldar instead. Volkan had an ease about him that she could easily fall prey to.

Shivers pricked her skin when his thumb swirled around her stomach, firm and unyielding. He rested his chin on the grooves of her collarbone.

"Will you be my Lady Luck?" he asked.

"I don't think you care if you win or lose. You'd find any excuse to undress," Yara teased.

Thaddeus barked out a wild laugh. "I see why you fancy her."

"Will you give us a moment, Thaddeus?" Volkan asked.

Thaddeus left the room, tucking his cards close to his chest. "If you think I'm leaving my cards unattended, you are mistaken."

Volkan snorted, and when the door clicked shut, he tilted her so she faced him fully.

"How have you been?" he asked.

"I'm wondering when I can go back to my chambers," she said. "Pomona is dead. There is no threat to my life anymore."

"There is someone out there killing vampir. I shudder to think what they would do if they got their hands on you," he said with a dramatic shiver. "You should stay until the threat has passed."

"That sounds like an excuse to keep me locked in your tower like an evil sorcerer," she said.

"Eldar cannot perform magic, last I checked," he said.

Yara giggled. She loved when he made fun of Eldar. It always brought a smile to her face.

"You hate my brother, don't you?" he asked.

Yara had buried her father's finger in the garden. It had been silly, but she hadn't known where else to put it, and she vomited anytime she looked at the box. Her hatred for Eldar was unlike anything she had felt before. It was coated in poison and seeped from her pores.

"He makes you look like a gentleman," Yara said. "You know,

when I first met you both, I thought you were worse. But he has far surpassed you in cruelty and harshness."

"He's changed," Volkan said. "He was always a bit of an ass, but I think he's so focused on his plans that he's blinded to everything around him."

"What plans?" Yara asked.

Volkan only smiled, patting her cheek good-naturedly.

"It is a secret between brothers," Volkan said. "But take my word for it, Yara. In the end, it is better to stand with Eldar than against him."

⸻⸻◦⸻◦⸻⸻

Volkan rarely locked his bedroom, and Yara snuck in when Thaddeus and he disappeared to the bathhouse. When she entered his bedroom, she realized *her* bedroom was the spare room. This one was well furnished with a high bed covered in black damask sheets embroidered with a nest of peacocks. There was a mahogany chest at the foot of the bed filled with jewels and trinkets. In the armoire there was his vast collection of fabrics from Greece and Rome and India. Golden candlesticks shaped like tulips were strung around the ledge, illuminating the space. The walls were concealed in paintings of naked men and women, conjoined in intimate acts that made her skin flush.

Yara walked to the curtains, no doubt imported from the Ottoman empire. It had the design the weavers favored: the thin feathered leaves surrounded by rings of artichoke. Yara tore back the silk fabric to find a second door. She twisted the doorknob to slip into a second identical bedroom. How delightful that they were so attached. Even their rooms were conjoined. Yara didn't waste another second in Volkan's bedroom. She slipped into Eldar's room. Their rooms were identical, except Eldar's walls were devoid of the lewd portraits. And he also had a prisoner strung up on the wall. The boy had a cloth in his mouth, and his limbs hung from the chains on the wall.

Yara was about to turn back when his head rose. His eyes were removed, and all she saw was a bloody torn socket. A scream bubbled up her throat. She knew that face. It was Lysander.

"Lysander," she whispered.

"Yara," he said hoarsely. "Is that you?"

"Yes. Yes, it's me," she said. "What did that monster do to you?"

"He...he caught me that night at the dinner. I picked the lock to his bedroom. Zuri thought advanced spy work might be too hazardous for you. Days later, he found me. He said he smelled my scent in his bedroom. It...it was impossible for him to smell me not after so many days had passed. Their senses are not *that* heightened. But he's becoming something else. I saw his hands; the claws are twice the size of a vampir's, and the veins beneath his skin are poisoned."

"What has he done to you?" she asked, cupping his cheeks. He smelled of blood and sweat. There were deep slashes on his chest. And the nails of his fingers had been torn, leaving behind bloody scabs.

"I told him many things, Yara." He sobbed. "The pain overwhelmed my senses."

"I'm going to release you," Yara said.

"No, no," he said, frightened. "I will be put to death by Zuri for revealing our secrets. It is best to die here. He will kill me soon."

"I don't know what to do," she said frantically. "How do I help?"

"Go to Zuri and tell her what I've relayed. Tell her that Eldar has a power that far surpasses any I've ever seen," he said. "When he is angered, his eyes are pools of darkness, and his teeth descend past his lips. Tell her that he is becoming something."

Yara nodded. Tears dripped down her eyes at the thought of leaving him to his fate. She kissed his cheek, knowing full well she would never see him again.

"Goodbye, Lysander."

Yara ran back to Volkan's bedroom and down the hallway, passing the blur of portraits and marble statues. She found the hidden staircase to their secret spot. It was almost noon, and Zuri would arrive soon. She always arrived at noon and midnight for the reports from her network of spies. Yara often awoke early to see her when the halls were silent and the vampir nested.

Yara paced back and forth, biting her fingernail. He'd know she was in his room. He'd know the way he knew Lysander was in his room. Mircea had to arrest him. He had to contain him before he came after her. Zuri arrived in a blur of shadows.

"You seem agitated. Is everything well?" Zuri asked. "I could hear your heartbeat miles away."

She led Yara to sit on the dirt-stained floor of the tunnel. Yara didn't know where the tunnel led, but she could hear a stream of water from the right side. Zuri had said it broke out into the ravine behind the property.

Yara tripped over her tongue to explain everything Lysander had shared. Zuri's face grew grim the more she spoke.

"We must warn the prince," she said. "It is outlawed to perform any act of cannibalism. And these traits you described are a transition from man to beast. He must be stopped."

Zuri wrapped her arm around Yara's elbow, and her legs dangled as she raced them to Prince Mircea's bedroom, walls passing them in a blur of color. Inside his lush chamber, Mircea relaxed in the seating area with tea and biscuits.

"My lord, we come with grave news," Zuri breathed.

Mircea sat upright and beckoned for Yara to come to him. She hadn't seen him in a few weeks, and she was surprised to find his eyes filled with concern. They hadn't spoken since he had left the fate of her marriage to Augustus in the hands of the Undying King.

"How do you fare, child?"

"Well, considering everything that is going on..." she said.

Zuri relayed Lysander's words, and Mircea was struck with silence. He stroked the end of his beard.

"We need to speak with the Undying King," he said. He spoke to his guard by the door. "Summon Radu to Dracul's chamber. Tell him that it is of the utmost importance."

They made their way to Dracul's chamber in pitched silence. Yara was surprised when Mircea bypassed the main room and headed straight towards Vlad's private bedroom. Vlad rested in a silken robe atop an ornate bed reading a set of ledgers and scrolls. It was the most extravagant bedroom she had ever seen.

"What is the meaning of this?" he demanded.

"My lord, it is Eldar of House Demirci. He has broken one of your cardinal rules. He has devoured the flesh of one of our own, and he is descending into a path of madness and power that we cannot fathom."

King Dracul arose just as Radu, and his sentries arrived.

"Find him and arrest him," Dracul barked. Yara noticed that his fist shook when it curled in anger. And when she looked upon his eyes, she saw terror blossoming like a red poppy. He was frightened of Eldar. They were all frightened of him.

His sentries and soldiers assembled and split out of the room in droves of steel and fangs. Yara felt her chest deflate. It was over. It was all over. Eldar would be found and executed. Yara had won. She had destroyed Eldar. He would pay for all his sins. And Yara would stay to watch until the bitter end.

It was strange to think that Yara had ever been anything less than who she was now. To think she had been a girl haunted by monsters. The one who had wept and broken down, only to be reborn. Now she would watch him break and splinter. Now she would taste her freedom.

It was all over.

Eldar was nowhere to be found, and dinner that night was stilted. Yara sang to distract them, but she could see that everyone was on edge. The rumor of what he was becoming had infested the Grand Hall, and everyone moved in a stiff, wary manner. Tension bled through the air with each shift of the sentries. Mircea and Radu had their heads bent together as they spoke. It seemed a threat could even bring the princes together.

At a quarter to sunrise, the gates were breached. A sweat-stained guard came to tell them there was an attack.

"It is hunters, my lord," he said. "Dozens of them. Carrying blades and torches."

Yara could hear the door being bludgeoned. They had a ram with them, and each rock of it against the door made the ground quake beneath them.

"Who are the hunters?" Yara asked.

"Humans who seek to burn us down," Mircea said with a curl of his lips. "We will finish them."

Everyone shot up and got into position. The guards and soldiers made the first line of defence while the sired vampir made the second line and the trueborn took the rear. Cloistered at the end of the room beyond the throne were the wide-eyed blood slaves.

"Go to the back with the blood slaves and servants," Mircea growled.

Yara shook her head and yanked out her dagger. "I'm not leaving your side."

She had missed his somber company. And she knew deep inside that she forgave him for not fighting for her when Augustus sought to entrap her. She could understand his need to defer to his brother, who ruled them with an iron fist. Even Yara wouldn't risk the wrath of Dracul for anybody.

Mircea stared at her almost fondly. The tip of his claw stroked her cheek. "You are a good child, Yara. Your father would be proud of you. *I* am proud of you."

Her heart swelled with his words. She hadn't known how badly she had needed to hear that.

Yara stared out at the unknown. The attackers trickled in like shadows. Their faces were concealed with sheaths and their black robes twisted in the breeze. A silver cross was painted on the breast of their dark armor, and their blades were sharpened to thin points. They charged at the crowd of guards while the courtiers held rank behind them, their claws lengthened, and teeth descended to attack.

In the back were the princes and their guards and behind them, the Undying King sat upon his throne and watched as madness descended on his hall.

The vampir attacked first. And while the guards had speed and strength, the hunters had military training. They stood in impeccable formation and used their shields and blades to jab at them.

Yara watched as several guards were stabbed in the chest and their faces grew mottled and grey. She had never witnessed a battle before, and she was surprised by the mix of human blood and immortal blood that coated the marble floor.

A crash sounded behind them, and Yara watched as Dracul arose and stared at an inky blotch that hovered by the wall. It peeled away from the corner and descended in a crouch. A vampir. Eldar had his hair falling down his back in a severe manner. It made his skin look almost translucent. Veins as black as the night sky trailed beneath his skin like cracks. His eyes were as dark as the void. And she wasn't the only one who shuddered when she saw him.

"Protect the king!" Mircea growled.

A man climbed up the stairs, and Eldar whispered a small "stop." The man froze like his body had been tethered to the ground.

"I challenge you, Vlad Dracul," Eldar said in his strange, raspy voice. "I challenge you to a combat to the death. The last one standing will sit upon the throne."

"You are corrupted and will descend into madness," Vlad spat. "You are not worthy to sit upon the throne."

"Let us speak no more," Eldar said in a bored tone. "Let us fight to the death."

Vlad lunged, and Eldar met him halfway. The dais rattled beneath their footfalls. Vlad's claws dug deep into Eldar's chest tearing out the flesh, while Eldar merely gritted his teeth. He punched him in the jaw, and the bone shifted to a gruesome angle. Vlad was quick to push the bone back in place and grip Eldar's throat, squeezing as hard as could be. Eldar snarled and dug his claw into his eye, shattering the iris till fluid and blood trailed down his skin. Vlad cried out in pain, cupping a hand to his injured eye.

Eldar raced behind him and kicked his knee out from under him, swiftly grabbing his neck.

"You betrayed my house when you aligned with the Maleinos," Eldar said. "For three years, my brother was brutalized and raped at the hands of his wardens. I killed them. Pomona and Titus fell by my hand, and you will be next."

Even now when he was mere inches away from power, he protected Volkan. He had taken the blame for Titus' death.

Vlad struggled under his hold, and the princes watched with grim faces. Eldar dug his fist into his chest and ripped out his heart. He clutched it in his hand, and only a few gasps escaped when he dug his feral teeth into the wet pulp and devoured it in several quick bites.

For a moment, Yara thought he would shatter. The black veins beneath his skin multiplied and his claws grew another inch—long enough to impale someone. He picked up the crown that sat upon Vlad's withered corpse and placed it upon his head.

"Bow," he said. Yara felt her limbs move of their own accord. Panic tightened her chest. It was like when they drank her blood, and she was forced to do their bidding. But he hadn't bitten her nor those around her. Yet they all fell. Anyone within listening distance dropped to their knees. On the outskirts of the room, the battle with the hunters raged on, but here in the back, they hailed the Undying King.

Yara had to escape. It wasn't safe for her here. Not after all she had done to ensure his sins were brought to light. The panic in her chest eased when he said "rise." Yara pushed her way through the bodies and into the battle. Volkan was tearing the humans apart with a gleeful smile. He grabbed one by the neck and when he shook him hard, the sheath that covered his face fell to the ground. For a moment, Yara was alarmed by the youthful face of a boy. But when she looked closer, it wasn't a boy.

"Aylin," she whispered. She would know that sharp little face and big brown eyes with her eyes closed. "Volkan!"

The world stilled as she stared at the face of her older sister. Aylin. Aylin was here. A sob ravaged her chest, slipping past her throat in a broken cry. It was mere feet that separated them, but it felt like oceans. The spell of shock broke, splintering like fragments of glass. And before she knew it, she had begun to run to her, yelling for Volkan to stop. His head snapped toward her as she ran to him, waving her hands like a madwoman to catch his attention.

"Put her down, Volkan," she cried. "Put her down."

He loosened his hold as Aylin gasped for air, but his hand still clamped around her slim neck.

"I don't care to hear about your pesky mortal sympathy." Volkan snarled. "I'm going to cut down all these hunters. I'll shred them to ribbons."

"That's my sister," she said. Her lungs ached from tearing across the room. "Put. Her. Down."

Volkan lowered her till her feet touched the ground.

"This bald cretin is your sister?" he asked.

"I'm going to kill you," Aylin promised. "And when you're dead, I'll make a pretty cloak out of that white hair and fashion a necklace from your eyes."

"Your family is charming," he said dryly.

Yara fell to her knees and wrapped her arms around Aylin. A sob escaped her, and she felt Aylin's arm strangle her. Her ribs ached, but she would let them shatter to dust if it meant another minute in her sister's arms. The battle around her ceased to exist as she clung on to her sister. She smelled of blood and sweat, and Yara wanted to absorb it into her skin. To carry the bloodshed she witnessed and partook in till it burdened her no more.

"God, I missed you," Yara breathed. "I thought I would never see you again."

"I missed you," Aylin said. "I was so scared that I was too late. That you were...you were gone."

"I'm still here," she said. "I was strong for you."

"I'm proud of you," Aylin said, kissing her cheek. "So proud of you, my little bird."

"We have to leave. It's not safe for us here," Yara said.

"I'll go grab Ilyas," she said. "It helps that he's the size of a giant. Give me one second."

"Ilyas is here too?" Yara said, delighted.

"Of course," Aylin said. "As if he'd let me venture off on my own adventure. He's far too selfish for that."

Aylin teased, but Yara knew her sister had always had a bond with him. Yara had always said they bickered like an old married couple. When they had been young, Yara had been swayed by his beauty and grace, and sought to catch his attention anytime he passed. But she soon learned that Ilyas cared for nobody but her sister. His eyes strayed toward no woman but Aylin.

Ilyas was fighting off two vampir, and Aylin was quick to jump into the thick of it. Yara marveled at her technique and courage. Her curved blade swung madly until it sank into the chest of one, and then she climbed Ilyas's back and stabbed his assailant in the throat, weakening him long enough for Ilyas to finish him off with a fatal strike to the heart. Ilyas's spare hand gripped her leg while he hunted for any threats.

"You can't go," Volkan said.

Yara stared at him. She had almost forgotten he was standing there looking at her with an unreadable expression.

"Eldar will kill me," she said. "And I no longer have the protection of Dracul."

"I won't let him hurt you, but I won't let you go either," he said.

"You didn't see him, Volkan," she hissed. "He is a monster. Look at him!"

Yara pointed to the dais but he wasn't there. She didn't know where he went, but she wouldn't stick around long enough to find out. Volkan's arm gripped her elbow.

"Is that what you want? To return to mediocrity and stifling rules?" Volkan whispered. "When you could stay here and blossom?"

"I am not made for this world, Volkan," she said. "I am the weakest creature in this room. There will always be a greater threat. There will always be another enemy."

Yara felt a strange ache in her chest. A part of her would miss him. A foolish part that had begun to see the trickle of humanity within him. Volkan was monstrous, but he was not a monster. He was broken, and a part of him hadn't yet recovered from his imprisonment. He had picked up the pieces and aligned them, but there were still pieces that hadn't quite fallen into place. He didn't love her, and Yara wasn't certain he was even capable of love. But he wanted her, as fiercely as he did his next breath.

And there was a beauty in being wanted.

Yara leaned up on her toes and pressed her lips to his in a kiss good-bye. She tasted the cold of his breath and felt the bristle of his claws scraping her neck. Before she turned back to her sister, it was time to return home.

XXIV

AYLIN FELT THE weight on her chest decrease as Ilyas cut through the vampir to get to her. Blood drenched him like a second skin, and Aylin felt the thrill she experienced anytime she watched him fight, cut and maim. As if each stroke of his blade were a caress along her cheek. He killed in a manner that could only be described as beautiful. In the distance, she could see Domenico hacking away at limbs as if he were a butcher. He plunged his blade into his victim's unprotected eye before ripping it out to bury it in their chest. There was no finesse to the way he killed, only a mad glint in his eyes that told her he enjoyed this far more than he let on.

Yara was alive and well. Aylin could still feel the phantom touch of her hands around her sister, squeezing her so tightly she could feel bones. Every limb in her body quivered with the force of her emotions. She had cut down many of them, and Ilyas had cut down twice as many, but it had all been worth it to be reunited with her sister. Every sacrifice she had made had been worth it.

It was reckless and dangerous, and they were in the middle of a battlefield when Aylin yanked Ilyas's sheath from his face. He twisted to stare at her where she was perched on his back, limbs tangled around him like the vines of a tree. His harsh face was covered in sweat, and his thick brows descended with irritation.

"What?" he asked gruffly. "I can hear you perfectly well with my mask, Aylin. Where is your mask? Do you want to get scarred?"

Something sad flitted in her chest, even in the midst of such victory. A tear in her chest that hadn't sealed up even when she held her sister. Though the emptiness had lessened gravely, as if a missing limb had been reattached, she still felt empty.

Her father had always called Yara her shadow, but a shadow disappeared during the night. Yara had always felt more like a piece of her heart.

"Ilyas, I wish to tell you something, but I cannot speak it into words," she whispered.

He didn't belong to her. He belonged to God and the sultan, but she wished for one small moment that he was wild and mad enough to choose her. She wanted so terribly for him to want her, to be with her when it all ended. She wished that she was more like Yara, who captivated men with a single glance and brought them to their knees. It was selfish to want more when he had risked his life to bring her sister home safely. He owed her nothing, certainly not his fealty or devotion. He had broken every rule and law that governed his life for her family, and to expect him to forsake his most sacred vow besides his *shahada* was selfish.

"What is it?" he breathed.

"Nothing," she said with a tight smile. She swallowed past the pain in her chest. "It's not important."

She slid off his back, putting a good bit of distance between them. He stared at the empty space between them with a frown, like it offended him.

"We must go," she said. "Come."

Aylin spun on her heels, surprised to find her sister entangled with the white-haired vampir—the one who'd almost killed Aylin. His arms wrapped around Yara like a shackle, his hand fisting her curly hair in a brutal grip. If it wasn't for the fondness in his eyes, Aylin would be concerned.

When they untangled, Aylin hissed at him, delighted to see his eyes widen.

"Are you sure this is your sister?" he asked.

"I hope for your sake that is a compliment," Ilyas growled.

"Ilyas!" Yara said, ignoring their bickering. "You've been missed."

"You as well, Yara," he said. "I'm glad that you are well."

"Come, let us go. I know another exit from the castle," Yara said. She led them out the double doors in the corner of the room that broke out into an empty hallway. It was eerily devoid of people.

Aylin didn't complain when Ilyas enfolded his hand in hers and pulled her close to his side. She wished he would stop these small gestures; they only made the weight on her chest tighten. Now that they had found Yara, it seemed that all she could think about was the future. Of what awaited them when they returned to Constantinople. No doubt a good chiding from her baba about running off into danger and a fierce hug from Aunt Sevda. She hoped the return of Yara would ease the sultan's temper regarding Ilyas's desertion. She didn't know what she would do if he were punished.

"There are tunnels that run beneath the castle," Yara said. "I heard water nearby when I was down here. And was told it spits out into the river."

"The Arges River lies below the cliff, but it is freezing out there, Yara," Ilyas said. "We could catch our death."

"We can't go back in there," Yara said. "*He* could find us. The Undying King."

The way she referred to him, Aylin knew she feared him. From the title, she assumed it was one of the vampir monarchs.

"We'll take the tunnels and deal with the consequences after," Aylin said.

"Why would the king concern himself with us when there are hunters killing his kind?" Ilyas asked. "Let us go back in and make it to the front door. There are horses there with provisions enough for our travels to the next port."

"You underestimate his desire to destroy me," Yara said. "I betrayed him."

"Yes, you did," an inky voice said behind them.

Aylin spun around with her sabre raised to look upon a familiar face. One just as beautiful as the fair-haired vampir in the hall. They shared identical features—the same carved nose and slim jaw and overly full lips. Except this one's hair was as black as obsidian. And his eyes were pools of darkness. Something within him was terribly wrong, and Aylin shivered at the sight of his canines slipping past his lips like daggers. He had a crown on his head, one with interlocked silver thorns.

"There's two of you," Aylin said. "I could hardly stand the first one."

"Are these your pathetic saviors?" he asked Yara.

"Who did you call pathetic?" Aylin asked, swinging her sabre over her shoulder with a dramatic slice of the air. She was going to gut him until he was nothing but dust. "Let's see if you can speak when I stab your heart."

"We don't want any trouble, Eldar," Yara said in a placating tone, as if he were a wild beast that would attack at the smallest provocation. "We just want safe passage home."

"Do you think it is that easy, Yara?" he asked. "Did you think you could betray me and stand with the Draculs, and now that they have fallen, simply flee?"

"You will be a wretched ruler," Yara said evenly. "And I don't care to watch you burn this place to the ground. I'm going back to Constantinople."

He smiled, the thin points of his teeth scraping his jaw. Aylin didn't think Yara should taunt him. He looked unstable. Unlike like the other vampir, his teeth were sharper, and his eyes were nothing but blackened shells.

Ilyas reached for Yara to yank her behind him, but before he could touch her, the crazed vampir snatched her. He held her by the neck while his other hand draped around her waist.

"Shall we play a game?" he asked.

"Does it involve sticking my blade in your chest?" Aylin growled. "And Ilyas eating your eyes?"

"Disgusting," Ilyas said under his breath. "Why don't I kill him, and *you* eat his eyes?"

"Where did you find these two idiots?" Eldar asked.

"Don't insult my sister," Yara snapped. "And Ilyas is twice the man you'll ever be."

"Sister?" He raised a brow. "Interesting."

Aylin lunged forward.

"Stop," he said in that deeply sweet voice.

Sweat beaded Aylin's forehead as her limbs locked. Ilyas stared at her, his eyes wide with panic. From his rigid posture, she knew whatever invisible hand held her back was wrapped around him as well.

"Shall we play a little game?" he asked again, speaking into Yara's ear.

"Let them go," Yara said, squirming beneath his hold. "Let them go, you wretched beast."

"I'm going to kill one of them, but I'll let you pick which one dies," he said. "Is that fair?"

Aylin's heart lurched in fear. She fought as hard as she could, but it was as impenetrable as steel. Fear began to creep into her veins.

They had made it so far. They had crossed seas and trained night and day to infiltrate this castle in the hills. Aylin had taken up the garments of a man to join an exclusive order of hunters. She wouldn't lose Yara and Ilyas to anybody but God. No man, vampir or mortal, would take them from her.

"I'm not playing your games," Yara whispered.

"Then I'll kill them both," he said. "And you will live with that decision for the rest of your short life."

"It's okay, Yara," Aylin said gently. Tears streamed down Yara's face, and she could tell she was tormented. They had grown up with Ilyas; he was like a brother to her.

Aylin didn't think she could live knowing that Ilyas had died for her. It would eat away at the shell of her till nothing remained but misery. She had brought him here for her sister, for Yara. He would have been safe in Constantinople if it were not for her. He deserved to grow old and live a full life.

"Pick me," Aylin said. "Save Ilyas."

"No," Ilyas growled. "Don't be an idiot, Yara."

"Insulting her is not going to make her listen to you," Aylin snapped.

"Nor is your childishness going to endear you to her," he said. His nostrils flared. "You are all I have, Aylin. You are all I've ever had. When I was brought to Constantinople on my knees, you were the only thing that made me want to rise to my feet. You are the only woman I've ever wanted to possess. You are the light that guides me. I am *nothing* without you."

Aylin turned away from him. His words twisted in her chest like a living entity.

It was difficult to dissect her feelings toward his words when they stood before true evil. The man before them was scarcely a man, but rather shadow stitched into the shape of one. No inkling of humanity twisted in his eyes. It was impossible to decipher his true intentions from the void that made his gaze. Only that his head was tilted to face Yara, to drink in the pain that darkened her pretty face.

There were many men who adored her sister, for there was much to like: Yara was innocent and clever and beautiful. The fact that she had survived all these months amidst these monsters was proof of her tenacity. But the way the Undying King looked at her made Aylin's skin break out in goosebumps. It was an obsession that loomed above them, like a stained cloud prepared to drench them in its wickedness. He stared at Yara like she belonged to him, mind, body, and soul.

Yara licked her lips. She stared at Aylin with an apologetic look before she stared at Ilyas, her chin lifted in determination. Aylin knew before she parted her lips that she was going to sentence him to death.

"No, no, no," Aylin said desperately. "Yara. No. Yara, please. Not him. Not him. If you love me, you will spare him."

Her heart cleaved in two, and she fought hard against her restraints. It felt like pushing against a wall, but she didn't care. She didn't care so long as Ilyas lived.

They hadn't had enough time, and staring at his resigned eyes made her sick. Blood trickled from her nose as she struggled.

"There is another choice," the Undying King called. His hand rose, and those black-tipped claws stroked Yara's cheek. "I can unmake you and raise you from your death. I can make you a creature of the night. An immortal. A lady made of darkness. In return, I will spare these pathetic mortals you care for."

"It's a trick, Yara," Aylin said. "Don't fall for it."

"I will send them away with those treasures the prince promised you. I know of the promises you made with Mircea. Lysander told me much before I ripped his tongue out. In case you were wondering, it takes forty-five minutes for one to bleed to death from multiple wounds," he said. Yara flinched, and Aylin wondered if she knew the poor fellow he'd murdered. It did not sound like a peaceful death. "They will have their lives and enough wealth to keep them satisfied for the rest of their days."

"What do you get from that exchange?" Yara asked as if she were truly considering his words.

"You."

The words echoed along the ceiling like a doomed prophecy. Like a curse. Aylin didn't believe a word from that pretty mouth. He was a deceitful vampir who was toying with her sister like a pawn.

"Yara, he lies," Aylin said. "Please, please do not consider it. You have a life to return to. You have a bright future in Constantinople. Your return will be rejoiced and celebrated, and Baba misses you terribly. The sultana worries for you, and I'm sure the imperial prince's attention will bring forth many worthy proposals."

"Weak human men will not satiate her appetite," Eldar said. His lips curled in disgust. "She will have all she desires and more in my court."

"Fine," Yara said in a resigned voice. "Do your worst."

"Yara," Aylin whispered. "No."

But her sister had her shoulders drawn back, and her eyes stared unwaveringly at some distant point over Aylin's shoulder, as if she couldn't quite meet her eyes.

"It will be a lovely end," he promised. "And a wicked beginning."

Aylin screamed when his teeth sunk into Yara's neck. Her eyes shuttered blissfully closed, and her hand drifted to his cheek almost fondly. Salvatore had told them of the poison in their teeth that convinced their prey that they were safe. It was strange to watch them perform this act that reeked of intimacy and false seduction. Yara's chest heaved, and his hand gripped her hip so tightly that his claws sunk into the fabric of her dress.

Aylin felt her limbs twitch, and the command that stiffened her bones grew lax with each passing second until she could finally move with ease. She looked at Ilyas, who nodded that he was free as well. They drifted in from opposite sides, their blades raised and their footfalls as soft as a whisper.

He was so absorbed with draining her sister, he had fallen to his knees, clutching Yara's slumped form like a doll. His monstrous face was lost in the rapture of her lifeblood.

Ilyas raised his twin blades. The Undying King spun around just as the iron plunged into his back. The angle was wrong, and Aylin knew Ilyas hadn't struck true when he released Yara to attack Ilyas. He caught him by the throat and slammed him against the wall. A loud crack sound when his head collided with the stone.

"Ilyas!" she cried.

"Do you want to test me?" he growled.

Aylin stared at Yara's lifeless body. Her blank eyes were turned to the ceiling, and her body was still.

"Yara," she said, her voice quivering. "What did you do?"

"To be reborn, one must die first," he said. "Now don't distract me. If I don't awaken her soon, it will be too late. Her soul will have departed." He bent down, the ends of his long, dark hair falling onto Yara's chest. He bit his hand, and black blood spouted from the wound. He pressed it to Yara's lips. For a long while, nothing happened. His brows twisted in concern.

"What's happening?" Aylin asked.

"Shut up," he growled. "Something is wrong."

"What's wrong?" Aylin demanded, falling to her knees.

Yara didn't blink. She didn't breathe. She was as dead as any corpse. And Aylin bit her lip hard to contain the emotion trapped within her. "Wake her up."

Aylin didn't care if she was no longer human. She didn't care if it was unnatural. She wanted Yara back in any way she could have her.

"It's not working," he said, speaking to himself. "My blood is altered. I thought it would work. Find Volkan and tell him to come, quick."

Aylin didn't have to ask who Volkan was. It had to be the twin. She ran as fast as her feet could carry her. The battle had faded, and a small fire burned in the corner, climbing up the drapes. The hunters had retreated. All those who hadn't died at the hands of the vampir were long gone. The sun had begun to rise, so they couldn't be hunted either. The creatures couldn't follow them into the light.

Aylin thanked God that Volkan's hair was so bright it was easy to pick him out among the crowd.

"Yara, Yara is in trouble," she panted. He gripped her elbow, and before she knew it, he was running, the walls fading into a blur of color. Before she could blink, they were in the hallway where the Undying King sat cradling Yara in his arms. Looking down on her as if he cared about her. His arms were clutching her so tightly, Aylin feared he would snap her in half.

"What have you done?" Volkan whispered.

"I was going to make her one of us, but her body is rejecting my blood. You must try yours," he said. "I won't let her be sired by anyone but us."

Volkan crouched beside her and bit his wrist, pushing it to her mouth. A strangled sob broke from Aylin's lip when nothing happened. It was too late. Yara was gone.

Ilyas was slumped in the corner, injured or dead. She didn't have the strength to discover which, and she was frightened to find out.

"Please save her," she whispered. "Please. Please. Please."

If she lost them both, then she had failed the only people she had ever loved, and she wouldn't dare show her face to her father. Not after everything.

"I'll do my best," Volkan said between gritted teeth. He pushed his wrist deep into Yara's mouth. "I know you're in there, Yara. Drink for me, darling."

It felt like ages before Yara's red eyes shot open. Her hands dug into his wrist, swallowing mouthfuls of his blood. It trickled down her chin, slipping between her breasts.

"She needs human blood to complete her transition," Volkan said.

Aylin extended her wrist without hesitation, and Yara blindly took it, sinking her teeth into her flesh. Aylin felt a sense of peace drifting through her while her troubles floated away.

Yara was safe. Yara was alive. Ilyas would be okay. He was too stubborn to die. He'd promised he would never leave her. He'd promised he would always follow her. And Ilyas never broke his promise.

Aylin felt herself being pulled away from her sister, and Volkan dutifully licked the wound on her arm till the skin sealed.

"No. Aylin, Aylin are you okay?" Yara asked frantically. Blood dripped down her chin, and her eyes were wide with guilt. "I hurt you. I'm sorry...I'm..." She clutched her head in her hands and began to sob.

Aylin crawled to her and pulled her to her chest.

"Shhh, it's fine. You are alive, that's all that matters."

Aylin smoothed her hair. It didn't even matter that Yara was a vampir. That she had become the enemy she hunted. She would always be Yara to her.

Aylin glared at *him* behind her. She infused as much poison as possible into her gaze. His eyes were locked on Yara. Both of them stared at Yara in a manner that left her with unease. As if Yara were a possession that belonged to them both, and they would split her in half if it meant they each claimed a piece.

"Say your goodbyes," Eldar commanded. "Volkan, see to it that they are given provisions and coin."

"Send one of your soldiers," Volkan snapped. He lifted Yara, cradling her in his arms. "She needs to rest and feed properly."

"I don't want to leave her," Aylin said. "She needs me."

"We had a deal," Eldar said sharply. "I hear the boy's heartbeat. Perhaps if he receives a healer in time, he may yet survive."

Aylin stared at Ilyas. It felt like an impossible decision. But it was not a decision at all. The Undying King had no intention of sharing Yara. He would hoard her like a fine jewel and pick her apart at his leisure. Enshroud her in a darkness of his own making until she saw no one and nothing but him. He had already manipulated her into becoming one of them. He had already twisted the knots of fate with his monstrous hands to bring her closer to him. To shut out her friends and family was his final step.

"I'll find you, Aylin," Yara promised. "I swear it."

"Don't make promises you can't keep," the Undying King said. His dark brows descended like a flock of crows while his pink lips remained twisted in cruelty. Aylin remembered his face. The face she would destroy someday. Death would come for him as surely as the sun would rise from the east and set in the west. And when Death called his name, it would be Aylin who stood above him with a blade of silver and ice.

XXV

VOLKAN LIFTED YARA, drawing her to his chest. They watched as Eldar summoned a guard to carry Ilyas out the front door. Aylin looked back at her sister, a hopeless look in her eyes. Yara knew the words she spoke to Aylin without her parting her lips. Be brave. Be strong. Be vicious. It was what her sister had always advised her to do in the midst of great despair.

Her body ached and her gums felt sore. Everything was too loud. She could hear the shouts from the Grand Hall. The moans of the fallen humans and injured vampir alike. The smell of the blood from their wounds twisted in the air, and she felt her stomach twist in hunger and her teeth slowly descend from its sheath.

"I'll feed you soon," Volkan said, sensing her hunger. "Let me see your teeth." He peeled back her lips to assess her canines. "They are coming in beautifully. Should be fully grown overnight."

"I'm scared," she whispered.

"It will be a pleasurable life," Volkan promised. "I will be your hand in the dark and I shall never let you go."

"You're his brother. You will always belong to him," she said. Volkan was not an ally. It would be foolish of her to think of him as such. Yara could not trust anyone.

"I don't agree with what he did. He shouldn't have forced you into this choice. But it was his mistake," Volkan said. "I can make you cruel, Yara. I can make you wretched. You only need to say the word."

"I want him dead," she whispered. "I want his bones to rot and his skin to fester. He nearly killed Ilyas. He tore my sister away from me. He mutilated my father, and he *killed* me. He killed me, Volkan. Drained every last drop from my body and made me into a monster."

"Now, now, there is no need for any insults," Volkan said in a chiding tone. "This is not an excuse, but Eldar has been the head of our family since our father died. Our father was a wretched man, and it was a relief when we found out his torment had come to an end. Everything Eldar has done was for me. I think his quest for power was to avenge my wrongful imprisonment."

"Men will always find an excuse for violence. It is always a war for king, for God, for family. As if justifying the reason for carnage somehow makes it acceptable."

Yara was tired of being the victim. It was time for her to twist herself to resemble these creatures. Volkan brought her to her room in the quarters he shared with her brother. The one that had slowly begun to feel like her own. During the weeks of her stay, her clothes and jewelry had begun to fill the room. She hadn't realized how many of her belongings were there. Almost as if fate had known she would never leave. As if it knew she was tied to the Demirci boys.

Yara sat on the bed, staring blindly up at the ceiling. At the sturdy wooden beams that ran from one side to the other, intertwining like clasped palms.

"Everything hurts," she murmured. Her eyes felt too dry, and her nails were reforming into something sharper and darker. It was a metamorphosis that could not be stopped, and she wondered if she would recognize herself in the end.

Volkan lay down beside her, and she felt a sense of ease when his shoulder grazed hers. It bloomed in her chest and spread like poison.

"Does it feel better now?" he asked.

Yara felt the pain lessen, and she stared at him in surprise.

"Do you have magic?" she asked, frightened.

Volkan chuckled. "When you are reborn it helps if your sire is nearby. The transition can be painful. After all, you are being remade. My blood will run in your veins till the end of your days. I will always be your comfort."

Yara laid her head on his chest, and she felt the pain disappear, fading into embers. She drew closer to him, feeling the hairless skin of his chest. His tunics were always loosened, revealing a sliver of skin that was just a touch immodest. Her hand fell between the gaping and her panic faded at the feel of his un-beating heart.

"What does it mean for you to be my sire?" she asked.

"It means that you will always be drawn to me. Thaddeus described it as a sense of belonging. He says I feel like home," he said.

"What does it feel like for you?" she asked.

His hand stroked her hair. His claws were gentle and scraping.

"I have a fondness for all those who I've sired. I consider many of them family," he said. "They always take my surname."

"Do you consider me family?" she asked.

"I would not describe the things I wish to do to you remotely familial, but rather depraved," he said.

Yara tucked her hand beneath her cheek and stared at him. A strand of his pale hair danced in his black eyes, and she had the unbearable urge to tuck it behind his ear. She curled her hand tightly and forced it beneath her chin.

"Do you think now is a good time to flirt?" she asked with a small smile.

"I would consider my deathbed a good place to flirt."

Yara laughed, a light, tinkling sound. It was strange to her ears. She couldn't recall the last time she had laughed. But when she gazed at him, he had a somber look in his eyes.

"Will you take my surname?" he asked. His black eyes were intense as he awaited her response.

"I don't know," she said. It felt wrong to carry not just Volkan's surname but *his*.

"I'm sorry," he breathed. The words were strange and clunky in his mouth, and she wondered if he had ever uttered them before.

"For what?" she asked. "This is all your brother's fault."

"For picking you that night when you arrived. For letting his obsession with you grow and fester as poisonously as my own," he whispered. "We've always had the same taste in many areas. It would make sense that we would desire the same woman."

"Do you like me?" Yara whispered. It was strange to feel the absence of her heart beating and the warmth of blood that often flooded her cheeks. She was as still as a wild animal hunting on the plains. Her nerves were tightened into a ball of doubt as she awaited his response. It felt like an eternity before his lips peeled in an insufferable smile.

"A little bit," he said. He lifted his claws and measured a small gap for her understanding. "Do you like me?"

"A little bit."

"Is that so?" he asked.

Yara was tired. She felt her eyes shut. And when she fell asleep, it was a single thought that ran through her mind unbidden.

A strange, sorrowful thought.

I will never look upon the sun again.

The Grand Hall was empty. The hunters had retreated, but they would return. Eldar's footfalls echoed along the high ceilings as he surveyed his broken empire. The fire had been put out, and a mountain of human corpses twined with mangled vampir limbs were piled by the door. The battle had turned in their favor, as he'd expected. He made his way to the throne, running his claw down the glossy onyx paint. It was an ugly, gruesome chair, and Eldar decided then that he quite liked it. It matched the inside of his soul.

A figure stepped out from behind the pillars, and he stared at the leader of this pitiful human cabal. His fair hair was streaked with blood, and black ash coated his handsome face.

"It was you," he said. "In my dreams. The one who told me to come here."

Eldar blinked at him. He had known about the Silver Cross for a long time. His father had lived centuries and witnessed all forms of mortal history. He had watched the First Crusade unfold and had been present for the Battle of Nicopolis. He had seen the destruction of paganism for monotheism. His father had a fondness for tales of war and bloodshed and plagues that devoured babes like rot. Eldar was no foreigner to religious zealotry. The Silver Cross believed vampir to be abominations, cursed beings risen from death to torment the living. They often hunted their lesser counterparts who ran in solitude, as opposed to those who had a coven.

He'd known the Silver Cross was prepped to attack. They had been gathering information on them for years. Just as he knew Salvatore Di Mazi was their young and enigmatic leader. The Hand of God who came to strike them down. Eldar had found him on a night alone, unguarded by his retinue but instead regally clad in his priestly robe. He had disappeared weeks ago to confront him. To bring his plans to fruition. He had caught him with a strange, solemn look in his eyes, like he was contemplating his existence. He had pinned him to the wall, torn the gaudy button that pinned his collar, and drank a pint of his blood. He had whispered to him when the pleasure of being drained had eased his mind to his influence.

"I am your prophet," he said into his ear. "And I have a mission for you."

The vampir were an old race built on tradition and lineage. Usurping the Dracul clan would not have been taken with ease. But if the vampir faced a common enemy, it would band them together. It would silence the echoes of rage. He had Radu and Mircea knotted together in the dungeon below. He hadn't quite decided what he would do with them both. It would end in blood, that much he was certain of, but the *how* was left to his imagination.

The hunter climbed up onto the dais. His blade scraped the ground in a terrible screech.

"I had dreams about you," he whispered. His chest rose and fell. A wild, manic gleam in his eyes. "You've infected me. Cursed me with your devil's touch. I thought you were a prophet. I thought I was carrying the torch of light. But you had me in your shadows all this time. I was merely a pawn in your schemes."

"And what will you do?" Eldar asked, amused. "Will you slay me?"

"I will not have you tempt me to stray. I will not be the vessel for your corruption," he said in a quivering voice. "I will not turn my back on God."

"But you have turned your back on Him. You're here, aren't you?" Eldar asked, tilting his head. "You've come for me. You've prayed for me. I was your prophet once, wasn't I? I can still be him."

Eldar wondered how he was the monster when the vampir hunter appeared just as ghastly. With his blood-soaked hair and pale features, he looked rather ghoulish, like something that had crawled from the grave.

Salvatore did not hesitate to press the gleaming end of his blade to Eldar's throat.

"You're going to have to inch a little lower to kill me," Eldar said. He wasn't certain why he was tolerating this. He wasn't like Volkan; he didn't play with his food. But there was something pleasurable about corrupting someone steeped in such innocence. It reminded him of Yara when she had first arrived, scared, and broken. She would cower from her own shadow. But he had made her into something vengeful and cruel. He wouldn't forget how she had looked at him when she awoke. Like she would carve out his heart with her teeth. He could see her descent into villainy as clearly as he saw his own the day they had taken his brother from him and tortured him for their own amusement. It was poetic to use her sister as a catalyst. To know that soon her cruelty would match his own. He had made her, and she would be his.

"I can't kill you," Salvatore hissed.

"Why is that? You have a clear shot," Eldar said. He sprawled his arms. "Cut me down. See if it erases your sins."

"You're not like the others. There is something ungodly about you. Who is to say striking your heart clean will even kill you?"

"Go home." Eldar sighed. His cautiousness was tiresome. "Hide with your knives and fear-drenched comrades and lick your wounds. When I come for you, it will not be in an empty room. It will be where everyone can see your downfall. Your death will crush the morale of your little crusade, and it will raise me in the eyes of my people."

Eldar swatted away his knife, and it crashed against the wall. He stood up, fixing the folds of his kaftan. Salvatore was a tall man, but Eldar had many inches on him, and when his claw tilted his chin—a demeaning and crude gesture intended to emasculate him—Salvatore glared at him with a hatred that burned.

"Pray to your God. My death will not be your comfort tonight. You must find your salvation elsewhere."

Eldar left the room, his back turned to his enemy. He had meant what he said: there would be a time for their final battle. Their paths would cross again, and when they did, he would send him back to the God he worshipped.

It was hours later when Eldar returned to the Grand Hall. He had visited his miserable prisoners, changed his blood-soiled clothes, and checked on his little vampir. He was surprised to find the bed next to Volkan had been empty. The sheets crinkled and cold to his touch. She had been gone for some time. He wondered faintly if she was foolish enough to escape the castle. It was afternoon, and the sun hadn't yet returned to its slumber. If she had gone outside, he would find nothing but her withered body.

He was powerful enough to tolerate the sun now, in small increments. It had felt strange the day he had tested his power. The sun had stung, but it didn't tarnish his skin, melting it like candle wax when a flame was lit.

His means of coercion had grown stronger, and his prey was no longer influenced by the venom of his tooth, but rather the echo and timber of his voice. It struck him then that *all* vampir were now his prey.

He opened the double doors to the Grand Hall to find a figure on his throne. He felt the knob splinter beneath his finger, crumbling to dust. He stood beneath the dais in the blink of an eye. She looked different. Her brown skin was hard as stone. And her eyes were as dark as night. She hadn't yet learned to retract her canines, and he admired the small, sharp points. Volkan had dressed her in a black linen nightgown with puffed sleeves and a long trail. It was his brother's overly indulgent taste, dressing her like the lady of a manor. He was already molding her like clay beneath his fingers.

"I should break every bone in your body for daring to sit on my throne," he said. They were not the words he wanted to say. He wanted to tell her she looked beautiful. That death suited her.

"I should slit your throat for daring to stand before me," she replied.

Eldar leaned down, his fingers wrapping around either armrest. He inhaled and was mildly disappointed to find the addictive scent of her blood gone. It was a small sacrifice for a greater reward. The price of immortality was not cheap.

"When I was a little girl, I dreamed of marrying a prince," she whispered. "When we arrived at the Ottoman court, it felt like I was one step closer to that dream. As my father's role at court grew, it felt as though I could become more. The imperial prince desired me, and I knew then that my wish to marry a prince had never been for status, but rather a desire for power. I wanted to be revered and feared. Just as Aylin desired freedom, I desired power. It felt like for a moment perhaps I could fulfill both our dreams. If I had power, then I could set her free."

Yara stared at him with a hatred that would burn a lesser man.

"I will never return home to my family. I will never walk in the sun. I will never marry a prince. I will never be that girl who had dreams and desires," she said. "I will be the monster you made me. I will be the torment that breaks your soul. If you don't kill me now, then I will kill you," she said. "One day when I am stronger and the grip on my blade is tighter, I will drive it into your chest and watch you come undone."

Eldar wrapped his hand around her throat. His thumb found the spot where her pulse had once throbbed, and he stroked her empty skin. He drew her closer till their breaths collided.

"What if there is another option, one that does not end in death?" he asked. His lips grazed hers when he spoke, and he could feel the shivers run through her body. He could hear the hitch in her breathing. In time, she would abandon these little human gestures she clung to—breathing, blinking, eating, and sleeping. All of those would fade till she was as still as a corpse. Many of them still performed the latter. Sleeping did not give them energy or make them feel well-rested. It simply silenced their minds and gave them a reprieve from the sun-drenched day when they were trapped behind barred doors.

"I don't see this tale ending any other way," Yara said. "It will end as it began. It will end in blood."

"Isn't it better to marry a king than a prince?" he asked. "To become the bride of Death?"

Yara stilled beneath him. Her entire frame locked up. She was silent for what felt like hours, and he tightened his grip just enough to capture her attention.

"Answer me," he demanded.

His words haunted her. *To become the bride of Death.*

When she had slipped out of Volkan's arms, she hadn't moved with any true intention. Yet a small piece of her wanted to return to the place where it had all started. She had entered this room a girl, and now she returned as a monster. Her only consolation was that her presence had surprised him. She had seen his pupils begin to enlarge till they consumed the whites of his eyes when he saw her sitting on his precious throne, and a thrill had run through her stomach.

She didn't know what had become of him. He had gone through his own metamorphosis. Veins as dark as night twisted beneath his ghostly skin. His eyes were shuttered in pools of darkness, and those poisoned veins crawled up his face like cracks on porcelain. His teeth

descended monstrously past his lips, scraping his jaw. He wasn't looking at her with anger now, and perhaps that scared her most.

"You're betrothed. To that sweet, shy girl," she said. She was everything that Yara had once been, innocent and pliant. Before her innocence had been twisted and misshapen into this monstrosity. A girl
who was now nothing more than a beautiful predator. A girl who
hungered for the misery of her tormentors.

"Betrothals can be broken," he said. "I don't need alliances anymore. I hold the title of the Undying King."

"You hate me," she said.

"Do I?" he asked.

"I see it in your eyes," she breathed. A hatred as pure as her own.
It tangled around his heart like a snare.

"Perhaps I hate that I want you," Eldar said. His words were layered in disgust. "I hate that you've made me crave your despair. I hate
that I want to see you come undone and I want to pick up your pieces
and assemble you for my pleasure. I want to infect you as you've infected me. To ruin you as you've ruined me."

Yara stared into his beautiful face. It was unfair that someone so
dreadful could be blessed with the face of an angel. It was a face that
could tempt even the most pious woman. It wouldn't be difficult to
pretend. Pretend that she was poisoned by her desire enough to forgive him for his sins. To trick him into making her his, and then stabbing him at his moment of weakness. She would look him in the eye
when the day came for her to rid this world of him. She would let him
see the monster he had made. She would let him see his damnation.

"The Undying Queen," he whispered.

"And you will crown me?" she asked.

"If you pass my tests, I will," he promised. "If you cut out the softness within you to become the vicious woman, I know you are, I will."

He moved with both speed and grace till it was he who sat on the throne, and she was sprawled on his lap, her legs firmly set on either side of him. His hand never left her throat much like a necklace, or perhaps a shackle was a better depiction. Eldar could never be anything less than frightening. He demanded utter possession. His current title and status were proof that he dominated anything he put his mind to.

He drew her down till their mouths hovered inches apart. It must have been her transition that made her stomach tighten with desire and longing. Volkan said her emotions would be heightened until the end of her transition. That they would sway as rapidly as a turning tide. Even in that bed with Volkan, she had fought the urge to pin him and kiss him till her lips were bruised. That feeling had been building ever since she awoke. This all-encompassing need to lose herself in the arms of someone, anyone. To fill them with this loneliness that spread like an infection within her.

It was Yara who sealed the space between them. Her kiss was hard and merciless, and she felt the sharp edge of his teeth. His grip on her throat tightened, and for a moment Yara panicked that she couldn't breathe. That was until she lost air for several seconds and nothing happened. It both delighted and saddened her that she didn't need to breathe.

Eldar's mouth was cold and firm, but unbearably soft. His tongue licked the corners of her mouth like he intended to devour her. And his hand—the one that didn't grip her throat like a doll—was draped on her thigh, stroking her like she was a willful beast.

"It isn't going to be that easy," he said. His lips brushed hers with every word.

Yara's brows furrowed in confusion.

"Take her," he commanded.

Shadows slipped out from behind the pillars, and Yara saw the familiar uniform of the castle sentries. Their all-black garments and stern faces and pointed teeth rushed toward her.

"What are you doing?" Yara asked as they each gripped one of her arms. She heard the click of shackles sliding around her wrists. If her heart could beat, it would have been racing. She fought as best as she could, and it made her smile when she swung her arm and one of the sentries stumbled in surprise. But he recovered easily and secured her again.

"Do you think a few kisses will make me forget your betrayal?" he asked, staring at her beneath his nose. He looked like he belonged on the throne, like a stain on the polished black enamel that would never be cleansed. "You will spend your nights with your beloved Prince Mircea and his weakling brother until his sentencing. You will see the fate that awaits anyone who dares to betray me."

"I hate you," she growled. It didn't feel like enough. There had to be a word stronger than that to convey her emotions. He would never stop punishing her. It didn't matter what she did or said. He would *always* hurt her.

His lips lifted in a cruel smile, and his claw scraped his armrest with a screeching sound.

"This will be good for you, Yara," he said. "It will teach you some respect. It will teach you who you belong to. It will teach you to submit, unquestioningly and wholeheartedly, to me."

Yara was dragged away before she could respond or curse him to the farthest pits of hell. The hallways were eerily silent, as if the courtiers knew that a monster sat upon the throne. It was the way cockroaches scattered when they sensed something more powerful approaching. It was both instinct and self-preservation.

The guards led her down a dank stairwell and deep into the cellar beneath the servant's quarters. The walls were packed with soil, and it smelled like rust, blood, and feces. Her stomach rolled as they went down the steps. It felt like the stairs were leading her into the belly of a beast. At last, they came upon a row of barred cells. Most of them were empty except the last two. One of them held the sharp-faced

Radu, who paced back and forth, a calculating look on his face. The second one held Mircea, whose eyes were closed, and hands folded neatly upon his chest, as if he were resting.

They rattled the key in Mircea's cell, and the guards tossed her in pushing her forcefully inside before quickly clanging the bars shut. Yara fell on top of Mircea, groaning in pain. His eyes snapped open. Fury coiled his face until he saw it was her. It softened considerably when she moaned at the crunch of her nose as it landed on his chest.

"Hold still," he said. "I need to put it back in place."

"It hurts," she murmured.

"Don't be a child," he teased. His hand wrapped around her nose, and she yelped when he set the broken bone in place.

"What are you made of stone?" she asked, rubbing her sensitive nose.

"I could ask you the same. Your skin is cold, and I can't smell your blood," he said.

"I was turned," she said. "Eldar killed me and Volkan awakened me."

"How do you feel?" he asked. "Have you fed?"

Yara nodded. Volkan had brought her a chalice of blood, and she had been so grateful that he hadn't brought her a human to bite into that she had hugged him. She recalled his lean body wrapped around hers and the safety she had felt standing with him in the dark. Perhaps it was because he was her sire, but Yara wished she had never left his side, that she was still tangled with him in that massive bed. She missed Volkan, and she wondered if the ache in her chest was her connection to him as his sired, or if it was her true emotion. She wished that the connection between a sired and their master ran both ways. She wished he cared for her the way she suddenly cared for him. The thought of him in pain made her hands tremble. She wanted to protect him, to keep him safe. It was the way she felt about family— both her baba and Aylin. It was strange to feel this way about him.

"It can be rather nostalgic, transitioning into a creature of the night.

You will feel unsettled for some time. You will miss your humanity, but there are many gifts that come with being a vampir," he said. "There is much that you will have to learn."

"I can't do any of that, considering I'm imprisoned," she said dryly. "He's going to kill us all."

"Not quite," Mircea said.

"Do you have a plan?" she asked.

He pressed a finger to his lips, and discreetly nodded in response to her question. Yara felt hope blossom in her chest. It was strange to hold on to something so foreign after all she had suffered, but she believed that Mircea would find them a way out.

"I'm sorry," he said.

"For what?" she asked.

"For involving a mortal in vampir politics. It was foolish of me to think you would come out of it unscathed," he mused. "I suppose I never quite cared for humans. Their lives started and ended in the blink of an eye. But when Zuri couldn't locate you during the attack, I worried that some harm had befallen you."

"I never regretted being your spy. You've never treated me with anything but kindness from the day I arrived. You gave me a fair audience with Dracul, and you promised me my freedom in exchange for information. I've always trusted you, Mircea."

"Your trust is safe with me, young one," Mircea said. "I am far too fond of you to harm you."

"If I had to pick someone to rot within the dungeon of this castle with, it would be you," Yara said with a smile.

"Shut up!" Radu snapped. "We are on the verge of meeting our maker, and you both are exchanging your sad monologues. Pathetic."

"Do you think pacing until your shoes are worn thin will mysteriously solve your problems?" Mircea asked. "You may as well conserve your energy."

"This is ridiculous," Radu said. "How were we bested by Eldar Demirci? I was present at the birthing celebration of the twins, and now he has unseated and murdered Vlad and seeks to do the same to us. He has walked the earth for less than two decades. We hold *centuries* on him. It is absurd."

"He's dangerous," Mircea said. "You know he's been eating the hearts of the vampir. He has centuries of power coursing through his veins."

"He will be the end of our race. A mad king on the throne. It could lead to exposure, or worse, a war with the humans," Radu said.

A tap sounded behind them like a rat scurrying behind the walls, and Yara shuddered at the thought. The cell was covered in cobwebs, and a decayed skull lay in the corner beside a silver chamber pot. The presence of rats was not an unlikely scenario.

"How do you think he'll kill us?" Yara asked. "I suspect it will be the Bone Garden for us all."

"Must you be so dreary?" Radu asked.

"How does it feel to be burned by the sun?" Yara asked.

"Like being set on fire," Mircea said.

That scratching sound continued. Yara opened her mouth to ask about it, but Mircea pressed a finger to her lips, looking warily at where Radu paced.

"The walls are filled with rats. I can hear them clawing. It's maddening," Radu snapped. "How dare he imprison us? How dare he make an enemy of our family? We were the first, and he will not end us without turning our people against him. We are the Draculs. Our house shall never fall."

"What do you think he will do with Little Mihnea?" Radu asked. "Will he kill the child? Dracul's son will no doubt be a threat to his rule. Should we worry for our nephew?"

"He will not kill a child," Mircea said.

"He will," Yara said. "He possesses no compassion."

While Radu rambled, Yara stared at a hole slowly broadening in the wall of her cell. Her heart thudded as she watched it grow until it was wide enough to fit a person. A face appeared in the shadows, and Yara smiled at the sight of Zuri, whose head was covered with a hood.

"My lord," she whispered. "Yara, make haste."

Radu turned then, his eyebrows rising in shock. "Mircea, have her do the same to my cell. You cannot leave me here, brother."

"I'm afraid I can, Radu," he said. "Only one of us can reclaim our fallen brother's throne, and it will be me." Mircea pushed her to the hole, and Zuri pulled her into the damp space behind it. It took her eyes a second to adjust to the dark, but she was surprised by the strength of her vision.

"We must make haste," Mircea said. "That bastard will call for the guards. Run."

Yara ran, and the walls around her blurred into a mass of color. She followed the trail of Zuri's robe and could feel the cold breath of Mircea behind her. She could hear the rushing sound of the Arges River and the thin flap of fishes swimming in the deep. Zuri stopped, and Yara almost barrelled into her before Mircea caught her with a chuckle.

"Newborns," he said, amused. "And their untrained limbs."

Zuri pried the latch open, and water poured in, soaking their feet. She crawled through the opening, disappearing into the dark.

"I...I can't swim," she said.

"Nor can you breathe, so you won't drown," he said. He ripped the ends of his stained tunic and wrapped it around her wrist and his. "I will drag you along."

"Thank you, Mircea," she whispered. "For saving me."

"I will always protect those who serve my house, child," he said. "Though you are not sired by me, I feel as though my blood courses through your veins."

"I've lost my family. I've lost everything," she said. She would never return to Constantinople. She would never embrace the day. She would never see her father or Aylin. "You are all I have now."

"I will try to not disappoint you then," he said with a faint smile. "Come, let us go home."

She had never heard any word quite as beautiful nor quite as painful as *home*. It had never been a place to her, but rather people—Aylin and Baba and Aunt Sevda and Ilyas.

Yara didn't look behind her as the climbed out into shallow water that grew more treacherous the deeper, they swam, or rather, Mircea swam. She was simply drawn behind him, water clogging her mouth and nostrils as faint glimmers of the evening sky made her skin burn in sensitivity. The sun hadn't completely fallen, and she could feel each painful lick of its gaze scalding her skin. Yara settled deeper beneath the water, ignoring her body's instinct to rise up from the punishing waves.

In the distance, the castle of the Undying King stood like a dark mark upon the snow-encased land. Its high-necked pillars pierced the sky and its windows shaped like a multitude of disjointed eyes looked upon her as if their owner watched her from within its depths, peering at her with his cold gaze and unforgiving nature.

Yara promised then that when she returned, she would take twice as much from him as he had her.

XXVI

AYLIN STARED AT the gates as they lowered to the ground, splintered in several places by their invasion. While Eldar the Undying King was a cursed man, he kept his word and had his soldiers provide them with provisions: a strong black stallion that Ilyas was currently draped on, along with a pouch of dry fruit and bread. Aylin led the horse by the reins, staring at Ilyas in concern. He still hadn't woken, and she wondered if some greater damage had been done to him. A lump tightened her throat. She had failed so miserably, and now her sister was farther from her reach and Ilyas was incapacitated.

She followed the directions Salvatore had told them to take when they retreated— north of the mountains and east of the fortress. Aylin could hear their faint voices and found them in a pathetic state. Many men groaned and wailed into the night, deeply enough to wake the wolves. Salvatore paced with bloodstained hair, speaking in hushed whispers with Cristifano, who was dressed impeccably and clean of any stains. He had stayed behind with their horses and tents while they embarked on their journey.

"Aydin," Salvatore called with relief in his voice.

"Elijah needs a healer," she said. "Now!"

Salvatore nodded at one of the men to place him on a cot while Vincenzo, their healer, looked him over.

Aylin saw Domenico tied with a thin rope to a silver fir tree. He struggled against his confines and bellowed for them to release him. His fair hair was streaked with blood, and it ran down the side of his face. There was a small cut on his high cheekbones. Her chest lurched in a feeling she could not describe at the sight of him alive.

"Why is he tied to a tree?" she asked.

"He refused to retreat from the castle until we found you. It took three men to subdue him, and we had to keep him settled until we departed," Salvatore said. "You may release him."

His ropes were unwound, and the moment he stood on his feet he barrelled toward her. His green eyes had darkened with some unnamed emotion, one that frightened her but also awakened a part of her that had always been dormant, rousing like a slumbering beast. Domenico raised her off her feet in a rib-crushing embrace. His fingertips dug so deep into her waist she wondered if he could feel her bones. She wondered if it would leave behind the imprint of his fingers.

A surprised laugh escaped her.

His hand tightened around her wrist when he released her, as if he feared she would disappear. He quickly began to drag her to an unoccupied tent, as if he couldn't bear to have so many eyes latched on their heavy reunion.

He stared at her with his green eyes, and she saw that there were tiny flecks of brown within the orbs. In the light they reminded her of a river, clouded and drifting brackish water down its thin arms. His hand curled around the back of her head, sinking deeply into her dark hair.

"I thought I lost you," he said in a gruff voice. His eyes roamed down her body, searching for any sign of injury. There was a small cut on her stomach that soaked the fabric of her shirt. Domenico slowly peeled back the fabric, staring at the small gash. "We need to clean this."

Aylin shook her head. Her throat tightened with each word she spoke. "I failed her. He...he turned her. He made her a vampir. If Salvatore ever finds out, he will kill her. I saw the look in his eyes. He is even more determined to win now, but Yara's life is at stake, and I don't think I can be here anymore. I can't fight against my sister."

Domenico's grip on her neck was the only thing that kept her upright. If he let go, she would sink to his feet and weep for days to come. She didn't know how to function without Ilyas, without Aylin, without her father. She had never felt so unbearably alone, as if the world were conspiring against her.

"We will find her," Domenico said. "We will return to the fortress, and we will find her."

"Salvatore won't wait for our return," she said. "Besides, it's too dangerous."

"We don't need Salvatore or that dead weight who calls himself your brother," he said. "And I fear nobody, not even God."

"Don't be blasphemous," she said. "And don't insult him."

"Do you want to save your sister?" Domenico demanded. "Yes, or no? If yes, then we must strike while there are still tears in their foundation. When they have not yet picked up the pieces from our attack. When they are still disoriented and unsuspecting."

Aylin hesitated; he had a point. "What if Elijah needs me?"

"A man afraid to claim you is no man at all," Domenico said evenly. "Your sister is your family, your blood. Perhaps turning her was the first attack in a future filled with pain. She could be in the midst of being tortured, her nails ripped from the stems, her teeth uprooted and discarded, her entrails unraveled and pooling on a tabl—"

"Stop!" she cried. "You are being cruel."

"Then come with me," he said, offering her his hand. "Come with me, and I will give you everything your heart desires. Come with me, and I will give you the world."

Aylin looked out as if she could see beyond the tent, see where Ilyas lay unmoving with his mind so far from her it felt as though there were oceans between them.

Beyond that she saw the picture Domenico painted: Yara strapped to a table and the Undying King above her, his claw prepared to slice her open. As much as she despised him, Domenico was right: Ilyas could only be saved by trained healers, whereas she could be of some use to her sister. She could save Yara. Even if she wasn't the Yara she had always remembered. Even if she was changed. She was still her sister. She would *always* be her sister.

Aylin let her hand slip into his big palm. He folded his hand around hers, a satisfied smile on his lips. She knew he had his own motives behind it all. He could never be so self-sacrificing. He wanted her far from Ilyas so he could chip away at the cage that protected her heart until she was blinded by his obsession and drowning in his dark promises.

Aylin knew that while he may have had her hand, she would *never* give him her heart.

XXVII

ELDAR WASN'T PREPARED when the guards roused him. Sleep had not come to him, and he suspected it had much to do with the power coursing through his veins. He ached to silence his mind, but rest remained beyond his grasp. It would be a great tragedy if he could no longer sleep.

"My lord, he has escaped," the guard said, grim faced. "Prince Mircea is gone."

"How?" Eldar growled. His fingers itched to throttle him, but he wouldn't make a move until he'd heard the rest.

"Well, it's no secret Prince Mircea had a network of loyal spies. We've found a hatch in the wall that tracks out into an underground tunnel and spits out into the Arges River. I have men searching for them as we speak."

"So, the princes are gone," he murmured.

"No, he left Prince Radu behind."

"Of course, he did," Eldar said. There was bad blood between the brothers; his betrayal was hardly surprising. "Bring Yara back to my chambers. I want to question her myself."

The guard hesitated. A gesture that was enough to make Eldar wrap his fingers around his throat and squeeze till he felt the bones shift under his touch.

"Where. Is. Yara?" he asked slowly. He could feel his body quake with fury.

"She...she is gone with the prince," the guard said in a raspy voice. "My lord, we will find them."

Eldar squeezed until the bone and flesh snapped between his fingers and his head rolled to the floor, falling with a soft thud.

"Burn him," he demanded. Eldar yanked his leather tie from his wrist and pooled the length of his hair into a tight coil. He left the confines of his bedroom and entered Volkan's bedroom through their shared door. It was identical to his own. While he and Volkan were different in many ways, they shared the same taste in many areas, in clothes and finery. All except for Volkan's rather crude taste in art.

He was coiled in his sheets like a serpent, laughing with Thaddeus, who lay beside him.

"We should teach her how to hunt," Thaddeus said. "She'll be a marvelous huntress. We should bring back those court games Dracul led. You know, the ones where they released blood slaves into the woods, and we hunted them? I suppose, now that your brother is the Undying King, we can have more revels. Dracul was growing old and tiresome."

"Are you both done gossiping like old hags?" Eldar asked. "We have a problem."

Volkan turned, folding his naked arms behind his head.

"I thought you were so independent. You plotted this grand coup without even telling me," Volkan said. "I'm sure you can fix your problem without me."

Eldar knew from the sharpness of his tone that he was not pleased to be left out of his plans.

"Oh, don't pout, it is unflattering," Eldar said. "I would know, I have the same face."

"In truth, Volkan is prettier than you. We put it to the vote a few months ago amongst our acquaintances, didn't we, Volkan? And you won!"

"It doesn't count if you're sired by him," Eldar said dryly. He shook his head. These two brought out a childish side of him. It was best to keep the chatter to a minimum. He already regretted giving back Thaddeus his heart. "Yara is gone."

"Gone?" Thaddeus frowned. "But we haven't even taught her to be a true vampire. Volkan and I had planned to travel the world with her. Introduce her to debauchery and hedonism."

"What do you mean she's gone?" Volkan demanded.

"I had her imprisoned with Mircea for plotting against me. I received word that he's been aided by his network of spies, and she has fled with him."

Volkan barrelled into him, elbow pressed to his throat.

"You had her imprisoned? Mere hours after she awakened?" Volkan hissed. "She has barely completed her transition. How could you do such a thing?"

"She's softened you," Eldar said, his lips curling in disgust. "She betrayed me. She was going to see me burn for my plot to usurp the throne. She pinned the death of that Maleinos wretch on me, and she's been aiding Mircea in his schemes to expose me."

"You've done nothing to warrant her loyalty. She owed you nothing, and you already punished her when you took her life," Volkan said. "This wasn't necessary."

"I won't let her come between us," Eldar said. "Release me, Volkan."

"Not until you admit that you want her," Volkan said.

If it weren't so early in the night, he'd wonder if Volkan was drunk. Eldar didn't *want* her so much as he wanted to destroy her. All those words he had told her had been a trick to lull her into a false sense of security. To make her believe that he was her savior, only to watch the pain on her face when he tore his promises away from her.

But that kiss, that kiss had been for him. He could admit that. Even if it was only to himself.

"I need you to find them. I can't leave the castle until my rule is secured. And you're the only person I trust to do the job," Eldar said.

"Admit it," Volkan said with hard determination. "Admit that you've never wanted a woman before, and it frightens you, so you're pushing her away."

"I'm not you, Volkan," he said. "I don't tolerate distractions."

"What do you call your obsession with her then?" Volkan asked.

"If this is how he treats the women he likes, I dare say I don't wish to see what he does to those he hates," Thaddeus said.

Eldar pushed Volkan away and lunged for him. But Volkan caught him, wrapping his arms around his torso.

"Easy, brother," he whispered. "Your defensiveness is showing."

"Release me," Eldar snarled. "If you won't be of help, I'll find my own way. I was foolish to expect any help from you. I suppose I have myself to blame for your laziness."

"Oh, Thaddeus and I are going to find Yara," Volkan said almost calmly. "But we won't be bringing her back to you, if that's what you're hoping for."

He pried Volkan's hands off him. "Where will you take her?"

Volkan smiled, that secretive little twist of his lips. It was strange that they shared the same face, but Volkan had always been far more expressive. He had many variations of the same smile, and many flickers of his eyebrows rising and falling as if they spoke their own language. Whereas Eldar's own face was carved of marble and devoid of expression.

"Where will you take her, Volkan?" he repeated.

"Home," was all he said.

"You're going to pick her over me?" Eldar asked. He felt something stir in his chest, and he lifted his hand to scratch at the sensation.

Volkan pressed his hand to his cheek. "Never, my brother. I will return to you. But it is time for me to take charge of my destiny. I suppose protecting innocent maidens from my evil brother is as good a purpose as any."

"This is not a joke, Volkan," Eldar said tightly.

"I thought it was pretty funny," Thaddeus said.

Volkan walked toward the door with purpose to his steps. It was strange to see him so enlivened, and it was worse that she brought out that side of him. She made him want to protect her. To fight for her. To keep her.

"I could stop you," Eldar whispered.

He had power and he had soldiers. He could keep Volkan contained in the castle until she was brought back. The thought was sounding more and more appealing the longer he thought of it. He could easily snap his neck until he fell unconscious and have his body secured in one of the bedrooms under lock and key.

"Careful, you are beginning to resemble Pomona, or better yet, our father," Volkan said in a scathing tone. "He had a way of disguising his love as manipulation and cruelty."

Eldar blinked in surprise. Their father hadn't let a day pass without hurting them both. He didn't see them as children but rather as competition. He had always feared that one of them would unseat him for his place as head of the family. So, he had beaten them and broken them. While Volkan had grown smaller under his heavy hand, Eldar had risen and grown stronger. He was glad his father had broken him so he could reshape himself into his worst terror. So he could watch his blank eyes as he ate away at his soul.

"Enjoy your throne and power, Eldar," Volkan said. His eyes were hard when he looked at him. "I hope it was worth losing everything."

The door clicked shut behind him.

"Don't worry, I'll take care of him," Thaddeus said. He hesitated for a second. "He didn't mean it. The bit about your father."

"I don't need your comfort," Eldar snapped. "Leave before I take my anger out on you."

The door shut behind him, and Eldar felt his hand quiver. He tightened it into a fist before it barrelled into the marble statue Volkan had commissioned of his likeness. The artist was long dead, and he knew how much Volkan adored it. It shattered to dust beneath his touch, and Eldar didn't stop until the posts were ripped from the bed and the wallpaper was shorn with imprints of his claws. It didn't lessen the rage in his chest to see the room come undone. It didn't quiet the voices in his head that begged for him to punish them all.

His entire life he had been Volkan's crutch. He soothed him when his night terrors would awaken him, wiping the sweat from his brow. He had carried him around those years before he transitioned, when their father had broken his legs. Volkan had been so upset he couldn't walk anymore Eldar had been tempted to break his own legs so he would find some comfort in their shared pain. But he knew he needed his strength to protect them both from Cetin Demirci.

And when he had destroyed his enemies and punished the families responsible for his imprisonment and his pain, Volkan had turned his back on him. He had chosen the girl who hungered for Eldar's death as she had once hungered for her next breath.

If they thought he was a monster, then there was nothing holding him back from becoming one. Eldar would soak his hands in blood and become the vision they painted him as.

He would become their monster.

GLOSSARY

fajr: the first prayer of the five Islamic prayers

entari: a garment and/or robe worn by Turkish women during the Ottoman empire

kaftan: an ankle-length garment with loose sleeves

gömleks: an undershirt typically worn beneath an entari

salwar: loose trousers

hassa nakkaşları: court designers during the Ottoman empire

shahada: a declaration of Islamic faith

bey: the governor of a district or province in the Ottoman empire

beylik: the territory under the jurisdiction of a bey

audubillah: I seek refuge with God

janissary: a member of an elite infantry unit in the standing army of the Ottoman empire

don: derived from the Latin word Dominus used similarly in a manner such as "mister" or "lord"

reverendo don: the revered lord

zecchino: an old gold coin used in Italy

bacari: a wine bar

DRAMATIS PERSONAE

THE TRUEBORN VAMPIR

Draculesti Family
Vlad Dracul: The Undying King
Mircea: The Undying Prince, Brother to Vlad Dracul
Radu: The Undying Prince, Brother to Vlad Dracul
Mihnea: The Undying Prince, Offspring of Vlad Dracul

Demirci Family
Cetin: Former Patriarch of the Demirci family (Deceased)
Eldar: Son of Cetin, Current Patriarch of the Demirci family
Volkan: Son of Cetin

Ramose Family
Bahiti: Matriarch of the Ramose family
Akila: Daughter of Bahiti
Kosey: Relative

Maleinos Family
Pomona: Matriarch of the Maleinos family
Titus: Partner
Vita: Daughter
Augustus: Cousin

Sired Vampir
Zuri: Sired by Prince Mircea
Thaddeus: Sired by Volkan
Defne: Sired by Eldar

THE MORTALS

The Ottoman Empire
The Sultan: Leader of the Ottoman Empire
Beşir Ağa: Chief Black Eunuch
Aylin: Eldest Daughter of the Chief Black Eunuch
Yara: Youngest Daughter of the Chief Black Eunuch
Ilyas: Janissary and childhood friend of Aylin
Sevda: Nursemaid to Aylin and Yara

The Silver Cross (Vampir Hunters & the Holy Brotherhood)
Salvatore: Leader of the Silver Cross
Cristifano: Council Advisor
Antonio: Council Advisor
Domenico: Warrior and son of Cristifano
Borza: Warrior
Pietro: Warrior
Gratiosa: Cook
Leandra: Maid and Daughter of Gratiosa
Vincenzo: Healer
Franca: Bar wench

ACKNOWLEDGMENTS

The Court of the Undead is vaguely based on real and fictional historical figures and countries. I was inspired much like Bram Stoker by the source material inspiration for *Dracula* which was Vlad the Impaler. Of course, I've taken a lot of liberties with my version of Vlad and as witnessed he is less like the caricature we've seen represented in media and is not really all that evil. This is because as can be seen, he is not a primary character in this novel, but one of the building blocks I used to craft this world to introduce a set of original characters.

Furthermore, this book is not set in a specific period as can be seen by the lack of naming notable Ottoman figures in the initial chapters such as the Sultan. All except for Beşir Ağa who was a true historical figure I read about and was fascinated by. Various other subjects I found of interest such as religion, culture, and monstrosity are explored with as much nuance as possible. I've used my own lived experience as a person of color to explore themes of race and prejudice with both Aylin and Yara's characters.

To conclude, I'd like to thank all the alpha and beta readers who read this book and provided me with their excellent feedback. Thank you for obsessing over the love triangle and answering my desperate questions about which brother you liked most. Thank you to my editor Lynsey for catching all the things I missed, and all the professionals who collaborated on this project with me including my cover designer, and interior cover designer. I'd also like to thank my lovely friends and family for their continuous support. Thank you to my best friend Nawaal for listening to me talk non-stop about this book and every other book I've written since the tender age of fifteen. I wouldn't be here without you.

And for anyone who has ever heard me talk about my vampire obsession all these years and Damon Salvatore from *The Vampire Diaries*, I am sorry, and I love you.

To my future readers, thank you for picking up this book and giving this world a chance.

ABOUT THE AUTHOR

FARHIYA ADEN has been writing ever since she learned how to hold a pen. She grew up in Toronto, Canada, and is a lover of all things dark, gothic, and romantic. She likes to spend her free time drinking iced coffee and baking. When not reading or watching T.V, she can be found traveling across the globe and discovering new ways to make her characters suffer.